Burning
Desire Fades

Burning Desire Fades

*The Psychopath and the Girl
in Black Prada Shoes
Part 2*

M. L. Stark

To order additional copies of this book, contact:
Xlibris
UK TFN: 0800 0148620 (Toll Free inside the UK)
UK Local: 02036 956328 (+44 20 3695 6328 from outside the UK)
www.Xlibrispublishing.co.uk
Orders@Xlibrispublishing.co.uk
805069

CONTENTS

ACKNOWLEDGEMENTS

To everyone who has supported me in the difficult process of writing the book. Thank you. Writing is not a simple task!

Special thanks to my family, my childhood friends, and my many friends around the world. You have been a substantial support with my obsession with my many travels.

I want to express an exceptional and heartfelt dedication to "Laila" in The United States. Thanks for all your help with research, and for believing solidly in the story.

A special thanks to my friends in Cayman Islands.

Special thanks to my readers, without you the book would not have been a success.

Cover art by Elena Dudina. Thank you, Elena, for your fantastic artwork, I can't wait to show the next cover creation for book number 3.

I understand now that genuine love can either be seen in reunion or goodbyes. I chose a last goodbye!

I forgive, but I also learn a lesson.
I won't hate you, but I'll never get close
enough for you to hurt me again.
I can't let my forgiveness become foolishness.
—Tony Gaskins

Enjoy the reading.

CHAPTER 1

Run For Your Life

> You cannot escape the responsibility of tomorrow by evading
> it today.
>
> —Abraham Lincoln

It's a hectic petrifying day at the hotel in Hong Kong. Early in the morning, we go to the reception space to retrieve our belongings. Holy mackerel! Hell breaks loose.

'We are checking out. Can we get our belongings?' Drake nervously paces in front of the welcome desk, gazing around scared and confused. The mafia can be here any minute.

'We cannot hand over your things, Mr Bates. You have not yet paid the bill,' the reception guy says and stalls our precious minutes to escape from the hotel.

'Mr Chang Chen will take care of it,' Drake responds in anger and refuses to pay.

'We know nothing of that strange arrangement with Mr Chen. You must settle now, Mr Bates; otherwise, we can't give you the items,' the receptionist explains.

Fuming, he grabs his phone. 'Hi, Terry. It's Drake. They have not paid the bill at the hotel. Why?' *What a rude way to ask him*, I reflect.

Terry calls CC to get the weird situation confirmed, then I am getting uneasy when I hear the reception fella asking for Mr Chen. *Who will handle the invoice? Strange*, I speculate, while the front desk fella is talking to someone from CC's company and next, the staff wants to delay us. Holly crap! Now I get petrified. Argh! Damn it, I'm frightened as hell. Holy moly; I am involved in a terrible mess.

'Mr Chang Chen does not allow you to leave the hotel without permission from him.' The reception dude informs Drake and calls the security guards to detain us.

Auch, this suck! I become annoyed. My blood is fast boiling inside, and my blood pressure rises to dangerous heights. 'No one is deciding if I'm allowed to leave or not. Such horrifying mafia methods you are forcing on us,' petrified I yell as a barking angry Terrier. Now being more scared over this entire mess.

Drake tries to hush me, eyeing around to see if the gangsters are coming.

'Pay the damn bill, Drake!' I'm shouting as a frantic woman and stare with anger at him.

'I don't have the money for it. CC promised to settle it.' And he paces to the automatic entrance door, to see if CC is coming.

I realise he can't handle it, and CC will not pay until he has spoken to Drake. I've never been in such panic and distress, as Drake continues shouting and quarrelling in anger with the front counter and the security guards. My heart is pounding with madness, frustration, and distress while I am monitoring the entrance door, ready to flee.

CHAPTER 2

The Talking Imaginary Painting

Painting is silent poetry, and poetry is a painting that
speaks.

—Plutarch

Fiction cannot live without reality. There is no way around it. The
so-called reality will always appear in even the wildest fiction.
People who write have nothing to write about, except for what
exists in everyday life. There are good reasons to use reality in fiction.
In fact, there are no other options.

This is a work of fiction but based upon ideas of actual events.
Names, characters, places and incidents either are the product of the
author's imagination or are used fictitiously, and any resemblance to any
actual persons, living or dead, events, or locales is entirely coincidental.

My name is Mary, and the continuation of my heated dangerous
love story has the focus of an enchanting, humorous, gripping and tragic
part of my life, that can depict a real-life event. As the telling unfolds, I
realise I can't have wealth, thrill, fun, and bliss at the same time. So, I'm
exploring the genuine affection with the charismatic doctor, Drake L.
Bates, which was almost fatal for me.

For me it's been an immense challenge to write *Burning Desire* part
1 and 2, as I wanted the story to be as realistic as possible to the real
life we as humans are living. Also, for the readers to get a decent sense

of what kind of an intense desire you can have as it is in the dreadful thrilling drama between Mary and Drake. I grabbed the magic pen and got the inspiration to write about the psychological drama when I moved to my new apartment, facing the front row of the sea on the southern coast of England. I had to rip up in many emotional traumas, backtracking the heated love life with a devious, calculated psychopath who manipulated and ill-used me. It's a tough thing to do, when you most want to forget everything. Though, there were too many unanswered questions in my head, so the many years of writing, has finally put the pieces of the puzzle together, about Drake and Mary's passionate and dangerous love affair.

*   *   *

Let's backtrack to where it ends in Part 1 when the gloomy day arises as Drake drives me to the airport, and we stand in the pouring rain, when he dropped me off at Hong Kong Airport, where I broke down before we say goodbye. Wet from the rain I'm following in his hasty steps at the hectic, noisy, packed Airport, with millions of rushing people heading to their destinations around the world. I can only see him among the crowds of people and want to scream my heart out as loudly as I can to him. I want to stay with him—not fly back home. We hug intensely, while I have tears in my eyes, I hold him tight to me, and clench his lovely soft hands before we say goodbye in an emotionless and insensitive, unimportant loud Airport, as he kisses me tenderly goodbye and let go of my hand. He turns around and takes his last graceful steps while I grief-stricken watch his stylish figure disappears, without him looking back. With cries in my eyes, I desperately continue to watch him elegantly fade farther and farther away from me with hasty footsteps. He is resembling an opaque shadow on the horizon, as my beloved ghostly disappears, as if everything only has been an unrealistic ghostly dream in my head.

Twenty-four hours later I sit on my empty balcony with my loneliness, on a chilly winter's morning in Southern Spain, and faced with my hardest decision of my life. Should I run from my previous life

I had with Paul or stay in my enchanted romance and remain in Drake's muscular arms?

It's incredible how one human being can have a profound impact on another, despite ten thousand kilometres. Being loved by someone one day and having him completely unrealistically upset the next is turning my life upside down. I'm facing an incredible emptiness in my heart as I enter my penthouse, because neither Drake nor my dogs nor my family are there. I throw my heavy suitcase into the corner of the room and go straight into my bedroom. Weeping and desperate, I throw myself lifeless as a dead doll on the soft bed and curl up in the foetal position and hide under the soft goose down duvet as a scared little unhappy crying child. Grasping the pillow, I desperately hug it, with my knees drawn tight against my chest, and fall asleep.

Gently, the glow of the Sun shines through my window the next morning. I slept comparable to a baby the entire night, still wearing my clothes and having my head in the foot end. While seated on the edge of the bed, I reflect deeply about Drake, and ponder if my decision to go back to Spain is wise. Next, I'm speculating roughly of my hateful husband, who doesn't want me to come home for Christmas though, it's difficult for me to imagine a life without both men. However, I want to be with Paul, but mostly, I miss Drake. I ruminate of him dearly as I take off my clothes and get into the steamy shower, presuming Drake is the best thing that's happened to me. Am I wise in my consideration?

Despite that, both fellas exhaust me; I still have many unanswered questions in my head. I'm content Drake for five months ago, picked me up from my miserable sadness, so should I better forget everything about him? Stay in my marriage? I don't know what to do. Whom to choose?

The lukewarm water trickles gently down my body, while I turn around and let the gentle drops run through my blonde hair and splashing my tanned face. I'm pausing as if I'm spellbound under the therapeutic shower, then ponder my future destiny with Drake and Paul. Who will it be?

It's three weeks before Christmas and it's snowing and freezing in Denmark, and on the southern coast of Spain, it's twenty-five degrees and sunny. I'm getting dressed, grab my newly brewed hot coffee, pour the milk into the mug, snatch the smokes, and my computer. As I read emails, I'm pondering; *A nice meditative stroll on the beach can do me right, then sit and listen to the sound of the waves crashing on the beach.*

Instead, I entertain an ideal vision, watching a light brush beginning a graceful dance with a painting on a canvas leaning on an easel in the middle of the room. In the bare garden, the brush paints gorgeous flowers—majestic lupines, gladiolus, lilies and lots of colourful herbaceous perennials—surrounded by various green low plants and shrubs. The flowers radiate a scenic harmony of colours and define the composition as a floral frame. With my imagination I sense the comforting and reminiscent of something I experienced in the past which makes me reflect on it. Maybe it's from my dream or my déjà vu. A light blue sky appears at the top of the art. The Sun's rays glisten over the flower sea, with a striking, magical, bright light. In the setting, I weakly hear a relaxing melody from my stereo, which makes me extra aware that something enchanting will happen.

A small white wooden chair stands in the garden. The brush glares inquiringly around and notices that something is missing in the portrait, so the dancing brush draws a black spot and glances at it in amazement! *What to do?* It considers and then continues the art.

White splashes appear here and there, and a few tiny, thin black strokes appear. What is it? It's resembling a small soft muzzle so it could be the whiskers of an animal. The brush is content, diligent and inventive. The black and white spots turn into a black kitten with a fine-looking white marking on its chest, and white blurring surrounds its pink muzzle. Four small white paws turn up, resembling as tiny white baby socks. Full of health and vigour, the kitty bends its back and joyfully; it spins an adorable little meow, wandering curiously around in the green grass. Enthusiastic and excited, it tumbles wildly everywhere on the plot, but her play is not seemly, as she overturns few empty pots. Frightened, she tries to jump out of the pictures' left corner.

The confused brush eagerly chases the little cat—paints it back into the image, behind colourful delicate plants in the many pots. The brush won't let the sweet kitten vanish, because it has excellent value for the paintbrush and its potential painting. The kitten finds a red ball of yarn the brush had, with great pleasure, created in kindness for the kitten. Kitty should not get bored and disappear, so Kitty glances with full-sized green eyes at the new exciting toy. She plays with the lovely ball of yarn, and during her play, the thread rolls out of the canvas. To catch her new, adorable toy, she pops out of the painting's corner again.

The brush gets frustrated and makes another decision—then jumps into the image in search of the kitten. For nothing in the world must she disappear. She stares at him in amazement and can't understand why she must return to the garden. *I don't belong here. I don't know the garden. I'm afraid of the brush.* She muse. The kitten only desires to explore the world *alone* and doesn't hunger to stay with the brush.

The brush is brave and considers he must hold on to the precious little treasure, because he imagines; *I alone have created her!*

So, he entices Kitty to stay and paints a small light blue bowl on the tan garden tiles. Next to it, he paints a similar pale blue milk jug with fresh white milk and pours the chill liquid into the small light blue bowl. Kitty gets happy and excited for her new loving friend and bounces back into the light. She jumps into an unfamiliar world with her new master—licking the delicious milk and playing with her white paws in the fresh milk. The bowl is rowdy, and tumble in her play, and over the entire floor flows the milk. Kitty begins sorrowfully to mew over the spilt milk, then she glances at her master who comforts her.

She can't see on the canvas that the brush is a calculated puppet master, steering her around with his string. Her new puppeteer makes sure that the picture does not fall into gravel, because the brush is gaining something of its efforts to keep the lovely cat. She surrenders to the charming soft black brush and becomes a permanent part of the art.

As she has licked up all the spilt milk on the floor, the brush master ponders; *oh, my, the kitten is missing something in her life.* She can't only lick milk, play with yarn, and topple pots. *What shall I do with her?* He ponders.

He paints a soft small red heart pillow on the white wooden chair. Kitty tires of her efforts, and her inattentive playing, so she lies down on the red heart pillow. She falls asleep, dreaming of her amazing day in the garden, and falls in love with her beloved brush—the disguised puppeteer with his invisible strings.

The brush is pleased with today's brilliant efforts, so finally, he declares an excessive love for the sweet kitten. 'I love you with a passion that I haven't tried before in my life. Darling, we belong to each other for eternity. We are created for each other as God specifically created you for me. Yours forever, with my loving heart.'

Who is the soft little kitten and the handsome, obscure, artful, crafty brush?

* * *

It's the first thing I see on my computer that December morning after twenty-four hours of travel, from Hong Kong to Spain.

The day before yesterday was the last day; I saw Drake and thought everything only had been a ghostly dream. But it wasn't a dream; it was real-time—and so was the Kitty and the brush, as I'm reading his enchanting card. In the bright light of the Sun and the blue sky on a mild morning, I sit concentrated, wearing a warm sweater and drinking my hot fresh coffee. With my hands gently folded around the hot white cup, while I gaze at the stunning picturesque mountains and breathe in the gentle fresh mountain air. I want to write a letter to him after being reminded of the lovely brush and the kitty card and tell him how much I miss my everlasting love.

The tears I lost on the previous sad departure day have turned into sparkling stars the past night. They flash across the night sky of the entire universe, watching and blinking over us, just as the angels protect us in our peaceful sleep. When it's late at night in Hong Kong, it's early morning in the southern part of Spain. In my early morning, it replaces the stars by the Sun's glowing rays on a gorgeous morning in Spain, getting warmer hour by hour, as my love for Drake grows day by day— more than I ever imagined it.

CHAPTER 3

Arms Made Of Steel

There's a plot in this country to enslave every man, woman
and child. Before I leave this high and noble office, I intend
to expose this plot.

—President John F. Kennedy

My life is a petrifying mess, and I was suicidal when I first
met Drake that gorgeous summer day. A stunning man
where a part of him appears mysterious and exciting.
He always presents himself as the picture of normalcy and he acts
educated, possessing an outstanding personality. He appears healthy,
seductive, handsome, and charming at first, as my doctor, and quickly
I get caught up in his intrigues. Having a doomed marriage makes me
consider a divorce with Paul, so Drake offers to help me through the
complicated procedure if I want a split-up with Paul. I trust Drake with
my fragile life, not realising how talented he is in tricking people; hence
I continue to have contact with him in good faith. Quickly we enter
the honeymoon phase and the first four months with him begins in
good and evil. Is it doomed to be the end before it begins? You might
think; *Oh, my God! She must be naïve and unwise.* That's okay. Despite
everything, you don't know me, but I'll do my best for you to know me
better during the story. Though, I'll not deny; you might be right! So,
what is behind the ominous shadow of Dr Drake Lucifer Bates?

Few months back, before Drake travelled from Spain to Asia, he with proudness showed me a box with paper clips, many letters, business proposals, and more that he thought were significant.

'This is not a secret what's in the box. Babe, you can make it electronic. I mean; if you help me. You are talented with computers. Will you do that for me?' He pleaded.

Among it, there was a funny letter written to the royal establishment of the Crown. I laughed while reading it. But I'll get back to that part later.

I don't know so much of calculating people, so will I figure out what I can expect from such evil people? I think such people never show empathy for others, and it's all a game to them, when a person fall victim to such horrifying manipulations and psychological abuse. Some say; it's as being a chased Hitchcock character in a horror movie, because such persons are *that* talented and can memorise all their lines and win awards for their incredible performances.

They can lie about their professional experience, their private life, yea, I tell you they are a habitual liar, a perfect predator. And you are their prey.

With a massive drama they will tell you disturbing grim stories about your family, friends or people at your work and about you and your past, of how horrible you are, and much more.

Only *your* demoniacal behaviour badly and negatively will affect your common lives, in the psychopath's opinion. Only *you* have all the damn depressing demons, not *him*. That's why he thinks he is the prince in shining armour and so determined to rescue you, and in his opinion, only he is the person who can help you get rid of all your devilish demons. Possessed and threatening demons run in your family, not in his. So, he'll save you from the evil devil who he considers might be your husband, boyfriend, family or friends. He is the man with arms made of steel.

As a woman you can easily become petrified and insecure, and don't dare to leave him, because all the disturbing stuff can truly frighten the hell out of you. They can be an excellent con artist and get anyone to put work or money into their project or believes.

They can be quick-tempered if something doesn't work for them, and some never physically harm you and can give you many caring and stunning days in between the madness. But they can be extraordinarily manipulative—a psychologically violent person, which for some can be worse than if they beat you up, because it's difficult to escape the psychic terror. Emotionally, many women get badly manipulated and mistreated by such psychopathic men. Believe me, it plagues these women with confusing thoughts that are constantly swirling in their minds as they slowly get poisoned by these abusive men. The bruises after the physical violence fade away, but the impact of the psychological abuse doesn't disappear, and keeps haunting you for the rest of your life. Not that I'm saying physical violence is less harmful, both are dangerous and horrifying, because the psychological abuse also follows the physical abuse.

You might remember the disturbed, handsome, and charming lunatic, like Ted Bundy or John Meehan. They used people—victims who couldn't figure out what was happening to them before it was too late.

The problem must be me. There must be something wrong with me. Was I the 'demonic psychopath' and not Drake? Could be your thoughts. A hairy thought! How frightening.

If you are a vulnerable, trusting woman who loves too much, is caring or just too trusting, a sociopath uses this, and controls and abuses people and takes advantage—to get as much as he can. The charming prince knows you have a heart of goodness and possess unlimited trust in him, and then he drains you as a bloodsucking leech.

I knew nothing of such people, though; I figured it out, what you can expect from them. They're dangerous to their surroundings, and there are billions of them worldwide. It is dreadful getting out of such a muggy, creepy spiderweb when you first get trapped as a fly in their foul snare. It's all a play to the predator, and you are the target.

The storyline is told as an insight of what to expect from such people, and how the emotions and feelings can give you a massive crack in your life. Listen to the warning signs and take them seriously, or it can end up fatal. Living with such a wolf in sheepskin is not a love game nor a walk on rose paddles nor floating on a soft tender pink cloud. It's catastrophic! You turn every part of your dreams to shame, because the man you love has killed the dream you dreamt.

By now, everything is a romantic dream between us, so after musing over the kitty illusion, I swallow his lovely words as it is sweet delicious honey, easing my sad-hearted and desperate state. The lack of love from my husband makes me weak, because Drake has entered my life, with great understanding, warmth, and passionate affection for my bouncing heartbeat. In my gullibility, I can't understand what I'm doing, so in my privation, I get more involved with Drake. I want desperately to go back to Asia—to be with him—but I must decide if I want a divorce or stay in Drake's caring arms. What will be the reality?

CHAPTER 4

THE FEELING OF LONESOMENESS

I feel as I'm stuck between two worlds, wanting to be a part
of the new but feeling at home in the old, now I'm not a part
of either and I'm alone and lonely stuck in nothing.
—Idle Hearts

Do you know the emotion of loneliness? It's a vast loneliness that is sad and long, and to me, it enquires smokes, and superb wine to endure the pain, while I am sitting with it in my heart, soul and mind. It's impossible to understand when the night is so lovely, with the sky full of sparkling stars, that glances on my solitary, while the calm wind blows my loose hair wildly. I fill my glass with a superb French red wine, sending a delicious bouquet up to my nostrils. I take the last drag of my ciggy and exhale the greyish smoke into the dusky universe. Shortly after, I crave to light an extra one but write my lonely thoughts instead.

Earlier, I had a perfect Skype afternoon with Drake, we laughed, his mood was high, and I was also in a pleasant state while he wasn't busy with something else. The fresh chilly night gradually crept in from Asia with him, while the last Spanish warm sunbeams were still shining on my body. We said goodnight, and he went back to his solitude, while I sat alone here on my balcony, drinking delicious wine.

I'm isolated. Then my heart becomes broken again, and my soul is empty and sad, while the loneliness is back. My secluded thoughts swirl in my head, speculating; *If I'm smart, sneak in a nice warm bath and prepare myself, so I'll appear good-looking.*

In the late afternoon, I enjoy a warm foamy bathtub, drinking a glass of chilly Chardonnay and enjoying the lively flames from the candlelight's standing around the tub. I find my white dress with the black polka dots, take my sexy black lingerie, then put on my thin stay-up stockings and slip into my fancy sandals. Next, I put on a gentle makeup and make my lips shine with a glossy cherry red lipstick. I sense this action will allow the loneliness to go away.

I can't escape from it so I'm gathering energy then walk to my car, though the action requires something from me for it to happen. While seated in the driver's seat, I drive off, hoping my joy will overthrow my lonely soul. I head downtown to find an excellent restaurant serving nutritious quality food, then I'm doubting whether it's a marvellous idea.

At the city square, I park my car in the underground garage, then take a small stroll on the major street, as I'm trying to be content, while browsing in few shops but buying nothing. It's boring, so instead I sit in the city square and admire the nearby stunning Catholic church, noticing the sun has set. There are many black metal benches with fine-looking ornaments on the backrests, and it fills the benches up with local Spaniards, young and old. Noisy children run playing around, close by the splashing water fountain, so I find a vacancy and sit next to an old wrinkled grey-haired man, grinning and staring sweetly at me so I can see he is missing few front teeth. A formal and boring text message jingle in on my phone. It's from my friend Lucy, and as I read it, the lonely thoughts re-enter my lonesome mind.

OMG! I don't understand the freezing cool message from someone I fancy so much, so my loneliness sneaks more up in my sad mind and gets more precarious, as I realise she is unhappy with my friendship, with Drake. I try to call Lucy, but she doesn't pick up the damn ringing phone.

Spain is no longer as it used to be, and deep in my thought; *Mary, you are so lost and abandoned when your life is not with the one you love.*

It's about time for me to find a restaurant, so I raise my booty and stroll to find one. I'm heading to the superb restaurant we visited several times before, while Drake was with me in this godforsaken land. The content waiter recognises me from past times, then smiles and waves caring at me, as he has found a secluded tiny table for me.

He gazes pondering at me. 'Only you?' he asks. 'You are alone. You look so lonely!' Handing over the menu, then he smiles.

I try to keep a straight face, mumbling in Spanish, 'I want a glass of red wine. Oh, and icy sparkling water.' I'm starving! My blood sugar is at its lowest, so I must have food, here and now. It makes my greedy hungry eyes to order a big Angus steak, medium done, mashed potatoes, spinach and bread in a small basket.

It's delicious, prepared on the plate with the garlicky spinach on the side. The loneliness doesn't allow me to enjoy it; I can't eat the food, so I might as well pay and want to leave.

The waiter frustrated takes the food away.

'Was it not good?'

'I'm not hungry anymore.' Instead, I sit watching the noisy people walking on the street as a herd of roaming cattle. 'Big', 'trivial', 'ugly', and a few gorgeous ones. 'Tall', 'tiny', 'thick', and 'thin' people. Lots of Danes, German's and English, and many tourists I can't understand. Some Spaniards glares at me as I'm an obsessed demon, and hundreds of screaming and quiet children, playing around. A bunch of gleaming dogs piss on every palm tree they pass. Noisy cars lurk back and forth on the promenade, playing loud cheerful Spanish and English music. Young bragging car dudes' shouts in the distance as they set their foot on the accelerator and race off at high roaring speed. The early evening is still summery, but you need a sweater not to get cold. The breeze from the ocean causes the drops of the water to settle on my lips, so when I moist my lips I can taste the salty dewdrops.

I glare at my kissing pictures of Drake and me on my phone. Oh my, I trouble the thoughts as an obsession, and now I'll soon be sleeping alone again, as I did last night too. *I can no longer be without him.* The waiter comes to my table, and with a gentle smile, I pay my bill, give him €5 in tip, and walk away, as the thought strikes me, *Shall I go out dancing or not?*

But without Drake, I can't dance, because I don't want any other men in my arms. It's only him I want close to me in a dance—and he's great at it, and has the salsa rhythm in his body, when he swings me on the dance floor resembling a snowy swan.

Before I walk to my car, I stroll on the boulevard, then someone calls my name, and I stop, gazing around and pondering it is Drake, but I can't see anyone. It's not him!

In solitude, I turn to the parking lot and settle into my car, glaring at the empty seat next to me, and drive home. From our gloomy garage, I take the stairs up to the fourth floor, lock myself into the empty penthouse and write my solitary on the lonesome blank white paper on my table.

The paper is no longer blank because now it's filled up with many words on my loneliness—though, in my mind, everything is emptiness. My apartment is hollow without Drake, empty, without my loving family, the barking dogs, or my funny friends, or people who before filled my alien life with value and joy. Everything has disappeared. I miss his presence, his physique, his gentle hands touching my body, the words coming out of his lovable mouth, his kiss, the look in his eyes that makes me plunge in the deepest warmest forest lakes on this glorious earth. I miss his gentle laughter, the pleasant smile, the way he walks, and me touching his good-looking firm ass. I miss his loud coughing, the crunchy voice, the way he speaks and laughs when he hilarious pretends he is gay. I miss everything about him, that I can touch on him—his delicious scent, his minty breath when he sleeps nearby me or speaks close to my face. I miss all that exists in him in my awful lonely moment, and it's hard to understand that I'm so isolated now, when he usually fills out my loneliness. *Why are we apart when we need to be together?*

So dear you, who fill my loneliness, fill me with joy and love of great value, and let me no longer be lonely. Exhausted with concerns, I go to sleep alone, musing I am travelling back alone to Denmark the day after tomorrow.

*   *   *

It's a chilly morning while I'm waiting in Malaga Airport on my way home for Christmas with my family. I muse of Drake, while I melancholy listen to Hurts playing 'Stay' on my iPod. It describes so well my feelings for him and reminds me of the day we said goodbye at the same Airport, when he for a few months ago travelled to Asia. Today the girl in her black Prada shoes sits on the same hard creaking metal chair in the check-in area, and it makes me want to cry.

I recall my last minutes with Drake, 'Baby, we will not say goodbye to each other. We will soon see each other again,' he said, trying to comfort me.

It was awful back then, watching him with quick steps disappear farther away from me.

The last minutes we had eye contact now and then, while he was standing in the lengthy winding queue of expecting glad people on their way to travel. Other guests were entering the zone, following him in the lengthy line, until I could no longer see him, nor his lovely warm-hearted brown eyes.

I want to cling to his tender hands, but they are not there and then it spins in my head, pondering; *did he know how I suffered letting him leave?* It was terrible back then, watching it until he disappeared into the duty-free area, and the *Burning Desire* of a shadow was fading when the opaque glass door opened in front of him. Our last goodbye turned into a final silent wave as he hastily turned to face me before the door shut. I broke into unhappy crying, watching him to vanish at the corner, as the shadow disappeared, closing in behind him, and I screamed inside with my heart. *Stay! Come back to me.*

My tears rolled down my cheek and fell heavily on the stony granite, so I could no longer sense the heat or glimpse his presence; thus, I was eagerly waiting for him to come back. He didn't, so I had to give up my

Burning Desire, and my longing turned into the most torrential wet tears I have ever shed.

Such Airport goodbyes are the hardest moments, when I must pick myself up again, then pick up the tears and send them to Drake through the night—glittering sad tears became comparable to stars, and would gleam at him as he sat in the plane gazing out of the tiny window, that devastating day.

I wished the stars of the night were smiling at him while I was sending a kiss to the blue Moon, knowing our hot lips meet again under the sparkling night. Only his name was on my lips.

Don't let your tears flow into the Spanish mud, lest I showed my loneliness. The fingers tried to wipe them off from my swollen eyes and blushing cheeks, as if I might have caught the massive drops. They were heavy as the rain in Spain, a vast pool, as when the Spanish sky bursts open, and God cries many drops. I shed the tears for him, and I recall his promise before my trip to Jerusalem and Bethlehem, 'Mary will always gather up the tears.' He comforted me.

'Collect them Baby. Take them in your hand. Put the hand in front of your lips. Then blow a discreet breeze over the crying tears. Send them to me, into the night's twinkling sky.' That's what I did, and he would be at sleep while the stars would blink in the night's darkness, shinning in the moonlight, so he would never forget me.

Although, he is no longer close by, it makes me sentiment as he is my entire life, thinking he is the man I have been waiting for, and I am lost without him. What shall I do? Choose between Drake or my cheating husband Paul and the life in Copenhagen?

The affection appears right, but I don't know how Drake's craving is for me. My thoughts float to another space, of how intimate we have been, and I don't want to give up our friendship. Everything is okay, I'm so convinced, and soon we will be together again, and then with his muscular arms he will embrace me. Before he came into my life, I have had nowhere to escape by being a prisoner in my unhappiness. Since then I have come out of my captivity, of my misery and having been close to happiness; I don't want to give it up.

No more goodbyes in an Airport again, there have been too many farewells, similar as we had at Hong Kong Airport, not so many weeks ago.

I need Drake here with me, and I'm waiting in a meaningless, unemotional Airport again without him. It's too hard for my heart and soul, and it's creating a gloomy fear in me of Airports.

After a four-hour flight, I land in Copenhagen, and King winter rages. It's freezing, it blows, it's snowing something awful, and I'm not prepared for the cold, so I freeze and quiver. Staring across at the street, I walk into the designated smoking space and light a cigarette to calm my nerves, because I'm anxious about being back with Paul. I glance at the many waiting black taxis, trying to pick out who I want to drive with. I'm dumping my finished fag in the trash, jump into the black Mercedes that will drive me to my next destination.

The friendly driver chatters uninterruptedly of the harsh weather, but I'm not in the mood of listening, because I'm only thinking of one thing—to gather my powers for an upcoming high-pitched discussion with Paul. Thoughts swirl and buzz madly in my head, pondering; *I must get it to work with Paul*, and it needs to get resolved, although I can't forget his cheating.

CHAPTER 5

TRUTH FORGOTTEN AND
LIE REMEMBERED

Fake friends are like shadows. They follow you in the Sun
but leave you in the dark.

—Everyday Power

At the time I'm arriving outside my home, and to my
astonishment, I discover that I don't have the apartment keys
with me. Shit! The ones in my bag are to the penthouse in
Spain.

Thankfully, Mark is home alone, and he gets somewhat surprised
when I ring the doorbell, and he imagines it is unreal. 'Mom, please
repeat. Is it you?'

'Yea, my love. It's me.'

Fast, he shots down the stairs, then flies right into my arms, kissing
and hugging me, and will barely let go of me. It's nice to meet him again,
so joyful he helps me with the luggage, loudly laughing when we take
the stairs up to the third floor.

The entire apartment has a pleasant fragrant of cleanness and
appears very tidy. Exhausted, I slap my booty on the leather sofa in the
living room, talking with Mark until Paul comes home. It distresses
Paul I'm there, then he stops surprised and is almost walking out of the
apartment again. The reunion is not the best, as I'd hope for. Besides,

I'm also somewhat irritated and flabbergasted, because he has changed most of the apartment without my consent. He has removed the white leather furniture and replaced with fresh black pieces, then removed our stunning Asian pigeon blue hand-knotted rugs and instead, bought modern oriental red carpets for the entire apartment. I can no longer see my hundred-year-old teakwood heirlooms, but I notice fresh pictures, ugly designer lamps which have taken over the two stylish crystal chandeliers in the living room. A new fridge and changes in the kitchen, so it felt as Paul had removed everything reminding of me.

Paul has transformed my office to be his office now, so his old workplace is now a wine-and-bar room. He has redesigned the bathrooms with black tiles in the shower cubicles and on the floor, which looks as a massive black box of hell. He has bought new folding curtains throughout the apartment. Yuck! So ugly! At least I don't fancy them, and finally, they got all walls painted, and the floors sanded and re-lacquered; I have been asking to get it done for years. It's nice he has redone the children's rooms, and it's only for their benefit.

Overall, I got miffed that Paul had done so behind my back, though a lot of it looks good. Within a brief period, he has been busy changing our home, though it's not okay that he removed items without us agreeing to do so, therefore I complain.

'Well, Mary, you told me I can keep everything. I'm in my right to do as I please,' Paul argues, standing stiff and ice-cold in front of me and staring heated at me with his stunning blue eyes.

I get crossed. 'Is our estate divided? I'm not sure, according to our agreement.' I point out. And the aggressive discussion begins between us.

'Are you not hugging and kissing each other?' Mark asks to ease the situation.

'It's not such a grand idea, Sweetie. Dad is not so content with me being home again.'

'Um-hmm, mom, where are you going to sleep tonight?' Mark asks with a sad voice.

'Daddy has told me I may *not* sleep in the bedroom. It's better that I find another solution, as Daddy suggests.' Sadly, I glance at Mark and try gently to explain the situation.

'You can sleep in Adam's room until tomorrow.' Paul interrupts. 'Or in the living room.' So, Mark and I carry my stuff up to Adam's room on the first floor.

In Hong Kong, I had bought an eighteen-carat golden Chinese astrology Ox and a chain for Mark. He is playing on his PlayStation when I enter his room to give him the present. Sitting on his bed and watching him play, I sense a sudden sadness. *The day has been extraordinary and hostile between Paul and me*; I reflect. Sincerely, and no matter how much I love Drake, I expected Paul and I could find a solution for us to continue the marriage. Sadly, Paul had expressed the opposite. *Not sleeping in the bedroom.* There was nothing more to fight for. The marriage was *dead!*

The next day, Adam comes home, and is sincerely glad to see me, then he gives me a mega hug. For him, I have a unique silver coin hanging on a chain as his present. However, he's disappointed that I don't have Spotty with me.

'Mom, when will Spotty come home again?' Adam asks, staring hopeless and heated.

'Sweetie, he won't come back home anymore. Daddy has told me that both of you agreed that it's okay for him to stay in Spain. Spotty is being taken good care of by Lucy and Cliff.'

Outrageously, in a brassy chorus, the boy's yell at me, 'Daddy didn't ask us at all whether it's okay for Spotty to stay in Spain.'

The fierce anger between all of us begins because of Paul's massive lie concerning the dog.

Every time the boys ask me something, I answer them truthfully. That's my most important promise to them, because I'll not allow Paul to spin another lie to them, and I make sure he can hear my definite and honest answer. I want the boys to understand how big a liar he is, and that one of the biggest disappointments I've in our twenty years of marriage is his many lies.

The next day, Mark and I visit Sandra and Tony, and they get delighted with our visit.

'Mom, where have you been? Have you just landed from Spain?' Is Sandra's first question.

With her, you can't lie. You'd better tell the truth, because she always finds out.

'Sweet Pea, I arrived from Spain yesterday. I've also been in Asia.' I glare around carefully, not saying more. Grabbing my coffee, slurping it, and next I sly peek at my iPhone. To my great distress, I haven't deleted the pictures of Drake on my wallpaper.

What a blow! Sandra came too close to discover the picture on the lock screen with my favourite photo of Drake, in his red T-shirt. Smirking, I glance quickly at it then allow myself to enjoy the sight of our magnetic kissing picture. Next I hurry, to see if there are any messages from him, and next, I check my mail, and rush to close the phone. I notice Sandra's suspicious way of eyeing at me, following the question, 'Do you want to stay for dinner, Mom?'

'Yes, please, sounds lovely, Sweet Pea.' And at 10 p.m., we walk back home.

The unbearable quarrels between Paul and me escalate, and peace between us can't endure my being at home. Most of all, he sees that I disappear again.

After a few days, I book into a hotel at the Airport and consider travelling back to Spain again. Finally, when I'm alone, I call Drake on Skype. I urgently need to tell him of what's going on in the freezing frosty home in Copenhagen.

'Darling, imagine—it's almost as if the entire world is in decline with Paul at home.'

'Wow! Where are you now?'

'I booked a hotel room,' I say, whining as a petty girl. 'We loudly quarrel continuously. Argh! I can't stand being there anymore, darling.'

'Baby, I've for a long time thought your kids believe you take everything from their father. "Flopper" (Paul) tells them he only speaks nicely of you. It might be as he does.'

'It's awful. Everything is in ruins. Paul can only see himself. Jeez, all his negative actions.' I wanted to scream into a pillow, so no one could hear me.

'I'm sure Flopper uses the manipulation technique of sneaking things into conversations. He wants the listener to perceive that what he says is right.' Drake smirks.

'I understand the technique well. Darling, I let myself getting manipulated too easily. That's a problem. It's indescribable how Paul can make everyone believe in him.' Relaxed in the chair, I gaze at Drake.

'Flopper will surely tell the children that their mother is "sweet and lovely" to the boy's. They can look forward to seeing her—to being with her on vacations. Then tell them he must stay at home. And can't travel, because Flopper has to save money.' Drake didn't perceive that Paul had spent a lot of dough on redecorating the entire home.

'Darling, I don't know what to do. I'm not welcome here.' I'm distressed with tears and sorrowful while talking to him.

'Flopper will tell them he has to give their mother everything he saves.'

Why does Drake presume so? I wonder, scratching my neck in frustration. 'I'm glad that you can understand me. Sometimes I guess you've been a fly on the wall—seen what has happened through my marriage. I imagine you've always been inside me but haven't been able to catch me—make me realise the evil I'm going through.' I'm not aware that it might be Drake manipulating me.

'The boys will then say to Flopper, "Is mom having it all?" And he will respond, "Yes, mom gets all our money I saved. I must save up again."' Drake says ironically.

'Is that's what's happening? I don't know,' then wrinkling my forehead.

'The boys say to him, "It's not fair for mom to have everything." Here you must grasp, Mary, that the boys already conclude you get everything you guys own and have.' He says dramatically.

'Mark also told me yesterday that Daddy often asks him if he has talked to me of you.'

'There you see! Flopper manipulates them. Next thing he'll say is that it's all that he has saved up. It puts you in a critical position against the boys. So, he adds the motive to say many other snide remarks that gradually put you in a merciless place.'

I feel awful, Drake saying these things.

'Paul asked Mark, "Is Mommy speaking to or living with Drake?"' I made it clear to Mark that he can tell his father, 'Sure mom is talking to Drake. He's the best friend mom has ever had.'

'That's why the boys are nervous. They will ask Flopper, "Well, what do we do, dad? Don't you have enough money for us?" Flopper will respond, "Yes, but we have to save even more; otherwise, there won't be enough."'

'I don't get it. What has it to do with Drake? I told Mark, "If your dad wants to know, tell him, that I meet Drake occasionally when he treats me. Sometimes, I help Drake with charity work—when there are projects with children, animals or other things." I told Mark, "I don't understand why daddy wants to know. But don't lie to Daddy." Then he glares at me, shuddering his shoulders.'

'Mary, do you understand what I mean? Here Flopper has laid out the case and the cause for not spending money on the boys. Flopper blames you for everything!'

'We never talk of the money aspect. I don't understand why Paul would backbite me.'

'But Flopper doesn't talk evil of you—not directly! He does it indirectly, Baby.' I ponder how Drake can come up with such ideas.

'Indirectly? What do you mean? Mark can easily tell his dad I help you with some office Work. Fixing brochures for you.'

'I imagine Flopper manipulated you in the same way so he could fulfil his sick dreams. Yuck! For him to persuade you to his nasty foul plays.'

'I ended up telling Mark he should notice one thing—thieves believe every man steal. His Daddy is apparently like one, with him judging I've had other men during our marriage. Blaming me while Daddy has had several bimbo's during our marriage. Christ! It's not such a brilliant move. Mark becomes saddened to hear it. Hmm, mostly because he realises that I want the divorce on that basis.' Ruminating, *it makes me sad that this is the end of my marriage.*

'I'm sure Flopper has gradually slanted your thoughts. He wishes to be sweet and evil in between. Then he gives you various reasons you must do what he wants.'

'I've done what Paul wanted. What more can I do?' I panic over the strange conversation we have.

'Flopper makes you imagine and feel that you are exceptionally cool. A woman who can do something no one else can in bed.' Drake smirks.

'I've never felt "cool" doing anything for Paul. I did it of love for him. I hope that you don't believe that I'm a sex monster. What we did went too far. More always want more. We couldn't stop.'

'When you give Flopper the filthy service, he will be happy with you again.' *What kind of service does Drake mean?* I ponder.

'I feel terrible of telling you about these nasty experiences with Paul. I should not have told you.' Embarrassed, I turn my head the other way.

'You should, Baby. I feel for you. I must know everything about you.' he grins.

'I felt, if I did as Paul wished, I got peace of mind and soul. He got what he wanted. I felt I was living with a calm man in a pleasant marriage. Then I could maintain a fitting standard of living for my children—give them what I've never had. Simple things, as chocolate, sweets, milk, and toys, were not part of my childhood. When I was eight years old, I stole milk bottles sat every morning by the milkman in front of people's door.'

'Poor you, little milk baby.' He smirks.

'Ha-ha, darling, did you have those in Sweden? Glass bottles with fresh milk?'

'Yes.'

'I had a big craving for milk. I didn't get it at home. If I had seen a cow, I would have emptied its udder for milk. I love milk.' I smiled sorrowfully, recalling of the childhood memories.

'It's when Flopper says to the boys, "We have to save, because mom takes it all from us."'

Will I grasp how the puzzle pieces of Drake's sick dreams and manipulation will fit. He's falsely sweet, then next, he's evil in between, and then he makes me feel as a marvellous woman.

'Flopper is a dangerous man with his words. He couldn't—and can't—do anything physically. He has learned to be dangerous with his words.'

Was Drake talking of himself? 'My problem is that I've always been better at expressing things in the written word. I'm not good at defending myself verbally.'

'Flopper can make people believe that he is speaking the truth by mixing truth with falsehood.'

Talking to Drake regarding this, I realise I honestly don't want to go to court with Paul. 'Yeah, it's so easy for people to run away from the spoken word. I get it.'

'If Flopper just uses 90 percent truth, then he can make the 1o percent lie count more. That's what's remembered.' What did Drake mean?

Will I find out who spoke the truth? 'Maybe that's why Paul hasn't written so much. I've nothing about him. That makes me an inferior in case of a lawsuit.' I get nervous of what will happen if it ends up in court.

'Do you understand why? Because the truth told, it was so boring that it's forgotten. And the lies have higher value and seems more trustworthy.' He smirks, clapping his hands.

Can you imagine? As Drake says all this, I believe in every word he tells me. I can't figure it out.

'I've been trying to figure out the manipulation technique. It's almost impossible. Perhaps you're right, darling. It's difficult to see through people using such a skill.' My forehead wrinkles.

It's incomprehensible to me what Drake was explaining to me. It's not, as he claims, what Paul is doing to me—especially the above manipulation technique, involving the ration between truth and lies. Whose lie percentage is higher than 10 percent?

'Baby, manipulators come through with their requirements and desires they have. Both private and work. Such people are dangerous with their words in their power.' Grinning and squeezing his eyes as Drake slurps water from a glass and continues.

'Flopper also drives you financially tight in the same way. He can then do with your joint money—meaning *his money*, he considers— whatever he wants.'

'Probably true. It disappoints me. I beg to get money earned in marriage.' That irritates me.

'He will take you on advice, pro forma. Afterwards, he'll say, "I told you," and, "Don't you remember that you agreed? What? What? What?"' Drake is very ironic! Smirking devilishly.

'You can't understand it, Mary. Augh, you don't know what he's talking of. He makes it sound as the most rigorous science. Flopper will say, "Can't you comprehend that, Mary? Eh?, Huh? Well, Mary. Eyh? Got it, Mary!"' Drake's mocking speech pattern turns over to rude anger. In this moment, I don't like his feisty, staring eyes, as he continues his mocking game.

'Do you get it, Mary? Christ! Oh, my, you're such a stupid head! Mary hasn't gone to school so much. Gah, such an institutional child! Aren't you stupid, bwahaha!' And Drake's mocking, harsh speech pattern continues.

His pitch is mean and sarcastic, and it feels as if he is pointing the finger at me.

'Darling, I'm not stupid. I don't suppose that's what Paul thinks of me. He apparently forgets that I also took part with the finances until Mark was born. After Mark's repeated illness, Paul wanted me to stop working.' I had no problem doing so, if we mutually respected our roles.

Paul was enormously supportive back then. Is Drake manipulating me by accusing me of being a stupid, uneducated, and misbehaved orphanage child and of not understanding shit. It frustrates me; I can't comprehend it and don't see it in my strong affection and blindness to him.

Is it Drake who wants to save money? I still don't know of his game.

'Flopper then puts you in place, imagining you can't say anything,' Drake continues. 'You become insecure about yourself. He sets the family up against you too. Remember that his stepfather Carl wanted to bang you. I bet it's because Flopper let it leak. Told that you are a whore. That you love lots of fooling around.'

'Huh? Oh, my! Why bring that to the surface, darling?'

'Yuck, Such a sneaky old dude. Carl thought he could put his ticket in by inviting you on a secret naughty date. Recall of the scene in *Pretty Woman*. Where the lawyer expects he could screw Julia.'

'I can't see the comparisons. I'm not a luxury call girl for a man with money. The difference is, though, that Richard Gere treats Julia Roberts nicely in Pretty Woman. He gives her everything.'

'What do you mean, Baby?'

'Oh, my! Gere has such an attractive hot appearance.' I can see Drake getting jealous when I mention Richard Gere.

'Are you trying to make me jealous? Hahaha, Baby, I know I resemble him! What I mean; Flopper has put you "down" to everyone. He wants you to be little. Then he can have full control of you.'

I'm analysing his comparison. Does Drake believe I'm a whore? What I grasp is that he compares me with a whore, and he is the one inviting himself on the secret dates as a *gigolo*, maybe hoping I financially will support him, to be my lover. I'm only seeking love from him, but I'm insecure, and he sets my family up against me.

'Baby, you're too strong for Flopper. He can't control you. He knows that! He's afraid of you. By putting you in chains, he has the power.'

I ponder, *are both men putting me in chains?* 'It's likely I have been mentally too strong for Paul. Yet, I must also have been a weak person.' I can't see my way out of the manipulation. Am I also too strong for Drake—even though I'm also weak in the moment of desperate love?

'It's fear of the unknown. And coming back to the old life.'

'Baby, you must understand Flopper is a sick man—a fool of a man.' Who is the sicko?

'It's not the first time someone has threatened with my children being removed from me if I leave a man. There, I've a much of my anxiety.' Stupidly, I gave Drake a new hint he could use.

'Flopper will do that. I read that through his behaviour. Therefore, he has a top position in the business.'

'I dread it! As a leaf shakes. Uh, oh, if someone deprives me of my children and I never see them again.' I shiver only by the thought.

'Flopper is good at controlling everyone. It's not because he is skilled. He has just understood how to manipulate with his words,' he smirks.

I consider Paul as skilled. 'I've promised myself that my children will never experience what I experienced as a child. I'd rather stay. Then be strong to them and me. Not to be weak.' I didn't see that Drake used the fear I had.

'People as Flopper stand as believers. You know? With the truth and lie ratio from before.'

'Darling, what will I get out of it in my life? I don't understand it.'

'Flopper can do this the rest of his life. And with many people. Few realise that they are being fooled.'

'Fooled?' I'm falling into Drake's melting pot and then believe Paul is wrong. 'Isn't that how psychopaths run their entire life? I can't figure out such tricks.'

Could it be possible I will figure it out?

'I'm glad you're getting away from Flopper.' Drake smiles sweetly.

'Darling, you are right. I must get far away from him, if that's the case.'

'Baby, you are on your way to healing your soul. You can only do it with me.' Bambi smiles.

'I realise it'll take time to heal and lick my wounds. Now, I lick and lick. Nothing helps! At first, when you came into the picture, it helped. What happened to me?' I wanted to hug him. And Drake's eyes glisten suddenly so gorgeous.

'Baby, you have not reached the end of the road yet. I've seen a slow improvement in you.'

'I'm convinced that I'm healing. I want an enjoyable life with you, darling.'

'I'll keep on helping you. Trust me, Baby. Don't stay with Flopper. He's not worth it!' Drake smiles and slowly blinks his dazzling brown eyes.

'I wish that my open wounds will heal one day. I hope you will tell me how well I've managed—without too many injuries to my soul.'

'Before you left, Mary, you went through many internal crises. It made you resort to the damn fags instead of me.'

Oh, my goodness, now he's starting on that road again. 'Darling, I sense it's been hard for you to see me resort to tobacco. Believe me when I say how much I hate them myself.' My brain receptors crave a smoke.

'Oh, Baby, I'm always there for you. You know that. You don't need the smoke demons.'

'But you're not. It hurts me so much.' He blames the smokes and me for being weak.

'I'm always in your corner when you have to fight—which includes fighting the ciggie's.'

'No. You blame me all the time. I'm not allowed to kiss you. I love to kiss you. But during the in-between period when the taste is disappearing, until you finally want to kiss me again—well, then I give up and take a new ciggy instead.' Woah! I'm sick and tired of this subject.

'You must understand—and you know it too well, Mary. It's not nice.' He lectures me.

I sense it smells, but I brush my teeth, wash my hands and head every time so he can't sense the unpleasant odour. 'You constantly remind me of them. My brain cells tell me, "If he still doesn't want to kiss me, I might as well take a fag."' I'm depressed again in my quiet mind.

'Jesus Christ, Babe, I hate that the damn cancer sticks are stronger than your love for me.'

With Drake talking of the smokes, I glare at my package on the table. I want to smoke *now*!

'Your love, embrace, and your kisses are all so gratifying to me. I sense that we are separating ourselves because of the tobacco,' I peep.

I want to end the conversation and get outside to have my smoke. The worst thing that can happen to you when you try to quit is the other person continually blaming you. Or when people are talking of your fault, then reminding you of being a smoker. It's so hard to stop the habit.

'Bloody hell, Mary, the damn smoke demons in you come up and pull you down occasionally.' He criticism me.

Christ! I'm seeing demons in every corner. It's comforting he can't see the "demon," pack on my table. My glands desperate drool for a cigarette the more Drake talks of it. 'Darling, we barely live with each other. I get nervous and scared. Sometimes I presume you're like every other man. You can't accept the faults I unfortunately have.'

'Baby, everything hurts so endlessly for me.'

So now he is the unfortunate victim. 'Unfortunately, in our relationship, I have the mistake of smoking. Tobacco is the only comfort I have in my life.'

'It's hard to see you suffer.' He pities me.

'In my childhood, I had nothing to comfort my cravings—not a mother's breast nor a pacifier.'

'Good damnit, Mary! Why do you need anything? You can have my tongue and Willy.' He pranks as if the comment is funny.

'I don't know. Apparently, the only thing I can get in my mouth is a man's nasty cock when he's horny. Afterwards, I can taste their nasty butter milk from their wiener. I can then wash my mouth and rinse it with mouthwash. Next, I can plague it with a cloud of smoke.' Holy shit. Somehow, I got pissed at his stupid remark.

'Christ! Holy mother of God. Sometimes, I don't grasp it of what to do with you.' He grumbles.

My brain cells shout inside me. *Damn you, Drake! Stop talking of those damn smokes all the time!* 'I try so hard to stop smoking! While we were together in Asia, I did not smoke. Isn't that good enough for you?' I get no answer. I ponder, *Is this some misunderstanding?*

'You know I'm subjected to too much mental terror now. My soul and my brain can't always cope without the emotional comfort you give me.'

'Oh, my goodness. I get it! You don't want me to care for you—or so it feels.'

I want Drake to take care of me. Doesn't he get it?

'Huh? What? We're both under a lot of stress now. Darling, I mostly want to give up. The only thing that's keeping me up running now is what I can give you—to give you a fresh start. Help you financially for you to survive.'

Drake seems ungrateful.

'It's hard to see you suffer that way, Babe. Christ! Am I not good enough?'

Why can't he realise I'm supporting him 100 percent in all his ideas—his amazing projects? I'm slowly becoming more depressed over my own miserable life.

'Baby, I realise there's a fight going on inside you.'

Yeah, but you're not supporting it ultimately! I contemplate. 'My life is hell when I'm not with you. My life is a deep black hole when I'm with you. Then I can't kiss you or hug you—because I smoke a fag now and then. That I don't understand! I understand tobacco is shit. It's destroys the body—and now to our love.'

'Babe, I can't get a foothold in your ring corner,' he criticises.

That's because I was hoping to save my marriage. Perhaps it's because Drake is pushing me away. Smokes and money! 'I never doubted that you were in my corner. You have spent many hours, days, and weeks supporting my cause. I'm forever grateful. I've never been used to someone stands in my corner.' I proudly praise him.

'I mean I've proven to you how much I love you, my precious Mary Magdalene.' His tone shifts to tenderness.

'That's what makes it difficult for me—to let you all the way into my private sphere.'

'My sweet little girl. You mean everything to me.' Then he sends an air kiss. M-wah!

'Oh, my, I'm afraid of being knocked out—of not having control over the situation. And myself.'

'Geez, Baby! I'm affectionate towards you for the right reasons—genuine love. What more can I say?' He blinks with his divine Bambi eyes, so I melt.

'I only want one thing, darling. It's letting you all the way in. I'll never let you go again.' It disappointed me deeply that a fag or two is ruling our relationship.

'Oh, my, I've been thinking of how Flopper turns your kids against me. It happens through his manipulation.' He changes the topic. 'Damn, it's times when he says to them in a devoutly way that mom takes it all from us.'

'Huh? It's difficult to tell what he's saying to the children. It's only guesses you come up with.' The lengthy conversation was boring me.

'Bloody hell, Baby, Flopper says to them, Drake is behind mom. He tells her how she can get everything from the poor fella, (Paul). That way, Drake can take everything. Worst is he also takes Mom from Dad.' The conversation has now turned to something weird with Drake as the victim. He keeps on complaining.

'Geez, darling, I've told you, I distinctly tell the boys how it's all connected.'

'Yah, yah, fine and next, Flopper puts in the sneaky context, "Yes, and then Drake does it only for his gain."'

'Eh? I find it difficult to bother. Paul might or not might manipulate them.'

'Christ, later, Flopper tells the kids, "Drake is probably not at all interested in Mom." Oh, boy, it may get the children to speculate, "Aha! Drake takes her for money?" because now Mary is a kept woman.' I believe Drake is suffering from persecution mania. Or is it because he *is* doing it all for the *money?*

'I don't sense if the kids understand. I hope they someday will understand the full context.'

'Ha-ha, and next Flopper will complain, "Poor daddy. I have to start all over again." Yeah, right! Start over at the top with a super salary. Gee! The rich damn dandy gets far more than the poor mocking heads of Danish men. Blokes who bother to run for a paltry lump sum.' Drake is soooo ... jealous, because he is the poor Swedish mocking head. He is behind everything, and I let him help me with everything.

'Phew, yesterday, the boys overheard a conversation between us. I told Paul that I have received nothing from him. I have not gotten it all.'

'Babe, it's clear to me Paul will always try to drive a wedge between us.'

'Oh, my, Paul doesn't want to sign our agreement. The divorce agreement hasn't come into force.'

'Oh ... la ... la. It will become difficult to make it last when Flopper sees how well *I'm* doing.'

'I told the kids; I don't get everything—if that's what daddy claims. No. Daddy will buy me out of his life. I'm getting money for some of our contents. Otherwise, we'd to split the entire home and each get half instead and there will then only be minimal left.'

'Ha-ha, but he will surely make trouble for you.' Obviously, it's only Drake who is doing good! He's the trickster getting all the dough out of me.

'Oh, my, the boy's must understand it. Jeez, I won't do that to them and take half the stuff. Then they'd have to start over, with new furniture, kitchenware, TVs, and much more—unless they conclude it's a better idea than having dad to give me money so I can start over.'

'Damn, if Flopper doesn't get the adjustable support, he might challenge you at the public administration. Oh, my goodness, Babe, then you must go to court; with the ammunition you have.'

'For the good of everyone, I've considered that it will be best for the family that Paul buys me out.'

'We need to have a lot more clarity on your story—even if it hurts to tell. Oh, boy, that hurts me too.'

'Then it's only one person, me, who needs to start over—not the entire family.'

'He-he, Babe, I've built a defensive wall inside me so I can deal with it.'

'Darling, I grasp Paul is mad at me. He will make it troublesome for me and, thus, our relationship.'

'I think it's harder for you to talk of it.' It's only about Drake—him, him, *him*—and how terrible it will be if he loses and Paul wins.

'I don't want to argue with Paul about who is getting what. *It's not ending in court.* I must resolve this sensibly between us. So, I don't understand your arguments.'

'Ohhh! Baby, you have the choice between this confrontation. I hope you can respond to your views. Then the court will find that you agreed with Flopper under pressure from him.'

'I get it! If it ends up in the public administration, I probably don't have complete control over it myself. Then they will decide it all—not him and me.'

'Oh, my, Flopper may still have the list of things you did during your muddy marriage—or, rather, improving your dirty life. It doesn't say that it was on his request. Um-hmm ... unless you have emails telling this side of the story,'—Drake turns the conversation to the dirty relationship during my marriage, — 'um-hmm ... something saying it bored Flopper with your way of banging.'

'Hmm! I'd rather not worry of those kinds of flaws now.' I get anxious of the many things Drake scares me with. He deliberates about everything.

'Ahem! Something exciting had to happen. Oh, yah, Flopper will lie in court. Geez, and say that it was *you* who made him find topics on dirty sites. And *you* approved of it. Oops! If these things get separated, he can create an alternative story that benefits him. Aha, therefore, it makes it harder for them to trust you. Uh oh, then it'll be more difficult to get support for your memoirs.'

'Oh, gosh, I must deal with this stuff when the time comes—if it ever comes.' I sense as he tries to scare me a lot.

'That's why I believe you must find the best deal. Then you must write the book.' It sounds as the worst *Dragon* horror movie.

'Fine! I'll let the lawyer decide if I should agree to that deal.' I'm trying to get around the conversation.

'Baby, you must move from Copenhagen. Now! After a year, you are in another jurisdiction. There you get a different managing than in Denmark. If Flopper stops paying, we find out why and under all the circumstances.' Drake is talking in a more threatening manner.

'Eh! I can't cope with another country's laws now.' I don't understand him or why he presumes it must end so drastically.

'Ahh, then you sue Flopper under Hong Kong laws. There will be a pressure on him he never imagined. In Denmark, you stand weak, but not here. My advice; push the divorce through roughly and send everything to the lawyer. Now!'

'Ohhh, I don't imagine it will come so far. Paul is not like that.' I try to defend.

'Baby, you should not take the Spanish apartment as the opportunity. Let him keep it.'

'Um-hmm, when I spoke with Paul, he asked whether I wanted to rent or take over the flat in Spain. I said I might not take it. And not with the uncertain clauses he has entered the contract.'

'Hey, rent it for a year. But with a month's notice. Cancel it whenever you want. Or stick to the reason of his adjustable contribution. Therefore, you will not take it over.'

'Okay? Paul asked if I want to rent it. I didn't know yet. But if he wants to rent it to others, he can do so. I don't care.'

'Will he take the apartment?'

'Paul is fine with taking it. He'll rent out, even use it for vacations himself. Therefore, I will go for that solution. I'll get all my stuff packed and put it in storage.'

'I advise you to meet with the lawyer before she invites Flopper to the hearing.'

'I suggested, if it's okay, I could rent it for a shorter period. Um-hmm, but now, I already pay for the mortgage through our joint costs. He also confirmed the rental rates are, as we've agreed.'

'You need to get everything in place. Bring the strategy in order. It's important.'

'Eeeh, Paul is not horrible to deal with.'

'Yoo-hoo, my darling little girl. I suggest you come back to me after talking to the lawyer. Then you can make plans.'

'Hmm, fine, I'll write to the lawyer. Then find out whether I must go back to Copenhagen several times for meetings.'

'Hey, while you're in Copenhagen, you can stay with my friends Casper and Jane. Ha-ha, it's cheaper than a hotel. Oh, boy, I wouldn't advise you to go through a lawsuit in Denmark. Nothing good will come out of it.'

'Gee... but it can quickly add up to a lot of travel costs living with Casper and Jane. I don't know them.'

'Instead, you can prepare everything, so you can sue Flopper under Hong Kong law for non-payment. Write that you sign the adjustable part of the agreement under "duress."'

'Huh? What is that?'

'It means under pressure. That you don't trust that Flopper will be honest.' Drake considers of everything.

'Okay, okay, fine. I'll write to the lawyer.' I raise my voice.

'It will help under Hong Kong law. There you can go after him, when or if you need to.'

'Darling forget the scary scenario with Hong Kong.'

'Oh, my God, we must look at all matters in time. Best to do it before you are entering a lawsuit from Flopper.' Drake's voice is getting more desperate.

'Oh, I see, so we carefully need to plan what I need to talk to the lawyer about. I don't suppose it's necessary.' Luckily, Paul and I will find a decent solution between us. Thus, I believe in most of what Drake says.

'Jeez, oh, my, as for my relationship with your children, I have to wait for what happens.'

'Darling, don't worry about my kids. They are unaware of the mess.'

'They will either like me or not after they get to know me.' Blink, blink.

'They don't sense what is good for them. Nor for me.'

'If Flopper continues to manipulate the kids, there will never be a pleasant relationship between us. Then I'll accept it. It's not them I want. It's only you, my love.' Mwah!

'I take it calmly. Don't blame the boy's. In time, the issue will probably resolve itself. I don't need them to know too much of us.' So, our "secret," relationship becomes more secret.

'Baby, that I'm grateful to have you with me is an understatement. I've been in love with you since we met. It's an honour for me to be by your side. We'll manage it.' Mwah, mwah, mwah!

'Our love holds us together—even when things are going tough.' His tender voice calms me.

'Well, what more can I say, darling? Too many things are floating around in my head. Maybe you feel it's not fair. Are you upset with what I say?' I try to excuse myself.

'Oh ... la ... la, Babe, in terms of money. Gee, yea, you are one of the *most rewarding people* I know. You are never afraid to "spit in the box". Yah, to help someone in need. I want us to get this done.'

'Oh, my love. Mwah! You mean everything to me.'

'We need to move on, Baby. Mwah! Are you ready for it?'

'Yea, I can't do it without you.' I depend on Drake massively.

'Great! Baby, I'm ready to find money for our lives together. I need to find out what I can do if you're still interested in living together. Will you let me know tomorrow?' He smirks, and I trust him.

'I believe I'm very loving to you for the same reasons you may be. My love for you is genuine love. Mwah, let's talk tomorrow.' I can't cope anymore, and we disconnect Skype.

In my search for a dreamy life, I must decide if I want to take the chance with Drake or stay in my marriage.

Though everything was not always wrong with Drake, we also have a lot of fun and foolish stories to tell each other. Especially with some of my silly nightmares.

CHAPTER 6

THE PUPPET ESCAPES THE PAST IN NEW STRINGS FOR THE FUTURE

A dream is your creative vision for your life in the future.
You must break out of your current comfort zone and
become comfortable with the unfamiliar and the unknown.

—Denis Waitley

As it's evening in Spain and morning with Drake, I call him on Skype.

'Good morning, my darling. I love and miss you. Jeez, I had a weird dream.' I pause briefly and take his smile into my memory.

'Okay, tell me, Babe. You can always trust me.' He's smiles sweetly at me.

'We were in Copenhagen. I was meeting with Paul to find out if I still love him. I wanted to ruin his relationship with Christel. You were at the hotel in Copenhagen. I was with Paul.' I giggle.

'Ha-ha, that can't be so bad. It must be because of what we talked about.' He grins broadly.

'Well, I got drunk. Then spent the night with Paul. I wanted to test him—to see if he was still unfaithful. Hi, hi ... I slept in the same bed as him. Christ, he tried to bone with me. I then cuddled myself close to him. Paul held me tight in the same way you always do. Oh, boy, the dude suddenly cried like a baby. I told him I wanted to leave him because I felt nothing for him. My only purpose was to take revenge.'

'Yuck! Disgusting! Flopper can't keep his pestilent cock to himself,' Drake yells angrily.

'Please darling, calm, it's only a dream. Paul became happy after I deceitfully told him I wanted to stay with him. Oh, my goodness, he gave me an enormous surprise.'

Drake's forehead wrinkled with worry. 'No, no, Baby. Don't leave me in favour of Flopper.' I'm not sure if I want to continue to tell him about this silly nightmare. 'Bloody hell, Mary, he only wants to take advantage of you as his little luxury whore.'

I leaned back in the chair over his strange and rude outburst.

'Calm now! I only wanted to use my chance to take revenge on Christel.' Smirking with my explanation.

'Oh, dear! This is a peculiar dream. Do you want to go back to Flopper? I mean, in actual life?' He sighs nervously.

'Oh, no! You know, I'm appalled by his so-called surprises. I feel nothing for Paul.' I lean forward to get closer to the screen. 'Tsk, tsk. We went to a luxury hotel to enjoy the weekend, with dinner, mellow music and dance. After a walk in the lovely fresh nature, I returned to the hotel lobby. Grunting and bossily, the woman at the front desk told me to go with the staff.' Just the thought of telling Drake the story makes me uneasy. 'Inside the restaurant, I was told to wait at a wobbling table, with two plates, glasses but no utensils. Why? I wasn't hungry. Then I sat down on the creaky green plastic chair. Through a half dirty window to another room, I could see friends and family, smoking, drinking and chatting. Blah, blah, blah ...'

Drake stares at me as something terrible is about to happen.

'The grunting waiter came, "grr ... get up!" and they squeezed me into the tiny claustrophobic smoky room. Everyone shouted, "Cheers and congratulations." I didn't know why.' I take a slurp of my coffee. The mug clunks when I put it too hard, back on the glass table, and I glimpse at Drake, sensing he's confused about the tale.

'Um-hmm ... That's a strange dream, Babe.' He takes a glass and gulping the water. I can see he's worried.

'Yea, can you imagine, I was in a boring pair of black pants and a worn-out T-shirt. Oh, no, I was not ready for a wild brassy party. Just a second, darling.' I get up, walk to the kitchen and grab a bottle of icy water from the fridge, and slurping some of it on my way to the computer. As I sit down again, I continue. 'Ha-ha, guests bring me from table to table in these various small restaurants comprising one room. They have different themes with garlicky, fishy and lemony food from around the world. Yuck, the food is poor and inedible.' I laugh, wondering if it was the chef's fault that the food smelled funky and tasted of plastic.

'Paul bossily told me, "Go to each guest." Suddenly he commanded, "Go to the nearest bank and get a lot of money."' I could hardly stop laughing.

'Huh? Did you go to the bank?' As he is wiping the sweat from his forehead.

'Yep, I withdrew the stinky dough. I gazed at the cash when the cashier gave it to me. Wauw! It looked as fake as paper notes, resembling Monopoly money. On one note, there was a message. It read, "Go to a locker in each room! Take eighteen diverse keys!"'

'Ha-ha,' he chuckles his crispy laugh and leans back in the chair.

'I was told first to use a passcode. Eighteen-fifty-two! In each room, I would get a lovely surprise.'

'Shut up! It sounds messy, Babe. Did Flopper really have eighteen diverse surprises for you? Was it banging with a bunch of other men?' he asks eagerly and leans closer to the screen, tilting his head in his hands.

'Oh, dear, the peculiar thing was that I could recognise the ugly handwriting. It wasn't Paul's,' I clarify, speaking in a severe tone and trying to keep a poker face.

'Huh? Whose handwriting was it?'

'It's weird. It was your ugly handwriting. Ha-ha, ha-ha,' I laugh out loud and take my hands to my stomach.

'Grrr ... my handwriting is not ugly.' Drake has not understood he has an ugly scribbled handwriting—typical of a doctor's ugly scrawls.

'While I was trying to pull the clattering keys out of the locks, their came some noisy tourists. They became impatient with my fumbling key show. Damn! Some keys were tough to get out again.'

I notice his bare torso, and the sweat is dripping from his forehead.

'I told the tourists, "I'm only missing six keys." Shut up. They got crazy. Clank, crash, they violently dragged me around so the staff could arrest me.' I seriously said.

He is dying of laughter. Holy mackerel, I miss him—missed his fresh way of laughing, the delicate scent of his skin and holding his tender hands.

'They put me in front of a squeaking door I had to enter. With all my moving things next to me, I noticed a staircase. It resembled a slope.' Then I realise how silly my story is, and I'm laughing. My excellent mood has come back with this whacky story.

'*Oh my*! Babe, now you're messing around a little too much in your visions and demons.'

His stupid comment annoys me. My lips face downwards in a sour smile. Again, he wipes the sweat off his forehead, so I sense it must be warm in his room.

'God damn it, Drake, listen. Otherwise, I'll forget the point,' I yell in frustration. 'There were two cats. One was black with white socks, pink muzzle and a white spot on its chest. It was a strong, healthy fat cat. The other one was white and awfully ill. I snatched the healthy cat, and before I left, I whispered to the sick kitty, "Don't worry, sweetheart. I'll be back soon and help you." Ohhh ... it glanced sweetly at me and was sadly meowing.'

'Oh, so sweet you are.' He glares at me with his stunning Bambi eyes and smiles pleasantly.

'I slid down the steep metal slope, and suddenly it turned into wooden stairs. Scared, I fell with the cat. Shit! It was falling out of my arms.'

'Oh, that's horrible. What happened?' Asking as is shaking his head.

'It fell far down. Uh, the cat hit some other stairs and died. I continued up the stairs again. Man, it got sincerely steep! I worked hard to get up to the first landing.' I take a momentary break and swallow some icy water from my bottle.

'Ohhh ... there lay the sick cat waiting for me. I picked it up and wanted to move on. The rest of the stairs turned into a slippery greenish slimy ramp. I hide the cat under my T-shirt.' I can't stop laughing. The dream is so unrealistic and funny so, I'm about to pee in my pants.

He listens intensely as I jubilantly gabble out the story. 'Aaaahh, I couldn't get up. Then I saw a door. I went in. Eeek, creepily, the door was creaking. I closed it without slamming it after me. Suspiciously, I hasty and scared walked into the eerie hallway. Then through many ugly squeaking brown doors. I noticed something was wrong when I turned around. I reached some other stunning carved black doors with golden doorknobs. Suddenly, they began loudly slamming in front of me. Bang, slam, bang.'

He stared at me and rubbed his eyes, listening to my strange adventure.

'Someone behind me gave me a sharp scare, booh! I couldn't see any. Then I got gripped by anxiety.'

He stares, surprised, into the camera with enormous eyes.

'Next, I entered a peaceful room where there was a mother and child. They said, "Go that way and then that way," pointing in different directions. I only wanted to get out.'

He leans his head in both of his hands.

'Geez, instead, I got deeper and deeper into the tumultuous flaming hell.' My eyes are wide open with excitement, telling the nightmare.

'Oh, my God, I ended up in a restaurant again. Man, it was the same principle. Though, it was a foul whorehouse.' My voice softens with sadness. 'Bugger! You were with another stunning harlot. Damn! I was sitting between two cute gay guys. They did strange things with me while I laughed. I also got drunker and drunker.' My mood gets a little gloomy.

'Suddenly the room was empty. Shh ... it was dead silent. I was almost naked and had only a red T-shirt on. Damn! My panties and pants disappeared, so I found a pair of dirty lady panties. Yuck! They weren't even mine. Anyhow, I put them on. Ugh! Then, I tried to find my belongings and money.' I've been talking continuously without a pause.

'Barf! How disgusting.' He appears as he wants to vomit.

'Yep, I bet it is. Finally, I got outside in the fresh air, ahh, nice. Can you imagine it? I was running as fast as I could away from it all. As I fled, a strange, handsome man caught me. He said, "Come over to me. I want to help you." Uh huh … It turned out he was a gloomy red beach devil.'

I notice his disappointment. Ha-ha, he probably thought it was him who was the handsome man.

'This beach monster wanted to take me down to his murky hell of fire. Paul had given the order to the beach Mafia to kill me. I would die as a demon. Then fade in the burning desire I have for you.' I realise it all sounds utterly ridiculous.

'Ha-ha, that's what I've told you all the time, Babe. Even in dreams, the demons and freaks possess you.' *Shut the hell up, Drake.* I muse.

Why can't he just be serious? I'm tired of his demon accusations all the time. 'I wriggled myself out of the devil's nasty grip. Uh-oh, suddenly, I ended up in another country. Ha-ha, with a different religion.'

He wrinkles his forehead and scowls at me.

'Auch, a Buddha monster, who appeared as a petrifying Spanish nun caught me.' Even as I'm telling him this, I know it sounds laughable.

He grabs his water and hastily empties the rest of the glass. 'Oh, how did you escape the devil's grip?' he crunches with his crispy voice.

'I don't know. The nun walked with some children on a narrow path in the forest. The leaves crunched and crackled under her bare feet. Then she stopped and stared evilly at me. I shouted for help in Spanish, "*Ayuda!*" (help) and shouted many other filthy things to her. As I approached the children, puff … they vanished into the sucking crunchy black sand. "It's your fault" The nun shouted and got furious with me—utterly red in her face, as over-ripened tomatoes.'

He listens with excitement over the drama.

'I got scared, and the sister caught me. Next, she gagged me and hung me up in chains.' It reminds me of the worst bondage scenario from a porn movie.

'I could hear the sand crunched under someone's flip-flops. Suddenly, I saw a chanting monk. I got out of the nun's grip, and the clattering chains. Fast, I ran after the monk. Screaming and panicking, "Help me. I live in a Buddhist country." He screamed back, "Don't touch me, don't touch me." Angry he glared at me, then cried and yelled at full blast, "Now I have to cleanse myself for many days."' I pause and fall back into the chair, exhausted with my brilliant way of telling the story.

'Ha-ha, ha-ha. You get things mixed up. What does the humming monk do?' he laughs and points a circling finger at his temple, as I am silly.

'Oh ... he helped me, together with another deaf and dumb younger monk. Ha-ha, we ran into a lot of problems. Some dangerous, hideous men chased us while we were driving around in a rusty squeaking car. Whoops, suddenly, the monks transformed into strange roaring creatures so they could protect me. The other villains were trying to capture me. They wanted to assassinate the monks.' It is difficult to explain it to him, or to describe the many Buddhist myths in my dream. Recently, I have read a lot about Buddhist and Hindi fairy tales.

'Finally, I got out of the inferno. Vroom, a strange car popped up. Woah, it resembled a submarine. Swiftly I was in the car. Yee-haw, it flew rowdily up the ramp at top speed. Yep, right into freedom.' I imagine myself as the leading character in a new *Fast and Furious* or *James Bond* movie.

'And you, darling, came in a white limousine with a lot of other men. They didn't allow me to have you. Oh, boy, they kidnapped you! You went through the same hell.' I grin.

'Ha-ha, ha-ha.' He laughs loudly at my endless imagination.

'I'm not done. Do you want to hear the rest?' Getting up and reaching out for my coffee thermos.

'Baby, I think it's a funny dream you've had.' He chuckles.

I pour more hot coffee into my mug. 'Yea, the monks were chasing the limousine. We caught the car, and you stepped out and asked me, "What have you done today, Mary?" I came up with a counter-question for you. "What do you want me to say? Do you want to hear the truth, or shall I lie?" You preferred the truth.' I laugh at him as he glances at me.

He does his cute trick with his head tilted, slowly blinking his Bambi eyes and giving me a crooked, silent smile.

'Do you remember what I precisely asked you in Spain?' It brought me back to the time of the text message in Spanish. 'You eagerly called me and asked, "Is the message for me, Mary?" Next, you questioned, "Did you send the message?"' I hope he remembers, and I laugh.

'Sure, I remember, Baby. You use the same words as in your dream. Wauw! How funny thoughts can play with us in our dreams.'

'Okay. Do you want to hear the ending? What I answered you?' He nods and grins. Smilingly, I give him the answer. "Before I tell you the truth, it's important first to tell you how much I love you. I only want you. And spend the rest of my life with you. I can no longer trust Paul."

Drake's sensual gaze almost makes me faint when he glances blissfully at me, and it thrills him with my response from the dream. 'That's not what you said, Babe.' His crunchy, sexy voice makes me even crazier about him. I want to hug and kiss him.

'I know! Let me tell you the rest of the answer. "Once again, Paul had shown he was lying. He tricked me into get nasty with him." Then I woke up, staring directly at the picture standing on my bedside table— of you and me.' My dream story has ended. 'That's why I had to call you and tell you this cracking story.'

'It's somewhat a strange story.' He laughs at me and leans back in his chair.

'Baby, humankind has ruined the good of life. Most are selfish. Too many rotten apples.'

As I glare at his bare torso, I want to cuddle next to him, and I daydream of hot intimacy with him, right here and now.

'Huh?'

'We have to do what we have done back in Jesus's time. We must once again be an outstanding example for others. They can see our love is real.'

'Huh? What are you talking about?' I can sense his speech is going in a different direction than I want.

'Baby, they may want to mimic such perfect happiness as we have with each other. You must come back to me. Write to your family that you are *leaving* forever. *Trust me.* I only want the best for you.'

Is Drake confused about the situation as I am? And I can feel him fighting a big fight to keep me. I spent a lot of time fighting for my marriage, so now I mostly want to escape from it all.

'Baby, travel with me to Taiwan. If you want to. Leave now. Take part in the seminar there.'

'Oh!' He knows which buttons to press by luring me, as he knows Taiwan is my big dream.

'We can celebrate our first Christmas together there. They are all expecting you to come.' He smiles, pours water in his glass, and slurps from it.

It does not take me many minutes to exclaim, hugely thrilled, 'Wauw! Yes, yes. I'd love to travel with you!' I shout with joy, clapping my hands in eagerness. My happiness is a never-ending story of wild excitement. What more can I dream of? My biggest dream has come true! I'll be visiting the country of intoxicating blossom trees, though it's winter.

'Let me think about what I want. I'll call you back soon.'

'We can meet in Hong Kong, before I leave.'

'Fine. I'll let you know.'

We break off the conversation, and it doesn't take me many seconds to search the internet for a ticket. I'm ecstatic, even though it's not the season for delicately blooming trees. While contemplating what I want to write to my family and take a warm foamy bath while I muse over the situation.

I decide impulsively. And will you believe it? The sweet little puppet is dancing with the tug of Drake's strings and trust the puppeteer.

Leaving the past behind me, I'll let his steady puppet strings steer me back, because I want to be with him.

I calm myself again and think about what the dream means to my actual future with Drake.

I believe the vision reflects what I have faced in the past, maybe it's a reflection of what I'll experience with Drake.

CHAPTER 7

DELUSIONS OF GRANDEUR

The megalomaniac differs from the narcissist by the fact that he wishes to be powerful rather than charming and seeks to be feared rather than loved. To this type belong many lunatics and most of the great men of history.

—Bertrand Russell

Before I'm leaving, I send a letter to my family. However, it's irrational to think so selfishly that it makes me feel uncaring towards my family.

The letter reads:

My dear family,

As you know, things aren't working between Daddy and me. That's why I've made a recent decision in my life. So, don't worry, because I've an innovative mission with the journey I'm embarking. If it goes as I wish, I hope it will mean a lot to me and your future life.

I don't want to hear all kinds of negative nonsense from the family of my personal goals. It's tedious! I don't want a repeat of how it was when I started school again at my adult age. That's why I haven't told you what I want with my life.

What I'm doing could give me an intellectual challenge and great future work possibilities. I hope for success, and I believe I will get it with my recent venture. Then I will tell you about it next time I come to Denmark again.

I want you to accept that I need serenity to concentrate on this task. Please be patient with me, because it could take weeks or more. You'll hear from me via SMS or by email when I have more positive news. Don't worry! I have complete control over it.

Paul, you must do what you promised me. Then I will do my best, so the future can make me strong and independent again. I'm sure you will be glad you have supported me and given me the space I need.

I love you.
Mom

* * *

After over six hours with Qatar Airways, I have a connecting flight in Doha in two-and-a-half hours, and I go straight to the shower room and the sweet lady brings towels and great bathing products, scented with fresh citrus, for my refreshing warm shower. Next, I enter the large and hushed business lounge, with a large restaurant, and get delicious red pepper hummus and halloumi salad and ask for fresh sushi. Fantastic! Then it's finished with hot coffee and a choice of sweet-tasting peachy cake desserts. Bright as a bird, and satisfied, I'm ready for the next flight.

I settle into 10A, a rear-facing window seat and appealing for me as a solo traveller. Great, and with an adequate size footwell, so I don't feel super cramped, even with the seat in bed mode. I find a decent privacy, and the bed being comfy. It is quiet in the business cabin, so you can only sense people nearby me buzzing as bees. The flight attendant brings a welcome drink; I can choose between chilled juice or water. Next, she brings a kit of Bolton amenities, along with an eye mask, earplugs, and socks, but I must find the toothbrush in the lavatories.

The flight attendant brings me two pillows, plus a comfortable blanket, so I manage later several hours of sleep. The entertainment system has loads of movies, ranging from the latest releases to classics. The food and beverage menu look delicious, as they also offer an exquisite à la carte menu, and I order the Arabic food, served with a breadbasket, and, next, seasonal fresh fruit. My overall impression it's a great crew and a super experience, and after nine hours of pleasant journeying, we arrive in the noisy Hong Kong Airport.

My stomach swirls with happy, eager, energetic butterflies as I walk from the gate through the passport, then next to the luggage section. Consistently, I have a radiant smile on my face and pleasant thoughts of joy spins in my head as I imagine seeing and embracing Drake again, and suddenly I can see him standing there.

He smiles with a skewed head and blinks his eyes in surprise when he spots me coming outside the whooshing sliding door. Even though I'm exhausted after so many hours of travel, I pace as fast, I can and straight into his arms. It's a fairy-tale I never will forget when I saw his delightful expression. He does it so often, so it's solidly printed into my memory as a great remembrance of gladness. It's humid outside, so I get a heated blow in my head, heading to the taxi who brings us safely to the hotel.

'Well, Babe!' He begins with a cluck and slaps his body thump on the bed. 'Come and lie next to me.' He smacks hard on the bed, and I lay beside him.

Cuddly, I crawl into his open embrace.

'I told Kuan-Lin Wang and the physios you come from Denmark.' He whispers in my ear.

I take a deep shallow breath and let my inhalation whisper out through my mouth.

'They want to meet you, Babe. We will travel to Taiwan and see if we can work there instead of working in Hong Kong.'

'Well! Phew! Good! Exciting.' I slowly breathe and lick my dry lips to moisten them.

'I'm glad that you are back. Now we can continue as usual.' I stare at his soft hands and give them a gentle squeeze, relieved that he's given me that message, so I feel this it set. Daily life can begin. Everything continues in the same way, as I have never been away.

'Well!' He makes a rapid smack with his lips and jumps up and sits on the chair in front of his computer. 'Let's go through it together. This is what I did while you were away.'

Worn-out, I get up from the bed and review the few patients he's treated.

'You just continue to be my secretary while I treat patients. I've five new physio girls.' Ay, this suck! This isn't what I was expecting. Well, I never! Again, I must be a bloody secretary. I want to scream and protest. Behaving, though, I stay calm and scream angrily inside my head.

Drake is a flawless puppet master, and his perfect technique of controlling my strings is indescribable. He has devious words and is controlling others and my emotions unmistakable.

It shows my brain is overheated and on constant overtime, because I'm confused, however my heart is bouncing in eager beats for love. Soon I get a hot flush—and then chills! Then I'm scared or joyful. My heated wish for love makes my rushing warm blood tingling through my narrow veins, while I gaze at him or hold his hand, I'm excited. When he commands me or snarls, I don't fancy him. God damn it! I think it's damn flabby of him to behave so with me, when he talks to me as I'm a minor ill-behaved child—as if I'm treating him unfairly. It's frustrating! I don't admit to myself that he slowly steers me around to his interest. I take the risk of being with him, and I genuinely want to be there. His steady invisible puppet strings handle me as a blind clattering wooden Pinocchio doll being in deep love with the master. Isolated in my unfamiliar world, I'm far away from my secure haven in Denmark. Suddenly, I can sense how he shadily glares at me as I sit, lost in my mind.

'You're pondering something. What's wrong with you?' He breaks out sceptically, then gets up and takes me into his embrace.

It gives me a shudder the second he asks his question. 'There has been no response from the family about my letter.' Glaring into his sparkling eyes with my sad stare.

'Listen,' he says with a wry smile. 'Either you write to them again, or you forget of them.'

'Yea, maybe you're right.' While glancing at him, seeing his behaviour is controlling and calm.

Tomorrow we will leave for Taiwan. Drake has packed his heavy suitcase, and I pack mine. During our flight to Taiwan, I'm continuously connected to him with my body. Relaxing in Business class, with bubbling icy Champagne and a bowl of warm, tasty nuts, we hold hands. After boarding, we get our warm meal, fruity wine, and chilly sparkling water, and while we rest, we cling to our hands tightly. I love his hands, and I'm obsessed with them, so I can't get enough of them.

'Do you want more of this delicious wine?' He drinks the rest of his wine and calls a flight attendant.

Mostly, I want to ease my body and crawl under his soft white skin to hide, then abduct him, and hide in a mystical cave in Israel. 'Yes, please.' And I drink the last drops, and hand over my glass to him.

Musing, I convince myself it's right what I do, by running off with the person I believe is the love of my life. Then I can have him to myself, and I sense it's the best of peace, of happiness. I can't survive without him, because his love is my biggest strength, and not for one second am I thinking of my selfishness—abandoning my family and friends. Drake is the most fantastic person in my unknown world, but he has flaws too. I try not to overthink the flaws, putting my tension aside in my desperate pursuit to know more of him.

Unquestionably, Drake can pursue the smallest detail. Whatever the physio girls or I say or write, he turns it around a thousand times—until I believe he's right. It's bothersome and sends sometimes ghastly frigid chills along my spine.

Suspiciously, I fear whether I'm sane. Despite that, I fall more and more in love with him, and every time I glimpse at him with greedy, loving eyes, I get more possessed. My love for him makes me unwise and wobbly, and I can no longer think normally, and then I love him even more. Does he understand he is forever a part of me? When he tenderly hugs me, I feel more comfortable and as he is my loving home, but sometimes things are swirling frustratingly around in my head with our strange relationship.

Instead, I enjoy his presence and the firm, warm grip he has on my hand. After a two-hour flight with Tigerair Taiwan, we have a two-hour stopover in Taipei. In the hectic business lounge, I grab the hot coffee, pour milk in it and slurp it before I refresh myself in the ladies' room. Drake checks his emails, and time flies faster than I expected.

The beginning in the country is not adventurous. What a bummer! After a tedious transfer and another security check-in in Taipei, the staff is troubling me of something in my bag. I don't understand a word of their horrible English.

'What do the security want? What is it they're searching?' It irritates me, so I ask for Drake's help.

'Argh!' Frustrated, I open the zippers and then turn my bag upside down. Clash! Clatter!

Clank! Shit! Loads of stuff is toppling out onto the cold metal table in front of me. Lipstick, iPhone, purse, iPad, candy, earplugs and much more. It's a gigantic mess! Shit! Damn it! Oh, my goodness! From one of the small pockets, a stupid lighter falls out and then my smokes. That's the culprit of the entire heated mess! The fiery security staff jabbed something utterly incomprehensible to me, while one of them points irritated at the yellow gas lighter and takes it away from me.

Drake flusters at them and is furious at me. 'Why the hell do you still have a pack of smokes and a lighter in your bag? Are you stupid? What the hell is wrong with you?' He yelled.

Darkness is over me, then it panics me of his wrath and makes me unable to breathe. I hadn't told him I had the smokes only for emergency reasons—nothing else. My eyes gaze at him in frustration and then at the staff, barely daring to bark back.

'Bloody hell, Mary! You promised me. No smokes! This comes of your disrespect. Shame on you.' He is furious and shouts at me as I was his child.

'Hmm, um-hmm, oops! Well, at least you can be happy, darling. They confiscated the lighter. Enjoy it! I can't even light up a smoke if I want.' I let out a fake laugh. 'Damn!' I'm baffling of his unpleasant manners. How stupid of him to get angry. 'Christ!' I roll my eyes. The boiling blood is still raging in my body with a fast speed, and I sense a not so good pressure inside my veins.

I get afraid of him and his many snide remarks, so now I mostly want to escape back to my family. But I can't, because he is twisted firmly into my heart, so I have a hard time of letting go, and besides, I'm stuck in Taiwan. In a situation like this, my relationship with him is sometimes vastly confusing, with him continually running as an uncontrollable full of ups and downs freak. Love and hate.

It's as he wants me here one moment, and the next, he doesn't want me here. Then thoughts drive madly through my mind, and I doubt if I should love him. *Sometimes he truly frightens me. Should I leave him?*

I have learned one thing—don't argue with Taiwanese security in an Airport. God almighty! They almost kept us from continuing our trip to Kaohsiung City, but we leave after Drake's lengthy discussion with them.

Sweating, we rush through the Airport, and arrive at the gate at the last minute. He growls angrily, and his chest pumps the blood through his fuming body, raging as a bull.

'Geez, Mary, you are not so clever as I thought. Oh, boy, smuggling cigarettes in your bag. Shut up! Christ! You disappoint me deeply.'

So, the love trip has started badly.

Next, we're boarding the flight to Kaohsiung City, although it's Business class, it's not the big cabins with beds, so I plant my bum in 2A and he in 2B. In a comfortable position, with my head relaxing on his shoulder, I cling to him tightly, while my hand is resting peacefully in his, and we sit in great affection. I'm tired, so my heavy eyes close, in pleasant thoughts of Taiwan and him, as the citrus scent of his great aftershave makes me joyful, so I want to snuggle my nose deep into his skin.

'Oh, Baby, you have changed my life. It gave me fresh opportunities. My, God, I will not lose you, my beloved.' His voice is crisp and calming, then he squeezes my hand.

'Oh, likewise, darling. I love you deeply,' I mumble.

His lovely rasping voice makes me fall into a deep universe of shooting stars, with dazzling small cherry blossom flowers swirling in my head, together with the stars. His chest heaves in gentle movement so I can hear his bouncing heart beating in smooth rhythms—*bum, bum*. I wish my heart were following his calm pace, but mine is pounding fast.

The flight last only one hour, and I wake with a start as the plane at full blast lands. Hallelujah! I am so excited. A new experience is to begin.

After many hours, the trip has been exhausting, and finally, we arrive at the southern tip of the coastal town on Taiwan's island.

Mr Kuan-Lin Wang's driver is waiting outside for us, a funny dude, bowing several times. He grabs our suitcase and drives us to our accommodation in Kaohsiung City. Wow, such a stunning drive, passing areas of scenic landscapes and an active volcano, of the Tatun Volcano group. We are so excited. It's December, and the climate is chill, but it's still lovely, fresh and sunny, and it's great we have packed warm clothes, as it turns out to be of excellent use to us.

The first days, we will stay at a luxury hotel where they've booked us for the imperial suite, overlooking a volcano and the blue sea, from the panoramic window, and I gaze at it, taking it into my memory. 'Hey darling, have a look!' I call when the volcano suddenly erupts with smoke.

Immediately, he stands by my side, and from the 1,400 square-foot hotel apartment, we enjoy the stunning sight. The suite has a vast living room, a kitchen, and a massive bedroom with a connecting bathroom and an enormous bathtub—overlooking the city from large panoramic windows. Bubbling Champagne, sparkling and still water, soft drinks, and beer stands in the cooled fridge. Drake loves beer, so we grab one and he plants his tush securely in the antique rococo sofa padded with a light beige flower design.

'Come here, Babe.' He slaps hard with his hand. 'Sit next to me.' Stroking his hand firmly several times on the seat, showing I must sit there.

'It's a shame we don't have time to try the hot spring bath,' I add, glancing at the brochure placed on the table. 'Wow! An aromatic flower bath,' I exclaim and bring the advertisement to him and sit next to him.

He put his arm around me and pulls me closer to his body.

'Oh, my gosh! I could use a firm body massage at the spa. It's needed after a lengthy trip.' Next, I thought, *Well! Better luck next time.*

'Ha-ha, I can give you a *dirty* massage, Baby.' He grins. Oh my! I want to throw my clothes right away. I draw closer to him, take his soft hand, and kiss it, imagining his sliding hands on my oily body in a tender massage.

'It's a perfect hotel. Tomorrow, I will first have a one-day seminar for Mr Kuan-Lin Wang.'

'Oh, that was new information.'

In one quick slurp, he empties the rest of the bottle of beer and gets up to grab one more. Drake grabs the menu, sits on the chair by the table, and orders food for the room. Energised, I get up, sit astride him, and kiss him, then let my rotating hips over his crotch show that I prefer instead to screw him then eat food.

Irritated, he grabs me by the hips and moves me insensitive away from his cock. 'Not now, Babe. Later. I'm hungry.'

Disappointed, I get up and smack my bum on the couch instead. After we have eaten, he goes to bathe, so eagerly I throw my clothes off and jump into the shower with him, clinging to him tightly and intensely with my over-sexed nude tanned body. On the glass shelf stands lemony soap. I take it and wash his body, while my hand slowly slides to his inner thigh, and then I grab his shaft. With gentle touching, I massage it back and forth and then get on my knees, ready to put Willy in my mouth and suck him.

'Stop! Not now, Babe.' Agitated. He removes my hand and head and walks out of the shower.

Bummer! Disillusioned, I wash myself and jump naked into bed.

'Oh, yea, darling, can I have my *dirty massage* now?' I smile, begging as a puppy.

'In a minute, Baby.'

Joyful, I cuddle up against his well-scented lemony body and try to make a fresh try on him, despite he is in a T-shirt and boxer shorts. *Yeah, easy access*, I ponder and sneak my hand up under his boxers.

'I'm tired, Babe. I have an endless day tomorrow. Sleep well.' Kissing me goodnight, he turns his back to me.

What! Second massive bummer! No boning tonight. Shit! I'm so horny. Screw him!

*   *   *

Oh, boy! The next morning, Drake is awful, stressed and cross at my presence.

'Morning, can I help you?' I want to help as much as I can. His mood is grumpy, and he sends me annoying glances.

'Eh? Doh, have I done something wrong?' I ask. He says nothing, and it frustrates me, then I get heartbroken. *Why am I together with him?* It might be much easier if I cut off contact with him—went back to my miserable life in Copenhagen instead. We hush the rest of the morning until we must leave.

The driver takes us to the convention centre, where Stephanie stands waiting in front of the entrance and greets us. Walking along a long wide corridor, she first shows us a red room with two flimsy high wooden tables and stools in the middle. No one speaks. To the right facing the wall are two long tables, and underneath stands folding canvas stools without backrests.

'Eh? I do not understand why we have to see this,' I question, giving Drake a confused stare.

'Shh, be quiet, Mary. Don't complain,' he growls, miffed, holding his finger in front of his lips.

I enjoy the silent show and glare at the tables with the flowery flat milky plates with their decorated golden edges. In the middle of every flat plate stands a deep red plate sitting upside down, which perfectly stands straight, as if they had arranged it with a ruler. And at the end of the room is something resembling a small ornate temple. *Umm ...*

looking weird. In front stands a flimsy bench, and a long table with peculiar little dark ashy wooden blocks.

'Oh, strange. It looks as there's a hole in it. Does it resemble as a small birdhouse?'

'Hush!' Drake glances at me with vile eyes.

'I do not understand what they use the room to. Is it something religious?'

He doesn't answer.

'I must admit, though, they have a sense of correctness and precision. They line everything up straight in the room,' I whisper to him.

'Argh, can't you just keep quiet, Mary? I can't hear what they are saying.' *Grumpy dude! Idiot!* I muse, and I want to be despiteful and contradict him; *Well, no one says nothing.*

Then we go out of the room and continue to the massive hallway. And on the long wall in a large framed hanging glass display is a spectacular kimono in golden yellow and orange colours.

It's stunningly, decorated with white flowers and a flaming orange sky. Next stands a stunning white wedding dress in a tall glass display, with the mannequin holding a pink flower bouquet in her folded hands. It reminds me of my wedding dress. Dreamy, I'm sent back in my thoughts, recalling my enchanting wedding—with Paul.

'Oy, Drake, wait for me.' Holy crap! He walks fast with his hands in his pockets and is twenty steps in front of me. His head raises proudly, and with his elegant steps, he marches towards the enormous hall, and ignores me while he is chit-chatting with Stephanie, Wang's secretary.

It's as to him, I'm not there. I'm as thin, icy air—puff!—gone as *Puff the Magic Dragon.* I might as well disappear; he wouldn't notice it.

Instead, I take my time taking in a massive painting on a linen canvas, with fringes. It's in stunning golden colours, with fantasy-like small islands, a vast lake, and low green plants in the foreground, and resembles the fantasy world from the movie *Avatar*—except for the missing blue characters.

Before entering the hall, on the wall next to the entrance door hangs a vast bronze relief. It's massive and depicts, eight wild horses running in an open field, and a few of them elegantly and wildly rear up towards the sky. They have written something in Taiwanese on the top right corner, which fascinates me.

'Wauw, have you seen this? I wish to take it back home with me.' I say, and he stares furiously at me and walks away.

The hall will soon be full of four hundred Taiwanese participants, who will occupy the forty round tables covered with white tablecloths and the fake beige leather chairs. They have decorated the tables with red and white carnations, table stands with numbers and table arrangements for the dinner following the presentation. Along with the organiser and Stephanie, Drake goes up to inspect the vast stage. OMG! It's so big that it looks as they are small ants when they stand on it.

Deep in concentration, they check the massive podium and inspect the equipment to see that everything is ready, then connect the projector with the gigantic TV screen hanging in front of a vast white curtain. He glances at me and points with proudness at the giant sign over the screen, written, "Doctor Drake".

In the backroom, Drake and Stephanie prepare the rest of today's program for his one-hour speech to the congregation, and ignores my existence, talking only with John and Stephanie. I sit still, as his obedient housewife, and listen to everything. Maybe I've spoken and asked too much today, and the little ill-mannered bird in the cage gets quiet.

The time has come for the big moment, and while waiting outside the enormous hall doors, we can hear that it's buzzing with millions of bees in there. A sneak peek shows us its full of expectant people. Stephanie puts a big blue paper flower, with blue and white ribbons, on his suit over his pocket. It doesn't match so greatly with his purple tie. I get one too.

The pre-presentation has finished, and Drake is nervous and pushes me to the side, then he enters the hall. We must wait a bit, because it's only him who may come in first, but we can hear a massive applause, and next, we can go in. I glance at him and see his gigantic proud smile, which pleases me because he looks great, and then he trudges up the stairs to the giant stage, as if he were the mighty emperor. We have our table right in front of the scene.

Auch sucks! Frustration pops up on his face when something goes wrong on the podium, as the technique won't connect to his computer. Oops! He gets irritated, staring questioning at Stephanie, and she hurries up there to help him, and finally, it works. His prepared PowerPoint slideshow pops up on the big white screen, and the congregation sits politely, waiting for his speech. It's the first time I'll hear him delivering a speech, and I believe he will do well.

Years ago, I studied rhetoric and got good grades on the subject, so I'm aware of his way of delivering a speech. *Oh my*, I muse. *He needs an update on how to behave at a podium.* He is unsmooth, saying 'um-hmm,' 'ah,' and 'oh' all the time. Saying phrases, 'I am', 'It's only me', 'I can', and, 'It's only because of me they succeeded.' So, it continues, and it's only about him being the best in the world.

He jumps from one subject to another and not being consistent, and has a problem finishing sentences, so it's difficult to understand the purpose of what he's saying. I feel sorry for him, so I make notes I can show him at another time. I ponder why he tells many strange jokes that don't belong in this assembly. Politeness in Taiwanese culture calls for avoiding explicit disagreement, and this was one of the few simple rules he forgot along with a few others: Never criticize in front of outsiders. Never brag! Don't use honorifics for other people while they are not there. He honours himself based on another people's success. The name-dropping is not good (a try to make yourself famous on another people's celebrity, claiming you know them better than you do to appear more unique). His arrogant comments are hard for me to endure. Geez, has he forgotten the Taiwanese rarely brag? He speaks low of other kinds of physicians and treatment protocols, and that's a big *no go!* It's good indirectly to praise others and always downplay one's own accomplishments. Taiwan has a distinct culture compared to many other countries. Kuan-Lin Wang is Japanese of origin. I'm not saying they are perfect, but they are proud in their manner, posture, and clothing. The Taiwanese and Japanese avoid expressing their power and leave it for others to do for them in flattery. Talking of your excellent leadership or knowledge, they considered it as bragging. It's hard to predict the rules for foreigners, but I believe Drake breaks too many of the rules. I'm not perfect either, but I appreciate constructive criticism on what I make wrong, so that's what I'll give him. Still, I know he wants the best for everyone, so the entire presentation is a success.

After his one-hour speech, many possible new sponsors ask him many questions. Gee, he's able to boast about himself even more. It's as if he is a massive bull who has won the glorious game in the arena. It's too much for me, but fantastic for him, that they respect him. His way of bragging and triumphing in front of the many tiny women makes me surprised, but I understand them. He is tall, handsome and charming. A women's man. They ask questions of their medical issues, touch him as a God and he says, 'only I can help you. Come to me.' Jeez, I'm not used to such cocky behaviour, and I have never seen that from Paul or any of my friends.

Appearing tall in my black dress and short high-heeled boots, as I stand in the background and see everything. The black boots are stylish, decorated with a leather bow and marked with a silver chain around the edges of the bow. I listen, smile, and watch as a well-behaved and polite woman. It's interesting how I can view over the tiny petite women's heads, and see Drake surrounded by them, with his fake smiling appearing. Christ! He feels as he's a big hotshot and loves being at the centre of everyone's attention. It's excessive! He only sees him, him, and only himself.

With his peculiar flirtatious expression, he gazes at an elegant younger woman and has unique eye contact with her. It makes me suspicious and somewhat jealous. Imagine him doing such things in front of me. *Shame on him!* I try to ignore it.

In the hall, small children run wildly around and chuckling, while they try to get in contact with me. Oh my, they're so sweet. Jingle, jangle, and we're interrupted when a bell ring, then a monk enters the hall, and it gets dead silence. People shows deep respect for the monk, and next he is giving a speech before they allow us to eat.

On the table stand small trays with small bowls of appetizers—raw tuna, shrimp, and salmon on green leaves, along with vegetables, soy, and pickled ginger. Noodles, wontons, radishes, and we get chopsticks. The waiter brings icy still and sparkling water, a big hot ceramic flower teapot, beer, and chilly delicious white wine, together with bread snacks reminiscent of hand-cooked crunchy English crisps.

Suddenly they bring a present to our table.

'Ha-ha, open it,' Stephanie grins when this strange packet arrives. Inside there's a big round wooden thing.

'Push the handle down to the box,' she says.

I do not understand what it's about. 'It's a strange experience. Pop, pop... oops! Darling, I'm not sure what I'm doing, while fumbling with the thing.' I laugh broadly, eyeing at him, while he tries to help me. I never figured out what it was.

After the dinner, there are several greetings, bowing and more bowing, between the investor and the participants, and the day's events end with photographing and more bowing before we leave. The spectacular day is over, and the private chauffeur takes us back to the hotel.

When I give Drake the constructive criticism, he gets furious at me; 'What do you know about it? Nothing!' He grumbles as a roaring Grizzly bear.

'Oh, sorry. Fine. I see that you want to do your best.' And I try to highlight more positive things for each negative thing I point out. I should have kept my mouth shut, although I showed sympathy and interest in his presentation.

I think he didn't flatter the audience. He had one choice; he should ask his rhetorical self-answering question for self-verification. Did he do his rhetoric correctly? The answer must be a big fat, *no*!

CHAPTER 8

A TAIWANESE FAIRY TALE

海千山千
Ocean thousand, mountain thousand.

Meaning: A reference to the sly old fox, someone who's seen everything and can therefore handle any situation, usually through cunning.

—Japanese Idioms

Today we're driving to an insignificant town, about fifty kilometres west of our first hotel, as this is our last two days at Mr Wang's private location. The small Japanese luxury boutique hotel, the friendly staff, and the delicious Japanese food specialities make my life worth living together with Drake. It's peaceful, it's only us, and arranged everything personally for us at the lush tiny romantic spot. I sincerely appreciate the splendid adventure, because there is a unique reason we stay here alone. Mr Wang wants us to enjoy everything in quiet harmony and cheerfulness. Let me try to take you back to a previous Chapter in part 1 and imagine the picture of the large tattoo on my body. Do you remember it? Such a piece of body art they told us I can't show to other people, so I must cover them at any public sites. With deep respect for Mr Wang's culture, I meet his request. At the place it divides the spot in a unique spa spaces into men's- and women's facilities, so no one will see my tattoo, and we can enjoy the entire spa together in peace, alone. It's euphoric! What a grand gesture from Mr Wang.

Many people in Taiwan 'don't dare to' get tattoos, rather than 'don't want to.' Those who do get tattoos, they often hide them from their families.

In Taiwan it's not outright banned as it's usually outright banned with tattoos in Japan, and they have looked down at them for centuries. It's said that it's only outcasts among those who have them, so now I'm nervous. Will Mr Wang consider me as an outcast?

The first written records of tattoos in Japan date from AD 300. Japanese men had them on their faces and decorated their bodies with massive symbols and, between AD 300 and AD 600, tattoos become more negative. It shows in records the most dangerous criminals get tattooed on the forehead, showing that they have committed a crime. The Yakuza began using tattoos to show they were a gang. Once again, they banned such body symbols in 1868, and they thought of tattooing oneself as barbaric and distasteful. When China and Japan got into the war in 1936, they considered people with tattoos problematic and undisciplined, so they banned tattooing until 1946. Today, it's become a popular fashion and symbol of toughness, but the negativity associated with tattoos remains deeply rooted in the Japanese psyche. Therefore, there's still a stain on people with tattoos, and I don't want them to relate me to criminals or the Yakuza, so I respect the rules and cover my body art wherever I go. Though in Taiwan the indigenous people such as the Atayal, who have tattooed themselves for hundreds of years.

At the boutique hotel we enjoy every minute alone in the stunning surroundings, with special seasoned dinners in our room, sitting on the wooden floor at small low wooden tables, while the elegant petite women bustle quietly around us, as tiny delicate dancing dolls in their embroidered hand-sewn kimonos. Sweet and smiling, they prepare everything for our first spicy, mild and sweet-and-sour different small prepared meal until our private chef has finished everything. Bringing us sake, aided with an "oblong" plate of unique kinds of tasty nuts. Mushrooms and small dishes of raw salmon, tuna, and cooked shrimp adorned with small green leaves. In addition, they serve pickled ginger, white and red creamy sauces, and soy. The main course is hot spicy chicken soup, tempura of shrimp, fresh vegetables, tofu, and sashimi of fish. Next comes a steamed dish of grilled wild boar and deer. On the side is a salad of seaweed, Chinese radish, and carrots in strips turned in vinegar. Everything in loads of tiny portions with different vegetables. I've never seen such a spectacular colourful meal, adorned with tiny pink, white, red or purple flowers. After the main course come rice, miso, and pickles. To complete our fantastic dinner, we get a dessert of crunchy nutty cake, colourful fresh fruit, and glacial coconut ice cream—served in the perfect traditional Japanese style. Oh, my, it's so delicious! It's much better than what I've tried in one of our most famous Japanese restaurants in Copenhagen.

We are more than full, so we don't go hungry to bed. The tiny women silently clean the room while we get more ginger tea, and then its comfy time; we're going to the spa area.

Picture yourself bathing Taiwanese style. Wauw! It's interesting! You begin by rinsing the body, by splashing the lukewarm water over you with a wooden washbowl. Then you clean the body with a lump of aromatic white Jasmin soap. Blissful, we slowly soak our naked bodies in the hot spring, an Onsen. Ahh, so nice. This you must experience to imagine the gorgeous natural scenery of a black and greyish stony back garden. Taiwan is a volcanically active country and spreads thousands of onsens across all its major islands. Ahh, great then in stillness and relaxation, I slide my nude body close into Drake and mwah; I kiss him, gliding in between his legs with my back to his chest. He embraces me from behind, with his hands firm on my breasts.

'Ooh! See those many large square black jars, darling. Wow, such amazing green bonsais.'

And turn my astonished gaze to the many small well-cut trees, as we talk about how they keep them so well. Slowly, I let my hands slip into the warm water and gently caress his inner thighs.

'Fantastic how they can shape them in so many shapes. What do you think, darling? Is one more gorgeous than the other?' Meanwhile, I sneakily try to get my hands on his bratwurst.

'Hmm... uh-hmm...' Grumbling, he moves a little to the left, showing that he doesn't want me to be *that* close. Gently, I remove my hand from his floppy danger noodle and thighs.

'Let's observe the blinking stars in the black night. Um-hmm, then enjoy the luminous milky Moon,' I whisper, hearing the leaves rustle faintly in the background. 'Darling, I believe you are the genuine love of my life. No one else matters but you.' I've lost my heart to him, and now he brings so much happiness into my rainy days.

'Pee-yew, what a strange nauseating odour out here. What is it, darling? Pew!' Squeezing my nostrils.

'Yea, it's stinks of many components. Yuck, its hydrogen ions and lithium in the water. Yuck, it has an awful mix of smells. Hmm, somewhere between a rotten egg and a clean chlorine.' He wrinkles his nose, ewww ... when I peek at him.

'Ohhh ...' and we laugh at his comic description. It's impossible to describe the rotten stink.

In inner peacefulness, I send a prayer to my Jesus and the Virgin Mary. *Thanks for the pleasant life you are giving me with Drake.*

I can hear his deep relaxed breathing, and suddenly I sense his excitement between his legs growing up against my lower back. With soft touches, he plays with my breasts and tickles my nipples, so they get excited, stiff and set me on fire. Sexy burning fire ants crawl under my vigorous skin and sends naughty signals to Minnie. The lukewarm water brings him into a sexual arousal, so I take another chance to move my hand close to his inner thigh and grab his tool, but he is not iron-hard in my hand.

His sensual rasping voice whispers into my ear, 'Baby, tell me more about the erotic things from your marriage.'

'Umm ... well ... fine ...' I close my eyes and go into a deep relaxed concentration, while he's holding my nude body in his tender, muscular arms and turns me slightly around. While lifting me up, he puts his lips around one of my nipples. Comparable to a tiny kid. He gently sucks my sensitive stiff nipples, so I get lusty goosebumps all over my body. Excitingly, they jump satisfyingly deep into my horny Minnie, and I'm squeezing her with joy. *Mary, are we going to have sex tonight?* She shouts with excitement up to my brain. I push my body closer against his lips. Oh, Lord! I get heated with a wonderful arousal, and pondering, *Yee-haw, Minnie, today we can ride him. But calm girl, first I must tell a naughty story.*

A few minutes later, all the wicked spicy memories come back to my brain.

'Okay, fine,' and he lets go of my nipple and turns me around, as I tell the wicked narrative of 'the rough-cut gigantic man and his petite wife.'

I can sense the growing stiffness of his peckerwood against me, while he keeps on caressing my breast with excitement. His gentle touch seems stimulating that I randy gasp many times for breath while telling my story. I notice he enjoys getting me excited. Oh my! I get hornier. *When are his hands coming down to my Minnie?* She shouts savagely to my brain, hoping he can hear it.

Hmm ... well, nothing happens, and when I finish the story, he only hugs me. Downer! My pussy is bawdy and enormously disappointed.

'You are the love of my life, darling' I fast whisper, expecting I'm about to bone with him.

'Ha-ha ... well, funny story. Let's get up, Mary.' he utters and pushes me aside.

As he's gets up, I notice his bird is not stiff, though, my imagination and body have prepared for a hot enjoyment with him. Will I get disillusioned? I'm awful horny and want to bang with him. *Now!* But he walks away. I ponder; *what am I doing wrong?* We wash again and then grab the bath kimonos (yukata) and go to bed in passionate embraces of love as he gives me the impression he wants to put his P in my V. I'm still nude under the kimono, then open the belt for his view as an invitation. While resting on the nicely prepared soft futon floor mattress, he kisses me intensely, Christ, he continually transforms me into a wet and randy humming siren. Out of lust, I change to a dangerous randy Greek mythology creature, who lures nearby sailors with her enchanting singing voice. I spin my music of the bawdy desire for a magnificent night of wild banging. With his magic fingers on my little eager pearl, he teases Minnie. *Finally*; she muse; as he is playing on all the piano keys, and spreads my shaved labia, so my juices moisten the area, and I gasp with delighted pleasure.

'Oh, Baby, hold yourself. Feel me. Take in the pleasure of my soft fingers,' he whispers.

Aya caramba! I'm shining in a powerful desire for his teasing touch. The pleasure is gigantic when he gently satisfies me in an exhilarating trip of multiple orgasms. Only one thing is missing. I want him entirely, but the sleeping Willy is not pushing wildly inside my flower. It's a half act of lovemaking, and I get disappointed, thinking; *what a flaccid 'woodcock'.* What the heck! I'm a woman with needs, but you can't always win. Instead, as a well-pleased little kitten, I quietly fall asleep in his arms, resting there most of the night—dreaming of an iron-hard cock. What a magical world.

In the morning, tiny, fast clacking footsteps wake me up, and a petite woman serves a well-prepared delicious local breakfast in our room and some hot Jasmin tea. Drake smirks at me and seems content that he has satisfied my naughty Minnie, but we are not talking about his failure to take part in a consummated sex act. I keep my disappointment entirely to myself. Sex at our age can be better than before and getting older can also bring some changes. I'm at my best age for sex though, I'm not sure what is going on with him. Many mature couples have better love lives than they did when they were younger, so thinking of, at our age, we don't have so many distractions. We don't have to think of pregnancy and being busy taking care of a bunch of kids, so it should give more time to us. Plus, we also have more know-how, though I know that hormones take a dip when you are middle-aged. But I'm not aware of how the man can suffer from erectile dysfunction. Can that be the case? If so, I feel sorry for him. Or is it more than something else going on in Drake's brain? *Does he not love me?* Pills might be an answer. I know he's not suffering from any medical issues, so I don't get why he can't stay hard. I must talk to him about it, though he or I might not find it easy to talk about this subject.

One hour after our breakfast, the driver and Stephanie pick us up at the hotel for a day tour, heading to an astonishing red building called a Shinto shrine, originated from Buddhism. The journey is beginning at the temple's torii gate.

'Out of respect, bow before proceeding underneath it,' Stephanie dulcet tells us and continues the lessons on what we must do. 'Please walk along the sides in respect for the spirits to pass through the centre.'

Hush and in silence, we enter off centre of the gate.

'Before approaching the shrine, go to the large rippling water basin. You must purify yourselves. I'll show you how to do it.' She smiles, sweetly.

At the cold-water basin, we respectfully fill one of the bamboo ladles with pure water. Washing the left hand with the right. Next we switch hands and do the same process again.

'Next, purify your mouths.' Stephanie kindly tells us. 'Don't swallow the water. Spit it next to the basin. Then the spiritual ritual has purified you,' she smiles.

'Now you are ready to enter the main hall. It's for donations and silent prayers.' She points in the direction we must walk, heading up the massive black stone stairs.

'Please ring the large bell, Doctor Bates,' she points, 'yea the "*Suzu*", hanging above the box.'

'Huh? Why?' he asks, content to get the honour.

'It's telling the deity of our presence. Next, we must bow. Then clap our hands twice. Then bow again. Then make a secret prayer.' Stephanie smiles, pleased. Clink, clink, clink and Drake ring on the large bell. Like monkey see, monkey do, so next we pray. My secret prayer is of Drake, and he asks me curiously about it.

'Well, I won't tell you,' I smirk, 'ha-ha, it's my secret.' I mockingly chuckle.

Stephanie points towards some green trees. We walk alongside enormous rough stones, while the gravel crackling under our feet, and the leaves rustle in the many trees. It's a glittering, sunny, crisp, chilly day, a cloud-free blue sky, and a slight refreshing breeze blowing in my loose hair. It's magical, a spiritual experience for my mind and soul, though I don't know how Drake takes it in, because he is reticent. They have decorated the enchanted part around the shrine, with carved wooden elephants, dragons, and lions and stone lanterns stands in the gravel. Pondering of the great orgasms, the night before and walking around in this paradise, gives me a bliss of peace and happiness. I can't be more delighted than I am today, so I stroll continuously around with a cheeky smile.

After all the religious parts, we drive to a famous observatory Park. Holy smokes! The views over downtown are spectacular on this bright shiny hushed day, with the sight of the smoking Volcano in the distance. We can't hear the rumbling of the eruption, but it's so clear to see the massive greyish smoke. The Taiwanese people accompanying us show us their country with great pride, and they can be proud of their country and their friendly behaviour. It's spectacular! It's an enjoyable, fantastic experience for my soul, and enchanting is the country. Ooh... I love it!

In the late afternoon, Mr Wang invited us to a special event. His family is dressing both of us in unique *"Hikifurisode"*, and apparently, it's the most favoured type. Mr Wang's mother, Christine, and few loving female members of the family will dress me. Oh, my Holy Lord! It's a mind-blowing white silk wedding kimono I've ever seen—diligently decorated with yellow and darker pink flowers and long sweeping sleeves, as the elaborate pattern runs unbroken across the back and around the entire body.

'It's worn at the wedding ceremony at the reception,' Christine explains.

'Gosh almighty! I am proud.'

'These kimonos have an elegant silhouette reaching down to the trailing hem. It gives it an overall effect that is feminine and sophisticated,' she tells proudly. 'They embryoid the silk in dyed gold or silver threads. Showing the style is both elegant and radiant.' Then she undresses me to prepare the next step.

'Wauw, the colourful designs are themselves works of spectacular art.' I shine as the brightest Sun.

'It's the same kimono Mr Wang's sister wore at her wedding,' Christine proudly says.

'Wauw! Now I'm even more proud to have the honour of wearing it.'

'It's said that the gorgeous handcrafted kimonos are a dying art. It's the most enduring cultural symbols of Japan.'

'Oh ... how tragic! Such a picturesque culture must never disappear.'

I will later read in an article:

> Most craftsmen today are over eighty, and within the next ten years, many will pass. We are in actual danger of losing thousands of years of kimono-making techniques. From the silk cocoon to the ultimate product, there are more than a thousand processes involved in one kimono, each carried out by different specialist craftsmen. It can take forty years to master a single technique. (*The Telegraph*, Sunday, 18 August 2019).

'The kimono is a T-shaped wrapped garment with long sleeves. It's often worn for important festivals. Holidays and weddings,' Christine enlightens me as she shows me the procedure for dressing.

'You must fold it from the hip and wear it left over right. That's important. It's worn that way unless the person is deceased. They tie it with an obi,' she is so gently, pointing out the sash, 'and knotted at the back. They call the knot a *musubi*. They can tie it in many special ways.'

She carefully tells of every movement and meaning of the kimono, so it will take the women several hours to dress me from top to toe. As I stand undressed, except for my bra and thongs, the family sees my large tattoo.

'Oh, my days! It's impressive. What does it all mean, Mary?' The women seemed amazed.

'It's a cherry blossom tree. And Chinese animal signs.'

'Oh, why Chinese signs?'

'It's showing the years of my children's and my birth. I also have some different Christian signs, showing my Catholic faith.' And I gladly tell them the story behind getting the tattoo. Lucky for me, they don't see me as a criminal. Our chit-chatting and laughter fill the room with a rhapsodic atmosphere, and its genuine girls' time, with lots of giggles. They are as cute as tiny wiggling fairies around me, and I'm over two heads taller than them. Incredible hours fly fast, while they dress the "Japanese doll" and accomplished the stunning task.

'Hi, hi ... Mary, let's fix your hair a little.' Christine laughs and combs my hair, while another woman brings some white socks.

'Stick your feet into these, Mary,' one woman says, pointing to a pair of split-toed socks *"Tabi."* 'Then you must wear these traditional footwear.' She shows me a pair of 'Geta,'.

'Oh, my goodness,' I giggle, 'they are impossible to walk in.' I feel as a wobbling geisha and stumble, insecure, on my feet.

'This is a traditional wedding item,' another of the girls says, handing me an oilpaper umbrella. 'You must have it with you.'

Its stunning, in purple and beige colours and decorated with pretty flowers and a landscape painted on it. And it's the last thing given to me.

'Tradition says the matron of honour will cover the bride with it. To ward off evil spirits,'

I gladly take the umbrella in my hand and protect myself against evil spirits. 'Ha-ha, well, I'm sure I'll need it for the future.' I chuckle and hold the umbrella with pleasure to protect me.

I still have the umbrella. It's a dear item to me, in remembrance of an intoxicated time in Taiwan, together with these amazing women and a glorious memory.

I look drop-dead gorgeous, as I watch myself in the mirror, realising the women did stunning work.

'Wauw! You are eye-catching, Mary. The dress suits you well—in the same way as it did with the bride. You're like a real native beauty.' They all smile sweetly and clap their tiny hands.

'Thank you so much, Christine,' because I'm deeply grateful for the tremendous work the women did on such a special day.

'Wauw! Mary, you have stunning almond eyes. Such a lovely smile.' Christine claps her hands and holds them in front of her lips, while I am over the Moon of happiness.

I don't know how to respond to all that flattery, so I glance embarrassed and shyly glance down at myself upon hearing the sweet words from her. The captivated women gawk intensely at me. *Snap,*

snap, and it's photograph time! *Click, click*. And it immortalises the memory for me.

Next, they escort me into another compact room, where Drake waits with excitement for his 'Japanese bride'.

Trembling and uncertain, clack, clack, I wobble in my clunky sandals and enter the room.

He breathes deeply, surprised at seeing me in my striking outfit, and our fictional ceremony can begin, but first more photography. Snap, snap! And another camera clicks, snap, snap, and it immortalises the stunning picture for me.

'Wow! Oh, gosh! You look stunning, Baby.' His eyes get big as teacups. He wears a black kimono, that is what men wear at weddings, tea ceremonies, or on special occasions. He looks kind, smiling, gorgeous and ecstatic, and I fall even more in love with him. Click, click and Christine take fantastic snapshots, while Drake and I kiss intensely. What a memorable event, a one-off and a breathtaking experience—ok, besides my actual wedding.

'I've loved no one with so much passion as I love you. I will only love you, darling,' I whisper proudly to him when I hug him close to my body and kiss him intensely.

'My angelic Mary, you are stunning. Now we are ready to get married.' He grabs my cheeks, and I glance straight into his loving glinting brown eyes. 'My love for you grows more and more every day. It will never stop growing,' he smilingly whispers and glances gently into my glittering green eyes and hugs me.

'That lovely kimono on your graceful body is gorgeous,' he adds. 'For the love of God! You walk right into my heart, Baby.' He gently caresses me over my set hair and does the lovely elevator stare from top to toe and takes my hands.

All his lovely words creep directly under my skin. *I want to hear more of his sweet honey words*; I muse.

'Baby imagine you this; I'm finally allowed to have a woman who loves me so much. Oh, my, such a passionate woman. You're so closely attached to me. I'm on cloud nine!' His intense, lovely gaze burns into my cornea. 'You are unique in every way. I love you more than life.'

His lovely words tremble deep inside me, as he is driving me to divine madness of hunger for more love from him.

'Oh, you look lovely. Madly lovey-dovey hot. I can never get enough of you, Babe.'

I slurp all his sweetness directly into my heart as he hugs me. 'Well, darling, it's all for you. I can only have you. I can only let you touch me. It gives me peace and harmony in my soul.' My deep, intense love grows massive in this very instant.

'Darling, I want to be with you in this paradise. To live a joyful life with you.' I squeeze myself closer to his body, then let my hands slide down his back until I end at his nice firm Butt Cheeks and gives them a tight squeeze.

'It's nice that you don't want other hands on your body, Babe. I'm pleased that you only want my magic hands.' He whispers.

Instantly, I'm imagining his soft hands touching my nude body, and it makes me lustful.

'I know you feel as I do, Babe. Only my hands belong on your lovely body.'

It makes me think of the stunning orgasms he gave me the night before. I stare lovingly at him and can't get enough of his words, and he continues.

'It's only me who will lead you forward in the dance to a new fresh life with me. Like me, you can't have others either. We have no room for others in our lives.' Crisper his lovely voice.

With his gasping whisper, my happiness is complete. I'm speechless as he continues his lovely words.

'Our bond is unbreakable after this ceremony. It can't be different for us. It's for all the right reasons.'

With every second he says something sweet to me, I fall even more in love with him.

'You are mine! Mwah! I'm yours, my beloved MM. It has never been different. Mwah! It will never be. I'm yours forever. Mwah, mwah.' Ooh, he is so romantic, so I melt.

Every second with him, I melt more into a liquid lump of butter. Together, and in great love, we walk into the next bigger cosy room, where our next surprise is waiting.

Wang's family gives us a special ceremony, including Japanese tea and a fabulous dinner. Then we get 'married' in a traditional Japanese way. Okay, I must be honest with the reader; it's not valid. But, though, it's exciting and an enchanting act! The romance is unstoppable, and I'm in a shiny Disney fairy-tale enjoying my delighted moment to the fullest. With the mesmerising surroundings and Drake, I'm the most ecstatic woman in the world, when Cinderella gets her prince on the white horse.

The last day, we drive to The Sun Moon Lake, a caldera lake in the Yushan National Park, the home of the Taiwanese Loch Ness 'Issie-Kanua'.

'The local legendary lake serpent is a nightmarish giant fish, with Plesiosaurus-like flippers. Uh-oh, it's lurking beneath its waters. They say the monstrous fish is over five metres long. It has razor-sharp teeth. It's the inspiration for many stories from ancient Taiwanese folklore. This is the largest volcanic lake.' Stephanie bravely tells the mystery.

'Wow! How deep is it, Stephanie?' Drake asks.

'Um-hmm, up to 240 metres.'

The impressive locality adorns the outstanding ocean-blue water with a spectacular view of Mount Yushan, also known as Mount Jade.

'It was once a religious site. The Shinto priests used to consider the lake the origin point of humanity. People still feel the site sacred. They pray at the local Kanua Shrine today.' Stephanie says.

It's a fun day, and I am sitting on the statue of the dangerous monster.

'Whee ...' Drake puts his head in between the razor-sharp teeth of the slippery fish, looking scared and stupid at me.

'Yeeha!' As a dominant mistress, smack... smack... I whip the beast hard, with a stick on its behind. 'Wee! Faster! Grrr!' I pretend the beast growls and bite his neck off, as we behave like two small children.

'Well, darling, the fish has no success today in biting your neck. Ha-ha, you luckily survive the nasty, dangerous bite.' I laugh, and we walk in the crunchy gravel to the tiny lake restaurant close by. It's well needed—some hot coffee and icy water.

'The scenery is spectacular,' and I take in the fragrant of the purple flowers in bloom when my nostrils get deep buried in the massive bush. 'Wauw! Have you seen the massive green bonsai?' I'm astonished while pointing at it.

The moment between us is passionate. Many things have happened in my life with him in such a brief time, and I can't believe I'm so happy.

Is this life for real? I muse with myself.

'Let's take some pictures.' The glossy still water in the lake appears as a mirror, and it is stunningly clear, looking fantastic with the many small boats. 'Stephanie can take a photo of us.' I'm beaming all over my face and behave almost as a child, when I suggest it to him, and hand over the camera to her.

'He-he,' Drake giggles, then carefully takes my hand and happily poses for the photo.

Before we drive to the next spot, Stephanie takes us to a small ice café nearby.

'Wow! Look at that, Baby.' He roars and makes gigantic eyes when he sees the hundreds of different flavours of frosty ice cream and behaves as a little boy.

'I'm not a big fan of ice cream. Coffee and nutty in a cone for me, please.'

'Jeez, yea, I love ice cream,' and orders vanilla and mint-chocolate, as he licks his lips.

After a brief break as we enjoy the ice cream, the lake tour got to a last chapter for today.

We jump into the car, and drive one hour to a prime Italian restaurant, Felice Di Aqua, with unmistakable Taiwanese flourishes. Another stunning locality.

'Let's go for a walk first. To explore the outdoor surroundings, before the Sun sets,' Stephanie suggests. Outside sit two small adorable children, three and five years old, playing and rattling with the gravel. Drake approaches them, squats in front of them, and reaches out his hand.

'Can I have some stones?' He smiles gently, reaching out his hand.

'Oh no! Darling, the kids don't understand English.' It's a sweet sight to see how the children stare intensely at him, with no fear in their eyes or any movement, nor a smile. It's probably not a sight you see in so many countries—kids interacting with a stranger, without fearing that the man might be a child molester.

'Oh, my! Those kids are so cute. Geez, look at their big, black, eyes. Ohhh... such innocent eyes. And their small, thick apple-red cheeks. Ha-ha,' I laugh and watch their thin shiny black hair fluttering in the mild wind as they play silently with the small stones. Well, he gets none of their stones.

'Let's go inside. We can start with an ice-cold local Kaohsiung gin and tonic. I can recommend a delicious meal.' Stephanie smiles.

'Yea sounds great. Which one?' he asks.

'A prize-winning Wagyu steak.' Stephanie smiles while we have a cheer.

The waiter helps us find some well-paired red wine with a delicious bouquet to go with the best prime Wagyu steak I have ever tasted.

'Oh, my goodness, darling. Taiwan is the most gleaming experience in my life. I wish to come back one day,' I gleam, as my heart is pounding identically as a hot steaming locomotive.

Drake and Stephanie smile, and I reciprocated their smiles.

'I want to experience millions of cherry blossoms tree. Oh, my goodness. Best when they are in full bloom. Can we go back next spring?' I beg, smiling lovely at him.

If you ever visit Taiwan, you sincerely must take it all in. I'm confident in that those who already have visited this stunning country will agree with me; it's a fairy-tale of the best variety.

一期一会
One life, one encounter
Meaning: Every encounter is a once-in-a-lifetime encounter. Sometimes used as a reminder to cherish every moment because you'll only experience it once.

—Japanese Idioms

We toast Stephanie and thank her for a breathtaking day, on our last day, as the days have been as a magical dream.

I don't know what lies ahead of my future or what his next move is for our upcoming. Our return to Hong Kong frightens me, so I am nervous about going back, because I am sure they are the Mafia, and CC is the boss.

While packing my suitcase, anxious thoughts run through my scared mind, as I tremble because I can't forget these two ugly chilling blokes, who intensely and ravenously stared at me, the first time I met CC in Asia. Will tomorrow be as coming from a magical heaven and then flying into a flaming horrible hell when we arrive in Hong Kong again?

CHAPTER 9

DANGER IN HONG KONG

Too often we don't realize what we have until it has
disappeared. Too often we are too stubborn to say, 'Sorry,
I was wrong.' Too often we hurt those closest to our hearts
and we let the most foolish things tear us apart.

—Angelic Cupcake

The turbulent flight is lengthy, and I'm exhausted when we arrive
at the luxury hotel in Hong Kong. Drake's next task is to figure
out how he can continue his business. His conflict with CC and
his concurrent work there is not such an uplifting task for me. Noticing
him going from being a kind, caring person to get irritated and snapping
at me makes me sad and frustrated. I'm aware it's not a peaceful mission
to get solved, so I do my best to support him.

While we sit in the taxi, Drake calls Terry. 'We are driving to the
hotel.' He snarls.

CC has moved the entire clinic to Hong Kong. Drake is nervous,
defending himself with stupid subjects over the phone, though I don't
know what it's about.

'I noticed your strict conversation with Terry. What's happening,
darling? Do we need to talk?'

'For mysterious reason, CC says he has found out there is
something shabby up with me. What? Shabby?' He wraths at me.

'Oh? What does CC mean?'

'Bloody hell, I don't know. Today, CC wants a meeting with me.' As we get to the Hong Kong office on forties floor at this massive glass building where CC has his headquarter. The ugly bloke with the scar stares ravenously at me, giving me the elevator glare. It panics me. Next he vulgarly fixates his eyes at my boobs, then staring at my legs. I am frightened shitless, trying to pull down my short dress. *I'll never be able to run out fast from the room, wearing my high heel black Prada shoes.* Shit!

What is the meeting about? Well, the only thing I know is that CC and Drake got 50 percent each of the treatment machine staying in the new clinic in Hong Kong. *What has Drake done?* I muse.

After half-an-hour, Drake and CC finished the not-so-pleasant meeting. Drake was peculiar and negative, as there was a hostile attitude between the parties. Wisely, I didn't interfere, keeping my mouth shut, and next we pace out of the building; and grab one of the black-and-white taxis to Grand Hyatt, Hong Kong.

'Um-hmm ... eh ... Baby, I must confess something.'

'Okay. What is it?'

'I don't have my private accommodation,' Drake bursts out.

'What, do you mean, darling? Why not? I thought you did.' I'm surprised.

'Jeez, I'm sharing a small, disgusting room with Terry.' He is the driver, handyman, and clerk of CC, yea, CC's goon and has an expert knowledge of the ominous shadow of CC's existence and how his life is.

'Oh?'

'Eh, Babe, do you want to see the apartment?' Asking as he stares odd at me.

After a brief rest in our room, we walk over to the apartment. I'm upset, and say nothing, staring at the awkwardly infested little room. Oh, dear! They share a disgusting toilet and a lousy muggy shower.

'Oh! Perhaps they want the best for you, darling. Um-hmm, but it doesn't show to me it's your cup of tea,' I'm gazing at the peeling yellow wallpaper. 'Christ, don't you get sick? There is mould in the corners. Yuck! It shows over the entire place.'

Drake stares at me, frustrated.

Eww! Golly Gosh! This manhole of shit stinks of old food, sour macho sweat, and nasty garbage.

'Can I sit on the bed?' The bed is screeching and nearly crashing. 'Um-hmm ... maybe you should open one window, darling.' I want to puke.

'Why?'

'It is musty in here!' I get up, and the windows creak and difficult to open and equally tricky to close again. Because the windows in his room can't close properly, rain is hitting his bed, and you can see the greyish fungus under the window.

'Why aren't your clothes in the closet?' Messy articles of clothing are hanging from various nails.

'There's no room in this small closet.' Drake opens the squeaking door, and the closet is nearly falling apart. 'There's barely room for my things.' He has tucked his golf gear away in the far corner. The shoes stand under the bed, together with plenty of dust, and he has stacked various boxes beside the bed.

'Yikes, when did you last wash your bed sheets, honey?' I'm close to vomit. My stomach is turning up-side-down because of the sour old man's sweat on them.

Dirty, sweaty and smelly clothes lie in the far corner of the room.

'Oh, my! Darling, are you okay with this apartment?' And I try to be kind and supportive.

'Drake, truly, I would get suffocated living here!' There's no room to turn around and I'm feeling choking. He doesn't even have a chair.

'How can you sleep in this awful noise from the street, darling?' The roaring honking cars and screaming people make me consider, *Christ, he never gets proper sleep.*

'Babe, do you want coffee or tea?' I go with him to the small, worn-out yellow and green kitchen.

'No thank you, love,' I say and have lost the craving for coffee or tea as I stare around the filthy kitchen, as it's piled up in the sink with dirty stinking plates, glasses, and mugs. On the mucky floor in the corner stands an overcrowded dustbin with old foul-smelling garbage from takeaway food.

'Where is the washing machine?' I notice the other guy's wet clothes hangs in the entire living room.

'Terry and I wash our clothes in the laundrette.'

'I'm upset to the deepest part of my heart.' I am touched with sadness at the thought of him living in such a miserable state. 'This can't be what you're used to.' I'm giving him a sympathetic, gentle hug.

He pushes me away, then glares at me and says nothing. I can't bear to be here anymore. *We must get out of this clammy and claustrophobic place—pronto!* I angrily muse.

'Oh, boy. Now I understand much better why I can't stay with you,' I comment unhappily.

He gazes with a sorrowful expression. 'No. I'm not content with it either. It didn't take a long time before things went wrong between Terry and me. I'm tired of his damn smoking. Yuck! The whole apartment stinks of smoke. I've had enough of him,' he complains, sounding miserable.

'I don't understand it, darling. Why didn't you tell me?' I'm frustrated and ponder of the unreasonable way they treat him. 'Didn't you tell me that CC is a rich investor? And he has promised you splendid chances in the country? Huh? Hasn't he? This doesn't look right,' I remark, and he pause resignedly.

'Honestly, Drake! Why are you staying here? It's unacceptable.' My street smarts and gut tell me something is wrong and fishy.

'Don't you worry with that, Mary.' He smiles falsely.

'This isn't what you told me so proud of. Where are the massive plans you agreed with CC?' I glimpse at him in astonishment.

'Ha-ha, Baby, I'm protected by a guardian angel. I am lucky I met CC,' *Such crap to say.*

Musing, I stare at him, *pondering what sort of guardian angels do they have in Asia.*

'CC asked me to hurry to come to Asia, but then he moved it all to Hong Kong. I had to solve the vast assignment. Including Asia with my massive treatment protocol. I told you that?' He defends the case.

I nod and ponder my own thoughts of his mess. So far, I have seen nothing Drake had *accomplished here.*

'Don't you worry, Babe.' He tries to calm me. 'While you are here, CC pays for the hotel. He promised. As last time.'

'Hmm. Okay, darling.' And I don't find it odd that CC is paying for our stay.

'Drake? May I give you any advice?' He nods and glares strangely at me.

'Frankly, I believe you are better off with the opportunity elsewhere.'

'Yea, well, I'm not sure, Baby. Do you think so?'

'I'm not interested in staying with you in Hong Kong. I fear these mafia goons.'

'Well, perhaps! They promised me my private apartment later. They still search for something.' He groans.

I believe him. 'Well, what with the extensive project on the medical city?'

'By the way, Baby! Tomorrow we will take part on the golf course for lessons. We will meet with a famous golf instructor.' He turns the topic to something else.

'Wauw!'

'He has trained celebrities in the United States. His son will also be there.' he boasts.

'Oh! What about your hospital's plans with the Americans? How did your last meeting turn out?'

He glares at me and doesn't give me an answer to my last question.

'Eh? What will happen to the Japanese? Are they still part of the project?' I am despairing with this entire mess of his.

'With the Americans, CC, and others, we will do the gigantic hospital project,' he brags. 'Mr Haruto has backed out. He is not interested. But there is another Japanese investor living in Taiwan."

Stupidly, I eagerly believe his many plans.

* * *

The next day at the golf course is exceptional, as it's my first time hitting a golf ball ever. The golf instructor tells me I have a flair for playing, so I'm motivated and want to play golf. Sadly, it will never come to fruition, so my stunning career as a golfer ends that day, but it was fun trying it.

While golfing, Drake's phone rings several times. It's Terry constantly on the other end of the line. He worries and gets petrified over an information from Terry.

'Are you okay, darling? You seem concerned. Can I do something for you?' I notice the fear in his eyes.

'CC is asking for a meeting with me tomorrow.' Concerned, Drake gazes at me. 'He doesn't want you to come.' He quivers strangely, and I perceive he's not okay.

'Strange. Why not, darling? Honestly, that sounds suspicious.' In this instant, I can't figure Drake out. *Does he not want me to be here?* I muse. 'Why am I not allowed to come?'

He glares at me over my question. No answer.

'Darling, CC expects me to invest. Then I'm not allowed to take part in the meeting?' I'm concerned and surprised at this shady business with Drake.

'CC insisted. It was specific that you don't come with me!' he sharply snaps. 'We go somewhere to a remote spot. I think it's nearby a beach. Terry will pick me up at the hotel.' He sneers strangely.

'*Secluded spot?* Where?' I yell.

'Half an hour's drive to Chung Hom Kok Park'

'This makes me more nervous on your behalf.' I insisted on attending in the meeting.

'No, Mary! You can't come.'

'Darling, it's as the worst gangster movie.' There is mystery with this. I imagine him as the key figure in the plot for a murder.

'Jeez, Mary. Don't be so dramatic.'

'Darling, I fear for your life,' I stammer, shaken.

'Nonsense! Nothing will happen. CC and Terry are my best friends,' he jokes with a smirk.

'You should not be best friends with the Mafia. Grr ... or whatever they are.'

The next morning, we walk to the front of the foyer. Terry is waiting for Drake at the front desk, and we go outside with him. In front of the primary entrance, they parked three black Mercedes, where the foul guys lean their backs against the first car. One has his arms across his chest; wearing dirty blue jeans, a black shirt, and a black jacket. The other dude pushed his coat aside, holding in his hand of something that appears as a loaded gun. *I have seen him somewhere.* Oh, yes! It is the daunting gorilla with a long ugly scar along his cheek. His skin appears blemished and unhealthy, and he is wearing a black turtleneck sweater, dark jeans, and a worn-out black jacket.

'Spooky! Both resemble the worst mobsters from a chilling crime movie.' I'm distraught and scared. CC sits calmly waiting in the second car with another guy. Who is it? I can't see who it is. Terry is alone in the third car and will drive it, with Drake in it.

'I'm deeply concerned for you, honey. This doesn't look reassuring.'

'Stop it, babe.'

'But have you seen the sneaky guys in front of the first vehicle?' I scowl, directing my eyes towards the car.

'I don't think he looks sneaky.' And he is trying to calm me.

'Darling, I will not allow you to drive without me. Those guys are gangsters. Mafia gorillas. Can't you see that?'

Annoyed, he stares at me with mistrust in his eyes, as I'm nuts. 'Come on, Mary! Stop your crazy paranoia.' He smiles insecurely.

'Darling, I refuse to let you drive off without taking me with you,' I dictate nervously.

He gazes at me, fuming now, and snaps. 'Oh, my goodness! You are too much. You see spooky ghost everywhere.' Then he calmly walks over to Terry and speaks with him.

He should be ashamed, talking so rudely to me, and by his aggressive response, my tongue gets paralyzed. I'm glaring at the dudes and try to hear what they're talking of. I can't hear it because of the funnel effect increased as it squeezes the wind through the narrow space in front of the hotel entrance.

Drake comes back to me, and Terry is heading over to CC It's as watching an energetic ping-pong game, with the dudes running back and forth. After Terry speaks with CC, he comes back again to chat with Drake. While speaking, Terry points at me, then with a firm finger points to the car where CC sits, showing that I must ride along with him and the fishy fella next to him.

'I will not do it, Drake,' I roar in Danish. 'If we are driving somewhere, we do it together. In the same car.' Pondering; *Is Terry out of his mind?* Crazy fishy bloke.

'There is something dingy with this.'

'Grr... *Stop* being so dramatic, Mary! Calm down now!'

'If we're together, I'm sure CC and his goons won't harm us.' I mumble the last bit in fear but believe in my self-assurance.

'Enough! What's going on with your stupid brain?' He hisses.

I feel as Drake doesn't believe me. 'I sense a nasty feeling with this.'

'Hush now! Nothing is happening. What do you think this is?'

'What the hell have you done?' My heart is beating faster.

'Bloody hell, Mary, you are too dense.'

'It's as they want to knock you off.' Shit, I'm scared, and my blood is pumping with fear, while my legs are as a wobbling jellyfish.

'I know the guys. You don't.' He sounds confident in his massive anger.

'God damn it! I can see the scarred guy has a loaded gun on him. Why don't you trust me?' I whisper harshly to him.

The scarred bloke glares at me, aggravated.

'I just can't bear to lose you.' I want to cry.

Drake grins in superiority, 'Christ, Mary,' and rolls his eyes at me. CC gets calmly out of the car, smiles, and walks steadily towards me.

'Mary, you can ride with me. Then we can talk.' Oh my, CC is so calm. 'Drake is driving with Terry,' he commands, kindly grabbing my arm, and I twist myself out of his grip.

'Darling, I'm scared!' I say in Danish and refuse CC's suggestion. Rather than follow him, I hastily jump into the same car as Drake. A strange expression slides across CC's face. I wonder what scary plans the others ponder.

CC signs with his hand that it's okay, so Terry lets me ride with him and Drake.

'Gee, Mary! How do you want me to do business with them?' He takes my hand and squeezes it gently. 'Why are you so suspicious every time?'

Terrified, I silently cling to him.

The buzzing bumper-to-bumper driving takes us far away from the loud, bustling town, passing West Kowloon, then driving over a massive bridge ending on another vast island until we end up at Chung Hom Kok Park. There we end up by a quiet deserted restaurant by a white sandy beach at the southern tip of this other island. The waves crash along the shore, and the powerful wind blows wildly in my hair, while I glare at the massive blue Chung Hom Wan Ocean. We're the only people for miles around this location, and it turns out the restaurant is closed at this time of year. I worry even more when I notice the chairs are still on the tables, and there's no sign that the restaurant is open. The chef approaches us and whispers something in Chinese to CC. Yuck; he appears greasy and smells of sour old sweat. Distrustfully, he glares frighteningly at us.

'It's unnerving!' I whisper to Drake as there's a shady meanness to the atmosphere.

'I ordered food.' CC smirks and constantly stays calm. 'Doctor, let's go out and talk.'

Several times, CC shows that Drake must go outside with him to talk in private. Each time I see, the creepy guys instantly rise from the worn-out squeaking chairs and ready to follow them.

'You are not leaving without me.' I whisper.

He sends me a nasty glare. 'Now, you shut the hell up, Mary!' Whoa! He gets mad.

'The one bloke has a big knife in his belt.'

'Christ! You are too much! It's me who decides what will happen,' he snaps harshly in Swedish.

I sigh nervously, telling him about my observation. 'But darling, I saw the knife when he turned.'

Every time I try to give these warnings, he gets mad at me.

'CC will knock you off. He'll cut your throat. Dump you somewhere.' I can hear myself saying irrational things that sounded dramatic.

'Come on. Stop it, Mary. Only I can and will handle this. Nothing will happen.' I can see the worry in his eyes.

'No, I won't! Then they will tell me you went off with them to see a new plot. Searching for a building for the clinic project.'

'Stop, Mary.' He glares at me as am I stupid.

'They will come with other foul excuse. Then drive me back without you.'

'Oh, yea, I see his knife now, Babe. When the dude turned around again.

'There you see. Next I can find you chopped up in a dumpster.' My imagination is immense, as I say these creepy conspiracy theories about them while I am distraught, musing; *have I seen too many gangster movies?*

'Maybe you are right,' he whispers, and refusing to follow CC.

Next he lies to CC 'You know what, CC? I don't feel so good today. I have a headache. I'm very dizzy. Let's talk another time.' Drake stares at CC, pretending he's unsteadied, and slowly he sits again.

CC may have expected it to go smoothly by luring Drake into an ambush. I'm sure CC hadn't expected my stubbornness, as I wouldn't leave Drake alone with them.

The restaurant does not serve the food ever, and CC gives up his foul plan, then drives us back to Grand Hyatt.

'Holy cow! I'm so terrified of what's going on today, darling.'

Back at the hotel, either CC or Terry phones Drake several times. Each time, he becomes more nervous and suspicious after their talk. Strangely, and during a conversation with Terry, he warned Drake that he isn't particularly popular with CC He wants to do something cruel to Drake, so he gets spooked.

'Baby let's go back to the apartment. I need my things.' He suddenly says.

'Okay, fine.' Unquestioningly, I agree with him. We grab a taxi back to the filthy, muggy residence; pack his things, including the other machine he has in the apartment; drive it back to the hotel and get it stored in the hotel's locker room. Next, we drive to the clinic, to gain access, as he wants his things, and the other machine; he has a 50 percent part in it.

Drake realises CC changed the lock as he tries to get into the clinic. We must leave the place with our task unaccomplished. He's fuming as a roaring and fiery dragon, and with a rage, he paces with hasty steps along the street. Turns sharp right, takes a sharp left and right again, stomping to the office to confront CC I have a steady grip on Drake's hand, as I run to keep up with his quick steps.

'Oyh ... Drake, can't you stop for a moment? Shit, so many potholes on this street.' I can barely manage this quick run in my close-fitting dress and my high-heeled Prada shoes. Damn!

He's fuming again as we stand in front of CC's building, and the receptionist lets us in, then we take the elevator up to the forties floor.

'Is CC busy?' Drake roars angrily at the next reception desk.

The spine-chilling, eerie guy approaches us and escorts us into the office. In front of CC's desk stands the other creepy dude too and sneers at us as he walks threatening towards us.

'Mam, you stay there!' The ugly goon stares strictly at me, almost body-to-body contact, and commands me to wait.

I slap my bum on the black leather sofa and wait for Drake for half an hour.

It's obvious to me when he comes out again—his face insinuates it, it's best to escape from Hong Kong. Now!

'What's going on?' I nervously ask when he comes out again.

No answer, but he is boiling red in his face of anger.

'The private chauffeur is waiting for us on the street to drive us back,' he roars.

'I prefer a taxi instead.'

'Mary, God damn it! Shut the hell up!' Then he stops a taxi instead. 'Get into the car. Now!' He snarls, and we head back to the hotel.

Angry and determined, he grabs his computer when we get back to the room.

'This will take a moment. I must write to the Taiwan investor. Kuan-Lin Wang wants me to come fast and train his five therapist.' he growls.

'May I know what you decided?'

'I'll confirm that I appreciate the offer of the job.' He snaps at me. 'We'll travel to Taiwan instead. Best within the next few days. Now shut up, Mary. Let me think.' He sounds outraged.

'Mary, search for tickets!' He orders and suddenly sounds convinced and responsive to my warnings. 'We have to make a fast run, Babe.' This last bit comes roaring out of his mouth, and he looks scared.

Grabbing my computer, I search for flights. 'Oi, darling, I need your passport, darling. Oh, and credit card to book your flight.' I reach out my hand to get a card and the passport.

'Damn, Mary. Fix it. Just pay for mine. Don't nit-pick with me now.' Is his rude answer while he angrily is clamping on his keyboard. 'I'll transfer money to you later,' yapping at me while he hands me over his passport.

Gullible, I pay for both tickets to Taiwan. Does Drake not have any money? Will I ever get the coinage back? In the shadow of darkness that night, we pack our stuff. Next, it's stored in the reception's locked baggage room, together with the rest of his stuff. Early in the morning, we go to the reception space to retrieve our belongings. Holy mackerel! Hell breaks loose.

'We are checking out. Can we get our belongings?' Drake nervously paces in front of the welcome desk, staring around scared and confused.

'Is the mafia after us? Damn! Then CC can be here any minute.' I'm scared.

'Just a moment, Mr Bates. I'll prepare the bill.' The reception fella says calmly.

'I'll not pay the bill. Mr CC will.' Drake roars.

Drake glares nervously and continues shouting and quarrelling in anger with the front counter and the security guards. My heart pounds with madness, frustration, and distress while I am monitoring the entrance door, ready to flee. I go back to the front desk.

Unexpectedly, the staff detains us. Holly crap! Now I get more nervous and frightened as hell. What have I messed myself into?

'Can you see if the gangsters are coming?' He asks me.

'What will it take to get our things?' Impatient, I clamp hard my fingers on the marble counter. With a fury I snap at the receptionist as a wild bull and star heated straight into his brown eyes. Oh ... my ... I could have killed him with my anger stare.

'*Pay the bill, Mrs Bates!* Then you can pick up your stuff,' he barks, resembling an ill-mannered little snarling rabies infested dog, while I stare terrified at Drake.

My entire body shakes and wobbles comparable to jelly. With no hesitation, I snatch a credit card from my black Prada purse, and throw it hard on the desk with a loud smash. 'Okay, I'll pay the damn bill. Receipt please. Now! Hurry!' I fiercely yap at the dude.

The rage in my fingers enters the pin code, and they accepted the payment, so I seize the papers.

The bellboy gets our things and prepares to get it outside, and I smack him $20. In a haste shivering with my jelly legs identical to a sick petrified donkey, I tremble, stomping fast outside in my high-heeled black Prada shoes.

A big black-and-white taxi is waiting for us, and hurriedly we load our stuff into the cab.

'Sorry I got so furious, darling. This horrendous mess is too much for me,' I sob, half crying and trembling, as I jump into the black-leather back seat of the station wagon with him.

'Think nothing of it. We are in safety now. Well done, Mary. Wauw, you're a cool woman.' He quivers, giving me a clap on my shoulder. In relief, I squeeze his shaking hand firm and turn my head to glance out of the rear window.

Shit! Two fast speeding black Mercedes with the driver at full blast honking the horns arrive at the hotel just as our taxi drives out of the front area. With lightning speed, three creepy guys, CC, and Terry get out of the cars and sprint into the reception space. That's the last I see before our taxi smoothly turns around the left corner of the hotel space. Hastily and relieved, we drive to Hong Kong Airport. Disappearing as two shifty lovebirds—running off again, as chased fugitives, comparable to Bonnie and Clyde, searching for an unknown life somewhere else.

I suspect that so far all other business is a significant disaster. It's going into the dark, stinky, slimy sewer. Drake has no money and no income, so he depends on the job in Taiwan, including me and my money.

What will Drake's solution be for us? As Abraham Lincoln said; You cannot escape the responsibility of tomorrow by evading it today.

CHAPTER 10

BLOOD DIAMONDS FOR THE QUEEN

> He denounced him openly as a charlatan—a fraud, with no
> valuable knowledge of any kind, or powers beyond those of
> an ordinary and rather inferior human being.
>> —Mark Twain, *The Mysterious Stranger*

Drake is hilarious in between his madness.

'It's not a secret what's in the box. We can make it electronic if you help me.' he said, as he proudly showed me his box with paper clips, and letters, that he believed were significant.

Occasionally, I must grab my head and contemplate what's wrong with him. I can't understand whether he is sane or has a fantastic imagination.

'Oh, Sweetie, monsters are real. Ha-ha, and they appear as people,' he jokes on a lovely night, telling me a story of the royals. During a lovely dinner under swaying palm trees in crescent moonlight on a blissful beach, I get by his tale of the royal king's house.

'Mary, can you prepare this for me for my online scrapbook?' He sweetly asks me.

'Sure, I'll do it for you,' along with Blogging and creating a Web site, I'm preparing for him. I ponder of what a person I'm living with, when he shows me the 'Nigeria' letter, written to the royals many years ago.

'I was so proud when I got in contact with the queen.' He smirks.

'Oh, ha-ha, it's funny,' and my jaw drops to the floor in bewilderment. I'm speechless and laugh as I hold the letter in my hand and read it.

'Finish the reading. This is serious, Mary.' He gets miffed at me. 'I want it in the online scrapbook about my life. Don't laugh!' He seriously stares unsmiling at me.

'Hmm ... ha-ha, ha-ha ...' It's amusing.

'Argh, Mary! Why is it so funny to you?'

Many years ago, he gradually became more desperate to make quick money. In the late hours of the night, he mused how he could make the next inventive plan for his day ahead.

Buckle up, friends, grab it with a special humour, though, in the way I'm expressing the letter. I often took a laughing break before getting back to my normal senses. Is this worrying? I have never seen such letters before.

When he was in his fifties, he had woken up early one morning with a set of splendid novel ideas. Being well-rested and happy in his upper pot lid of a non-functioning brain simmering on the sizzling frying pan, he had received a fantastic revelation during the night. OMG! These kinds of eye-openers of his, I have seen them many times. He wrote a letter to Her Majesty, The Queen of Sweden, of the imaginary project he had dreamt about during the night which had convinced him of the perfect solution for an improvement of his wealth.

'Baby, it's terrible. Many years ago, I got this new eye-opener. I had lost over three million dollars. It was on a strange business presented by others.' He plays convincing when he tells me this and I feel sorry for him. I'm not sure if his story is true.

'The other scumbags cheated me. It wasn't even my fault. When I accepted a payment of this massive sum, I lost everything with a single keystroke. Damn it! When my finger hit the enter key on my computer, jeez, seconds after—*puff!*—I lost my entire fortune.'

'Oh, no! What a terrible bummer.' I comment pitifully.

'Yea, the entire sum disappeared into outer space. Argh, jeez, to live its life on a fake satellite.' He sounds devastated over his massive failure.

'What the hell do I know of bogus satellites? Why are you sending money on a rocket to outer space?' I am asking him. 'Christ! It sounds somewhat weird to me.'

'It was my ignorant world for the future wire systems in its early age of development.'

I listen intensely to his story. I genuinely believe he invented the internet as his fantastic masterpiece developed on his idea of the nervous structure in the human body.

'What a genius guy you are. Wow, I'm proud of you.'

'Mary, it's for the future networks of the entire world within seconds. These stupid buffoons I was working with stole my entire project. And my patent.' It was revenge time for him.

'I got this magnificent idea. With the queen. How do I get my money back?'

What a ponderous plan he got during the night. The dude is so talented—or so he thinks. I muse, and it might be he is very boned headed, because on the outside, it shows he has a high IQ, above average. So, what does the genius do? The loss changed nothing in his innovative intellect, as a fresh idea was born.

During his night-time revelation, he had, in his sleeping mind, created a stunning letter to the queen. He's good at his various ingenious ideas on any novel project. That's why he's always in such an excellent mood in the mornings—when he so often wakes up with a new-fangled idea. He creates many of them during the shadowy darkness of his imaginative crooked nights; I have noticed. Though, the splendid plans rumble only in his imaginary mind, I suppose, but it's the most *amazing* concepts he can come up with where he promises it can bring in lots of cash. At least that's what he supposes. God damn it! Foolishly, I trust in every of them.

His letter to the queen reads:

Her Majesty, Your Royal Highness Queen Sofia of Sweden:

I'm a tremendous fan and citizen of the impressive Sweden, and still faithful to the king and queen. I'm in my best age, with brilliant innovative ideas and projects on wealth and welfare. Despite being overseas, I stay close and faithful to the throne of Sweden. Besides, I'm so fascinated by Your Majesty, and as by the monarchy, with its impressive history. I've always wanted to and dreamed that I could contribute something positive to its future. For me, the royal house is the strongest connecting link that ties the people of the kingdom together, and I want it to always stay that way.

My primary business is as a well-known professor in medical research. I'm, of origin, a famous and successful Swedish doctor, with a PhD and many published medical researches. Beforehand, as a successful doctor, I excelled in a system of complementary medicine, based on the diagnosis and manipulative treatment of misalignments of joints, which causes other disorders by affecting the nerves, organs, and muscles. I was, and I still am, the most famous doctor in the world. I owned the world's largest clinic in Sweden, and I am now processing, and building a new, more massive medical clinic in Europe and The United States. Patients' needs my hands and expertise, which no other doctor in the world can offer.

I am also a specialist in the development of electronic train components. Among my many patents, I've also patented unique bedding products, and an extensive wireless communication network. You will not believe it, but it is a giant hit in Europe and Scandinavia.

It's now come to me as a fantastic, unique idea that maybe I can contribute with something unique to the kingdom— only with your help and creativity for the arts. Together, we both can gain a real symbolic value in the royal's future house of Sweden. The inspiration for this initiative came to me as I enjoyed the festive days leading up to the marriage of your beloved daughter, Her Royal Highness Crown Princess Magdalena to His Royal Highness Crown Prince Jesus Alfonso.

I noticed that, your majesty was wearing a stunning necklace in white- gold, primarily studded with gems of glittering diamonds, stunning emeralds, and warm deep red rubies. You will not believe your own eyes and ears when you hear what I now will tell you, Your Royal Highness.

I'm in such a fortunate position as a business owner and financier. I am co-owner of a considerably large number of investment grade gemstones—it's the finest Pigeon blood rubies from the jungles of Burma, rarest Columbian deep intense emeralds from the mountains of Muzo, and flawless diamonds from Shaban Uri in Sierra Leone. Don't worry, Your Majesty, they're not blood diamonds from these states. They are perfectly legal and come with approved certificates. I know it could be a scandal if the Kings and Queens house gets enriched with conflict diamonds, used by rebel movements to finance conflicts to undermine lawful governments.

I want to think about these precious stones as we can use them to create a striking first-hand and elegant set of crown jewels. My idea is that Crown Princess Magdalena can wear it when she and Crown Prince Jesus Alfonso get proclaimed queen and king of Sweden. Then they can pass it on to the next generation in a lifetime, with such a unique piece of jewellery as a gift to the royal house. Later, the royal family inherit it, as they do with so many other jewels.

My artistic abilities do not work for design, but only for original financial purposes. So, not for elegant jewellery—I therefore of this allow myself to contact Your Majesty to ask for your artistic help, as an expert. I know that Your Majesty has a confident and uniquely elegant style in everything you do, and this includes your resourceful prowess. Only Your Majesty knows how a noble person should look—especially when it's done as exquisitely, strictly, elegantly, and correctly as only you can do.

My humble suggestion is to ask Your Majesty for help in designing the most stunning piece of jewellery ever made for the royal house. Then you can use it for the occasion mentioned earlier. There are many years leading up to this event, so there will be plenty of time to do everything correctly, as the Crown Princess Magdalena and Crown Prince Jesus Alfonso appear as the most stunning upcoming married couple imaginable. They suit each other remarkably well, therefore I know emeralds, rubies and diamonds will dress the crown princess incredibly well. When Your Majesty design the jewellery with your safe hand, I'm sure the world will see a piece that you will admire in retrospect. Perhaps a symbol of the royal house's safe space in the new era.

The value of our gems exceeds $6 million. I believe that we will have enough gems to create something unusual for queens of Sweden, they forever can wear. I'm sure they will wear it with special pride because it's Your Majesty who has created the jewellery. If Your Majesty believes it is interesting and you want to speak to me of how we can carry out such a stunning project and the payment, then I would love to hear from Your Majesty with great pleasure.

As I'm a private person, I don't want the press's attention regarding this inquiry, either now or in the future. I ask Your Majesty to understand that I do not make this inquiry for my private relations gain, nevertheless I'd love to carry this fantastic project in full confidence. We can only do it if the intentions are noble and come from the heart.

As Your Majesty can understand, my work is far from such a magnificent jewel project in every way, and together, I hope we can develop the stunning jewellery project. We will move a high-tech department to Sweden, and I plan to build communications facilities and a large private clinic in your country. I'll therefor travel often to the country over the coming time.

You can reach me on my phone, +29 (0) 908019470 or by email dlb@holeone.com or, we can meet in private when I visit Stockholm soon. Your written inquiries you can send them to our office, at the address included.

Yours most sincerely
Prof. Lord Drake, Lucifer Bates, MD and PhD in science

Business owner:
Hole One Ltd
66 Sham Road,
90847 Craven Pit, Conman Island

You can run, but you can't hide. The story will repeat itself. Is the Blood Diamond story about to repeat itself. Though, I'm not a Queen, nor famous, but an ordinary housewife. Will I be the next victim of Drake's mystiques and ponderous plans he gets during the shady nights, in his murky rabbit hole in Sham Road 66?

CHAPTER 11

FLEEING IN THE SHADOWY DARKNESS OF THE NIGHT!

> You're trying to escape from your difficulties, and there
> never is any escape from difficulties, never. They have to be
> faced and fought.
> —Enid Blyton, *Six Cousins at Mistletoe Farm*

Exhausted, we nervously grab two trolleys, then run fast as two shifty criminals to the busy Hong Kong Airport terminal. Sweating and out of breath; we check in with Taiwan Airlines, and next it leaves us only ten minutes before the gate closes. After the great relief of getting out of Hong Kong alive, we land, after half a day of travel, in Taipei—pretending as nothing happened in Hong Kong. It frightens us shitless, having in mind that the Mafia wanted to assassinate Drake.

'Babe, we can't tell anyone of what happened. Not even Mr Wang. It connects them.' *That's a piece of fresh information to me, I don't know.* I stare questioning at him. 'That's how I first met Mr Wang in Hong Kong.'

'Okay! Whoa! This is a fat secret you tell me to keep safe,' and we never speak of it again.

Mr Wang's chauffeur picks us up at the busy and noisy Airport and drive us to the Ritz-Carlton. Pooped, I sit on the wide window frame, watching the Sun, setting in stunning red colours behind the impressive beige building, enjoying swiftly, the Sun disappear. The sky turns black, and the buildings shine as glittering stars in the night's darkness. In front of me is a round glass building with its characteristic sign, Hard Rock Hotel in yellow light, surrounded with red lights showing each floor of the building. Next to the building is another enormous glass building, and its orange, red and yellow lights running as a whirlwind up and down. Many buzzing cars drive on the busy roads as red and white fast driving black tiny ants in each direction. I glance swiftly at Drake, jump from the window frame, and unpack our things, though I'm tired.

We slap our bodies onto the double bed, take a brief rest while he talks of his idea for the future in Taiwan.

'Wang has arranged the first meeting for tomorrow. I hope we can finally arrange of the new clinic. Hopefully, everything goes smoothly. I wish you'll still want to stay with me, little girl.' He happily gives me a kiss.

I mostly need to get embraced by him and not talk business. I turn to the side, gently put my hand under his shirt and cuddle his soft stomach. 'Yea, darling, I want to stay. Um-hmm, but I don't know if Taipei is a perfect solution for me. It sounds great. At least you must go for it.'

He gently kisses my loose hair and reaches for my hand I have under his shirt.

'You know, I must travel back to solve my issues with Paul. I have my promise to Lucy and Cliff in Spain to watch the dogs next month.'

I gasp as he pushes me aside and casts an intense stare at me. 'Eyh? Is it so important now?' Then pulls me up to his body again and hugs me tightly. 'My sweet Baby. It's a perfect chance for you to forget of them in Spain. Lucy only takes advantage of you. As a dog keeper,' he insists and blabbers many other loving words to me, so I melt in his embrace.

Mostly, I want to stay with him, but my integrity tells me another story, though. 'I must pick up Spotty. I can't leave him there. He is my dog. He must go back to Adam. It's actually his dog.' I appeal to Drake with my promises to Lucy and my family. 'I don't know how to solve the matter with Paul. He told the kids that Spotty is not coming back to them.'

'My little poor girl. I don't need you to be sad again. Remember what happened before you came back to me,' he mumbles, annoyed over my decision.

'I must travel back to Spain. To do what I have promised Lucy,' Ignoring his strange assumptions of Lucy and Cliff.

'Babe, it's only a dog. Lucy and Cliff can keep him. The kids don't care. Your family doesn't care of you either.' It saddens me with his unkind dog and family comment.

'Um-hm ... Perhaps you are right,' as I sense the unpleasant conflict between Drake and my family.

'What makes you think Lucy and the kids even bother? Stay with me, my gorgeous love. We will live happily. I'll do everything for you.' He smiles sweetly, and I vanish in his brown eyes and his gorgeous smile.

'My darling love, your wishes make it difficult for me to decide what to do.' He does everything to tear down my defences and to get my family out of the way.

I'm so attracted to him. But still I try to ignore him and to stand by my promises I've made to my family and friends. I have this energetic fluttering inside me—the notion that he can give me a perfect life. *Oh my, I can't handle this about him. It's too soon*, I muse.

'When we later go to bed, my love, I'll let my hot fingers warm up your bones.' He takes me closer into his warm embrace and kisses me intensely. Then touch my breast gently in a pleasing, chilling and stimulating way. 'I'll charge your warm bubbly blood too—something exciting and nice little girl.'

'Oh, you are is so crispy when you whisper such sweet words into my ears.' I get carried away with his teasing and exciting words and smooth touches.

Perfectly he knows how to hit me on my hunger for him, and instantly I always let down my guards. In my stupidity and selfishness of being madly in love, I brashly abandon my family and friends. That part of me is selfish, and I'm ashamed of my bold action. I hadn't taken Lucy's warning seriously that I was probably just another score among the many women in his life.

Drake goes to the clinic without me, though he didn't appear well. I need time for myself, and stay in the room, thinking intensely of him. Meditative, I glance at the massive glass skyscrapers, surrounded by artificial lakes and a park on the horizon. With my nose to the window, from twenty floors up, I enjoy the stunning views. The weather is humid and hot outside, and while sitting in the wide's corner window frame, I watch the Sun gleam from a bright blue sky. I sense dense smog rising on the horizon of the massive capital, musing; *how can you desperately miss someone you are together with always?* I miss him when he is in the same building as me and when he is near me. In my passion, while I miss him so badly, I write him a letter of my feelings and final decision.

Subject: Miss you like crazy!

Hi, darling love,

Here we are together in Taipei. Yet I can miss you crazy. How can this be? You are on the sixth floor treating a significant person, and I'm staying alone on the twentieth floor of this lovely hotel. Why I miss you come from the fact that, since we came back a week ago, you told me you're ill, and I'm concerned for you. We have not taken enough care of each other.

My firm beating heart and immense love for you have survived your deprivation, so I hope we can achieve more of enjoyment together, before reaching our next goal. As in a single prayer and a tireless quest to get you fresh and ready again, I find with you an unbelievable love for me. I love you for always remembering our great love—for making sure that it's nurtured, even though you sometimes barely can stand up because, you say, you are ill.

In the innermost depths of my heart, on its pulsating blood-red throne, I have a love for you forever. You will be my king, and I will be your queen. I will honour you forever and love you for the eternity we want together. If you stay on the throne of my heart, I will continue to be the queen of your soul. I'll love and honour it, if you will respect my love and stay in my life.

I love you much that it's sometimes hard to believe—to know whether it's real or just a fluttering illusion. If it's just a ghostly daydream, I never want to wake up from it. I'll keep dreaming of a joyful life with you and never let the illusion stop, then keep it safe and firm in my bubbly, warm heart and memory. Best I will wake up again and wish you're not an enigmatic illusion, but that you are the one my flaming love belongs too.

Stay in my dream, and let me love you more today than yesterday, but less today than I will love you tomorrow. For tomorrow, my love for you will be greater than today. I'll stay with you, and I'll build a fresh life with you, so we'll happily have our first enchanting Christmas and a sparkling and bubbly New Year together here in Taipei.

Hugz and kizzez,
Mary Liz

'My sweet love. You are as intense as I know I have felt you before, a long time ago,' as he, during the afternoon, cheerfully comes up to the room. 'Oh, Sweet Pea, it seems so real. And good inside my soul to get your lovely letter. It gives me warmth and love, as only we can enjoy it together.' He tenderly hugs me intensely and breathes a deep, lengthy sigh, relieved to learn of my decision.

'Well, are you happy, darling?'

'It's so great to be with you. Amazing to experience how strong our bond is. Your sweet words make me pleased. Baby, I will carry them in my heart forever,' he kisses me shallow on my forehead.

'I don't like kisses on my forehead, darling.' But I take it as a love statement, as he next glances intensely into my eyes.

'Tomorrow my love for you will be greater than today. It will continue to be greater for us. Even for the rest of today. Baby, and forever in our life. Thanks for staying. Thanks for believing in me.' he hugs me passionately.

I ran away and hide with Drake, with no one knowing what I'm doing with my life. Many will say, 'Why has she done this?' I undeniably don't know! I'm mighty drawn to him, and without this illusion of a saving Angle, my life is not be complete.

* * *

A mesmerising Christmas has passed, and the hotel has removed the stunning decorations on the stairs and in the vast reception area. The ten-metre-tall magical Christmas tree with the red, white, and silver Christmas decorations, and its many fake stunningly adorned packages, disappears, as the busy staff hangs up the impressive festive decorations for New Year's upcoming party. As specially invited guests of Mr Wang, we enjoy an explosive marvellous New Year's party as I wear a long black Roman-inspired pleated dress, with silver-studded stitches and Swarovski crystals worn as a trimming around my waist. Proudly, I enter a grand decorated hall for a stunning and vigorous party alongside Drake, in his dark blue suit and the purple pattern tie I gave him as a Christmas gift.

At Christmas, we each received a lovely wristwatch from Wang. Drake's in polished steel, and mine with a mix of shiny steel and gold, studded with 12 small diamonds in the clock case. Together with my other jewellery, including the stunning Swarovski bracelet he gave me as a present, I adorned myself with a stunning Swarovski silver necklace and long matching dangling earrings; he gave me for Christmas.

It decorates the vibrant hall with lots of swinging black, white, and silver balloons, loads of dangling, winding serpentines and hanging festoons in the same colours. The evening's singer and performer, reminiscent of stunning and sexy Kylie Minogue, gives a bomb-exploding fantastic energetic dance show, and at full blast she sings imitations of Kylie songs. With pomp and splendour, lots of bubbling champagne floats in our glasses and the New Year hit twelve. A fresh unknown life is to begin for us.

*   *   *

The following month is hard work, education, and make plans for the clinic, and we will soon get our permanent stay in Taiwan. Drake sold one of his machines for $42,000 to Wang, and the other one belongs to us—meaning it's the one I pay for every month, as we made a handshake arrangement, so I consider myself as a business partner. Was it wise only to make what he calls a 'reliable' handshake with Drake? Or should I have signed a legal contract with him?

Over the following week we view many residences and plan everything to the utmost detail, and decide for the three-bedroom, modern, furnished apartment on the twenty-fifth floor, with a stunning view over Taipei, surrounded with a vast gorgeous garden. The building boasts a massive indoor/outdoor swimming pool and a large modern gym. Until everything is ready for the move, Drake works, I'm his secretary and I continue with my swimming and exercises, every late afternoon, in the hotel's gym. Finally, I relax before the sunset, so life seems great on the outside.

Darker thundering clouds on the far horizon come floating over the sky, as the night is to fall. I relax on the sunbed, listening to the artificial waterfall, splashing gently next to me, and allow myself to let go of negative thoughts and am treasuring by the grace of the present moment's experience. It's peaceful and inspiring, and in the background, I enjoy the last symphony by the birds twittering on their way to bed. The last butterflies flutter around from bush to bush to find a peaceful plant to rest, when suddenly a colourful coppery red, yellow, and orange butterfly gently sits on my bare shoulder, glaring at me, then it flies away. The power of beauty and serenity gives me a peaceful ambience and offers a fresh breath to my soul, while sitting under a tree with red frangipani flowers. Few flowers land on my stomach, then swiftly a vast stunning black and blue butterfly sits quietly on my arm.

Carefully, I reach up to the beauty, now sitting on my index finger, then I watch it, and breathtakingly; it looks directly into my eyes, then instantly, it flies and disappears into the darkening horizon. I pick up the red flowers lying on my stomach and take in its strong, lovely and comforting fragrance, glance at the gentle glow of the fading Sun. Colourful in yellow and red, it's setting its last gleaming beams to the west, while I let myself into a slow transition, from deep inhale to a relaxed exhale. Holding the majestic red flower under my nostrils, I again take in its delicious fresh fragrant, then breathing in deep thought, as my chest glides in a deep relaxation, until the disturbing worries in my head, and the psychical tension disappears.

*　*　*

When I'm together with Drake during most of the day, he teaches the five physiotherapists, but not me. It irritates me because he is only using me as his bloody secretary and assistant to make videos. He has only a few patients on the list, and today Wang has an appointment with him.

'I've a new client for you, doctor. Gus will be here tomorrow,' Wang swiftly says during the treatment session.

'Oh, thank you. That's nice.' Drake smiles.

'During his latest stunts, Gus injured his shoulder and ankle.' Wang states, and Drake is over the Moon. 'You get three weeks to fix Gus. He is soon heading to a boot camp.'

'Oh, that sounds interesting.' As he realises, it's one of Wang's essential connections, so Drake's self-centred madness will not end. Though, I am excited that he gets the privilege.

'Yeah, it's an action movie.' Wang adds and gives us a copy of the first action movie, then the chitchatting continues.

The following day a vibrant, handsome, youthful man in his late twenties arrives. Gus is a fantastic, good-looking man with lots of sparkling humour, a badass too, and a Taiwanese stuntman, traditional hybrid martial art where his fighting style combines all the best parts of kickboxing, karate and Taekwondo. He is like Jackie Chan, one of my favourite badass martial art actors.

During the treatment session, I watch the guys, forehead against forehead, while Gus holds his arms tight and firm crossed. Distorted by pain, his face turns into angry mimic, but Drake laughs at him while he is treating him and shoots the damn snapping electrifying energy into his sore ankle. After that Drake treats Gus shoulder with laser.

'What is the latest movie about?' Drake snoops.

'It's about an elite team of commandos. Taking down a brutal crime lord. The villains want every cop's head.'

'Sounds interesting, Gus. Wang gave me a copy of the movie with your stunts.'

'Yea, there will be loads of action. I can't tell too much, doctor.'

'It's okay.' And then Drake's arrogance continues during the treatment.

Occasionally Gus lies sprawled out on the table, as a wild, funny, uncontrolled angry pistol shrimp, when Drake sends his insane clicking energy through his body. He rapidly jumps as a petrified chased rabbit, and several times and because of Gus's quick reflections and pain, he wants to kick Drake hard in his head or stomach. Spiteful as my thoughts may be, I sometimes wish he will hit him—send him to the Moon in outer space, along with his selfishness and exaggerated self-importance. I'm speechless, listening to how he can boast himself in front of the patient as if he's hoping to get a reward for his bragging performance.

At least Gus gets well after three weeks and is ready to join the SWAT team.

It seems perfect from the outside with our relationship, but it's also full of many flaws. It saddens me when I discover that Drake flirts intensely with another essential and wealthy female patient during three sessions. Mrs Lily, a famous actress, acted together with Julia Roberts once. Wow, what a stunning beauty she is, and sweet of nature, and ten years younger than me. I get jealous and angry with his flirting behaviour, because I recognise the same hardcore flirting pattern he did with me in Spain. Frustrated, I don't understand why he is doing it in front of me.

At night, it ends up with a substantial loud verbal fight between us, and in my desperate frustration, I harshly confront him.

'Why are you flirting so much with Mrs Lily?' I grumble crossed in frustration, staring as miserable as I suffer. I don't want to lose him to another woman. *Is he doing it to trigger my anger and jealousy?* He knows I hate such betrayals. What is he trying to prove?

'What are you talking of?' He puffs himself up in self-defence. 'Grr, I'm not doing such a thing.' Glaring angrily at me and throwing his arms up in the air.

'Darling, honestly. You eagerly flirt with Lily. The same way you did with me in Spain.' I'm Verdigris green with jealousy.

'Argh! Are you out of your mind, Mary?' Growling as a stupid innocent bear.

'What does your blinking eye to Lily mean?'

'Baloney! Jeez, Mary, your obnoxious dumb demons play stupid games in your head again.' His eyes open wide, and his right eyebrow lifted in anger. He denies every observation I've seen during her last treatment.

'Oh! What with your constant hugging, Lily?' I drop my face to my hands in rage and cry.

'Argh! Bloody hell, Mary. Geez! Humbug! Are you stupid? I never flirt with my patients.'

'Get out! You hug Lily every time you have finished treating her.' In the back of my mind, I have always known deeply that my happiness with him will not last forever.

'Rubbish! Baloney! You are crazy.'

'Gah, this is hopeless.' Filled with disappointment, I get up from the bed and enter the bathroom. 'I need a steamy bath,' I mumble and take furiously off my clothes.

Next, I sit in a foetal position in the shower's corner, letting the warm running drops dripping over my face and body, leaving crystal drops on my skin. I silently cry, as I've never done before. I'm allowing my imagination to follow my distress feelings, then imagine a picture of the white sandy beach, with the crashing waves along the shore from my earlier dream. *Nothing can hurt me*, I muse. *I'll not let him hurt me.*

I let my shoulder blades and back gently rest in a melted peace while resting in the corner.

'Mary!' he shouts and pauses. Abruptly, I hear him calling my name. 'Mary!' He continues several times. 'God damn it. Mary, answer, now!' But I don't respond. Yuck, I dislike him.

In anger, he rips up the door and enters the bathroom. 'Argh, what's wrong with you? Oh, boy! What pathetic behaviour you undertake. I understand none of it.'

Drake's behaviour is unimaginable. He frights me.

'My goodness, stupid girl. Get out of the damn shower. Then we can talk,' he is furious.

I stare anxiously at him without saying a word, finish the bath, and grab the big white towel. Putting on my thongs and a T-shirt, and glare at him while he still stands in the door opening.

'Come to bed, Mary,' he commands and claps hard on the bed. He moves the quilt to the side, and I crawl under the sheets next to him, and saddened, I tuck myself into his body and weep.

Next I support my head on his relaxed breathing chest and clench his hand in peacefulness until he abruptly interrupts the calmness.

'Ahem! Let's pray, Babe,' he jumps up as a wild rabbit, so my body and head fall to the side. 'We must find a church for you, Babe. Let's sit up on the bed and pray.' He breathes rapidly and tensely.

'Eh! What? Um-hmm ...'

'Come on, Babe. We do it face to face.' He commands with an awkward voice. 'Baby, do your lovely prayer.'

Next we sit on our knees with folded hands, while I say my Hail Mary.

'There you go, Babe. Can you sense it? It's good for you. Now let's forget of the fight,' He changes his voice to being slick and calm.

Something in his facial expression makes me still wary of him, because his eyes glare intensely at me while he's wearing a superficial, sweet smile.

'I only love you, little girl. God created us for each other.' He hugs me tenderly and kisses me while we rest in a passionate embrace.

'I'm so sorry. I get so jealous. I don't want to lose you, darling.' I excuse my heated temper.

In my grief, he touches my flower, and I get wildly excited. Of a sudden, he brings me to several orgasms, and then he falls asleep, without us having full intercourse.

These odd praying and finger screwing ritual repeats recurring many times. It's mostly when I am frustrated with his behaviour or if he wants to gain something from me. Or when I'm having an incredible need for my family, who I no longer talk to and when I go through desperate isolation. He often uses my craving for boning with him. Is it only an act from his part?

After a month, the therapists get their diploma. Upsettingly, I get nothing! Am I taken for granted? We have a closing meeting with the therapists and Wang's secretary, Stephanie. I'm proud of the girls and take loads of photos of them, including pictures of Drake.

'Ugh, Mary. Stop your damn photography!' he snaps, and hell breaks loose.

I'm flabbergasted and out of my comfort zone.

'Jeez, Mary. I'll not endure constantly having your camera stuck in my face.'

The girls stare on in fear and tremor when he yells at me. I'm speechless.

'Why do I not get a diploma?' I ask him, disappointed when we get back in our room.

'I'm glad you started learning anatomy. You are a quick learner, Babe.' Strange comment.

'Ohhh, well that's fantastic.' And personally, I felt privileged to have a private mentor.

'However, Mary, you still have a long way. If you want a diploma on this knowledge, you must learn more.'

'Ahh, okay, I see.' I am desperate to learn more, and I have done my best.

'You got the will, Mary. And strength to complete your education. That's good,' he smirks.

'I've learned as much as the girls,' I reply in disappointment.

'Maybe you have! Maybe not! We will see, Baby. Maybe you'll get your certificate.' There is a strange twinkle in his eyes as he tries to explain why I didn't get a diploma.

'I have a hard time seeing the difference between the girls and me,' I include, next pondering in anger; *are his scruffy diplomas even worth a shit or valid?*

On the outside, life shows perfect, and everything goes smoothly— or so I believe!

Unexpectedly, Wang demands a rush-meeting, and he appears chilly towards Drake.

'Why are you interfering in my business?' Wang is furious at Drake. 'Don't snoop around! Don't ask questions about me!' He thunders with fierce in his eyes.

Drake gets copper-red in his face. Dumbfounded, I peek between the two of them, trying to follow the heated conversation.

'What? Eh, I'm not snooping. I've no idea what you are talking of, Wang.' Drake grins.

'People talk. They ask why you're prying. It's vulgar what you do.'

'Eh, It's the patients who tell me of you.' Drake lies and comes up with more excuses.

'People don't like it. They tell me you're snooping. I trust them! *Not you, Doctor Bates!*' Wang angers.

'Whoa! Oh, my God, Mr Wang! I'm not doing anything dishonest. If it's wrong, then it's the fault of the other—*not mine.*' Drake's tension is noticeable as he harshly defends himself, facing downwards to the floor.

I've no idea what it's about, but often, I've noticed he is asking strange questions of Wang's powerful connections. I can sense his nervousness as I watch his bogus and deceitful reaction in the conversation. He's lying!

'Do what you are best at, Doctor Bates! But no longer in Taiwan.' Wang rages at him.

'Huh? What do you mean? Such baloney! I don't understand your anger, Wang.'

'If you can't mind your own business, I want you to leave. ASAP! You are no longer welcome.' Wang gets up and speedily walks away, and the meeting ends devastatingly.

Our future smoulders and slides to the next dusky, slimy drain, after Mr Wang has banished Drake from the country. At no point does he try to apologise. In his opinion, it's the fault of everyone else—not his own. Although, in our honeymoon phase, I see nothing wrong with Drake.

'Jeez, it's so imprudent of Wang,' he angrily complains when we go back to our room.

In the afternoon, the concierge pushes a letter under the door.
It reads:

> To Doctor Drake Bates,
> You have the rest of the week to pack your stuff. Please leave the hotel before Friday.
>
> Regards, Mr Wang.

Appalling! We went to the clinic, but they have changed the key card, so we can't get in. Drake desperate grabs his phone and calls Stephanie.

'I want an explanation. I demand access to my things in the clinic—today!' In a rage, he is walking back and forth in our room and screaming at Stephanie.

'You no longer have access to the clinic, Doctor Bates. Mr Wang has banned you from there,' she says, and Drake went into a further frantic rage.

'Damn it, Stephanie! I want my equipment now,' he shouts, behaving as a little man child.

This is too much for me, so I grab my sack and go to the pool for a coffee. Drake and Stephanie can talk in peace or in their collective furious rage.

When I return to the room after half-an-hour, Drake shouts strange information at me. 'Damn Wang! Damn Stephanie! Bloody hell, they cannot hold my equipment as collateral.'

'What? I don't get it. Why will Wang keep our equipment as collateral?' I curiously stare at him and don't know what he's talking of.

'Wang says we must first settle our financial matters. What? Hogwash! I don't understand what the hell he is talking of.'

'Eh? Wang has no reason. Does he?' That's at least what I believe.

'What the hell is the idiot doing? Wang sure has the nerve.'

'Eh? What financial matters are you talking of?' Staring questioning at Drake.

'Bloody nightmare, I owe Wang nothing! Nothing! Nothing at all!' He is raging and always waving wildly with his arms in the air.

Gradually, I realise that he must suffer from a split personality or paranoia, shifting from being sweet and horrible or calm and manic. While taking a deep breath, I muse, *is this some false story he is making up to blame Wang?*

The hotel sends large bills to our room for many instances of catering, phone calls and dry-cleaning bills during our stay and comes as a surprise to me. I don't know how Drake and Wang have arranged the business contract between them, so I grasp that something is wrong. Drake says he has no money and won't or can't pay. *What of the $42,000 from the machine?* I ponder. Again, he wants me to pay the massive bills, but I don't. We agree to call the Danish embassy and explain the case.

'Baby tell them at the embassy it's you who got caught in this fight,' is his strange ask.

'What? Why?'

'It's better if it's a girl trapped and deceived her.'

'Huh? Okay? Fine, I do it.' To protect him, I wind up telling the embassy it's me who has ended up in this mess. They got surprised of the situation. And next, it's blamed on me.

'What are you doing in Taiwan, Mrs Bates? It's not a place for a single woman,' Mrs Hansen tells me in a way as I should never have come to Taipei. 'Did you go to bed with the rich owner?'

'Eh? What? I didn't hear what you said.' What a rude question. I'm dumbfounded and drop my jaw to the floor.

'Oh, my goodness. This is how women typically get caught in Taiwan. Mrs Bates repurchase a ticket home—now! It's dangerous for you to stay.' And with those words, Mrs Hansen has accused me of being a whore for a filthy rich guy.

Mrs Hansen has understood nothing of the problems. Not much help from the Danish embassy then and I disconnect the line, devastated! Confused, I don't understand what to do.

'Mary, we have to get out of Taiwan—*now*! It's too dangerous,' Drake shouts at me. His tone sends frightened chills through my body.

'Where do we go? We can't go back to Hong Kong, darling.' At this flash, I deeply regret he has persuaded me to stay with him.

We discuss several options.

'Find a map on the internet, darling. Wherever our finger lands, that's where we're going.' I've done that many times at home.

'What?'

'Yea, pointing in my atlas with closed eyes. And dreaming of exploring the world.'

We do it three times. 'Vietnam. Um-hmm—not a choice.' Next, 'Russia. Brrr, it's too cold.' The third times, my finger lands in The Philippines. 'Ahh... let's go there,' I suggest.

'Yes! Wow sounds as a superb idea, Babe. A nice warm exotic country.' He agrees.

'When we are safe there, we can solve the problems with our equipment. How about that?'

This is the best solution I can suggest.

'Awesome! Near the beach, Baby. I've never visited The Philippines. Let's go!' He gladly smiles.

So, our next life experiences will move from Taiwan to The Philippines.

'As I have always said, Baby. Everything has a beginning. He-he, and everything a natural ending. Ha-ha, an end can often be the beginning of something new and exciting,' He's ecstatic.

Drake runs his hands through my long soft hair, then joyfully squeezes my cheeks and gives me a tender kiss. 'Perfect idea, Mary. Let's leave this behind us.'

My heart pounds with excitement as he agrees, and in the meantime, I'm browsing for options in The Philippines.

'I found something. The only part I know is Batangas and Manila.'

'Hmm ... Batangas sounds great, Baby. What do you suggest?'

'Um-hmm ... Batangas? Okay?'

'Accepted, Babe.'

'Fine, hand me over your passport. Well, also your credit card, darling,' I kindly ask.

'Please use your own card, Mary. I'll transfer the money later.' And in good faith, I do as he asks. Will I get the repayment from him?

We prepare the final countdown for our next escape in the shadowy darkness of the night—to The Philippines. I book the Premier Beach front room, with balcony and Sea view at the five-star hotel Batangas Marriott and buy two one-way flights on business class for the next morning, landing in Manila, realising that my life is not dull with him!

Will I ever be happy? The time I so far have spent with him in Taiwan, felt more than less the dream I had dreamt of. Worst was I don't know how we will sneak out of the hotel, with no one seeing Bonnie and Clyde fleeing in the shadowy darkness of the night!

CHAPTER 12

YESTERDAY'S FUGITIVE AND THE PHILIPPINES'S TOMORROW

> I can't go back to yesterday because I was a different person then.
>
> —Lewis Carroll, *Alice in Wonderland*

During the sneaky night, we pack our things and prepare to escape for the second time in our life. So much drama within a few months is too much for me, and this time our scheming shady escape is at three o'clock in the morning. From our devious and dangerous escape from Hong Kong, Drake has learned not to announce our checkout. As two shifty felons, we sneak straight to the front sector at the hotel and grab a taxi, disappearing as two fraudulent thieves in the shadowy darkness of the night. Bonnie and Clyde once more flee, as two run-aways who have not paid their bill. Shaken, I'm feeling more than a shifty criminal than an average honest person, though I go further with him. It's the second time I am saving his damn ass from a catastrophic disaster, and it's still dark outside when the speedy taxi drives off with us. Without saying a word, we sit staring into the night for a long time. The bright Moon, and the sky is full of glittering stars, me staring ghostly at it, while I'm pondering of everything; *what has he done with my life for the last many months?* It feels so unreal and not something a classy woman as I usually do. One hour later we arrive at Taipei Airport,

* * *

The woman sees the attractive paradise tree, as the sly snake stares intensely at her, and offers her the harmful crispy apple. She finds the taste delicious that she gives the man a crunchy apple, then it ends fatally, and soon, they will get thrown out of the spectacular, colourful paradise. The rest of the story, we know so well. In terms of who is the sly seducer in this game, we must admit it; it is the vicious, seductive snake. With the man's bite into the delicious crispy red apple, it's the fall of man. The rottenness of a remarkable life begins when Adam and Eve discover they are naked in paradise. The man is always onto something, while the woman's gentle seduction is more superficial, teasing as a play. With Drake, its aggressive meaningfulness, with his ulterior motive to uncover the visible and make it invisible, thus achieving his own satisfaction. His goal is precisely to score as much as possible, and I'm sure it's from me. My innocence in my love for him makes me discover too late his problematic and fatal truth—his actual plan for me.

I no longer know who I am and 'The girl in black Prada Shoes' has fallen into the cunning rabbit hole. Will I end up in the stunning green forest of the vibrant Wonderland? Or will I get thrown into the hot flaming hell with Drake and his sly rottenness? My life is weird, yet it's a fantasy. One moment, I'm Alice in Wonderland, and the next instant, I'm sent spinning to the Land of Oz as Dorothy. I'm feel happy with him, and allow him to be too close, while my heart is beating infinitely fast through my bouncing chest for his love, during my blindness.

'What an idea. A crazy, mad, wonderful idea,' Alice says.

It's the same thing I consider, because I'm in both exciting adventures at the same time, and I follow the Wizard of Oz, as we walk happily together on the yellow brick road. He gives me many unexpected and thrilling adventures in both fantasy worlds, so I'm lost with him, in both Oz and Wonderland. My fast beating heart tells me

I must travel with him, while I still am in good health and not too old to enjoy life.

Basically, I want to work hard once I've started on a project, then I stay for a long time and keep it going. It's him that's the reason to get it started, and I'm ready to stick around and want to merge the results. Usually, I do best with a monotonous job that requires patience and determination, that's why my writing has taken a long time. I know what I'm worth when I start something, so I have great wishes for our cooperation to be good. This concerns both private life and work, so I want to make it work out.

But it would be wise for me to show more caution, and in my eagerness, I'm getting carried away by his plans. Unfortunately, I sometimes fail, because I don't care enough for myself. As a physical person, I've an exceptional talent in terms of anatomy, so it's benefitting for me to learn more of it. This is where he fits well into the image as a mentor and for a fresh challenge for me in our business. My firm will mean I'll fight hard to keep what I have, so my stubbornness can easily lead to a conflict for me. Choosing not to change my mind, I overrule the danger.

As two devious runaways, we move from one country to another. It's time to find extra motivation and inspiration for our goals, and I feel we have the signs to help us; And it's excellent while we're doing it! Well, at least that's what I trust with his many upcoming ideas.

'I'm not crazy. My reality is just different from yours. Every adventure requires a first step,' smirks the Cheshire cat, so I sometimes ponder, *who is this smirking cat?*

* * *

As we land in Manila's massive pulsating Airport around noon, I breathe in relief when we have completed our sinister escape from Taiwan. I am tired of our flight as we sit in a fast-driving green/white taxi on the way to Batangas. It's so humid and hot, because it's peak season—December to the end of February. It seems stunning, and luckily; we have mesmeric weather to photograph picturesque, perfect snapshots.

Batangas is one of the most popular tourist destinations in The Philippines and to the well-known Tall Volcano. The majority in The Philippines are religiously affiliated with Roman Catholicism, and other religions include Buddhism and Islam. Batangas Province spans a vast area and is mostly getting their wealth from tourism, and now we are tourists among thousands of other tourists, so our next experience is to begin.

After two hours of wild and speedy taxi drive and over one-hundred kilometres from Manila, we arrive at our five-star resort on the west side of the island. It's breathtaking, overlooking the South China Sea and the rainforest mountains on the horizon. The location booms with four- or five-star resorts, along the most popular part on the western shore, so after checking in, we throw our luggage into the room. Before the Sun sets, we stroll along the pulsating beach and drink a chilly pint at the local bar. I'm overwhelmed by the bright blue and turquoise waters, while I stroll hand in hand with Drake, barefooted on the soft white sandy beach. I enjoy the sound of the many swaying palm trees and listening to the crashing waves in my romantic moment, and I enjoy my freedom outside, compared to being locked in a tiny cage in Taiwan.

The stunning sunrise in the morning gives our day a fantastic opportunity to be peaceful and extraordinary pleasing. The Philippines instantly becomes a fortunate life for us, and everything is as it was in my earlier dream over six months ago. Sometimes we drive to the eastern side of the island, where we find the many minor well-known islands on the horizon. We often drive to Batangas Viewpoint or Mauban Cape to watch the mesmerising sunset before we drive back home. It's a spectacular region where we enjoy the beaches, have a spicy or sweet-and-sour typical local dinner, and drink cool beers at the many tiny local beach bars.

Batangas city is an impressive bustling city, with its many hectic minor shop houses and restaurants. Sometime mooing holy cows and giant elephants walk among honking cars and spluttering tuk-tuk taxis in the middle of the vibrant city. Wow! What a buzzing town and my eyes are always wide open for fresh information and exploration of the locals daily life. At this time of year, we can find thousands of Scandinavian and European tourists among the millions of fast running bikes and yelling local Philippine's.

Unexpectedly, we meet a Scandinavian bloke at the beach who wants to sell us something as Sven speaks with Drake. A friendly chap and he invites us to have a chill beer with him, so we join him at a local bar, have a drink with him, then he tells us of timeshares and wants us to invest in one of his packages. This is too much! Typically, I get snatched up by such a tricky snake oil salesman. I'm not interested.

We meet Sven several times during the week and become friends with him, along with a few of his buddies. Sven is a tall mid-forties Swedish guy, blond hair, (he sincerely needed a haircut) has blue eyes and is un-shaven shoving his stubble. He looks somewhat of a sloppy person, wearing knee-long army shorts, a white t-shirt and flip-flops. Drake is happy to meet a fellow countryman, so together they arrange a viewing of one apartment. Why? I don't know. Who will pay for the show? I merely follow the dudes out of curiosity.

'Wauw, Baby, this is amazing. Let's stay here forever. What do you think?' His eyes glow.

'Yeah, it's fantastic,' I beam, letting myself get thoroughly carried away in impulsivity.

'Why not stay in The Philippines, Babe? You wanted to stay with me on a secluded island. Let's do it here,' he eagerly is assuming I will go along with the idea.

The joy of anticipation rushes swiftly through my warm love veins. It's a fast rushing stream in a boiling hot troubled sea when he eagerly requests that we stay in The Philippines.

'Well, I don't know, darling.' I hesitate. 'I'm not sure it's the right thing to do.' Taking in a deep breath to control my impulsivity.

'Baby come on. You're the most important one in my life.'

'Hmm, I like the country's splendours. The weather is perfect. Sure, I enjoy it here.' With my unthinking answer, I have confirmed that I'll be staying here with Drake.

'Super. You are my perfect match. We belong together. Oh, I love you, Baby.'

'I can help you with a great contact. This bloke rents out pleasant villas.' Sven cheers in excitement, believing we stay for a longer time in The Philippines.

I ponder our affair. *Will the cheerful couple walk the yellow brick road of new-fangled adventures?*

'Uh-mm, darling? Where are you going to work?' I'm questioning him and scowl lightly. He has no money, while I'm in the same moment also forgetting he has my vast saving's including his income of $42,000 from Mr Wang. Who will pay?

'Ha-ha, ha-ha. Don't worry, little girl. I will think of something. Everywhere, they can use a clever doctor as me.' He is grinning and eyeing at Sven, who has plans to introduce his contacts.

My bouncing heart gives in to staying here, and I'm as a queen on a mesmerising and exciting adventure. *Who doesn't want to stay in Wonderland?* I muse. The country is fantastic, and I'm thrilled, and don't notice any red flags!

'Invest in the sales packages. Start selling timeshares,' Sven suggests. 'It's good cash.'

Drake and Sven make plans for how much I need to invest in the first ten packages—around $15,000, Sven says.

'Baby, you can invest in it. I don't have that kind of capital,' he smirks.

'Nah, um-hmm, let me think of it, darling. I don't want to stress of the cash now. First, we must find an income for you.' I stare at him, trusting he can manage a job.

Sven helps us with new accommodations, and after two weeks, I settle the massive hotel bill. The daring experience begins, we rent a car, and get the most amazing furnished villa as I appear confident with the future and sign a one-year contract with the owner.

A large typical U-shaped yellow building, with a green lawn in the front garden and several tall palm trees. In enormous pots they have planted yellow, red, and white fragrant flowers, standing on each side of the brown wooden front door. While we face the front door, we take off our flip-flops—that's the standard procedure in The Philippines. Tenderly, Drake holds me in his tight embrace, and as a true romantic gentleman, he lifts me up with his beefy arms. Joyfully, giggling, he carries me over the threshold, as I'm in a romantic heaven with him, feeling I'm his newlywed bride. My veins gush with excitement over my exotic honeymoon image I have in my head.

'Picture? I do a picture?' the sweet cleaning lady yells in broken English, so I hand her the iPhone. The tiny Philippine chick takes many pictures—an everlasting, joyful, funny memory for my scrapbook. He puts me down, and happily, we lean up against the front door frame, overlooking the entire garden. In front of the house is an outdoor pool, with a splashing fountain adorned with a praying local sculpture. Everything nicely surrounded with greenery and lots of fragrant flowers in massive big dark-grey clay pots. In the living room, stands rustic furniture made of dark hardwood.

I stroll into the bedroom 'Woo! Two kissing swans made of towels and spread flower petals on the rustic dark hardwood bed. It's so... romantic!' I squeal, and a smile spreads across my face, taking in the pleasant fresh scent from the petals. My imagination tells me *it's as the swans are swimming around in a mass of fragrant reddish and yellow frangipani flowers*. Over the bed hangs a huge painting, with pink lotus flowers in a massive black and gold decorated vase.

'I'll make fresh coffee. Do you want too, Baby?'

'Yes, please.' I beam and are comfortable as I enter the front room again, but I rather want to have a sweaty shag with him at this very minute.

Instead, I slap my bum into the sofa, and my beige, orange, and pink flower sarong opens, so he can see my tanned legs and the lace of my thongs, when he is back.

'Do you know what I sense, darling?' I call out, loud and cheerful, my arms raised high saying, 'Yes, we did it!'

Drake brings the delicious smelling hot coffee and puts two mugs on the sofa table. 'What, Babe? Are you happy?'

I'm staring at the two tiny bowls sitting in the middle of the table, watching the pink lotus flower floating in the water. It's stunning and relaxing.

'Oh, I could use a hot stiff Willy right now. Ha-ha.'

His eyebrows lift as I reach for him.

'Huh? Not now, honey. Let's sit by the pool.'

I can hear the weak whoosh of the ocean, as the house is near the sea, and reminds me of my dream, walking peacefully around in my flip-flops with my beloved. And I'm deeply in love with the grand Wizard of Oz.

'Gosh, it's like being Alice in Wonderland,' and life cannot be more extraordinarily breathtaking, because Drake is changing to the most startlingly loving person.

Although I look forward to working hard for my goal, I enjoy relaxing. I'm easily seduced by the dream-filled life I grasp that he can offer me, and the sexual pleasure he will give me is important. No doubt he has discovered this need fast.

'Let's make love, Baby. I want you now,' the horny bull whispers, as he apparently has changed his mind.

'There is nothing I want more.'

I'm hoping for a better shag this time with my unimaginative, wishy-washy boyfriend in bed. He is good at many things, but he's not an Olympic gymnast with the last part of sex. He can bring me to oceans of climax when his hands touch my naked body with his teasing way of luring my flower to the edge of a coming that makes me roar as a hungry lioness. Then he lets me slide at a leisurely pace and drives me insane with his sly dirty torture of my little pearl at the prospect of exploding in a massive spasm.

'Not yet, little girl. I want you to come several times,' he whispers in my ear. Ideally, he keeps on using his soft right index finger, and drives me up and down several times, before he lets me explode. His index and middle fingers are the most amazing and magical, while he sensibly teases my little shaved spot around the labia's and the pearl. It's well tucked in its folds before it gets stiff in its little female head, then my heartbeats pounds crazily, and my body shakes with a strong dirty appetite. The sweat dribbles on my body, and my nipples gets stiff with wicked pleasure, as millions of goosebumps reach my desirable body to a massive dirty arousing.

'Oh ... yea ... oh ... ahhh ... yea ... wooo ... I can't hold myself anymore,' I shout in grand pleasure.

Then he sends me up to multiple climaxes. Not only once does he give me this grand pleasure, so I gasp with joyful bawdy lust, as his soft, warm fingers drive me up to ten wild orgasms. He is undeniably a specialist with using his hands diligently on my body—not least on my little Minnie. He can get every part of my emotions covered by his tender touches, and I'm getting awfully dependent on it. No dildos. No other sex tools to satisfy my yearning, as he is a master at sending me to an exotic heaven—floating on a horny soft velvet pink cloud, with a gratification I've not tried earlier.

Drake's hands, voice and eyes are his primary tools to seduce me, and the way he touches me and glances at me makes me wild in the fire. It sends millions of exciting goosebumps through my body, as I reached a nourishing climax. Just by glancing at me, he knows how to use his talents to his benefit, so he captivates my interest in him. The deep emotions crawl under my skin, as wild burning fire ants, and then as a sneaky spider, he catches me in his dangerous cobweb. I'm getting emotionally poisoned with his deadly bites, as his dangerous venom creeps around in my brain and heart. What unaware woman in deep love doesn't fall for such a spellbinding man?

However, it's more challenging to get him to his own ecstatic heights. I want his bodily juices into my inner wet hot universe, but his food lover can't stand, and it frustrates me. Christ, his thoughts flicker always elsewhere as I try to get the pocket rocket in position to shoot.

'Oh, now we are dirty again, darling. Mama won't think well of it. Hi-hi, not when I'm a wicked boy,' he often whispers during our dirty act.

Does he have a mother complex? Or is Drake gay?

The fun stick often and rapidly becomes as a teeny-weeny relaxed dishcloth. Apparently; it forgot what his purpose is. *Come on, Willy! Put your P in my V,* I dream in my arousal.

I guide the half-shrunken baby arm in the direction with my warm hands. Golly Gosh, he can't find the opening of my tight pussy.

'Oh, boy! I'm confused of this fussy bratwurst,' he fumes. Slam, slack, and as a sadist, Drake whacks Willy many times on the top of the floppy pecker with an angry hand, so his heat-seeking saggy moisture missile swings from side to side and gets blue.

'Oy, hey, easy now. Don't slap him. Let me try to fix him.' I gently grab the half-shrunken lizard and calm Drake, masturbating the bird stiff again. As the boning continues, I guide the woodpecker into my wet cave.

'Woo... Ohhh... No ... Yea ...' Howling as a tiny kid doing something wrong, as he gets his ejaculation, splashes out over my body, as a dry, wrinkled lizard, whispering in relief, 'Oh… Mom.'

Gasp!! I go frantic and can't understand a shit and comfort the little 'dragon boy'. Though I'm fulfilled with my climax; he behaves as a tiny child who got the long-awaited lollipop after seldom achieving his relief.

'I don't understand why Willy behaves so fussy.' He excuses. 'When I was younger, I could bang as a wild roaring bull.' His sudden rasping apology annoys me; he's ruined what we just experienced.

'Huh? Oh, no worries, darling. It matters nothing to me. You need not to be a wild roaring bull for me.' Deep in my wild cravings, I *want* him to be a *sprinting bull*.

'Gee, I could make the women howl. They whined as sirens as I pumped loose inside their pussies.' He continues bragging of being a massive stud with no *stiff* horns.

What can I use this information for, as he complains and boasts at the same time? *Yeah, okay. We get older over time;* I muse. I don't say this but try kindly to ease his worry.

'Darling, you are great at giving me exciting orgasms. No worries.' I'm faking it, but emotionally I support him. Deep inside, I'm disappointed in him. Oh, my God! It disturbs me, this timeless struggle to keep his pecker ready, because I want more intimacy than finger sex. Slaving away as a lunatic with this slick, overripe banana upsets me, as I suck and fiddle, it's zero and no reaction. It's as my boyfriend has a lifelong too old striking woodpecker as an over-ripened banana. *Is there something wrong with me?* I must talk to him off the impossible task, because our first home run was okay. Willy shone as the king of the entire universe, and he had no problems invading my wet and lusty inner universe. I'm sure he had taken Viagra the first night in Spain to impress me. It was more than me having a problem with a climax, though.

Drake has taught me the art of getting magnificent orgasms, using only his magic hands. Yet, his interest in satisfying me fades too. Despite our later failed lovemaking nights; *what if I suggest him to watch porn movies.* But is that possible in The Philippines? Is it legal to download?

I don't give up and encourage him in the dirty act, trying nasty tricks, and sometimes we succeed. If he can wean me off the dildo, then I can help him. However, life is not as I planned it in my head.

Excuses, excuses, and more explains arise. 'I suffer from cancer.' 'I'm tired.' 'I have too much in my head.' 'I must find a way to earn money.' 'It's been too long since I last fornicated,' and, 'It's my prostate.' 'I'm too old.' Then it's this and that excuse and it went on.

'Maybe I need some Viagra. Let's buy some.' He says, so we buy seven packets of Viagra.

'I want to research on female parts.' He proudly blurts. 'I want to know how women look down there.'

'Ha-ha, darling, study mine.'

He had found information when Kussomaten (Pussy photo booth) takes on the 2011 Roskilde Music Festival in Denmark.

'We want to see your pussy,' said the sign outside the photo booth. Sex & Society will make a Pikomat (Wee-wee photo booth) right next door.

'Ha-ha, ha-ha ... the Danes are crazy' I laugh with a twist of a funny theme they display.

'The association Sex & Samfund (Sex & Society) is present at the festival to challenge guests often hetero-normative notions of gender and sexuality, among other things through games.' Writes Politiken.dk 1st June 2011.

The many anonymous photos were afterwards studied thoroughly and discussed in the media. At least the displayed photos on the internet remain anonymous, though Drake studied them with high concentration.

'It's disgusting! Darling, what do you want with such ugly hairy pictures?'

'To study them!'

'Ha-ha, give them eight hairy legs. Yuck! Then they will appear as dangerous giant spiders.'

'Don't tell anyone here in The Philippines. It's illegal to download the material.' He laughs in great excitement.

'Fine, but study mine. It's nicely shaved.'

With eagerness he spends days on female hairy pussies, instead of studying mine. The considerations of downloading porn scares me if I'm doing something wrong. *I must find another solution;* and give him a kiss, pondering; *there are perhaps things I just can't change.*

CHAPTER 13

Chanting Five Times A Day

> God is the greatest. I bear witness that there is none worthy
> of worship except God. I bear witness that Muhammed
> is the messenger of God. Hasten to the Prayer. Hasten to
> real success. God is the greatest. There is none worthy of
> worship except God.
>
> —Beautiful Islamic call to prayer

The Islamic call to prayer gives me at times peace and shows me few worthy qualities. I don't understand Arabic, but I've heard few enjoyable Arabic songs and prayers in Qatar.

They can make me feel safe, happy, and peaceful, and they can stress me to a great extent. In my search of the different religions of the world, I've read parts of the Qur'an. As with other religious texts, I've discovered helpful hidden secrets and gems in the book. Each religion has a splendour and has enriched my life with more knowledge. While staying at this magnificent spot, I get a unique experience when they call the local Muslims for prayers five times a day—Fajr, the dawn prayer; Zhuhr, the early afternoon prayer; Asr, the late afternoon prayer; Maghrib, the sunset prayer; and Isha'a, the night prayer.

Both of us are strangers in our exploration of The Philippines, but we fall in love with the country right away. I buy two bicycles, a black for Drake and a white for me, so we can cycle to the beach daily, or drive by car to the city and explore the exciting local pulsating life. We enjoy the place and give it a chance now our love is spectacular. Every day, he walks around naked with me in the well-temperate swimming pool, so I'm in an absolute seventh heaven. When I curl up against his naked body as a baby monkey, pressing my nude body to his and clinging to him, it feels safe in his embrace. With confidence, I do every for my beloved, and feel surrounded with compelling romance, and forget everything about my past, while living in the present of my fresh life. He knows how to play his love game, and my romantic dream comes true. The question is, does he love me or is it more for the desire for the money? I believe he loves me, and he considers himself; he loves me. However, the love for wealth is more significant, so he plays his act well. Capital is what I can give him, and he knows it, so I spoil him, unaware that I am paying for the love I want him to give me. Thus, he gives me much extra sweetness, therefore, I don't see any warning signs in front of me.

If he were an authentic gentleman, he would never accept letting me pay for him. Is he a 'Casanova', as the most famous Italian lover Giacomo Casanova in history? Casanova was a womaniser who was a scam artist, a scofflaw, an alchemist, a spy, and a church prophet?

Quickly I realise that Drake doesn't care what decent rules says, and he does what suits him. Doesn't he care if he misleads people? It's difficult to see him as a church prophet, though he sometimes acts as one, despite he is a nonbeliever! Is he in divine contact to speak on his own entity's behalf; by delivering strange messages or teaching from private supernatural sources to other people? Is that what happens to me? I figured out people abuses the word of God and I became more careful with my religion. Whether he's an alchemist is challenging to answer, but I can guarantee one thing, though; the dude can't turn base metal into gold, but he sure knows how he can get the *gold* out of me.

He still has $30,000 of mine on his account. He doesn't contribute with finances or make any payment, and over the last eight months, he has been living on my and others' accounts. He has earned money in Macau, Hong Kong and in Taiwan, but he doesn't so much as buy me a cup of coffee, not to mention a delicious dinner or a chill beer, even it's cheap to buy beer, coffee or dine in The Philippines.

'Baby, it's your birthday soon. I don't know what to buy. I don't have any money,' he sounds regretful. And in my intoxication of love, I've forgotten everything about my dough he still *has* on his account.

'Honey, you need not buy me anything. For me, it is enough just having you by my side,' with comfort I sweetly answer.

'I want to buy a nice present for my heavenly angel.' He smirks.

'Oh, I would love that great horse painting from a local artist,' so as a trickster, he makes me lend him the smelly Philippine Peso.

'Happy birthday, my wonderful and loving sweetheart.' As he sweetly surprises me with the painting. I'm overjoyed and on the table stands a vast bunch of flowers. I happily read my birthday card.

> My darling love, my dream lady, my life.
>
> I wish you a happy birthday. Here I give you a bunch of flowers and each flower is my token unconditional love for you. I am thinking of you every minute of the day. I love you with all my heart. I love you more today, more than yesterday, and less that I will tomorrow. I'm glad we are together now and forever. Never forget. Love you forever.
>
> Yours always,
> Drake

For now, I believe he is right and kind, because he makes me laugh and treats me like a princess. I feel ecstatic and believe he wants the best for me and makes me see life from a unique perspective. I cannot contain my heated passion when he makes love to me, (finger sex) and when he with affection kisses me, therefore I can't see that my trust in him leads me to further blindness. As a headless chopped of chicken, I jump into his many plans. He is sly, dominant, but peaceful most of the time, and I'm attracted to what I believe is a perfect man. I trust he can give me confidence and contribute to a good economy, therefore I never doubted him, so as a faithful person I trust this to be true about him. Are my desires too durable and causing me to go wrong in my beliefs?

* * *

'I have a splendid plan,' he says one day. 'We must start up a clinic here in The Philippines. We must get hold of the machine in Taiwan.'

'How will you get it back?'

'I refuse to let Wang keep it. It doesn't belong to him.'

My heart bangs in my chest, beating faster and faster. My breathing becomes more intense as he rejoices while walking the clinging monkey in the pool. 'It's true, darling. It's yours. Wang cannot keep it as collateral.'

With support, he puts a hand around my neck, gives me a mild little confirming squeeze and a shallow kiss on my cheek. 'It's no problem. My little girl, you must be my negotiator.'

'Huh? How?'

'Wang is not mad at you, my precious MM.' he whispers gently.

Surprised, I glance at him, and see how he cheerfully smirks and continues.

'I will write a letter to Stephanie. Tell her we need the machine for a little boy's treatment.' He grins.

I wonder, *how is that going to work?*

'Are you thinking of Rajah? He is not here. How can we treat him? I can't agree to that.' I feel bad that we make Rajah a target for Drake's sinister plan.

'Yea, Rajah.'

'If you want to continue Rajah's treatment, that's okay. But don't use him as an excuse for your plan. It's not fair.'

'It's not an excuse. It's facts.'

'Wang doesn't know Rajah. But it's okay his family wants treatment. They can stay with us.'

He lets in an instant go of me and pushes me brusquely away. Determined, he gets out of the pool and grabs the towel on the sunbed and glances weird at me. I swim as he fixes the letter.

Over the next three months, the correspondences go back and forth between Taiwan and The Philippines, before we get lucky to receive the machine.

In the meantime, before we get our equipment, problems show up. After four weeks, after we had moved into the villa; Drake gets angry about the chanting from three different mosques close by our location. He is furious and behaves as a racist!

'Bloody hell! Five times a day! Damn them. We listen to this challenging chanting bullshit. Such crazy competition between the mosques.' he spews angry while we sit in the garden.

It ends up in an energetic conflict between him and the landlord Adolfo. Drake is stubborn and wants to break the rental agreement, so he has daily arguments with Adolfo and is often angry at me. Drake decides we must move, and he contacts another agency, who shows us other options. As two thieves in the night, we pack our belongings, and before Adolfo finds out, we flee, once again under the shadowy darkness of the night. Oh my God, it's horrible! Another run, seek and hide!

Adolfo sends Drake an e-mail as a reply to our request of getting the deposit back. He refuses, and at first, I get angry, but then I understand the guy and feel regretful. He writes:

Subject: Rental agreement

To Dr Bates:

I had lots of enquiries from January and refused a long-term rental, as I thought we had a deal for the entire year. Now you leave! *Why?* You never told me you were going! I find out you contacted a real estate agency, and then you purchase another property.

Please don't lie to me! Though I'm younger, I'm not stupid. Nor am I foolish, Dr Bates! You're such a liar! You're a cheat and run off after six week's stay during the night like a coward!

You lived next to my villa. Come on, man! I overheard every word of your meeting on the porch with the agency. By good luck, the Muslims didn't chant in their speakers.

Your wife spoke about how she liked the property. However, having our business relationship, you must be more polite to me. Had I known better; I would have found someone else to rent the villa too. Having people like you around me, I must sell coconuts on the beach in less than two months.

I called you and wanted to talk about your meeting. No one picked up. Nor did you possess the courtesy to call me back.

Our company is in the right to keep your entire deposit. However, I don't want to pay for an attorney and wait ten years to solve this matter. We'll close this friendly, instead of having a fight between 'Puti' (white foreigners) and Philippine in Philippines territory. We'll return half of the deposit. Please give me your bank details, and I will transfer the funds.

Adolfo

'I want every penny back.' Drake furious screams.
'I will accept the deal with Adolfo. Such a mess!' I calm him.
As we arrive at the new villa, run by an American diplomat, Hazel and Philip, I throw myself on the couch in relief. Pulling up my legs, philosophising about our dreadful escape. My life comprises a constant flight together with him, so I feel as a shady villain in the night. Am I as bad as him? The site isn't so far from the previous one but is not as close to the beach, but in a secured gated zone and quiet, except for the shrill, vibrating sound of cicadas.

Drake pours a cup of fresh-brewed coffee and sits next to me, then I say; 'It's been a long time since I've been so stressed and afraid.' Taking in a deep breath, I try to get my heart rate into an average level. With gently fingers he slides them through my loose hair, and I grab his hand and clutch it to me in silence.

'I want to build a clinic nearby. Mary, we need to do something. We need cash,' With affection, he smiles.

He spends days devising a new-fangled plan. I notice his way of forming his unorthodox methods while he sits in deep concentration with his calculator, and his many spreadsheets open on the computer and tries to figure out how he can earn his next shifty dough. When I get the occasional chance to glimpse at it without him noticing, I can see millions of numbers there. Why does a doctor need to make calculations like that? He's not professionally working with finance in a bank, nor is he an accountant, and we have no clinic at the time—not after our many escapes. *Is he calculating his future involving my funds?* I muse, because often he needs me to pay for new investment or strange ideas.

Shortly after we meet with Hazel and Philip to enjoy a glass of chill delicate fruity semi-dry white wine. Unexpectedly, Drake announces the plans he has in his mind for a living in The Philippines.

'I'm searching for a great plot. I want to build a clinic,' He with proud says as if he has the capital to build a large clinic.

'We own a great free area on our plot. Do you want to see it?' Hazel responds.

'Wauw! What a coincidence.' He gets excited.

'For a long time, we talked of building a rehabilitation centre for expats. Maybe we could partner up.' Hazel suggests. 'I can show you the plot tomorrow. It's too dark now.' Then a superficial negotiation begins, and fast we exchange unique ideas.

'Let's think about it.' He answers, then we go back to our villa.

Drake grabs two icy beers in the fridge, and we sit by the pool, listening to the high-pitched sound of cicadas while talking about Hazel's idea.

'I'm optimistic. I'm energetic of doing it,' is my suddenly over-the-head reply to him. My dynamic nature and positive attitude want success for our future. *But why can't I keep my mouth shut?*

'Baby, I understand the need to make capital. But I don't have the finances for such an enormous project. You can do it!' he murmurs.

'Well, darling, I possess great courage. I enjoy a pleasant challenge. You should *not* have told them you wanted to build a clinic if you don't have the money.' I try to support him, which is a central part to me in life with him.

'This can be motivation to something important. I want to further educate myself in anatomy. Honey, the idea is not that bad!' By fair means, I don't know what I'm talking about.

'I want 80 percent of the gross income.' He commands. 'I'm the brain in this project.'

'Woah! That's a lot. Was that what you calculated the other day?' No answer.

In his mindset, he takes it for granted that I'll invest together with Hazel and Philip. It's incredible how many ideas he comes up with and believes he's the mastermind behind both the future treatment and the entire project. So, we meet with Hazel and Philip again.

'We have great contacts to embassies and diplomats,' Hazel says while we inspect the plot.

'I can help you and Mary to get all the required paperwork prepared.' And she puts us in contact with the diplomats at the Danish and Swedish embassy. We get a work visa, including, clunk, clunk, forty-two stamps in each of our passports, and can now stay, at minimum, one year in The Philippines and fast after we put together the entire clinic idea.

Then Drake comes up with more fresh creative ideas. 'Set up a business, Baby. Then we can run all this from here,' he encourages me. 'Only you possess such a capital.'

'Huh? Where?'

'It's best to do it in Hong Kong. We'll run the clinic in The Philippines with the Hong Kong company.' He seems trustworthy, so a Hong Kong company is about to be born, and our contact helps us with that matter.

While staring at each other, we exchange varied ideas between us.

'Sweet baby girl, you will be fifty-fifty partner in my equipment. But you must continue paying the monthly leases on it.' He smirks, and some of my trust went straight to the drain. *Has he forgotten I'm already a partner?* At least I get collateral in it, *I'm convinced.*

'Excuse me!' I protest and say no more. Next, I ponder what he's just said, while the thoughts run fast in my frustrated head. *I'm a heedless woman!* I've not thought of this before. The aware reader might remember I already paid many instalments as a *loan* for Drake. Though, I continue paying the same monthly sum! Oh, boy! At this stage of my life with him, I have already paid more than $12,000 for that equipment.

'I can offer you the complete equipment in Sweden, for $56,000. We can talk about it later,' he smirks. Holy moly! Now he wants me to purchase on an extra investment for his machinery in Sweden.

Is that a rip-off?

What more does he want? I'm also paying the entirety of our living, for a person I'm *very* much in love with. My blindness and stupidity have no end, because I'm awful with money and too generous. Why do I keep on trusting him?

We travel in business class to Hong Kong, finding a lawyer, setting up the business, and creating a bank account. Holy crap! That's expensive—all on my expenses. I'm in deep distress, though I'm also excited with the Magic Dragon's fantastic plans. Then trust the best will come of the flaming energy he spits out from his mouth.

But everything has a price—including his hidden, sneaky promises of success, so perhaps it's not priceless living with Drake.

*   *   *

Five weeks after our moving to Hazel's residence, I must travel to Denmark, being away for six weeks. The first task is signing separation papers with Paul, and next, I pack all my private belongings in Copenhagen and ship them to my apartment in Spain. During my absence, Drake will prepare the future project with Hazel and Philip, so I rely on him to do well and to be honest. That's where my famous envelope solution comes into the picture. Paul often laughed at me when I created these envelopes for my housekeeping money.

Before my departure, with care, I prepared $5,000 in separate sachets. I'm attentive and want to make it easy for him, so I give him *cash!* 'Darling, this is to cover two months' rent. Amenities. Car rental, and food expenses.' I laugh, because I, vigilant, have prepared it all in his 'lunch box' of envelopes. It's as making a lunch box for the little boy before he goes to school, and I believe it's skilful and fittingly done, so I trust him with my life. Everything has a price, though, even I'm still walking on air with him. He drives me to Manila Airport in the middle of the night, and with a tender kiss we say goodbye. The trusting lovebird (me) flies to Europe, and I trust him to do his faithful part during my absence.

The flight lasts seventeen hours, and I fly with time, landing in Copenhagen the same day I left, during the late afternoon. Then check in at the Hilton Airport hotel, because it's easy and convenient for me. The jet lag shows up several times during the following days, and my inner meridian clock is up-side-down.

First, I need to get the separation papers signed, however we must wait another six months before we settle for the final divorce. Next, the family events I must take part in, and during that event, I tell Paul and the kids I want to live in Spain. No one knows *anything* about my hidden secret plans in The Philippines, so I lie to everyone. Whoa! It's not my best skills, and I bet they didn't even believe me. I'm the worst poker player in the world, and they can see if I'm lying. Drake has taught me well in the lying skills as he pulls me around on his puppet strings. It's no excuse! I know it's *my responsibility*. I confess the shameful acts.

* * *

After Denmark, I travel for a few weeks to Spain, and shortly after my belongings from Copenhagen arrived. I pack the rest of the stuff I've in Spain, then everything gets shipped to The Philippines over the following days. I'm determined to stay there and am looking forward to continuing my life with Drake, because I find everything so dazzling. My life has additional dimensions to fill up my hopeless, collapsed world, and my heart pounds for him. I see us as two people united in the intoxication of love, however none of us know how things will continue. Will our lives continue in happiness in the long run?

I'm a person who likes to be on the move and explore unfamiliar territory. Some would call me a nomadic person who moves from place to place, yet I consider myself as a globetrotter. That's why I travel so much. I want my dynamic attitude to expand my mental horizon, which can lead to success, and wishing I can meet unique people. Some might say I possess an excellent talent for negotiating, but sometimes, I lack the diplomatic ability in my enthusiasm, then I fail. I'm glad I have overcome my tendency to quarrel, because I know I would achieve more success by using my mental effort alone. This is a skill I've learned to handle much better during my later years. I'm motivated to continue educating myself, and I know that travel and learning additional information are vital parts of my future life.

Existence is a lifelong learning process—a lasting school. Drake fits in so well as a boyfriend and a private teacher and has a significant impact on my mental development—in both good and bad ways.

Sometimes, I will find that the mood between us shows as competitive discussions in my eagerness to learn, and therefore it ends in quarrels or provocations between us.

As a child, life forced me to learn how to defend myself, verbally, but sometimes it ended up through fighting. Although, I want to speak out and object to injustice, and others will think I developed a somewhat sharp tongue and, thus, may possess challenging opinions. Because of my sometimes-defensive attitude, I might be better off as a respectful spokesperson in community affairs, but I'm getting distracted by peripheral issues. I have learned and perhaps a little too late in my life to avoid many problems by listening to others, thus preventing my tendency to be provocative or sarcastic. I'm sure my brain had evolved into a far more excellent tool had I practised these skills earlier. I could have avoided all the turmoil it exposes me to; this is also something I seem to learn too late in life.

Every action I perform in life with Drake become coloured by the energy I'm surrounded with, and I'm split between two more significant and very different strengths in life. My family's power has turned into negativity, and the energy of my love has turned into positivity. But shouldn't that be the opposite?

I give it the chance but can't figure out what he wants with my affection, then I do everything for him, and my generosity is heartfelt. I give him all the moral and financial support I can and give him my ultimate and unconditional love. But sometimes I have my doubts about what his requirements are. Who is Drake? Is he a fake or a proper person? However, our relationship seems to be part of an enchanted life. Woo! I'm floating on a mesmerising soft pink cloud, and only hear gentle angel music from his tender rasping Clint Eastwood singing, then see dancing, glittering stars in the enthralling moonlight. I'm caught in his mesh, and I can't see the truth when listening to him. It appears, I am not wise enough on seeing it, so I can't avoid getting into these situations, minimising the damage and protect myself better. As a result, I sometimes get gravely hurt emotionally. Does he even care about that? Often, he seems glad when he in his plot thought I deserved it by him being 'nasty' so whatever happens is for him justified.

While Drake is 10,000 kilometres away from me, the frightening truth comes sneaking in with a bleep in the form of a sinister-looking email I receive. It is, in the words of Def Leppard, a moment 'when love and hate collide'. It should be, for me, a surprising eye-opener. So, is it?

He knows how much I worship him. He takes the chance of writing something disturbing.

It's evil and heart-breaking to me to justify himself. It comes after he knows the shipment is already on its way to The Philippines, so I'm in deep shit and trapped! I'm in an abysmal conflict with myself.

For unexplained reasons, he must feel like he's in danger. Or is Drake not sure if I'll come back to The Philippines? The fella needs my validation that his delusion is correct and, in his fantasy, that everything is okay.

What's in the disturbing melting pot for me when I turn to the next chapter of my life?

CHAPTER 14

A DEVIOUS BETRAYAL

> It's amazing how some people find it so easy to twist and
> turn a story to shed negative light over others just for them
> to play victim. What they don't know, though, is that they
> are unknowingly so transparent, even to those who believe
> them... if not today than tomorrow.
>
> —A Modern Divine Comedy

Unscrupulous and punitive male guidance characters may have
played an essential role in the development of my intellect. I
had no caring brothers that I could mentally compete with, to
assert myself through. It was the disciplinary men of the priesthood, or
it was my strict and violent stepfather, who were the dominant men in
my life, with their firm opinions. Both parties were rigorous moralising,
with a tendency to make lengthy boring speeches of what they believed.
Through my experience, they manifested strict principles, opining of
what was right and wrong. Often, when I was a minor, this came more
in the form of beatings on my tiny, fragile body than actual decent
conversations between child and adult.

I also experience the powerful beliefs of right and wrong with
Drake—not the beating, because he doesn't beat me. But his
Machiavellianism when he is so focused on his own interests, to
manipulate, exploit and deceive me, to achieve his goals. Then there are

his moralising and dominance; *Mary is only a little dumb orphanage child!*
She is stupid! She does not know the math! She sold her body to other men!
This is his mindset; but I often ignore it. I'm susceptible to injustice
and feel a kind of righteous indignation when I experience injustice. It's
important to me that a man to possess the same decent mental level as
mine. I must tell you, I'm not that stupid, as he thinks, but I am merely
in love with him. And that makes me unwise.

I'm not sure if the man, in this recent case meaning Drake, is
capable of truly to love, because I believe it's the woman who develops
the mental muscle through her childhood experiences. I'm vulnerable
to men who insist that only they are right, and I then challenge their
views. However, it's a projection mechanism that wastes my energy, so I
end up letting him 'gaslight' me with his higher level of self-interest, an
absence of morality, and his dark triad of manoeuvring me, so he can
reach the throne. With his narcissistic pride, egotism and grandiosity
he seeks to sow seeds of doubt in my mind and make me question my
perception, my memory, and my sanity. 'Illusory truth effect' becomes a
daily life for me. Whatever he repeatedly tells is wrong with me, or his
constant lies, I believe in him, even I know deep down in my gut, it isn't
true. I must have forgotten the text from Matthew 7:15; Beware of false
prophets. They come to you in sheep's clothing, but inwardly they are
ravenous wolves.

I lose awareness and ability to trust myself, and I'm sure it is a
damaging aspect of psychological abuse, when Drake plays on his
narcissism and Machiavellianism, as his power play gets more durable,
and he therefore has vast control over me. I don't trust my instinct
anymore, and I cannot escape!

*   *   *

Fifteen A4 pages as an attachment bump into my mailbox. That's
between twenty-seven and thirty book pages. I will spare the reader
by being kind to you, and only include portions that highlight the
persistent denial, contradictions, and misdirection of others and
Drake's lying. In this devious letter appears a straightforward attempt

to gaslight, to brainwash, to diminish, and to weaken his victim, and here, it's me he abuses. He tries to disorient and disarm me; however, he can, lest I find out of his past.

Here's how (In part) the attachment begins:

Subject: The story of Drake in good and evil

Hi, my eternal love. Since I met you and moved to Asia, I wanted to tell you the actual story of Drake on good and evil and in highlights.

Unfortunately, it's always the negative things that are most stuck in the memory. My story can get a little dark, so I hope you will continue loving me after reading these many pages of me. No doubt that I'll love you forever, therefore this will doubtless be the hardest letter I've written to you, my sweet Baby. I want to open for myself, so you know what I got in me. You are the most important one in my life. Therefore, you will know what I am and what I left; thus, I share my total life with you.

I realise you know me, but you don't know it all. However, as you, I haven't had a dance on the flowering meadow with soft green moss. I had my good ups and steep downs. Compared to you, I lived a protected life and I could develop into the right person I am today. I've had my great successes and my disasters, and I've done well. I have been an exemplary husband and father, but I've been stupid, loved and cried. I gave far more than I took, because my heart has always bled for those who did not—or could not—or were ill, then given myself to them and burned my soul for their sake.

My life as a doctor became my rough prison and my great happiness. There was no one to comfort me when I was in need. One must give and not take. One must build and not destroy. One must love and not hate. One must provide solace and not pain. Life is one extensive process that has a beginning and an end, so in life, it's hard to make many decisions. Who is the person God can look at? He is not a judge. God is pragmatic, and he separates evil from good and brings forth the outstanding qualities of a human being.

Sex has become an expensive acquaintance for many, since humans would destroy more and more, because of the power of this flesh. A moment's desire has come important to a little child as you, with no parents to take care of you. They threw you into distress and poverty, therefore the world was and still is frightening.

My dear beloved little girl, I have found in you the roots I have been missing and been searching for far too long. You gave me a fantastic fresh life, a fresh hope to do more for people who needed me. You are sweet, and you possess a heart and a classy style. Best is; you haven't pushed me to tell you what has happened to me throughout my life.

What led me to the place I am in now? It is crucial for me to be open and honest, tell you the truth of me—of the good, the evil and the economic development of my life. The banks back then threw themselves at my feet because everything I did succeeded. The same was true with stock trading, but I didn't know enough, and they presented diverse projects to me. Though I usually said no, I joined few and had both success and failure.

Today, I view my financial history as one with too many elements of good and evil in it. I feel it's a terrible story. One of those stories has totally undermined me because I was stupid enough to trust the wrong investors. I went from having a fortune of $5 million to under $500,000; it was a robbery of lofty rank. The poor leftovers were in real estate and not in cash. It totally knocked me mentally.

I had an arduous time, so I was calling out loud for *my* Jesus and Mary Magdalene, my support and the one who was always there for me. But you didn't hear me, so I called *my* father God and asked if he had left me. The answer; I must go back to my roots. What did God mean? What was I supposed to do? I couldn't find the answer. I was sad...

So far it sounds harmless, except for the way Drake belittles me. Though, I'm frustrated. I'm sure the observant reader remembers that, at the beginning of the story, he told me he is an *atheist*! If he is a nonbeliever, *why* call for God, Jesus, and Mary M? Would you do that?

Is his attempt to convince me of what I call 'damage control'? I sense as he wants to minimise the negative perception of his crisis following an unexpected event. Was he hoping to conceal something from me, to prevent me from finding out of the true Drake.

His letter (in part) continues:

> I made other minor mistakes in my '*not* being a doctor' career. Once, while they considered me wealthy, I invested for humanitarian reasons, so I wanted to see the products for sale at an acquaintance's warehouse. It wasn't a vast amount, but I could double my investment fast. The American guy had told me a heart-breaking story of his son, who had married an Iranian woman, before they declared such marriages illegal. Then they sent the wife and child to prison. They often beat them to a pulp, and they feed them with rotten food and putrid water, and then the wife was several times raped by the guards. Shortly after, the new rulers executed the wife and child, and they expelled the husband. He had brought out a few cans of Iranian caviar, which was a deadly sin to smuggle out of the country. It was sweet and touching when he told me the story, so he gave me a can, and I stored it in my fridge. I invested in several more tins, and it turned out that I lost my money, except for a few cans of caviar. Every time I got mad at the man, I stared at the tins and thought of the story. I wrote it in my education book of the hard school of life.
>
> I went from being an enterprising and capable filthy rich businessman to having to learn the hard way that few were happy to deceive. I never swindled no one! I made my fortune by honest trade, then built and sold properties

and did a lot of other things. Although I couldn't sell the building in Sweden after I left, even the mayor had offered to buy it for over $3 million.

I built houses in Cuba and earned $5 million, and next I moved to the United States, and sold land and real estate and a lot of other strange things. At one point, I had several clinics in the United States, none of which I worked in myself. Then my broker couldn't get on the floor to sell, so I lost half of what was on my stock account. Later, I turned it around and got my finances back to what they were before the crisis. But I had to sell stuff to cover other expenses for a living.

I lent money to a large car repair company, and suddenly, the company went bankrupt, where I lost $1 million. I was in the warehouse, repair, and sales section, then one day when I went for work, they denied me access to my office. Mr Williams had manipulated the company's ownership behind my back, and had taken control, so he could sack me. At that time, I lived with another woman whom I saved from a physically abusive marriage.

One day, I sat on my bed staring and couldn't see any solution to my life, so I got sad, and tears ran down my cheeks. But self-pity was not something I had practised before, therefore I shouted to my Father God, asking what I should do. That night, I received a vision, when God told me to peek at physical conditions in the universe. I should use human physics as a source of inspiration. I woke up thinking, with a lot of images coming through my brain, and I saw electronic phenomena no one could control. I started writing many notes on my latest invention, so it took over my mind, and I regained courage in life.

When I invented the electronic supersystem that was better than anything you've seen, a large corporation declared my invention worth $1 billion. Swiftly I got a minor capital together, then after a while, I hired a guy who helped transform my designs and innovations into useable form. That's where a guy from Scandinavia comes in. They introduced him to me as a fundraiser who could help me build my business, from research to production to distribution and to sales. I worked ten times as hard to get things back on track. I then built a new organisation.

Fred Pharrell, a famous soccer player, introduced me to a rich European man who they introduced to my fantastic concept, and he had a famous contact to a British pop group Hearts and Ace. Fred told me I should give them free shares, in exchange for them introducing my product into his network. *What?* I didn't want to.

The arguing between us began, and those cunning and heartless guys went behind my back. They forged a deal with the other cunningly people, and before I knew it, Fred had taken over *my* business, *my* inventions, and *my* secrets. Fred fired me after the famed proxy fight, and they could freely take what I had created. Besides, I lost my US visa and work permit, that's why I worked illegally for a time in the United States. Imagine how my miserable life became complicated. I made minor trades, then I wanted to sell the house to get capital, but it was too difficult to get my wife to help, and she also denied me a divorce.

I had applied for a loan called a home improvement loan for $200,000 and came on top of the actual mortgage. I worked on few improvements to the house and got it perfect and ready to sell, because I had planned a US exit strategy. With the work I did on the house, I could score a profit of $300,000. Unfortunately, during those years, we had the global financial crisis, and it was difficult to sell expensive houses. Economists considered it as the most severe economic crisis since the Great Depression of the 1930s. Can you imagine how *bad* it was for *poor* me? Sales had stopped entirely back then, and thus, the banks wanted to get their money again, so things became hard. In fact, I was in the abyss of deep debt. It was as if God would not give me a chance to come up again after my failure. Or was it a sign from God that I had not understood the message correctly?

I did serious mental gymnastics, trying to figure out what I was supposed to do. Few years before I met you, God led me back into my studies—this time with the beginnings of the biological life of stem cells. This to tell how to affect them with my therapy form I use today. Besides, I invented for science crazy models of how life starts. I alone solved the mystery of how a sperm can hatch an egg from millions of other sperm in a nanosecond or less, and everyone thought I was crazy. But it made me think of whether this was my lot. The individual! That's what I should concentrate on, God told me.

They cannot patent my thoughts and intelligent brain, we know that! There is no value in commercial exploitation. You can't make any product from it. These studies kept my head going, so I didn't break mentally. It seemed as if there was an endless ocean of strange partial solutions of so many kinds in my head that it was utterly crazy.

What should I do with that? Because of the street smarts I gained in my life and battles, and my bright brain activity, it was easy for me to make a business plan—to devise alternative ways to make things work. It was easy for me to find logic in my new electronic skills, and I became good at it.

Unfortunately, I was and still am so multifaceted and multi-skilled that I got too many options. I could and cannot handle and make everything at once, and I won't even be able to accomplish it altogether in a lifetime. Many people said to me when I was young that I had to be a wise old man, because no adolescent man could know and achieved so much in such a brief time. They measured my IQ; to 180 or 190—that is to say, you are far over a genius. I believe they label a person who scores above 140 a talent or near higher genius.

I am just petty me, who has succeeded, failed, lost and conquered. But what good is it to me to possess high intelligence when I lose my entire wealth? Lonely, I licked my wounds, and systematically I started working with what I do today. I realised the problems and found the mistakes that the machines I use today had made. I corrected that on extra tables, then told it to the developer in the hope of I could make further money, including in the form of my book on the subject...

What an exciting bragging life story. I muse during my reading and have still not captured what it's concerning. Any red flags? Can you see them? Am I overruling the red flags? So far, I have cut fifteen of his pages down to four, realising he has so far only been talking of himself—him, him, *him*, his cleverness, and his high IQ. Hah... he must be Einstein.

Though, I realise Drake enjoys bragging of loads and of how his wealth he once had and has lost. I'm not impressed, because money is not the most essential part for me. But nice to have, though. Such a poor church rat!

Why is it so vital for him telling me how important and famous he has been and still is? Einstein, Freud, Abraham Lincoln, and Caesar are famous. Therefore, what could I use his strange fame for? When I met him, I had never heard of the 'famous' talented dandy, heh... heh... with an IQ above 180 or 190. Famous? 'Professor' in what? Nothing! And let me tell the reader; *Albert Einstein's IQ was 160.*

Afterwards, the ugliest part of Drake's dusky shifty betrayal landed on my table, the most disturbing part of his self-important lengthy letter, will so far reveal, these instances ranges from denial to be the abuser himself, and he diligently plays the sufferer ill-treated by others. With his previous offending incidents against others, he denies them entirely, saying that they never occurred. In his optics, he stages these bizarre events based loosely on the facts, so it shows that the others involved were and are doing something wrong. Is it a cunning way of 'opening up', so he can disorient me? For me to feel sympathy for him.

He is clever. Will I fall for his trick, when I continue reading (in part) his letter?

> Shortly after we met, Baby girl, I then moved to Asia! As a wacko, CC locked me in a compact cage next to a smoker and CC took vicious advantage of me and my knowledge in their clinic. They tried to give me 'candy' as they call the 'little girls' who sell their bodies for men's greedy lust, though it didn't suit a decent man like me. And here comes yet another correction and confession to you, my darling Mary. I must get it off my mind. For, in fact, it's nagging me. I have been too embarrassed not telling you the truth.
>
> When I moved over there, Mr CC took me after a business interview, where he had drawn the golden palms for me, to a big dinner. There were loads of booze at one of his shady nightclubs. During dinner, he tried to get me roaring drunk, when whisky, cognac, gin and vodka came to the table. They paraded lots of giggling and barely dressed girls in front of us, and we could pick one. Then the girls' 'Big Mama' came. *Puff!* The girls quickly disappeared as dew before the Sun. She asked if we wanted to keep the girls, and if not, more choices were in front of us.
>
> I was out of my comfort zone, not knowing how to act, so I sat and played dice with the one I chose. I couldn't make myself say I didn't want the girl back. I promise, we *only* sat and *talked* and *played* dice. Trust me and remember this *was before I met you.* There was no cuddling or anything, so we sat quietly and enjoyed each other's company as two friends—only the one did not have as many clothes on as I had. I figured that was it…

Oh, my God! I am near to faint, and my heated blood is rushing in my veins as an erupting volcano. He is not only screwed up; He is *insane!* Does he sincerely imagine that I believe his foolish story? Sorry, my dear readers, I need a break. The privy is calling for me to vomit. *Come on, dude!* Does he believe his own story? He's such a *holy* turd! He lied! I'm sure he was never alone in Asia, but first when he left Spain for good. Hence, his *before-I-met-you* story, it could not have happened, because he had told me he only went to Asia together with Kate. The shifty dude contradicts himself, so he did it at the beginning of our relationship. Yuck, the bastard is fooling around. Pestilence! Grr, I'm in a massive rage. But he resorted to his Machiavellian tactics in order to get ahead, to protect himself of what those two so-called *innocent* friends did after they stopped playing the dice. Did they play cards? Yak, maybe strip poker? Ick, or did they fornicate?

Let's get back to his deceiving letter (In part) where he writes:

> It was getting late, and we were about to go home, and the giggling call girls disappeared. Suddenly the trollops came back fully dressed, and CC had arranged for me to walk with one girl to the hotel and had arranged that I should get it off with the little 'dice' girl. I got surprised, but then I thought I just had to try it once. To experience how it was to screw a tiny Asian courtesan and not be such a fluffy man.
>
> As soon as we had entered the room, the tramp took off her clothes. First, she took a shower and washed herself thoroughly, especially in her lower, awfully hairy parts. She asked me to do the same. I did. Then something funny happened, when I was supposed to wear a rubber so she could work with amazing Willy. She couldn't get the condom on my penis, because it was obviously a too tiny condom. And clearly their Asian danger noodles are not *that* big as my slaying pocket rocket. She remained frustrated and gazed worried, then found a few other condoms in her bag and tried them on 'Big Willy'. She could barely squeeze the biggest condom she found on my giant bratwurst. Then came her professional problem, because she couldn't fit the dirty stiff dog inside her vagina; thus, it was a disaster that night.
>
> The second time I went with CC, during our Hennessy cognac party, he tried to lure me to another visit with a girl. It went as the first attempt, but this pretty girl was far

better at making everything work, so it was a good enough experience. But not so good that I wanted it to be a part of my life. I thought, if I would stay in Asia, I would be emotionally neutral, and I could buy a 'night out', and not bond with the person. It could work until I felt lust for a woman again. I couldn't find meaning in such a life, because I'm a sensitive man and not a cold iceberg. My soul must have the warm passion of my lovely MM and the passion you so dearly give me. I only wanted to have the woman that would give me the love; *as you do*. And I had been longing for—the one that I would share my life with. That would be meaningful, and a great angle for me, because the other would tear me to pieces.

My sweet Mary, I'm so sorry I haven't told you this before, because I was, and I am embarrassed or perhaps shy about it. I thought, since I couldn't change it, I could keep it inside me, and put it in the box with forgotten and unwanted cases. I'm sorry for my unwillingness to tell you of this specific experience. I was so afraid that you would feel bad of me or that it would cause you to not trust me. It worried me if you would think I was as the other worthless men. I'm NOT! I'm telling you because I can't go on without having a pure conscience, and then I must take the beating. Sorry, my love. Please forgive me. I will keep no secrets from you again, and I will always be truthful with you…

I screamed loud, whoa! What the hell! I am shattered and crushed. In sheer frustration, I want to destroy something, throw things around, and kill him.

I will, in seconds, massively destroy his condom story of his lying excuse! Of nature, I am inquisitive, therefore; I research on the penis size and the tightness of the vagina. I will kill the myth of Asian women having tighter vaginas than other women in the world, including that Asian men have smaller danger noodles.

First, let me execute the myth of penis size and race. The belief in scientific evidence does not support that! Drawing upon the results of twelve relevant studies, a review detailed in *The British Journal of Urology (BJU) International* finds the average erect penis is roughly 5.5 to 6.2 inches long (13.97 to 15.75 cm). And around 4.7 to 5.1 inches (11.94 to 12.95 cm) in circumference. When it comes to **penis myths**, the findings also deflate a few other myths of male genitalia. The notion that penis size varies according to race, for example, is *false* (Wylie, Kevan R, and Eardlye, Ian, "Penile Size and the Small Penis Syndrome", 2007).

Now for dispelling the myth that Asian vaginas are tighter. Dr Valinda Nwadike, MD and obstetrics and gynecology specialist in California, Maryland, can see how this stereotype exists, and wholeheartedly disagrees with the premise. 'I honestly don't think [Asian women having small vaginas] is true. I would disagree with this stereotype. We don't make decisions about size—we don't have Asian speculums. That would negate the myth. It should be put to bed absolutely.' Instead, when the myth currently has more power to hurt than to help, the question we should be asking is, why does vagina 'tightness' even matter? (Healthline.com).

Studies have revealed which race has the tightest vagina. Caucasian women tend to have vaginas that are longer at the front of the body (anterior) and shorter at the rear. Hispanics tend to have a larger overall width (what you would term tightness), with the shortest length. A recent study whose aim is to find the race where women have the tightest vagina has revealed that black women are the likeliest to be tighter down there. (Pulse.ng, 31 July 2016).

Oh, my goodness! I hope you so far can see the strangeness in Drake's story, and his vast bratwurst. In 'Viagra, Sex, and the Dildo', you might recall that 'Big Willy' only stood upright as an 'insignificant *half-stiff* Adonis'. And we know too well Adonis is the mortal lover of the goddess Aphrodite in Greek mythology. But his biggie banger was not a vast mortal lover. It might well be that he assumes he is the mighty Adonis, but his 'golden gizmo' can't fill me when it is only half-stiff. I believe I'm okay firm in my vagina, Paul often told me.

What does not fit correctly into his story? I muse, and I'm close to get pissed off at his self-rectifying made-up imaginary fable. This is a time of my life where I still am gripped by a deep sense of misery and tragedy. I am once again cruelly knocked out by great suffering, and it gives me a wrong lasting impression of my philosophy of life—especially that I was not listening to the massive danger sign that consisted in the entire letter. Red flag! Red flag! Red flag!

He is *nutty as a fruitcake!* He is a *psycho case* I should send to the mental hospital.

I'm upset! Distressed! Heartbroken! He emotionally paralyzed me, and I lose total trust in him. My entire world collapses, and it set off an avalanche of events. It crashes as an exploding atom bomb straight into my open face, and everything blackens before my eyes. Deeply shaken, my heart bounces faster and faster as were I running a marathon— *boom, boom, boom.* It races, jumping to two hundred beats per minute, so I can't breathe, as I feel suffocated as the lack of air to my lungs puts me in a distraught condition, and the immense shock takes fatal control over me. The 'Avengers Thor Battle Hammer' knocks me completely out. *Crash! Bang!* I collapse to the floor with a smash. As an overcooked, dazed, flabby dead hamster, I lie passed out on my marble floor with a thump.

As I come back to myself, I still hold the letter in my hand, then I weep as if for the first time in hundreds of years, and my tears won't stop. My heart desperately screams and cries loud, but it cannot delete the love I have for him. That hurts immensely. I do not understand of the gross agenda he's planning. The worst part is that he crushes me completely.

I must read the rest later—or do I want to read the rest? *This is where my love story should stop!* This should be the end of my relationship with Drake, even be the last page in my book. So, what is wrong with me? Does he have that much control over me? And play Russian roulette with me?

After a glass of whisky, two or more smokes, I continue the reading, sitting unmoving and shaking on the marble floor, continuing reading (in part) his letter:

I stand again as a leader in a new field and have confident that Father God wants me to go back and solve problems in human bodies. The pharmaceutical industries are choking people, so they need new thinking! That's what I'm good at. Though, here is my massive dilemma. I have made an innovative plan for how *we* together can do this in Asia—how I can treat people's brain diseases through my alternative methods.

But what does it help, when I have failed to protect my values in the past? It always went wrong when I trusted others and trusted not my gut feelings. Back then, I made financial mistakes in my marriage, and my wife Laila didn't understand me, so we never had excellent communication. My head was too great and intelligent for Laila; my knowledge proved too much for her. My life was hectic, and Laila didn't understand she needed to take me in and say, 'Stop Drake! I'll give you oxygen so you can breathe.' So, we lived on credit. The balloon cracked. And we had to get the debts out of the way by finding alternative sources of income. But Laila had more significant deficits and was imaginative, moving her loan from one bank to another, and I had to earn the money so I could repay the debts.

When I came back to Sweden, in 2006, I rapidly earned $40,000 a month. Suddenly, the *tax mafia* wanted more than half of it. That's why I moved immediately to Spain. The tax collectors in Spain were not so smart, so I didn't pay taxes, everything was 'black money' I earned. Then I distributed the earnings between Laila and me, as well, with my monthly payments in Spain. Nothing went to savings, and I couldn't sell the damn house in the US. It became frustrating, and I lived a spartan life with my mother, Gretchen, in Sweden, where I worked, cooked, and slept, and did what I was supposed to do.

When I didn't get paid for my work for months last year, things went wrong for me.

What I had saved up was for smoking bills in the United States and paying for my clinic. I was keen on Asia, and CC promised me a great fresh, precious life. He had the capital I needed, if I came with the expertise, and I left Spain for a brighter fortune in Asia.

CC offered me only a low share of our income, and I felt it was the wrong distribution, because I was the mastermind, and did the effort. I wanted to work and thought we could negotiate later for a fresh business constellation. In compensation while you were twice in Asia, CC promised to pay for the hotel. Baby, you know how it went, as I had to pay both stays, therefore I lost some of your transferred money to pay the smoking bills...

The goofy confuses me. What don't I understand? He lives and works in Spain, so how can he then live with Gretchen in Sweden? What a mystery it is to me.

I don't understand—hold on to your braces and belts! All the sweetness I was enjoying first time in Asia came from my own transferred money, spent on this luxury! Holy crap! Besides, I paid for the second stay, and not him! It suddenly dawns on me why we had to flee from Hong Kong, because he must have been too greedy and gotten into a gigantic mess with CC. It must be there where the source of the problems was hidden—in Drake's, sneaky darkness of greed!

Let us laugh a little more over my ignorance and live a little more each day! Ha-ha, ha-ha, I have unquestionably paid for everything myself! For heaven's sake, what a strange move he had conducted with his baton. Though I must look at the bright side, and laugh, because I enjoyed the indulgences paid for with my coinage. Oh, sweet Jesus, one more lesson for the future.

I need a brief break and get up, grabbing a chilly sparkling water in the fridge and go outside on my balcony to smoke.

Let's continue (in part) the letter:

Today I feel as an idiot I could lose such a vast fortune. But when I think it through, I consider that, despite hard work and good earnings, I couldn't make it come together. When I read my previous business plans, I believed the business principles were in order. I merely trusted in the wrong people at the wrong times.

That's why I find it hard not to give my wife a livelihood, so Laila could live without suffering. I can't and don't want to send her money anymore, and we must get divorced, so I must help her survive, then we must move on. Otherwise, I cannot see my children in their eyes again. Baby, I promise I did what I could for her, as I know that, with your enormous heart, you expect me to do the right thing...

I'm genuinely appalled. I can't believe my own eyes and realise that he has lied to me. After roughly eight months in my romantic and enchanting moments, this shifty guy tells me he *is married* in the US. Something serious he had forgotten to tell me about!

So far, I have read fourteen pages where it is solely of him, him, *him*, and his many failures, the many millions he boasted about, how intelligent he is and his treacherous deception. If he has such a high IQ as he claims in the letter, then I don't understand his many failures. It's easy to see straight in hindsight.

By now, in my life with him, I'm trapped in the dangerous quicksand he has dragged me into. I can't get out of it, and only the top of my head is above the sucking black evil sand.

Drake's dark personality triads have more sweetness to say:

Then I come to our situation today, darling sweet Mary, where I feel unmoving. I've only a few funds left to create something new. You've been and are *extraordinarily generous* with me, and I thank you with my heart. There has been no one before who has taken me by the hand and helped me. However, it still hurts me when I can't take part financially right now. I know I'm on my way back to stability with the things we are doing, and I might take my turn too, because it's always been me who paid for others.

When I helped you through the troublesome time of the pestilent negotiations last year, at no time did I do so for my gain. Nor did you pay any bonus in form of payment for my help. If you give me your *yes to marry* me when I again will be brave enough to sit on my knees and ask you this question, then please know that it will come from my heart and soul. I will ask only out of love, not for your wealth.

It's not my fault you went through the fire of hell. For me, the man must provide for his wife, but each deserved penny you get from Flopper is yours. I'm sorry that, at this point in my life, I don't have the financial strength to do so for you. It hurts me inside, so I must hurry to earn enough to give you that confidence. I will once more dare to ask you for your hand in marriage. If I could do it with serenity today, I would immediately fall on my knees for you. You've had it so hard throughout your life, so I wish to give you security—not just financially but as well spiritually and in our incredible love and sharing for the future. Soul, love, and sharing can be fantastic, and I will give you these in plentiful amounts. I will get the rest of the equation to go up too.

Because of you, my love, I'm flying on a cloud nine in the seventh heaven, and I'm living my dream of the eternal love for you. I'm feeling eternally loved by you, and I've never felt so strongly about anyone before. I've never been in such total love! I thank you, Mary, for taking me into your heart and for carrying me forward. Thank you, little girl, for giving me unspeakable happiness. That's what I needed in my life. Thank you, Baby, for so gently healing my wounds. I can get back to where I once was—this time with you beside my side. My precious Mary M, *you* give me strength and shine the light for me, so I don't stumble. You give me back my confidence and belief in myself, day by day. The innovative Philippine project here is an opportunity; therefore, I can come back with hard work and proper planning. It will be a pleasure to share it with you, because you said that you will carry us through to the goal. With you and your money, I don't have to seek investors to get the funds for the project. As future spouses, we will therefore share everything we own and earn equally.

Let this long story stand as a testimony that things don't come by themselves. Even if everything looks as if you're on a floating pink cloud, it may not be so. It must give us a positive and forward-looking goal, so we must always talk of things before we act—and always do it together.

With this I have told you about me, you must have the chance to say that you would rather be without me. Perhaps I'm not worthy of you. Maybe I've made too many mistakes in my life. You must thoroughly weigh whether my love for you, my abilities and brain are good enough to make you happy—to give you what you've been searching for and not found. I wait with the trembling in my body for your answer. I'll take whatever it is with my head raised. I've put my cards on the table so you can see them. It's up to you, how you want to use them—or whether you want to use them.

Yours forever, I love you.
Drake

I am done with this douchebag. This is where I, as the reader of Drake's letter, *must stop* the relationship. He is gaslighting me! He tries to make me believe that I must be insane to cover his own lies and criminal activities. And simultaneously, he tries to convince me I'm everything to him, and that he wants to prove that he can change.

First, he gives me a stomach punch and ten uppercuts to my face! Next, he expects me to finance everything. Then he makes a massive declaration of his love to me! Following, he wants to marry me! What am I supposed to do? Forgive him or run? Okay, he is my star and the most precious person in my life, so I can't imagine my life without him. My love for him has grown *too* fast, and I love him more and more every day, and feel that my love for him will not stop growing. The most pleasing experience of waking up and begin a fresh day is I'm doing it with him.

He has succeeded to brainwash and manipulate me, and I have allowed him to take advantage of me. In this appalling flash, I want to give up and *run* as fast as I can. Screw it! Kiss my ass! I am an overheated, angry bitch, and I want to thwack him—punch him angrily with a fire-heated frying pan in his head. *I will end it right now!* Never go back to him and stop this cruel chapter of what I thought was a mesmerising love story. He is not worthy of me—the false, lying bastard.

Then a sudden panic is spreading inside my head. *Oh, no!* My belongings are on their way in a shipping container to The Philippines. Am I foolishly materialistic in this instant, and afraid of losing my things? What shall I do and what will be next, recalling a quote from The Divine Comedy, by Dante Alighieri; Midway along the journey of our life I woke to find myself in a dark wood, for I had wandered off from the straight path?

The heated dark triad cat-after-the-mouse pursuing begins for Drake to lure sweet trusting Mary and to benefit from her affective empathy.

CHAPTER 15

THE CAT-AND-MOUSE GAME

Cat: a pygmy lion who loves mice, hates dogs, and patronizes human beings.

—Oliver Herford

Gosh almighty! I have damaged my head by my extensive fall to the marble floor. Unwisely, I'm falling right into Drake's devious, cunning trap. Well planted with both my wobbling legs in the dangerous vile sucking quicksand, where I feel stuck. I am being pulled deeper and deeper into the deep black hole of the shabby abyss and am lost in the dark wood. This is where my earlier dream of warnings becomes a hidden reality. Oh my! The monster of a Southern (fe) male black widow (*Latrodectus mactans*) has consumed me with his dangerous poison and grabbed me with its repulsing ugly eight long legs.

Goodness gracious me! I don't admit to myself that his letter is a *massive* warning with multiply *red flags*. Can I not see it? I'm reading the letter repeatedly and I still don't understand why I fly right back into his cobweb again; despite he vastly has betrayed me. I have never been aware of the danger being manipulated by such a harmful person, and I am not aware of him as a potential sociopath. Not such thoughts swirling in my life and don't think of the danger I am in at that instant. I don't know so much of the dissimilarity between a narcissist, a sociopath and a psychopath. As many others believe, a psychopath is a killer, so do I, though Drake is not a killer.

The *sociopath* is more cunning and manipulative, because his ego isn't always at stake. He is more unreliable, rage-prone, and unable to lead as much of an average life and doesn't possess any actual honest personality. The *psychopath* can charm, influence the impression of an ordinary life, and it's being the most *dangerous* of antisocial personality disorders. Which one is worse?

Is Drake a talented and harmful narcissistic sociopath? A person who can wrap his victims into his perfect maze of webs—just as the black widow captures its victim before killing it with its superior poison. Can no one be safe when he is nearby, when he scatters his poison? As a hungry lion, he will break the victim with his sharp claws and teeth's and has masterly learned how to use his dangerous sneaky strategy on people as me. We know it too well; watch out for greedy wolves in sheepskin, rattlesnakes and deadly spiders. In my rage, I'm thinking, he is fifteen times more dangerous than the venom from a rattlesnake or the poisonous spider. We perceive the snake is deadly and the toxin can damage tissue, and it affects your circulatory function by destroying blood cells and causing you internal haemorrhage. Drakes venom has poisoned my entire body, heart and brain. I'm close to death—I'm a participant in my ongoing long-lasting suicide. I should seek professional attention, because he makes me very sick.

As nature states, the male spider plays death roulette with his own life, because the black widow is one of the spider species where the female eats the male after mating. It takes much of cunning and quickness to be born as a male spider to fertilise the female, because he must get her interested, mate, and get away from her alive. Maybe the roles got swapped between Drake and me, and instead it's me playing Russian roulette with my life. A lethal game of chance in which I will place a single bullet in a revolver. Then I'll spin the cylinder, put the gun against my head, and pull the trigger, hoping the projectile does not reach the barrel of the weapon and I fire. I should, after our first shag, have eaten him. Next spat him to the ground in disgust.

In my naivety, I don't see the dangers come, nor do I notice of the chaos in his description of life. I feel sorry for his first part in the story. Then I anger over the whores. The last part he smartly uses flattery and reverse psychology to convince me to stay, and that is what I mostly remember. Clever dude, but what is it Drake wants in life and with me? Though, his deceit takes my breath from my lungs, and it profoundly crushes my heart into millions of molecules. He is the man who used to be my happiness and has subtracted me from my sadness and given me joy in multiples!

In my devastated mess, I isolate myself, don't answer him and can't decide what to do. Shall I stop the affair? I genuinely don't know what to answer him, so I go dead silent for a week. Will I be able to forget him? Get him out of my head? *How can I forget someone like that?*

Drake keeps on writing, and now he's mostly hitting my cravings, so our love is as Tom and Jerry. Love and hate! The cat is hunting the mouse. Who is more talented? The cat or the mouse?

Love is a positive feeling, as it is an imaginative protective and it's often too irrational. I'm destructive, and the past days wanted me to do immoral deeds to him. Mostly, I want to hate him, but hate is harmful and often considered being an evil passion. I don't possess such an evil passion for hating other people, and you must tame hate. I got it tamed in me, so cannot hate him, even if I *hate* his last letter. I surrender to my calmness and my love for him, then give him the benefit of the doubt and try to forgive him.

'Excuse me!' You for sure loudly will shout. 'Is she unwise? She must be!' It's Okay, you may think so, because you're right! I am *stupidly* in love.

My sexuality is healthy, and I can achieve complete satisfaction through the naughty act. Drake knows it and enjoys using it to win my trust. All but equal, I have a healthy and cheerful approach towards sex, despite saddening experiences in my past life. But I need the intellectual respect of my partner before I'm erotic. I thought Drake gave it to me, so I was fast attracted to him erotically. He is magical. Though we run into glitches, we still experience much fun, and enjoy heart-stopping times together, in the middle of the repulsive things going on in our relationship. I will not deny the many glorious and hilarious sides he possesses, because he is an eye-popping man behind his crooked deceits.

With my sexuality, I've often experienced that it fixates him of my earlier marriage—especially our intimate activity. Drake merely can't get enough of the ludicrous stories of the lusty experiences I once subjected myself to, in the aim of satisfying Paul's dirty hunger. It's as if this idea is the only horny stimulation that can drive the nasty desire in Drake so he can get an erect cock. At time's it's as a significant pain for me to tell him of my earlier 'Fifty Shades of Grey' life. It has been a whacking porn and bondage store, where he picks fresh movies from the shelves. Mostly, I want to forget the past and the many pornographic experiences.

Drake calls his cock for Willy and is the hunting cat, and Minnie, the mouse, is my pussy. The cat-and-mouse game begins. The game is an English idiom that, in dating, means "a contrived action involving constant pursuit, near captures, and repeated escapes." So, it is with Willy and Minnie. Or is it more similar if you imagine the cartoon, *Tom and Jerry*? Before I left, and before the letter, we had one of his "whispering" get down and be dirty nights together.

'Baby, whisper something naughty into my ear.' That's how Drake starts his erotic talk.

'Hmm… I don't know.' I think of what to tell him. 'What is it you want me to tell, you, darling? There is so much.' But I don't want to tell more stories from erotic chapters in my previous life.

'It must be something that relates to your dirty experiences with Flopper.' He blinks with his glittering eyes. 'Tell me of the swinger club,' he whispers, and takes my hand then gives me a kiss on my forehead. 'what about this fatty bloke crawling around on the floor as a submissive dog?' He laughs as if it's funny.

'Ha-ha, the episode was hilarious.'

Drake's erection glitches make me suspect he is impotent; so, a funny tale can't do any harm. I believe it helps him; me telling the wicked narration. To be honest, my world doesn't consist only of shagging, and I don't appreciate it when he oppresses me so much by hitting on my desires. Does he think it's crucial to my life with him? For me, it's not the ultimate point, because my love is unconditional; so, it's not restricted if he can't get a stiff weenie. I talked to him before I left The Philippines.

'Darling, it's no problem you can't get Willy proud.' My feelings for him are heartfelt.

'I'm so confused that Willy doesn't want to get up. Baby, you're so nice.' He stared at himself and his hanging dead lizard.

'There are methods that can help you.' I take his hand and try to be understanding. 'We will figure it out. Don't worry, darling. Mwah!' And give him a tender hug.

'I should knock Willy yellow, green, and blue on the top of his stupid little head.' Slam, bam, smack, and with anger he frustrated whacks Willy hard, so he turns blue in the head.

'Honey stop that. That's heedless.' I grab the wobbly thing in my hand. 'Why don't we just buy Viagra pills?'

The next day, we drive to the pharmacy and buy seven packages of pills. It worked for Drake for a short while. Suddenly, he didn't take them anymore. It was a bummer to me; the boning went steeply downhill.

This is among the many things happening before I left The Philippines.

Before Drake's horrible letter, he worried of how we could continue our naughty hunger. How could two beloved control the relationship? And at a long-distance? Neither of us had tried this bad art before. How could we get wicked without physical contact?

Since then, the imagination has no set limits when we enjoy our daily conversations via Skype or email. We've written a bunch of love letters and funny stories to each other. Drake can be a hilarious guy—mainly when he is writing or telling stories, and what a great imagination he has. Even with him being in The Philippines and me in Spain, we talked every single day on Skype, off sensibly, of everyday life, chatted boldly of the future and sex. He enjoys me to touch on the secret flower and to watch me getting an orgasm.

Before the devastating letter, we had our latest naughty erotic Skype time, while he was watching and telling wicked stories of Willy and Minnie. With a six-hour time variation between our continents, it sometimes can be an evening with me and morning with him.

*   *   *

Now, while Drake continues working on our new rehabilitation centre, I'm getting back to myself after his malicious letter. Many emails pop up, and for a reason, time gets trivial and lonely for him when I'm not there. I'm still angry with him, so I lay him on freezing ice. *Leave him in the pillory*, I ponder, because I wish not to get back. Though, I read his many emails, but I don't respond, even as he writes that my belongings, my clothes, and the delicious wine have arrived. It's challenging to get excellent wine in The Philippines, so I'm glad the boxes of superb wine with a fabulous bouquet are there. We will enjoy them together on the sandy beach or by our pool.

My dilemma is vast, so what shall I do with my stuff? I regret everything, what I've done. I deceived my family and told them I'm only going to The Philippines for a holiday. Only Drake's family knows we are lovers, and they noticed my great happiness with him. But they knew him from another angle, then I did. Slight hints came to my ears.

'Look well after your money,' Clarise said.

'Be careful with Drake.' Kristen said.

I didn't understand it.

'No one can tear us apart,' I insisted. 'I trust Drake's loyalty.'

So, who was I trying to convince? The family? Or me?

'Drake is faithful!' I excused.

People gazed at me as if I were a naïve, blue-eyed blond Barbie doll.

'Drake is with me for love. Not for my possessions.'

Did I believe in that myself when I told others so?

'Happiness does not last forever.' Mike said.

'What you and Drake experience together will not last,' Julian said during a family dinner.

'One day, you will realise it—just as the other women in his life.' Amy gave me a friendly clap on my shoulder as a warning of my future misery. I didn't want to believe it.

Drake is different! I told myself. Will I ever get wiser?

*   *   *

New strange telling signs pop up from him now and then, and I sense there must be more that's pressing Drake. I go through trouble figuring out what his actual problem is, when he has not been loyal to me. Despite my anger, I answer his fifth teens ringing Skype call, so I suppress my frightened feelings and his strange letter. He always has a formidable ability to convince me of the exact opposite of my thoughts.

'Damnit, Mary, why can't I get hold of you?' Is the first rude nagging sentence he shouts as we connect.

Sucks to you! I shout in my head.

'Gee, darling, I'm aware many days passed in silence. But I don't care.' I was heedless enough to answer him.

'Don't you want to talk to me anymore now that I confessed?' He gives the impression of being agitated, nervous and trembling that I not replied or have talked to him.

'You crushed my world into tiny pieces.' I hold a finger in front of the camera, so he can't see me. 'You were so stupid with your damaging blast of a nuclear bomb. I don't know if I want to come back.'

'Oh, my God! So dramatic you are, Mary. It can't be that dreadful!' Careless he smirks.

'Ugh! Your big dark betraying cloud is swirling around in my head.' I want to cry.

'Well, Babe, your stuff has arrived. I'm very cheerful. Mwah!' He smiles, then blinks his stunning eyelashes and sends me an air kiss. Oh my God, those eyes! And I melt.

'Your bomb has sent the worst shattering *shockwave* into my fragile soul.' Yuck! I want to turn off the conversation.

'I started unpacking your things. Babe, please come back. Let's talk.' He blinks slowly as Bambi with his eyelashes.

'Well, inside my broken soul, I'm not sure I want to come back,' In angriness, I shout these harsh words, but inside, I whine, then I remove the finger from the camera. 'You have radiated me with the worst dangerous nuclear particles. I'm dying.' The anger becomes to sadness.

'Wow, there she is!' He joyfully barks. 'Baby, I have been honest with you. Doesn't that count?' He begs.

Hump!

I don't answer and end the conversation without saying goodbye. My fizzy gut and angry senses tell me the story with the prostitute is not valid. He did it at the beginning of our relationship; I know that for a fact, and not before he met me. It's indisputable. He lies.

The next morning, he calls me. I miss him so much, even though I'm so angry with him.

'Good morning to my forever-lasting love. My sweetheart. I wish you will get a mind-blowing day.' He beams and looks stunning when we connect on Skype.

'Good morning.'

'What a morning. I slept with the bedroom door open. Ahh... then I got fresh chilly air at night. Argh, then I heard a strange noise. It awakened me at 5 a.m.—not an excellent way to wake from a dream. It shouldn't ruin my morning. I turned around and thought intensely of my beloved and Minnie.'

'Good, you could cuddle again and get more sleep.' I'm frosty.

'Yeah, it helped, Babe. I fell asleep again with a smile on my lips. At 7 a.m., I got up and responded to emails while eating oatmeal. Nothing from you?'

'Hm-mmm...' I mumble.

'I did exercises. And swimming. Afterwards, I bathed. And I newly trimmed Willy. Wow, as he has never been before.'

'Oh, my goodness. You didn't?'

'Sure, I did, Baby. I pick up from the rules of your nasty sessions that one should be shaved. Ha-ha, "in the face"? Mainly, be well-trimmed around the pecker and purse. Right?'

'He-he, I enjoy the funny way you can describe it.'

'Can you believe how nice and proud Willy got? He was thinking *much* of his Minnie.'

'Huh? Great. I hope that you both will become more energetic.'

'I gave myself a treatment on the legs. Jeez, and the groin. The entire lower part of the pelvis. So, it was all about Drake and Willy.'

'Huh, great. Continue treatment and training.' I stiffly smile.

'It's with shame that I confess. Baby, it's the first time I ever have trimmed Willy around the ears in such an intimate way.'

'Ohhh, I see.'

'A little funny, right? This, although, I told male patients to shave under the scrotum before treating. Are you getting in a better mood, Baby?'

'Hm. Not really. I'm outraged by your letter. I have no words for you. I'm still furious.'

'Don't worry of it, my precious. Come home to me. I'll take divine care of you.'

'Might be I'll get back home again. I don't know.'

'Please love me much again. I miss you, Sweet Pea. I need you here with me. You are my greatest love. I will not live without you.' The begging Basset Hound woofs.

'Umm ... at this moment I don't love you. I hope my dark, angry clouds will disappear.'

'Argh, Baby. You are my eternal love. Oh, and I've found your secret of the 'pantomime phenomenon,' we've had together. I understand what happens when you make those 'sensuous flowing waterfalls'—the ones I've been wondering off since when you first did it during a massive eruption of your climax. Wow, Sweet Pea, you can do something *extraordinary* that few others ever tried.'

'Ohhh, I see. What is it?'

'It comes from the so-called Skene glands. When we experience the waved washboard inside you, it becomes active. It swells during sexual stimulation. It activates the glands. Then it can ejaculate during an orgasm. The scientists mentioned the glands in the literature as "G-spot" or "U-spot" and called a female prostate.'

'Oh, I've heard about "G-spot" not about "U-spot". What is that?'

'The flushing water is a transparent thin liquid that cannot lubricate your vagina during lovemaking, because they react during the orgasm. Then it's too late.'

'What do you mean about too late?'

'The tricky thing with the anatomy is; it connects the tissue around these glands. It's connected to part of the clit and the vagina. With the right stimulation, the two react together. The result is your "flowing warm waterfall" from your front yard.'

Oh, that sounds interesting. I didn't know that.'

'Do you know what, Sweet Pea? When I get better at caressing you, I will find the points. I'll give you the best climax you've ever had.'

'I'm looking forward to get the pleasure, darling.'

'Yea, but we cannot rush it. We must give ourselves a flirtatious time of foreplay. It will be the most stunning job I can get. I'll gently massage you until you explode multiplied with pleasure.'

'I'm so proud that we've been lucky to find the spot sometimes, so I understand the anatomy of it now. You said that you only experienced it rarely by chance and you did not know what it was. Science says that it is an enriched *rare gift you possess.*'

'Thanks for the information. It's nice to feel special. I also enjoy your humour about Willy. It makes me laugh.'

'Glad you enjoy. I love to make you laugh. Then I see your lovely stunning white teeth. Your laughter makes your green eyes glow, Babe. Oh, boy, they twinkle bewitching. Sparkling as stars.'

'I'm *maybe* looking forward to seeing both of you. Best trimmed and smooth, shaved on your face, he-he. Let's see what I decide.'

'I'm glad we chatted, Baby. But unhappy to hear your depressed voice. It hurts so damn much to watch and listen to you feel so gloomy.'

'Today is a better day. Darling, I still love you a little.' I try to smile.

'Baby, now I must start my diligent work. I need to finish my brilliant presentation to the American's. Afterwards, I'll write in my treatment book. Oh boy, then the day over. I hope to get a friendly chat with you again before I go to bed.'

'Okay, let's count the days. *If* I come back. I will let you know.' Did I give him hope?

'Could you do Willy a favour and read a letter to Minnie? I hope that will bring the smile and laughter to your gorgeous lips. Maybe flashes to your glamourous eyes.'

'Yea, yea, fine, let's talk later. I must reflect on everything. Mwah. Bye Drake.'

'Thanks. Love you, Baby. Mwah, mwah. Bye.'

It dings on my Mac and I read Willy's mail to Minnie:

> Here's a special secret greeting to my dearest sweet little Minnie. D, he gave me much more attention than he has ever done. What is he planning? Do you think he and M have agreed on something we don't know? If you hear anything, you'll give me a squeeze, right?
>
> God help me! Do you know what he was doing? D smoothly shaved me naked. The long-haired salt-and-pepper bush disappeared around my pendant, where I save my treasured wealth in my golden purse. Wow! It tickled so much. Christ! The fool was clumsy and fumbling stupidly. Auch! God damn it! *He made me bleed!* In several parts, his sharp razor blade cut me half to death! What do you say to that? Wasn't it a miserable bloody dripping day for me? I couldn't get your help to hold and hug me tight and to stop the dangerous bleeding. Imagine if I bleed to death! I've found out that you can! Well, might be not that much bleeding. I survived—but only relatively.
>
> When I saw myself in the mirror, after my master had finished *cutting me to death*, I thought, *I am looking fresh and superb.* At first, I got scared that my Sweet Pea might not recognise me. *She doubtless could.* Once you grabbed me tenderly and sucked me gently in with your sweet soft lips around me, you'd know me. Last, your hot cockleshell is smooching me into your wet peachy Venus cave. Something you usually do so witchery arousing.
>
> You are my little spicy naughty Minnie girl. Well, don't think I mean wicked. I heard the birds twittering, that you can say 'naughty' in a sweet little way.
>
> I will only be super honey to you, so we must enjoy being together again, when you come back to me. I promise you,

and I understand by now that is not fun not being able to snuggle for you and warm myself in your warm moist cave. I now understand what it means to hunger for you.

You'll now get thrilled, Sweet Pea—or for sure, wet. I'm so glad when D told me about your secret of the 'pantomime phenomenon,' when you bathed me in your 'sensuous flowing waterfalls'. Wait with excitement and enjoy my sweet little pearl, now we know that little rare secret Minnie has. Sweet Pea, and we tried it several times together. That's what I hear in the bush. I don't mean 'the bush' as the naughty other female bush, but, yea, well, I mean… I'm not running around asking female strangers' bushes. It's as something you just say.

I'm looking even more forward to you coming back home, Sweet Pea, because we get along so well. I love you madly and deeply. Well, but now I know it's okay with you, so in secret I train every day to make the technique perfect for finding the lovely spots inside you. That way, you can bathe me in your purling magnificent 'Venus waterfalls' more often. Oh boy, because it's just *so* lovely and unique. We must do everything possible to take D and M there. Don't you think? I can hardly wait, but D whispers; 'Willy, be patient.' Shit! Drake can easily say that. It's hard to be tolerant when I don't know how.

At night, I dream of you, Sweetie, so I'm very stiff in the morning, and then I am *so* big. That's when I miss you the most. When we are alone we whisper sweet nothings to each other and have our little secret meetings—when your cockleshell clings to me before D and M awakens.

Well, I'm excitingly waiting. I will never be unfaithful to you, little Sweet Pea. You are my only one. Only you can make me ecstatic and satisfied. 'Willy, arm yourself with tolerance,' says Drake. Arms? What the hell does that mean? I got the gun loaded, and I'm not allowed to shoot it at full blast! What rubbish is he talking of? Even now, it's ready to shoot, and it's so hard to hit the minor keys on the PC with my proud raised head. I just want to squeeze the icing off.

Oops! By the way! I have an immense surprise for you, Sweetie. I believe you will embrace it with great joy. You will look even more stunning in it than you are. So far it must be a secret. I can brag, I believe. Oops, now don't get scared and worried, because I don't mean the 'surprises' you hate. It's an actual personal one—for you, from me.

Can you tell me how long the hair is on your cute little Mohawk? Do you think it's long enough for a tiny thing to get tied into it? Now you are on the verge of curiosity, right, Sweet Pea? Ha-ha, ha-ha. But you won't be told anymore. You can tolerantly wait—yes, you can.

Wow! It tickles so great now so I can't take it anymore. I'm getting mega big and blue in the head with this sexy writing. Drake is holding tight on to me, so I don't explode. Ouch! Whew! Uh oh… he is doing strange things with me, and practice his up and down movements, you know? Oh, my, Sweet Pea, do you think there might be more ink on the keys? Whoops! Now a tiny of the white sugary glaze comes out of my 'eye'. Oh, boy, Drake is driving me crazy! And I only want to explode in your tight peachy cave. Damn it! And you are not here, Sweetie, to gulp it. I better hurry and see if I can suck it back into me. Then I can save it for you, my little girl. Well, we'll see what happens.

I long for you, my precious little pearl. I got to run for now and clean up Drake's mess. The most arousing greetings from yours forever. I'm done by now and am relaxed.

High five, yours forever, aphrodisiac Willy.

*   *   *

Millions of women around the world get ejaculation with varying frequency. Around 10 to 54 percent of them ejaculate during sex.

The leading French researcher in the field, Samuel Salama, assessed, 'Women have the ability if their partners know what they are doing.' Samuel Salama of the French private hospital Parly II in Le Chesnay, in his research, analysed the fluid from seven women's ejaculations. For two women, it was identical to their urine. For the other five women, we also found an enzyme from the prostate that was mixed with the urine. According to Samuel Salama, there is no doubt that a female ejaculation flushes the vagina and makes life easier for the sperm on their way to fertilisation. The ejaculation fluid also has a lower pH value than the typical vagina environment. Thus, the environment becomes significantly less 'hostile' to the essential sperm.

A Danish study of a single woman's ejaculation found that only 50 percent of the ejaculated substance was urine.

It's all humbug that ejaculation only happens if you stimulate the G-spot. Ejaculation orgasms occur both by vaginal orgasm and stimulation of the clitoris. Ejaculation orgasms are not a recent phenomenon. The earliest descriptions of date go all the way back to Aristotle's time—three hundred years before our era. For the first time in the fourteenth century, it's described in Europe by a Dutch doctor, Laevenius Lemnius. He mistakenly considers it to be a kind of female semen.

I believe we've established that my phenomenon is not as rare as Drake makes it to be. Might be I'm wrong, but it's a bold trick for him to make me feel special. Within the past week, he has written several of those sweet and humorous texts to me, trying to affect my longing for the fantastic orgasms he can give me, and it's touching my wish for him. His sweetness and when he cares of me. I miss him, despite his betrayal, and I find the letters amusing, with his glorious sense of humour. Though, Drake pressures me to deicide, and he succeeded to arouse me, to want him close to me. Hungry and desperate as a female lion, I fall once again for his charm. I don't understand why I jump right into his love trap again, with his cunning act when he plays with my feelings. And what is this 'happy ending' about? Hmmm. It seems to be naughty!

As I have answered Drake, he has succeeded with his naughty plot, but can he succeed to get Mary back, while he got the attention away from his confession of the 'candy girls' in Macau. What will I do?

CHAPTER 16

WILLY STEERS THE STRINGS ON PUPPET MINNIE

Other people are not put on this earth to be mechanisms for you to achieve your ends.
Think about this until it really sinks in.

—Srikumar S. Rao

I still don't understand how Drake does his exquisite master tricks on me, when he hits on my lustful, malnourished Minnie. She misses the touches of his magical fingers on my horny pearl. Imagine that Willy and Minnie end up having an online chat of their two crazy masters. It's funny when they chat as two humans. He can see I'm online and then the speaker jingles on my computer. A Skype chat is about to be born, and it's Willy who wants to do sweet slandering with Minnie about Mary and Drake.

'Sweet ML, 4yeo. (for your eyes only) Do Willy a favour. Tell this to Minnie?' Ding. moggie-cat, 05:56 AM.

It is over midnight in Spain when his message jangle on my mac. I'm ready to go to bed, but I'm curious and want to know what he wants 'Hi, my beloved Minnie. C2c? (Care to chat?) about The Philippines?' Ding. moggie-cat, 05:56 AM 'Hi. cwyl. (Chat with you later)' Swoosh. g4ngzt3rmouse 00:57 AM. I'm frosty towards him, however I answer, and our crazy chat begins, as it's as a hide-and-seek game we are playing.

'Just 2 let u know. Whoops!' Ding. moggie-cat, 05:58 AM '??? Huh?' Swoosh. g4ngzt3rmouse. 05:58 AM.

'It's crazy. It's embarrassing for me.' Ding. moggie-cat, 05:59 AM

'5n. ^(Fine) What do you want to talk about?' Swoosh. g4ngzt3rmouse. 05:59 AM.

'Huh? Oh, it's not that easy to see what's up in the dark.' Ding. moggie-cat, 06:00

'Dark? Dgt ^(Don't go there)' Swoosh. g4ngzt3rmouse.

'Hmm! I'm only a 1-eyed insignificant creature! I can't c in the dark. D is asleep.'

'But ur ^(you're) on chat now.' Swoosh. g4ngzt3rmouse.

'Oh, Minnie, we have always an enjoyable time together when they were asleep. We cheat on them. Ha-ha. When they wake up, they c what we're doing.'

'WTF ^(What the f*ck) r u talking abt? ^(about)' g4ngzt3rmouse seems agitated.

'Willy! ILU. ^(I love you) U R 2cute. The innocence itself, and always there when he is in trouble. Phew, when he whacks me on my head.' moggie-cat smirks.

'Sweet W. Thank u for telling. But don't tell more.' g4ngzt3rmouse finds it strange, however I go along with his game and let him talk.

'D got his ass full by an angry M,' Ding 'Holy cow!' Ding. moggie-cat.

'???' g4ngzt3rmouse clearly know what he is talking about.

'In the night, she called. Ugh! He couldn't sleep anymore. Oh, boy!' moggie-cat got scared.

'Yea, I could sense something dishonest was afoot.'

'Sry! ^(Sorry) D. "forgot" 2 tell a major thing, while we were in Macau.'

'What r u talking abt?'

'Yay. The stupid dude had exposed me 2 something naughty last year.' Minnie and g4ngzt3rmouse can sense how both dudes are trembling in their pants.

'R u changing ur story?' g4ngzt3rmouse is frustrated.

'Damn, no! I'll tell u when u come home 2 me again. He-he, soon. I miss u.' moggie-cat is full of excuses.

'Ha-ha, ur good @ funny fairy tales. What is D up 2 now?' g4ngzt3rmouse giggles quietly and sense Minnie is missing him.

'Oh, that's sweet. It's great when I can make u laugh. Aww, then she squeezes around me with my beloved Minnie. She laughs so much. Then rush to the bathroom. Then she's beaming.' More giggling ensues from moggie-cat.

'Ha-ha, they're nuts.' Minnie worries and tries to send horny signals up to my brain, but g4ngzt3rmouse plays the Frosty Ice Queen.

'They're crazy! Mostly with each other. Can't u feel it 2?' moggie-cat tries to get back in good grace.

'Feel what?' I'm upset. He apparently tries to rip me out of the torments of my misery over his last deceiving drama.

'Don't be afraid. M is stressed. Worried. She has not given me any thought.' Minnie sobs over my frustration, because my body is still trembling over his deceitful letter. Though I was trying to be kind and understanding.

'Whoa! That's awful. She must look after u. Tell me if she doesn't. Otherwise, I need 2 have a harsh word with M. Oh, my, and of the need for u.' moggie-cat plays the big hero.

'Mary has only 1 thing in her head—2 get everything stable. She can't relax.'

'She must be as wonderful as usual. Xoxoxo. When u come home, Mary must be as good as when we parted.'

I wonder if that's an order from Drake or Willy, and I try to shut my inner passionate feelings for him behind my safe icy iron wall.

'D disturbs her. And her kids. And Paul. She is stressed. Distracted.' I feel he sends more stress up to my brain, while reading his childish crap, and I get irritated.

'Put that bastard in a cage for monkeys. Flopper is a wicked baboon. Christ, every primate in his monkey cage is stupid. I will slap him hard in his reckless head. Yuck!' Drake's sickening thought of whacking Paul's swizzle stick scares me.

'Nte!' ^(Not that easy) Swoosh. g4ngzt3rmouse.

'What if I get infected from those nasty hookers he bangs? Awful!'

'U won't. I'm not banging with Paul.'

'Hmm, I should whack both of his heads.' Bizarre moggie-cat.

'Yuck!' His comment makes me wrinkle my face in disgust.

'I'm glad u bit him as often as u could. Ugh!'

'Bit him?' moggie-cat must have forgotten I suck Paul's massive bratwurst.

'Good, he didn't spread his nasty, inflamed buds to u. Oh, my sweet, beloved Minnie.'

'U know I did many tests.' g4ngzt3rmouse justify herself.

'Oh? How do u suggest 2 make M joyful again? What sort of funny tricks should we find? To make her laugh again?' moggie-cat smirks.

'DON'T SCREW AROUND WITH OTHER WOMEN!' I scream and get more upset.

'OMG! I got so scared. M wasn't happy with D; I hid near his thighs.'

'How could u?'

'Jeez, I'm wishing this hullabaloo in paradise would go over soon.' Imaginative, I see him whining and scared, as little Willy trembles and hides in Drake's boxers.

'We sobbed the entire night.' g4ngzt3rmouse weeps. Hopefully, he can sense I'm still angry and a frozen black Piranha to him. Where it defrosted, he should swim fast, because they consider the black piranhas the most dangerous and aggressive toward humans. Though, it's said the Piranha is not *that* dangerous as you might think, and I'm sure they ever have eaten any humans alive.

'Oh boy, Minnie! My goodness. Scared and upset I was. Mostly of how upset D was. I tried 2 calm him. Argh, it didn't help. I know he's always so honest!' Christ! Moggie-cat lies.

'Come on!' *Does Willy really believe that?*

'He got his neck full. M was furious, of the prostitutes he had banged.' moggie-cat tries to justify.

'Yea, u said so.' I wonder if he realises he has no control of his own lies. Jeez, when he suddenly changed the story.

'We must accept the bollocking that comes.'

'The bomb smashed her hard to the floor.' g4ngzt3rmouse gets a terrified flashback.

'Sweet Pea, it completely freaked us out of the box.'

'It's nice to know u got scared.' I'm satisfied if that's true.

'Drake wanted not 2 hurt M.'

'He should have thought of that sooner. He hurt me.' Angry g4ngzt3rmouse.

'Sweetie, D. luvs her more than I've ever seen him luv any other woman.'

'Bullocks! It upsets me. There was a thunderstorm and lightning in M's body.'

'I know him well. Trust me. We have been partners throughout our lives.' *That, I'm sure, he tells every woman in the bush.* Though full of worry, Willy tries to explain and excuse himself.

'Her heart pounded as a wild twister. Her blood boiled in rage. She wanted to smash him to the floor. Hit him with a hot frying pan.' g4ngzt3rmouse anger.

'Sounds dangerous!' Ding. moggie-cat 'M. fainted. Her tears rolled down her cheeks as an unstoppable flushing waterfall. Ay-yay-yay! Reaching my Mohawk.' Swoosh. g4ngzt3rmouse.

'Huh? Oh no!' moggie-cat get scared.

'Yea, M. hit the marble floor. She got a big bump back on her head.'

'Gosh almighty! Minnie!'

'A dangerous tsunami of sorrowful water came over me. No warnings of a catastrophe.'

'It's death-defying. Goodness gracious me!' moggie-cat gets shaken.

'Holy moly! I virtually drowned. Dear Jesus. I was damn lucky I survived the flooding.' It practically flooded Minnie when I break into tears again, grabbing a Kleenex and dry the tears that fall as I recall the devastating day.

'Don't swim in such a dangerous flooding, Minnie. I frightened can imagine poor u. Phew! Being splashed out into the sea. I hear it can happen.'

'Ha-ha, ha-ha.' I laugh in between my anger, tears and sadness.

'Yikes, little girl. I would have to conduct a rescue search for u. I promise u I would never give up. Phew, even if I had to paddle in a small rubber boat. Oh, boy, over the entire oceans.'

Drake has a hilarious way of saving his ass—painting himself a the titanic moggie-cat hero.

'Oh, no! Sweet Pea, I can't bear the thought of you lost at sea alone.'

'Sucks u! I can imagine you floating around there. Alone!' I rudely reflect.

'Oh, sweet Babe. Don't say that.'

'Yea, all alone in ur deceit.' *Best you drown!* g4ngzt3rmouse devious muse.

'Then u swim in the ocean, alone. Boohoo without ur W. It petrifies me. I'm ur solid mast—firmly rooted in u. And get dry land under us again.'

'U have not shown yourself to be a solid mast.'

'I'm ecstatic that things did not go that badly. I'm not a capable swimmer.'

'Ha-ha, W. D and u swim as a clumsy walrus.'

'I've seen when u and M swim naked in the pool.' Smirky smiley from moggie-cat.

'Well observed—even though u sound worried at first. Next you smirked.'

'It looks enchanting. I can c u enjoy the water soaking the Mohawk. Wow, tickling ur soft labia. Hitting ur precious pearl. It must feel good.'

'Shut up, Willy! It devastated me. D. ruined the relationship.' *That's the last straw! Get out of my way!* 'I don't know if I want to come back.'

'Oh, no! Sweet Minnie, I'm shattered,' Willy and moggie-cat cries crocodile tears.

'Can u believe it? That D could be like that? Honestly?'

'No, sweet luv, I don't understand him.' moggie-cat's next lie.

'We luv each other so much. Why did D. do it?' g4ngzt3rmouse is frustrated.

'Could M be so wicked to leave him?' His question is full of worry.

'Yup! I don't give a damn. I've had it up to here. He should have told everything. Before they got too involved.'

'I angrily bit him in his thighs to get him to confess to you.' Yea, moggie-cat believes he is a hero.

'Shame on him. It's appalling. Wicked boy! Awful. A pain!' Angers g4ngzt3rmouse. Minnie thunders and I want to smack the lid on the computer.

'It was ghastly of him. Yuck! Foolish Asian tries at that strip club. I didn't want 2. I was looking for u, my little Minnie.'

Whoops! *He admits it!* Gawky! This tells me right here that he did it during our relationship. Scruffy dude.

'WTF, Willy? After we met?. Honestly! Just u wait!' g4ngzt3rmouse gets more irritated and can't continue the conversation. But my angriness keeps on.

'I knew for sure u were not among the barely dressed tiny girls.' Smirks the cracked moggie-cat.

'I should leave u. Damn it. Betraying me.' An outrageous chill passes through my body.

Shut up! D. screwed up enormously in his eagerness to gossip.

'Shit! Oh, boy, the idiot had to check it out. Nutcase!' Bingo! *Does he even know what I write?* Willy is hissing and admits he was with a call-girl. The goofy can't control his lies.

'I will leave you to your own rotten state.'

'No! Don't leave us, Minnie. D. could have lived his life with his scruffy, gloomy secret.'

'Ur not a gracious gentleman. Not telling me the truth.'

'D. is always honest. He could not live with the darkness.' None of them are not rational with their head and tries to sneak around in their sneaky lies.

'I told D. he must tell u. I'm proud of him, Minnie. He's nice. An honourable man.'

'R U serious? M would have found out with time.' g4ngzt3rmouse let the conversation continue, even she didn't want to.

'D. hasn't drilled me into many nasty caves to search for u, my sweet Minnie. Our detective work was at street level. Ha-ha. We only played dice and cards. Not digging in shadowy, smelly caves.' Bizarre! Revolting moggie-cat.

Willy tries proudly to protect his cheating master. I'm shaken. Self-righteousness!

'Whoa! There is angry airborne suffering for him. M. struggles to find the luv again.'

'This is where u need to help me. Please, Minnie.'

'M goes through loads of suffering. Because of his dreadful deception.' Minnie fumes, I rage, and have yet not seen everything Drake gets Willy to write between the lines.

'Although I heard that M had forgiven him for letting me behave in that horrible way. She might not have forgiven him yet. Right?' moggie-cat worries.

'That's true! I've not. It's not forgotten.'

'Help me make M understand. D luvs her more than life.'

'Bah, ha-ha. Baloney.'

'True! More than anyone else on earth.' moggie-cat tries to sway g4ngzt3rmouse.

'Really?' and I lift my eyebrow. 'If you did, you would not betray me!'

'Baby, there are only the 2 of us. Thick as thieves.'

'Who does that if you genuinely love the other person?'

'No 1 can separate us. Nor being used for anyone other than 2 satisfy our luv.'

'Hmm... I don't forget such things.' I fall for his trick between my sobs, and I'm close to forgive him, but it's tricky.

'U and I are happiness. We're in luv for the 2 of them.' Ding. moggie-cat.

'Argh, it's that idiot she has lived with. It made her helpless.'

'I understand. U have been through much.'

'I hate when people lie,' Minnie complains in despair. And now I'm using my past as a heedless excuse.

'D. must make M. find the light in God again. Find faith and trust again.'

'Trust Drake?' Does Willy not know that his puppet master is a nonbeliever?

'Yea. He promises never to get separated. I heard that myself. He had a grave chat with his Father God.'

'Eh? God? U R an atheist.' I realise Willy got into the same snare as I. His words hit me hard, as he continues to exploit my religious beliefs.

'Sry. ^(Sorry) God is over my understanding and senses.'

'I hope he will never expose us 2 something as that again. Otherwise, it's over. *Completely*.' Did I give him hope?

'I'm not sitting on D's shoulders as a listening bird. I know my right place.' The answer confirms, the *dickhead* is a nonbeliever.

'No more chances!' Swoosh. g4ngzt3rmouse.

'I promise it will never happen again, my beloved. Xoxoxo.' moggie-cat is steering the strings on the sexy little Minnie puppet.

'Next time, the hot frying pan will hit him hard,' I'm bossily. Ready to give up.

'They luv each other—at least M does. That's why u and I r together. We need to express our luv for each other.' moggie-cat trusts.

'I hope u will be better.' Swoosh. g4ngzt3rmouse.

'Trust me, my beloved. There is nothing better in life than our special luv.' A smirky smiley. moggie-cat imagines I have forgiven and forgotten everything.

'Watch ur D They can't mess up again. This is crazy.'

'Deal, Baby. We'll stick together. Us 2. Right? Can I trust u? ILU.' Ding. moggie-cat.

'M might forgive him. Bye.' Swoosh. g4ngzt3rmouse disconnect Skype. I sincerely hope that Drake hates himself for what he has done to me. He genuinely has hurt my feelings. We say goodbye and disconnect.

CHAPTER 17

THE ANTHROPOMORPHIC CHICKEN GYRO GEARLOOSE

I have not failed. I've just found 10,000 ways that won't work.

—Thomas Edison

As days go by, suddenly a strange conversation appears between Drake and me, as he wants to tell his wicked nightly story. He must be bored, and I'm not sure he is normal.

'Hi Baby, you know what? I tested new skills on Willy.'

'Oh, boy. What now?' I ask.

'He tried to tell me he was nervous of hanging with his head loose.'

'Who hangs loose?'

'Willy! Imagine if I dropped him! He could get sucked into the exhaustion. Then it would go wrong with his poor bald head.'

'Ha-ha, ha-ha. That would look funny. A minced sausage.'

'I told W it was an exercise. Jeez! To do for his bodily release.'

'Well, well, what are you up to now, darling?'

'Yea, Willy was distressed. He got scared. Did I mean we should get divorced? Would I decapitate him?'

'Maybe I should decapitate Willy from his unfaithful master.'

'Oh, no! Willy would never see and touch his Minnie again. "No, no," Willy yelled to me. "Please, Drake, I will be nice and decent." I have always been too shy to let W. "hang loose" You know that, Baby.'

'I do not understand what you are talking of rubbish.'

'I have always protected W. in my pants. I told W., "I want to regain my confidence in territory again."'

'I'm worried. Hanging loose? Protected in your pants, darling?'

'Yea, Willy asked, "Do you mean the territory here in Batangas? Or in the pool and the house?"'

'Darling, who protected W. from the "sweet candy" in Macau? It was not you!'

'Sorry, Baby.' He looks worried.

'I don't like you walking naked around with W. hanging loose when I'm not there.'

'Baby, I need to get out of my shell.'

'Christ, Drake! I can picture a horrible image. What if the cleaning lady sees you running around with a dangling hairy sausage? He-he. Oh, my, and a sagging "purse" with no "gold" in it?' I joke.

'I feel jollier to get rid of that shell. Baby, I love to walk around naked.' Blink, blink.

I get it! Drake needs to flash himself around for those tiny wiggling women around him. He hated it when Kate did the same in her apartment or ran around, flashing her bare boobs in front of others. He complained so often of it. I wonder if it's normal when you get older. Well, it's not to me!

'In fact, I find it's depressing you expose W. like that. What if a foul person comes into the house unexpectedly?'

'Don't worry, Baby, we are careful. You are the most sacred to me.' He smirks.

'Oh, fuff and whoops, she tries to snatch him away from me. Uh-oh. Then Willy will stink awful after his nose has been in a foul reek cave. Yuck! No, that may not happen!' I can't picture Drake running around naked with a swinging, flabby W. 'Hide Willy safety behind your towel! Don't you think it sounds reasonable, darling?'

'Willy and I dream all the time of your sweetness. Your lovely apricot scents. It's nearly too much. But nicely as a special sexy bouquet of exotic flowers.' Drake indulges me, hoping he can get to me.

'That's why Willy should not hang loose, buddy! If you want me.' I crossly snare.

'I can't help it, Baby. W. is getting mad without getting deep into Minnie's cave.'

'Yuck, a dip in another musty, rotten cave will make him smell foul.' I snappily answer.

'Oh, my lovely Sweet Pea. Willy wants to cuddle inside Minnie's special washboard. It gives us so much joy and passion.'

'Are you trying to calm me, darling? Are you even being honest with me?' I growl.

'You are as passionflowers, Baby. I don't want anyone else but you.' Drake sure knows how to flatter.

'You don't always take care of W's shyness. You may let him peek to see the glittering stars. Then tell him to hop behind the towel again. Best in your boxers!'

'Tell M. not to worry.'

'Ha-ha, how much pot did you smoke? Well, best I find W. safe in your pants again.' I marvel and don't believe Drake will hide him there.

'We will always behave decently, Sweet Pea. Hide well,' Drake promises, but I'm not sure I can trust him.

'Remember to close the zipper. Imagine if Willy crash, bang, falls out by mistake. Someone could run him over at full blast. Shit, by a roaring crazy truck driver. Crash!' I imagine the worst scenarios of an awful pecker accident—smashed, howling as an injured dog and looking as an overcooked crushed sausage, lying dead as a flabby hot dog in musty bread.

'Yea, it's funny when I forget to zip. Willy can always feel the draft. He yells as a lunatic.'

'Ha-ha. Typically, you only realise it when I tell you, darling.'

'Then, I perceive that it's crazy. Ha-ha, it's witty in a way. But I have become good at recalling it now. Willy has no trouble in breathing since you left us. No way! He enjoys none of it in the surroundings here.'

Strange! Few minutes ago, Drake told me Willy was 'hanging loose' in the fresh air. Now I'm confused. I should compost Drake in the waste grinder to minced meat and flush the dude in the sewer.

'Darling, you often forget to close the lower door. You think it's a fast running train. Ha-ha, with automatic doors.'

'Holy cow! How funny that you said so, Baby.'

'Just imagine it. Living in a fast running train? Willy will fall out. Crash! Bang! Hit by it.' I worry, because Drake often is a careless person and forgets to zip his zipper.

'I might invent an "automatic zipper" for pants, Baby. Ha-ha, ha-ha.' He laughs loudly at his own joke of being the anthropomorphic chicken Gyro Gearloose.

'No. Oh my golly gosh! I must stop with these nutty, thoughts, darling. You always steal my ideas. Jeez, then claim it's your invention. Ha-ha.'

Drake does whatever it takes to impress me. He shamelessly stole my ideas and designs for some of our bedding products.

'No. It's only you who can protect Willy. Ahh... mostly when Minnie sucks him right into the cave. Wow! Minnie is good at that. I love it! Inside you, Willy feels protected from dangers. But no worries, Babe. I take wonderful care of him.'

'Huh? How?' I worry. What is that supposed to mean?

'It scares Willy if I don't do it. You have promised me a fuming beating if I'm not good to Willy. He is glad for your protection. You're the nicest lady on earth.' Smirking cat.

'Yeah, darling, I'm working hard on keeping the pecker in good shape.' *It's a tough job to do, when Willy won't get up from his sagging sleep,* spins in my mind.

'I also started to "shock" Willy—with my rhythmic impulses. Aw, he got worried. What if I burned him with my treatment?'

'Well, shoot loose. See if W survives! Ha-ha.'

'I do it up along the shaft. Ahem! Ohhh... It feels *so*... nice afterwards. So much extra-warm blood comes rushing into Willy. Baby, that's a wonderful sign, you know.'

'Let's hope you can keep it there.' Replies the frosty Snow Queen.

'It scared Willy! He thought I would execute him. Hmm... ahhh ... strange tinkling electrical impulses. "Oh, my, is it dangerous?" W asked and tried to hide.' I picture Willy as he tries to push himself into Drake's front.

'But it didn't work, buddy. Willy had to get out. Then accept what was coming. I told him he must prepare for Minnie. What do you think, Baby? Oh, my life! Then I sent "shocking laser booms" under W's purse.'

'Hopefully, there is a jackpot. Ha-ha, maybe the gold is coming fast to your sack.' I wish.

'Baby, I think I have prostate cancer. That's why Willy doesn't work. That's why I'm abusing him with these stunning effects.' (In the therapeutic world, it's used successfully to treat various health conditions.)

'What?' I scream. 'Now you lie to W. with a lame excuse.'

'I'm hoping I can get Willy out of his laziness. Wishing him to get up on the chair again. I am tired that he has retired. Can you picture us as a retiree?'

'Darling, I understand you're disappointed.'

'From the first time I met you, Baby—oh my dear, how nice it was. Christ, I fell in love with you right away. Willy behaved proudly with his long, sturdy neck. Right? Hurrah, and with his head highly raised. Right?' Drake waves with his hands jubilant in the air.

'Hmm.'

'Your little gem insanely captivated me and Willy. Wauw! You surely knew of the art of lovemaking. You were way too superior to me.'

'Aww, so sweet, darling. Are you trying to flatter me?'

'Good Lord! No! But I couldn't get enough of your little pearl. And your smashing body. Willy told me I should make sure we became lovers.' Drake exaggerates and brags proudly, as he is trying to sweet-talk me even more.

'Okay, darling, I must go now. Talk to you another time.'

'Bye, my love.'

Several days passed when Drake calls me as loads of my boxes with clothes had arrived in The Philippines.

'Hi, sweet Baby. All your boxes are here now.'

'Nice.'

'I could see that many exciting things reminded me of you. Sexy and delightful. I felt touched when I started sorting it out. Ha-ha, Willy played it cool. He wouldn't get up to show too much excitement. Jesus! I walked naked around in a daze and was talking to you.'

'Is it all there?'

'Yea, I think so, Babe. It arrived yesterday. But for heaven's sake! Am I stupid? You weren't even here. Imagine I talked to myself and Willy and you as an Old Norse from Jerusalem.'

'Eh? You know I'm in Spain. Right?'

'Yeah!. This morning Willy was so excited. Boo—I caringly removed W. to the side. "Downer!" He said. Please tell that to Minnie.'

'Huh? I sense that you want to justify something.'

'Aw, don't be like that, Babe. Well, I said to W., "It's only M's clothes I'm hanging up!" Ugh! Willy was sad. And went into a relaxed position.'

'I suppose it's my clothes, you're unpacking. I hope you treat W. with dignity.'

'Yeah! I was silly with the clothes I hugged.'

'Have you stopped swinging W. around naked? Stopped yelling at him? Ha-ha, not squeezing the life out of him.'

'Oh, boy. I'm whacky, Baby. Though, I'm becoming content with W. again.'

'Tell me if you still smash W. You will get ten times back by me.' I'm close to death in a massive bout of laughter asking this.

'Sure, Sure Sweet Pea, Willy will gossip. I'm so aware of his welfare now. I hope you're not sinful.'

I scratch my head over such an impudent remark.

'Has W. looked around the corners?'

'Yes. I'm working on fixing them firm. I don't know what I can use them for—because Willy is the primary star. Right?'

'Check if "buttock one and two" are doing well—you love when I ask of your balloons.' I truly enjoy D's butt.

'Who needs such a pair of Butt Cheeks? Christ, even I often pretend those two fellas are gay. Stupidly, I wiggle around with them. Do you think I'm gay?'

'I hope not, darling.'

'I promise I'm only for you, Sweet Pea! You can count on that. Willy will not stick his neck out between those two big Butt Cheeks.'

Given Drake's handsome face and the way he does his waggling booty act, Willy should know that Drake might want to use him for that. Willy doesn't know; Drake never came out of the closet.

'I saw them just briefly. They looked lovely when you were wiggling around naked. Greet the Butt Cheeks.' I wrinkle my face while giggling.

'Ugh, Yuck, not to greet those two old Butt Cheeks. W has different exercises to do. The star needs to rise proud for you. With devotion, W. loves you. Stay true to me, Sweet Pea. I promise you; we'll never fail you again, my sweetheart.'

'Okay. Promises I'm not so sure of I believe in.'

'It's time for us to take a bath. Willy says I have become much more aware of his well-being. It's about time too! I have neglected myself for many years. So, help me, God. I told Willy; it will help his libido.'

'Ha-ha, ha-h, ha-ha.' I'm practically lying on the floor laughing my booty off over this comical story.

'Without W knowing nothing, I took this fantastic, lifelike, black thing. "Yes, it should absolutely be black, so I can't see squat in front of me." W. shouted. Sweetie, will you believe it? I took one of your sexy nightgowns. Picture this, that I have put it on top of a pillow. Then it lies in bed as I cuddled the silky thing. Wow! It has loads of nasty tickling fringes underneath. I can't leave it alone. I sniff and pet it. Jeez, as if my nose and hands have "fringes fetish". Ha-ha, ha-ha. Yes, there it's again—my nuttiness.'

'Thanks darling, for the picture you gave me in my head. Yuck! But hilarious!' I ponder if he has tried it.

'It ended up signalling to Willy. Will you believe it? We thought you were back.'

'No, no, I'm not getting back. I'm still in my thinking process—whether I want you back.' I'm playing the cold-hearted, iron woman.

'Both of us were so delighted and floating. Wow, on a blue cuddling cloud. Ready to enjoy myself intensely with you. I looked at Willy and saw he was excited to get into your cave. I was sending hot impulses through my soft, warm hands to W. Christ! he got enormous. Spot-on into his swollen head. Imagine what it looked like. Big, proud and purple—it's true. I was!'

'Hmm, thanks for the image.' It gave me repulsive pictures in my head of what Drake did.

'So, Willy was pushing, as he could sense your delicate skin. Boo, bubba loo, long Pinocchio nose. Willy could not scent your orangey. Your sweet Minnie is always so nice and clean. He sensed you in a neutral attraction kind of way.'

'Please stop, Drake!' Sickening!

'Ha-ha, only you have it in you. You can get me completely out of my flips, Babe. Whoa! Willy rose from his otherwise oh-so-lazy life.'

'Well, now I know what to give you next time I want to fornicate.'

'I felt what made me wacko. It was the shady fake silky thing. Soft as your skin. On your stomach. And around your little Mohawk. It turned me on. Ready to be your action hero. Man, I was excited.'

'Next time, I'll give you a black negligee to hug.' I imagine how much I've been working on Willy, only to have nothing happen, so my work has been in vain.

'Ha-ha, Willy gently crawls up onto what he believed was you. Ay caramba! W freaked out! Something weird was going on there. He thought he could sense your Mohawk. Pointing as an arrow, so he knows which way he shall aim. It so smartly, Babe. Even a half-blind one-eyed bloke as him can find the cave. But he couldn't find you, as he hit the fake fringes. What the hell was I thinking?'

'Yea tell me. Sounds as a unique night.'

'Willy was completely blue in his head with concern. Could he have gone wrong in town? He asked; *has Minnie's virginity grown together?* Man, I confused W! He couldn't grasp a fiddly squat of it. Then the phone rang—*bling, bling*. I turned on the light. Shit!'

'Who was calling?' And Drake continues his blabbermouth.

'Jeez, it was you, Babe. I had tricked Willy again. Made a "fictitious Mary" out of a pillow and your nightgown. Yea, I tell you, it was loads I exposed W. to that night. Oh, it sucked—especially when he is disabled. Phew! And have only one eye to cry and splash golden happiness with. He had not an eye dry. What do you think? What should I do, Babe?'

'Wag it off, dude. Make space for the next part of gold. But leave my negligee alone!'

'Oh boy, I'm not in control when you are not here. Stupidly I arrange women's clothes! Am I a drag queen? Well, I have never known such a weakness. Baby, I want to quit now. I need to dry my exploded head. Nice talking to you. I'm so relieved. Phew, and relaxed so I could sleep.'

He is rejoicing in high relief and happiness. The silent wet splash of blobbing juice is on the sheet, pillow and my negligee.

Drake is trying to affect my sexuality, and it's obvious he speaks much of my hunger for intimacy, then of how good and robust he and Willy are. It sounds as an inferiority complex. Being a woman in my best age, craving for emotion, tenderness, and make love with him, I am sure he is hoping that he can control me with his nasty story—keep me turned on and captivated. It's a clever and bold manoeuvring of my yearnings for love and tender intimacy.

Will I ever get the full package, when he brags *so* much of what he can do with his woodpecker? There has been no actual boning—only finger work on my pearl, then talk, talk, *talk*, and Drake's writing. I think it's entirely in his mind, though he has once again got me on his track, and in the words of Joseph Wood, 'In a cat's eye, all things belong to cats.'

CHAPTER 18

SMOKING DEMONS AND A FACELIFT

> But even the craziest idea can work its way into your mind if
> you're lonely and grief-stricken and someone keeps harping
> on it. It can *wriggle* in there like a bloodworm, and lay its
> eggs, and pretty soon your whole brain is squirming with
> maggots.
>
> —Stephen King

Let's endure you with smoking loads of intoxicating pot, release the psychoactive chemical before we let the brain wriggling with nasty bloodworms. Next following a stunning facelift, because the women need a makeover, get big breast implants and do the liposuction.

After many weeks in Spain and numerous Skype conversations rapidly passed, Drake and I got friends again. After reflecting over the massive betrayal, I finally take the long twenty-hour flight back to The Philippines, because I must find a solution to our relationship. I get blushing hot on my cheeks, eyeing Drake outside the noisy arrival hall of Manila's massive Airport. With a gigantic smile, he holds a basket of sticky rice with a lovely scent and slices of the fragrant dark yellow delicious mango in his hand.

He is gorgeous, standing there among the millions of other rushing travellers from the entire world. My rapid pulsating heart immediately melts, as my worried thoughts of our sour issues disappear. A plopping wave of warm assurance passes through my veins, and I appreciate how he shows me genuine tenderness, as he embraces me, and thousands of butterflies' flutter mellow and eagerly in my stomach.

'Oh, my God! The Philippines has the best tasting sweet mangos in the world!' I cheer of joy.

'Oh, you are so adorable. I missed you so much, Sweet Pea.' Then he hands over the basket and hugs me tenderly, as his rasping voice whispers the loving words into my ear. I take it in together with his embrace, and pleasant hot chills remind me of how I love his tender hands, his caring embraces when he hugs and kiss me warmly.

So far, I have buried my entire life under an avalanche of secrets and lies, and my love for Drake only exists because I don't know how I shall feel of him. Love him or not! He closes his hand tightly around mine, and I'm floating on a mellow pink cloud, suddenly pondering, *I don't understand why he lies so much.*

I don't get it. It's not of what Drake has done to me, but it's of what he genuinely stands for—being mean with his lies! Unwisely, I'll not see it in the eyes, that he lies so much, but his betrayal broke my heart, and I'm distraught. It's so painful. I've always assumed I had experienced actual pain, but I didn't realise it before he sent me his awful letter. This is now my big issue, so I must get it solved before I decide if I want to stay with him. During our two-hour drive back to Batangas, we talk about the letter, and suddenly, he begins ruthlessly to psychoanalyse me.

'Baby, it sits in you from your childhood to be distrustful. That's why you so easy and often get those mood swings. I grasp you're working on it. I've seen a change in you so far.'

The seriousness in his voice sends a terrible shock through me.

'They're not mood swings, darling. I was distraught. You lied to me. I asked you many times; is there something I should know?' My comment seems to surprise him as I defend myself.

'I'm your Jesus. You are my MM. Baby, my love for you is unlimited.'

'Do you mean that?' Gazing at him while I'm blushing.

'I will always stand on the high bridge of the ship. Then steady hold on tight to my Magdalene.' He smiles worried, turns his head to me for two seconds.

'I disgust lies. I had a bad quivering response in my stomach that you had been with others.'

'Baby, I'll never let you go.'

'You were not honest with me, darling. You told me you always said no to other women. You lied!'

'I was not with other women. We only played dice.' He sighs profoundly.

'You proposed to me in Macau. And now in your letter. Then you tell me you are still married. Want to apply for divorce.' I stare at him with a grim expression, studying him carefully.

'Babe, you think I'm lying. I'm not. Then you get upset at me.' Clinging firm to the steering wheel.

'Honey, you can't marry another woman when you already are married. Not even ask for her hand. What are you expecting?' I shake my head. 'I'm not even divorced yet! It's cruel. It hurts my feelings.'

'Why not? I can ask when I want to. You are too dense, Baby.'

'I have based my entire life on the lying from others. It's too much. I don't need this shitty crap from you.' In anger, I pinch my eyes together and feel like crying.

'It's an expression of your own inner frustration. Argh, Mary, it's not soothing for you.'

Does he imagine I cannot recognise his toxic tendencies? I don't get it; he needs to lie and present a changed story than what is true.

'Argh! Your atomic bomb exploded right into my face. Damnit darling!'

'It gets better when the heavy sea has settled in the ocean. When there are no more high waves in your disturbed mind.'

'I was lonesome. Distressed. Missing you crazy. Reading it got the bloodworms to wriggle. They laid trillions of seeds.' Pausing and star bitterly at him.

'Baby, the rough waves will flatten out. Slowly slide out to sea again.'

'Jeez, my brain is twisting with angry maggots.' I sense it irritates him and hear my distress.

'The waves will reach the sand on the shore. Drown your angry maggots. It will over time disappear.' Damn, he is too calm.

'I do everything to make our lifestyle possible. Darling, you are not paying to anything.'

'I have no money. You said you wanted to live with me. That you would pay.'

'Yea, ha! I pay for equipment. Lent you money. Settled your accountant debt. And bank.'

'Sweet Pea, I'm with you—although it can hurt when you get into imbalance. I stand by your side as the rock. Lean on it. It doesn't move. My belief and confidence in you are fully there.'

'I don't know if my belief is there no more.' My voice appears worried.

'My love for you is still growing, Baby. Don't give up.'

'I fund you in every project. I have set up a company in Hong Kong. And the Philippines. It's frustrating if I can't trust you,' I want to trust him.

'I see you in despair when you fight against your demons. They are spinning as storms in your heart. You can trust your Jesus. I'll take care for you.'

'Eh? What do you mean by my demons?'

'With my calmness and guiding, it will give you peace again. Don't allow any ill intentions from others to tear you away from me,' Drake is too irritating calm, offering me a loving smile.

I notice he flip the roles where he pretends to be noble, right, virtuous, caring, and I am evil, selfish, cruel and immoral.

'Do you believe I'm possessed by the devil?' It worries me.

'Well! Yes! I see you sickly possessed. Your smoking demons are challenging to handle. We will get them too. We'll get your other angry demons, too. I'll drive them out of you.' He sounds as he wants to practice exorcism, evicting demons, that he believes I'm possessed from.

'Honey, you are aware of I quit smoking, right?' I try to defend myself.

'Babe, they do everything to push us apart. But they can't. You get frustrated and afraid that I will not care for you. The demons are grasping on the weakens of your faith in me.' The exorcist seems to enjoy of having control over me.

In a Roman Catholic context, exorcist may refer to a cleric who has been ordained into the minor order of exorcist, or a priest who has been mandated to perform the rite of solemn exorcism.

—Wikipedia

'Eh, I don't believe I'm possessed by demons.'

'You've been crazy obsessed with those fags. Is it because of what the letter said? The demons did everything to tear us apart. I guarantee that you smoked in Spain! I can smell it on your skin. In your kiss.'

'Okay, I smoked in Spain. You shouldn't be able to smell it.' Freak!

'They have taken over your mouth. Your throat. And lungs. It does not make you attractive as my girlfriend. Do you ever think you can do what I ask you to do?' He angers.

'What?' How rude of him. 'I don't get it. Where comes such a devilish idea from.' I am appalled and try to guard myself.

'Did you gain weight, Mary?' He suddenly changes topic. 'Ha-ha, you've got a bit of a fatty tummy.' Laughing loud he sarcastic taps me on the stomach.

'Shut up, Drake! What a cheekiness.'

'The doctors perform good liposuctions here in The Philippines. Ha-ha, ha-ha.'

'Huh? I don't want such.' His strange imprudent comment offends me.

'Your smoking makes your skin ugly, Mary. Saggy. It smells horrible.'

'What the hell is wrong with you, Drake?'

'You look as you have smoked too much pot, Mary. Maybe you should consider a facelift!' He grabs my non-wrinkled cheek and pulls the skin downwards.

'Facelift! What a prick you are.'

'That's why I don't want to kiss you. It's disgusting! Then you get frustrated.'

'Why so mean? First you were sweet and loving.'

'You stink.' He continues criticising me. 'I lose the desire to have sex with you. That's why I can't get Willy proud.' I pick up between the lines that, in his mind, I am not the ideal woman. I massively regret being back.

'What does it have to do with Willy? Jeez, that's not what we were chatting about.' The frustration shows over my face.

'Bloody hell, Mary! You respond with inner irritation—as you did it as a child.'

'My childhood? Why are we talking about that now?'

'Oh boy, as if it were your destiny. It makes you insecure. It sets you on fire. Then you set passion to the smokes.'

I am close to explode in anger over his petty arguments and want to smoke *now*, but behave and continue, listening to the complaining chatterbox.

'I'm glad you understand things are falling into place in our lives. Even if we must go through a process to get ourselves rearranged. And we will, Babe.'

'What the hell are you talking about, Drake?'

'We've so far succeeded much. So, will we continue to do it?' Then his sweet smile turns up, and he changes the topic.

'Truly! You lost me there.'

'Let's talk of the business instead. Your manuscript. Of your marriage. Your life.'

'Manuscript? Marriage? Life?'

'Yea! Your story is so full of survival stories. It will have the public's attention.' He gazes at me for a moment.

'Why do you think so? It's not that interesting.'

'*But it is*,' he insists. 'Backtrack of everything they have exposed you to.'

'I don't want to talk about it.'

'You should. From babyhood until you grew up. The extreme violence Flopper exposed you to. Ugh, for selfish reasons.'

'But Paul never violated me. Why are you so judgmental?'

'Your story has many elements in it. Sensation to tearfulness.' He is satisfied and annoyed at the same time.

It's as Drake tries to attribute his own unhealthy behaviour, perspective, and character traits to Paul, because it shifts attention and responsibility from him, and plays the sympatric guy here.

'I don't understand what you're saying, Drake.' While I'm speculating where he got that idea from.

'It's what I've picked up when you tell me. It tells me that thousands will listen to your story. Especially since women will learn much from the psychological violent side. They will learn from your suffering. And torture to get off the train in time.'

I don't have an earthly chance to interrupt the blabbermouth.

'Nothing is worth sacrificing as you did. Only to hold on to a marriage—living and hoping to get accepted and loved by your mate. Flopper does not love you. Your story is captivating. I've not heard something like that before.'

'You are twisting it.' I'm scared, and want to cry, because he makes it sound so tragic.

'I buy the sole rights to publish your story—to write a book in the form of a true story.'

'True story? No, I don't want that.'

'I want the options of making manuscripts. For films and TV. I trust your story is incredible.

It's heart-breaking. It's sexual challenging.' He's ecstatic and cheers.

'I do not understand what *book rights* means.'

'Baby best you get divorced. After that, we can finish the negotiations. Here is how I want it. $7,000 for the first year of rights. If I don't make use of the purchase rights, I will lose the payment option.'

'What do you mean?'

'You can sell to another bidder. All rights to your book and media publishing will be $75,000. Plus, 30 percent of the net sales.' He continues as an unstoppable chatting of a parrot.

'It sounds complicated.' I grumble and yawn loudly, almost falling asleep.

'I expect revenue to exceed $1.5 million for Denmark alone. Sales of the book in English- and Spanish may be even greater. We make three payments. $15,000 after the last contract. $50,000 after the last manuscript in Danish. Will you consider it?' He proudly brags with massive high numbers.

'Wauw! Fantastic. Too good to be true.' I'm captivated, but don't understand any of it.

'Ongoing sales revenue will go according to normal book publishing payment terms. If a major publisher offers to buy the rights, and the offer exceeds the amount mentioned above, you will receive 75 percent of the sum paid. Excluding my investments, though. Thus, we can resell the rights to third parties. If the transaction is attractive enough for both of us. Without your permission, I cannot resell the rights. You will get the final say on the price to be traded. How does it sound?' He opens his eyes wide and flashes several sweet smiles.

'I'm tired. It's been a time-consuming journey. I can't see through it now, Drake.' Yawning loud and support my head in a resting position on the headrest. Jeez, then the chatterbox continues.

'Baby, rights to your story for online media, film, and TV productions, is important. I'll be an agent for you. When selling movies or TV rights, you will share insight into how the films should be made. Final approval of screenplays and of production. Choice of actors, and so on.'

'Yea, yea, fine. You talk a bunch of nonsense. I want to sleep.' And yawn.

'As an agent, my fee will be the standard 20 percent of the total contract price. Including royalties. You own every movie right. If you wish.'

'Gasp! It's boring talk. Drake I don't understand a shit of it.'

'I will be there for you until you can sell your story.'

Finally, he stops. And no more comments of my manuscript. Shit! Then he begins with the next business matter. I'm exhausted.

'The timeshare business. It's a brilliant chance for us. Invest $30,000. That includes setting up an office space. Then 10 sales packages.'

'Let me consider it.' He wants to be in the right, so he can prove my 'false validation' to regulate his shaky self-esteem.

'Okay, Baby! We will prepare the business with the American's.'

His sudden switch, from one state of demonic business jabber to another, is jolting. I'm worn-out, and my head is being racked by the beginnings of a migraine.

'I don't need you to play the grand man. Or do a gigantic business for me.' Trying to be gently. I'm irritated and try to stand up for myself. 'I don't need you to pay my bills. I am not with you for social reasons.' Oh, my! I'm pissed. Now it is my turn to blabber.

'Huh?'

'I need to get changes made.' The She devil, grew in me, and I notice he seems to dislike what I'm saying.

'I do not need you because of sex. I can organise myself out of it. Buying myself a dildo.' I smile, and he gives me a weird stare, musing: "How dare you react or challenge me!" 'I want to live with you, Drake. But, it's not great to date a man who gets mad or tired of me because I don't answer emails. Or the phone. Or because I smoke few fags.' I sense my power to get off with my frustration. 'I wonder, *are you worth it?*' Then I stop talking as he gazes at me in surprise.

I can sense from Drake it's tough for him to live up to my comment—when he discovers, *Oops! Mary doesn't need me on any limits other than the emotional ones she craves.*

He doesn't reply. Instead, he changes the topic again and continues talking of business for over two hours, until we arrive at the house.

The outcome is that 'the pretty little Pinocchio doll' attached to Drake's strings accepts that *his* story is true and is so convincing that the demons are only mine. That the business projects are ready. And the 'candy girls' were from 'before' he knew the pretty Mary doll. Meaning; everything is my fault. It's never his fault.

For several weeks, I'm considering the timeshare project. Drake and Sven finally persuaded me to invest, and they perfectly organised everything among the group of five people. *What can go wrong?* However, I trust Sven and Drake's idea, wishing for a better life.

Ladies and gentlemen, attention, please! Let's see what the team of 'snake oil salesmen' really can deliver.

CHAPTER 19

THE SNAKE OIL SALESMAN CAUGHT THE FLEDGLING DEMON

Ladies and gentlemen, attention, please!
Come in close where everyone can see!
I got a tale to tell, it isn't gonna cost a dime!
(And if you believe than, we're gonna get along just fine.)
— Stephen King, *Needful Things*

Sometimes it's not as simple, and there is an unhealthy behaviour on both sides. What is a timeshare? I still don't know, though I trust that it's an excellent idea, and the team seems professional. Before I examine the dude's behaviour, it's too late for me when I notice they are full of crap. Not having my usual support system, and getting proper advice because I'm isolated, increases Drake's chances of others siding with him and not with me. The snake oil salesmen team conducted diligently the seedy profiteering, trying to misuse an unsuspecting trusting Mary Liz by selling her strange cures. Am I living with a person who is convincing me of the story of a 'cure-all', and believes himself to be the ultimate doctor and businessman? Inexperienced, I wind up in the hands of a bunch of other strange people with the timeshare project. Damn! Suddenly, it's me paying for an office in Manila.

Eventually, I figure it out and redraw from the business that the slippery snakes cleverly conducted with their idea. Over $30,000 went straight to the pungent drain on their deception. Again, he is smarter than me. I excuse myself by pondering; *well Mary, you're not such a financial genius or mathematician. You're more than a person who loves to help others and animals.*

Having set up the business in Hong Kong and The Philippines, gives Drake a fresh chance to prove himself. He can't accept that he may not be a perfect person, so he does anything to maintain a fantasy that he is always right, while perceiving me as evil. In his grandiose megalomania, he tells everyone the companies are his, and he has paid for everything. He creates slanderous, manipulative narratives where everything of what *he* says and what *he* believes is true and tries to convince others of it. Mine and others unfortunately are that we, in the beginning, cannot see the truth behind it.

Roughly so far within the first year; I have misused far over $120,000 of my funds—putting everything on the wrong angel on the white horse. I'm heedless of my love blindness by being a generous and optimistic person. Trusting and hoping he can change will prove to be a tremendous mistake, and as a result, I get seriously hurt emotionally, socially, and financially. Does Drake even care about it? I believe he is often glad of being able to conduct his deceitful schemes and might be he believes I as an "evil" person deserve it. So, whatever happens, he can justify it in his mind.

*　*　*

During our six-month stay at Hazel and Philip's community, they find out of Drake's scandalous bluff. He demands at least 70 percent of the entire profit, and a raging disagreement between Hazel and Philip, other investors, and Drake comes to the surface. The discussions between us won't end, and Drake pulls me out of the business. Hazel furiously commands him to leave the village and once again; we must escape! Hidden by the gloomy darkness of night—this time we move to

Manila. My life with him has turned into the life of an escapee, fleeing from place to place.

Before Hazel banished us from the residence, we get through the Swedish consulates, in contact with Dusit Dang, a doctor in aesthetics, who is interested in expanding his clinic. With Drake's hypothesis, it prompts him to suggest building a minor hospital with Dusit Dang, and his wife Apana.

However, Apana, the wife of Doctor Dusit Dang discover fast the sly fox in Drake, and she dislikes him significantly. Swiftly, the entire project falls to the ground after Drake tries to seize power and control over them, and everything ends fatally.

The fat is in the fire! Drake has no income, because we have no patients, and if any, our patient count is less than five.

Together with our Dutch friend Kris, we inspect a marvellous house, considering the possibility of purchasing it.

'Why are they selling?' I ask.

'The British owner had unpaid bills to a contractor.' Kris brings up the chilling story of the sale. 'He refused to pay because the builders hadn't finished the job.'

'What happened to him?'

'One day, he was driving on his scooter, a fast driving car with four criminals having their windows open. Bang, and they smashed him with a four-by-four in his head. Wearing no helmet. Then he overturned with his scooter.'

'Whoa! That's terrible. Is the Brit okay?'

'The car stopped. Out climbed four angry, devious men. Furious, they nearly beat the fella to death with baseball bats.'

'OMG! How gruesome.'

'The Brit was in a coma for a long time. Next, he died from his injuries. The scared wife fled thereafter back to England.'

'Whoa! What a gruesome story. I'm not interested in the house.' Within time, we heard several such stories, as they weren't uncommon.

The week after one of our patients makes a malpractice complaint against Drake for mistreatment. Ivan Petrovic, also called Ivan the rough is a well-known Russian mafia dude and furiously he commands his money back. He threatens Drake—meaning Ivan the rough will send nasty people to kill us.

Well, the dragon dude has the grip on me.

'My darling love. We need to talk.' Drake says while getting closer to the pool edge. 'On a day like this, phew, where I must think hard of the best course of action for us.'

'Huh? What do you mean, darling?' As I step out of the pool.

'Jeez, Ivan the rough has been in focus today.'

'Oh! What's going on?' Being worried, while wrapping my towel around me.

'Our lawyer just called. Patty says we must find a way to handle the case.'

'Eh? What do we do?' Surprisingly, innovative ideas pop up in his head.

'Patty's first response was; Ivan the rough was sure I didn't have a work permit.'

'Whoa! But you've a work permit. Don't you?'

'Nor a medical license. I have a problem if there will be a lawsuit against me, Ivan the rough said.'

'Huh? It sounds daunting! But you have. Right?'

'Yea. Patty advised me not to let it go that far. I must make a deal. Something that will end this forever. She will negotiate it. She only needs the details of the case.'

'I can't follow you. What deal?'

'Patty met with Ivan the rough. At once he asked for the cash. Ivan doesn't want to talk more with Patty. He'll come after me, because I have no medical license. Jeez, then Ivan has reported me to the police.'

'Christ. Oh, my goodness! You must give him the money back. ASAP!' I'm terrified.

'Patty negotiated with him. Ivan Petrovic must sign a cease-and-desist letter to stop his harassment of me. He must let the case rest forever; otherwise, he'll get no money! Finally, Ivan the rough agreed!'

'Phew. Okay, then you solved your problem, darling. Right?'

'Yup! I feel relieved. Phew! And more comfortable. Can you help me?'

'Eh? With what?'

'I don't have the money for Patty or Ivan. I want to get rid of this problem—*now!*'

'Excuse me? Drake, you have the money Ivan paid you.'

'No, you have them, Mary. I can't live with the threat hanging over my head. I must have peace of mind. Do you agree? Baby, we don't want a problem here in The Philippines. Not wise! Right?'

'Eh? You got the cash, not me. Give it back to Ivan Petrovic. Today!'

'Sweet Pea, I don't. I paid bills. I don't want a four-by-four beam in my head. Or get killed. Please transfer to my account.'

'Gee, Drake, so dramatic you are.'

'Baby, I love you. I'm sorry this happened.'

Having in mind of the story Kris told us, got me into a shudder! That's why he feared that the gangsters would beat Drake to death if he didn't pay Ivan the rough.

'Okay, for our safety, I pay the money to Ivan Petrovic. And Patty's fee.'

Although Drake doesn't give up on the search for a house, and dares coming up with another alternative plan he is to put into motion. While enjoying a chill beer in our garden on a late summer day, he begins with his most famous sentence. Then I know something new is about to come to surface.

'My forever beautiful Baby girl. I've another brilliant plan.' He smiles ecstatically.

'Hmm. Okay, what's going on.' And he gets right to the point.

'It's about the mansion we saw recently.'

'Darling, that's too big for us?' Grabbing my chilly beer.

'Together with the owners of the place, I inspected it yesterday; Wang and Tang invited me to lunch.'

'Yeah, I know. Did you have a great lunch?'

'Wang and Tang showed me the blueprints of the building. Wow! It's a bold deal if I make it as a special "Drake deal". With the investor financing precisely as I assumed with Hazel's place.'

'Oh! How much are we talking about?' Not knowing what Drake is planning.

'The mansion has ten suites with kitchens. There is room for a clinic. A surgeon's section for minimally invasive surgery. We will not work there. But be the owners of it.'

'What do you mean; by not working there? What? Owners?'

'We will sell the suites for $350,000 each. That gives us almost $3 million in revenue.

We'll buy the resort for $1.5 million.'

'Oh, my goodness! That's loads of money.' Realising he is getting above himself.

'Yeah! The retreat centre will rent the suites back at an 8 percent return on their capital to the investors. It will pay this in the form of rent. With one to two years prepaid.'

'You have such a swollen head. I can't follow your tedious numbers.'

'Come on, Babe! Each investor will take part in the rental income. We will let out for $500 each night. To wealthy patients. Living there while being treated. Getting pampered according to my rules of art. Luxurious treatment is expensive.'

'Drake, stop! I'm not interested in investing a dime.' I am much more careful and less impulsive, and tired of his many ideas.

'We hire doctors. Train therapists, as provided in my plan. We can live where we want. Not having patients being treated in our homes.'

'I'm not interested.' That I'm sure will save me from a massive destruction of my finances.

'Babe, I think we can buy a house with profits. Let's make the resort deal. With the $1.5 million profit for us. We can then buy the house I saw yesterday. Perfect with the maids' quarters.'

'Let's talk about it later. I must ponder on it.' But everything ends up in chaos, and no deals come to fruition.

Once again Drake gets an up-to-the-minute idea, and an extra project is once more born. I trust in this venture, because I'm educated in sales and marketing. I believe this can work out well for us and I feel in my comfort zone; therefore, I hire Kris and tree local Philippine's, Ram, Wirat and the IT guy Prem to help us with sale and translating from Philippines to English and reverse. It's a promising team that will help to sell our bedding products. The adventure leads us to several upcoming trips to China and taking part in many expos, so whatever the costs, I sponsor for trips on business class and for five-star hotels for us.

Will our wide-ranging concepts collapse to the ground as a series of explosive bombs?

What I dislike the most is his frequent complaints concerning capital and me. We drink a chill beer outside the mall during one of our shopping days and while we talk peacefully. Suddenly, he behaves as a minor ill-behaved spoilt child after I paid for our beers, as we next go to the bank to redraw cash and pay bills.

'I'm angry that I can't pay for anything when we go to a restaurant or a shop. Only you have money, Mary.' This is a phrase he frequently utters when he needs money.

'Jeez, you have nothing to nit-pick about,' defending myself. 'We don't have to worry.'

'I can't keep on living off your dough.' Screaming at me, trying to behave as a hero.

'Darling, I get my funds from Paul. Why criticise?' While glaring insistently at him. 'As a start-up cost, I promised to cover our expenses. Ha-ha, yeah, our extravagant lifestyle.' Grinning sarcastically.

'You don't even share fifty-fifty with me, Mary.' Staring at me as a furious bull.

'What? Eh, Honestly? I want us to earn our own money too.'

'You should give me half of your alimony.' My lower jaw drops in surprise when he greedily commands me to share. I'm outraged! He acts over and over as a petulant man-child.

'Huh? Eh, darling, I don't understand why you are fuming at me. When I withdraw cash, you always get half of the sum.' I'm uncomprehending of his anger and unaware of his financial difficulty with me. Whoa! That makes me extremely frustrated! It's a never-ending money story with him!

'We agreed the expenses for travel, rent, car, and whatever I pay.' With bravery, I reach out for Drake's hand to ease his anger. I always give him whatever he wants. Oh, my! I'm frustrated with him and feel as a wicked bitch who won't give in to his evil forceful willpower, then he refuses to let me hold his hand.

So, what does the indulgent puppet do? Foolishly, I give in to his raging and blasting jungle drums, then grab my purse and give in to his greed for the smelly dough. Afterwards, he is mild, as a loving baby who received his comforter and a lollipop in his hand. This goes on for an extended period, giving him cash or putting a fixed amount into his bank account every month. The petty dragon is joyful.

'Baby, I was the perfect lawyer for you during your divorce. Right?'

'Yea, well, I know. Thanks.'

'You have never paid me fee! You should.'

'Huh? For what?' I ask.

'To help you with your agreements with the divorce. You had never got such a perfect settlement without my help. I must, therefore, receive a decent bonus for the many hours I've spent helping you,' he insists and laughs. In his mind, it's a professional service, even though the fella is not even a skilled lawyer.

'Incredible! You are my mate! I've already paid a fortune for a professional lawyer.' The sneaky bloke forgot that!

Then I find out the reason for his angry outburst. The dude is broke, and he needs my money, and I feel a chilling pressure from him to pay for it all. Scandalous! Somebody has sued him, and he is 'wanted' in the United States, because of a debt with taxes, banks, and something else. I feel deceived.

However, during our time in The Philippines, I often also feel over the moon with Drake and his noble part. Our love affair works decently, though, despite the problems as in many other relationships.

'I need the $30,000 I deposited into your account. Please pay it back.' I ask again and again.

'I promise you I'll transfer the funds soon.'

Excuses pile up on top of other explanations. 'I have no access to my internet account.' 'My password is not working.' 'I can't get the ID card to work.' 'Don't worry, Babe. I know the funds are still there.' 'The bank has frozen my account.' 'Taxes have taken my money.' These are a bunch of his many lame excuses for not transferring the money back to me.

I keep on begging Drake to return it. Next, he conducts a calculated spreadsheet of incoming and outgoing sums. I'm displeased when he presents it to me, and my jaw drops to the floor. The scumbag has remarkably cunningly twisted around; in his calculation, as he has deducted $12,000 on the spreadsheet—coinage *I'm* supposed to owe him!

'*What?*' I yell. 'How did you come to that amount?'

Simple, I find out, because he has deposited the two times "lunch-box" cash of $12,000 in his other account and created fictitious calculations of expenses. Then he's claimed *he* had paid all the bills, and that I owed him money from previous trips to Asia. The dude believes he is smart, 'Here you can see it Babe.' then shows me.

'You can see I've paid for "rent", "car hire", "electricity", "phone"' pointing at the numbers. 'See it, Babe? Even much more—everything funded from my bank account.' Distressingly, not from the cash he received in envelopes.

'Strange! Where is the deposited cash then?' *Clever guy!* I next ponder, not having any evidence that he received the cash. *How did Drake get access to his account online;* I muse, as he beforehand had told me he can't access it. I've lost the game! Pig! Con man! I'm annoyed.

* * *

Abruptly, Drake again gets a new creative idea, and plans to set himself up as a pension investor for ex-pats from Scandinavia. He started with me!

It's my instalment annuity pension fund, and it isn't an insignificant bagful of peanut. I've shortened the proposal considerably, otherwise, I must write one more book to include at least the thirty projects I got from Drake.

I have already sponsored so much, yet he keeps on bombarding me with more fishy proposals. *Goodness gracious me!* This one, though, is rather chilling, and it's an astronomical risk. I enjoy my icy white wine while he drinks a cold beer and a Jack Daniels, when he talks of his fresh idea; Advantageous International Portfolio Management of Pension Accounts.

'Babe, you have this personal portfolio. It's under special Danish rules for pensions.'

'Yeah, and so what?'

'It's running in a closed loop until a specific year. Stocks and bonds, right? I suggest that you get it reinvested and not redrawn at this point.'

'Huh? What do you mean?' Being surprised we are talking of such a matter.

'For your safety, Baby. I want you to move and get it managed in a bank in China. Without Danish tax consequences. I can be your mentor.'

'Eh? We are talking of a lot of money.'

'Sweet Pea, I'll take the lead in the trading. The advising to include gainful Chinese securities in the portfolio.'

'That's not possible.' I wrinkle my forehead, seeing my first red flag.

'Sure. You can't move the money from the Danish bank. The bank will be responsible for the execution of trades jointly with the Chinese bank. They will take the lead in advising on foreign securities. The Danish bank will only take the lead in trading domestic securities.'

'This sounds complicated, darling.'

'You can easily move the portfolio to China. Baby, the bank will be responsible for every trade. They will take the lead in advising on the Chinese securities. You should sell and buy. But only on the advice of the bank account manager or me.' He proudly smirks.

'I already have advisers in Denmark. I don't need new once.' I'm getting nervous.

'The aim is to open a second account.'

'Eh? What?'

'Yes, with the value of the same amount as the current portfolio. I want you to borrow money from the Chinese bank. Then you put your pension fund in collateral.'

'Sounds complicated. I don't want to borrow money.'

'Sweet Pea, you will use it for a second portfolio. The bank will manage it, with advisement from me.'

'I don't understand such trading's, Drake. I'm not sure it's possible.'

'Both accounts will run parallel as a secondary "private" pension without the Danish tax. When they end the account, you must repay all the borrowed funds to the Chinese bank. Before the balance of the proceeds can get distributed to you.' He talks bogus.

'I must ask for advice from my bank.'

'You must structure your earnings. Transfer it only from the trading to a current account in the Chinese bank. You can increase your own cash infusion to the account. Then transfer to the secondary "private pension" account.'

'I will talk to a trustworthy friend. David knows of trades and pension funds in Denmark.'

'This format of investing can be attractive to all the pension fund owners in Scandinavia. It's for them to make money outside of any pension funds.'

'Sounds bogus. I will think about it. It's a lot of money. Let me talk to David.'

'Yours, and their capital, will be safe. The performance of the Chinese Bank management will be a vital part in the future marketing package.'

'I must talk to the bank first.'

'Babe, this is a fantastic opportunity for you to earn more than double the amount.'

'Huh? Come on! Maybe I'm in love and blind, Drake. I'll talk to David first.'

'Give me free access to the fund for a minimum of one year—without you having any say.'

'I'm not an oblivious stupid chicken with my head chopped off. Don't put me in the pot and cook me.' Appalling! Disturbing!

'Give me the entire fund to administrate, without you having the fund in your name.'

'What? Baloney! Honestly, Drake, I'm not your brain food.'

'Aw, don't be like that. Babe, please let me know your thoughts. I love you over the moon and back again. I will never harm you. This is a super concept.'

'Do you believe I'll fall for such a reckless worm-on-a-hook trick?' I am irritated.

Months later, while I'm in Copenhagen, I set up a meeting with my bank adviser, Mr Peter Jensen, and I talk of Drake's idea.

'We cannot allow you to do so! *It's illegal!*' Peter says.

'My grim feelings tell me someone is trying to lure me into something outrageous.'

'If you do this, Mary, we will report Mr Bates to the police for fraud.' Peter seriously warns. I'm shaken over Peter's response.

'So, are my feelings right?' To get a second opinion, I also meet with my friend David and explain the case.

'Oh, my God, Mary! It's incredibly unwise to put in hard and risky bets when there is a brief time for the pay-out to begin. You cannot make up for any losses in equities or in the market development in such a short-term time. My advice is to be cautious in the last five to ten years.' I glance at David.

'*Hm-mmm. Proposal one* is a proposal, regardless of which model you invested in Chinese securities. The one model suggested moving after the retirement of the pension to the Chinese bank. You can hardly ever move the scheme to them. Whoa! And not without serious tax consequences. Nor will the Danish deposit guarantee schemes protect you.' I don't interrupt and understand nothing, except for many red flags I was close to overlook.

'Um-hmm, Mary, it's foolish to invest in equities or anything else in a country where one's insights are limited. Oh, my, and where there is a substantial political risk. That's an even higher risk of investment losses. Mary, God damnit, be careful. Then at a phase when there will be a few years before the pay-out begins.'

'Sounds as someone is trying to harm me.'

'Oh, yea, and vastly. Whoa! *Plan two* is impossible. *It cannot be done!* It's advised to establish other similar savings. The cash must come as a loan from the Chinese bank. Oh, no, and with the pension as collateral. *It is not legal* to provide the pension fund as collateral.'

'Gee, really? Illegal?' Now I'm more scared. The bank also said it's illegal.

'Mary, you cannot do it. Preparing such a bid is evidence of a complete lack of insight from the person. Who gave you this proposal? *It's insane!* This guy doesn't sound nice.'

'Oh, my goodness.' And I don't dare to tell David it's a proposal from my boyfriend.

'Whoa, that it's further proposed "to gear the pension highly up." Jeez, it's not possible. It's *very* imprudent at a point. Uh oh! And a few years before the payment will begin. Jeez! You will jeopardise everything, Mary. Then risk being left with an enormous debt afterward. It's petrifying! The best thing you can do at this point is to let the pension remain in a major Danish bank. Let their investment advisors guide you.'

'The bank said the same. Oh, my, I will not do it.'

'It is an intelligent decision of yours. Don't accept this **outrageous offer.** *You will risk an enormous loss!*'

'I take it as an expression of a *severe warning* from you.'

'Be careful. Yuck, this deal sounds dangerous.'

There is no substance in the many points there is put forward to deprive me of my funds.

But I can see that there is a certain amount of entertainment value in every of his attempt. The bank and David end up saving my ass. Cheer up and let's see if you can look forward too much more there is to come. I'm not done telling about the ambiguous performance.

As I deny several offers, I sense the devaluation phase, and things gets heavier every day. Many things are taken for granted and he keeps on sending me invoices and bills for loads of nonsenses. I'm exhausted from all these bills and my account is getting drained severely.

Gradually, he shows his actual personality—his unpleasant, mysterious, controlling tendencies. He does what benefits himself; otherwise, he criticises and dominates me, and is demanding. One day, he tells me how clever and intelligent I am, and the next day, I'm dreadful and a stupid fool. This can be for the same thing for which Drake praised me the day before. It's so frustrating! He is frequently brash, so his commanding personality is often a nightmare. As a grumpy little man-child, he gets calculating when he doesn't get his own way, then puts me under tremendous pressure and isolates me even more. I've lost more contact with my family and friends, and become more afraid, getting closer to a mental nuclear meltdown. I've damaged my core from the unscrupulous boiling and overheating of his nuclear-powered atomic bomb, then put my sense of justice to a severe test, every time I discover his power plays and deceptions. Only time will show me when I will completely collapse—as the Fukushima nuclear disaster in 2011 in Japan.

The only thing I expected from Drake was closeness, intimacy, love, and not being his sugar-mama. These are problematic tasks for him, so he is often out-of-control on his rollercoaster ride.

After a lovely dinner at an exclusive five-star hotel, the brown snake is sneaking towards our table. He turns on his charm, hoping he can lure further capital out of me for payment of any extra equipment. The snake is hiding in the leaves close by the tree one meter away from me, and its appearance makes the evening somewhat petrifying and frightening. Aah! Eek, a snake! At full blast, a woman behind me screams hysterical.

CHAPTER 20

DANGEROUS DARKNESS IN THE BLACK MOUNTAIN

Just when you think you've hit rock bottom; you realise you're standing on another trapdoor.

—Marisha Pessel, *Night Film*

The snake is about to attack, and the woman's scream terrified me. Scared, I jump up from my chair, and at the same time I push hard to the table as I try to get up. Oops... clatter, clink and both red wineglasses knock over, splashing the colourful wine over Drake's beige pants. With a bang, the chair gets overturned and hitting the screaming women, who stand frozen behind me as a statue. Drake fumes and fast gets up, then a tremor went through him when he sees the snake, and quickly pulls me into him. As frozen figures with terror in our eyes, watching the snake, an upset waiter comes running as fast as he can. Eek, and distraught by seeing the beast, he takes his hands to the face and gasps! He screams and jabbers as a wild uncontrollable rapper to another waiter, whom none of the tourist can understand a shit of. Another waiter comes running to calm the panicking guy and the guests. There lies an eerie, dangerous pit viper. Its potent cytotoxic venom is deadly, and many people in The Philippines die from bites from this common threatening snake.

'At a slow speed, please leave the space. No fast movements. The snake bites fast.' The other waiter with a calm voice tells us.

The creep is unwilling to get out of the way, but lies not still, while the one-metre long serpent is as fixated at us and is again heading towards us. I'm petrified while we at slow speed take few steps backwards. Without the serpent, knowing the waiter is behind it, crash, slam, and rapidly the guy catches the bastard with a fast movement with his stick and a fishing net. What a horrifying dinner! I'm scared for the rest of the late summer evening, although the eerie night is not over.

The night is pitch-black on our way home from downtown after our chilling dinner, while a new horrifying episode is to happen. On the spur of the moment, a fast-driving middle-sized truck chased us, while Drake has an eye on it in the rear-view mirror.

'Mary, can you also see someone is following us? It doesn't look good.' He nervously notes.

I turn the side mirror on my side so I can view what's going on. When the truck gets close, driving along our flank, I perceive two terrifying guys inside the car, because their light inside the vehicle is on. The car resembles a dark grey Toyota Tacoma or maybe a Hilux. Drake honks the horn several times and tries to block their way, so they slow down, driving behind us again. So, the game goes several times, and I'm terrified, having in mind that the road in few minutes will narrow and be pitch-dark.

Out of the darkness, without warning, the chilling dudes at the speed of light overtake us, and Drake with no restraint honks the horn as a maniac. The truck pronto slows. No doubt the suspicious guys get aggravated that Drake honked the horn. The next terrifying picture comes upon us, as we can no longer glimpse any streetlights for miles around.

Less than a hundred metres in front of us, those daunting guys stop, and we stop. Fear fills me! Fast and furious they jump out of the truck, standing threatening behind the trunk and gawking at us. Our lights show us that one bloke is holding a baseball bat, and the other chilling chap is pointing a rifle at us.

'What can we do, darling? We only have a stupid little folding knife in my bag to defend us with.' I break the silence.

'For certain, they want to rob us.' He says.

'Damn it, we are in a risky situation.'

'Do you remember, Kris told us, if we ever get stopped, be aware.' Being stopped and shot is not so uncommon—first and foremost, if you provoke the criminals by honking the horn.

'God damn it, Drake! Do something! Shit, I'm scared!' I yell as a desperate woman.

'Shit! The road has narrowed on the stretch that leads us up to Black Mountain.'

'We only have one more chance. Less than twenty or fifty metres ahead, there's a small unlit road turning right. Can we drive that way?' Shivering, I ask.

'I'm trying to make out of what these insidious guys will do.'

'I'm sure the road is there.' I repeat.

'Shut up, Babe. I'm thinking.' He shouts at me.

He turns the headlights on full beam to blind them, and at full speed he gasses up the car. At the last second, he sees the minor gravel road. With a snatch he is tearing the steering wheel right, and screeches onto the narrow path, leaving a dusty cloud behind us.

'I don't know of where the road will lead us.' He almost loses control of the car, while we swerve from side to side while my heart pops up to my throat, and I can almost not breathe. At last, he gets control over the car, and I'm relieved as we continue along the dusty black path.

'We seemed to have escaped the two eerie dudes.' But Drake is not knowing where the road will lead us, despite we continue until we end up at the major road again.

'I told you to stop pushing and honking at them. I'm petrified shitless.' My heart is pumping at a top rate, while I'm shaking with fear.

Our trip ended up with a massive detour around The Black Mountain, and safe, we end up in front of our home again.

The day after we tell Kris of the incident.

'Ohhh, it sounds as what happened last year. There was an awful incident with a British man driving behind a lorry. The local lorry driver was provoking after being overtaken on an unlit country road by the British man. Several times, the Brit with lack of self-control honked his horn. Forcefully he pushed the lorry driver.' Kris tells the gruesome story during our meeting.

'What happened next?' Drake asks.

'Without warning, the lorry driver slowed. Then the Brit slowed and stopped before he almost hit the lorry.'

'Did they crash into each other?' Drake questions.

'No, no. But the local driver got out of the lorry. Furious, he took his rifle. Headed towards the British man's car. Screaming insanely. In the same second, he pointed the rifle straight at the bloke's side window. With a blast, he shot the fella in the head. Cold and cynical. The lorry driver went back to his truck. Jumped in and roaring drove away, as nothing happened.'

'Oh, my goodness. How terrible.' I burst out.

'The story was in the local Batangas news. The driver admitted the crime without blinking with his eyes. However, he got off the hook. He claimed the Brit was threatening him. Hmm, ironically.'

'But that's awful.' I am dazed.

'That's why you must be aware. Besides, they estimated if the Brit not stayed in The Philippines, this never would have happened.' Ironically, Kris said, 'what's the Brit doing in the country? He's just a simple "Puti".' Then he glares at us, shakes his head, lifts his shoulders, as if it's a normal behaviour in the country.

That isn't the scenario I want. However, life in Batangas with Drake is not dull. Everything is not only about danger, fraud, and nonsense. I will not deny that we also have a lot of delightful times together, because he can also amaze and to a great degree be loving when it suits him.

The countries many street dogs become my first-hand compassion. Every day, I lure Drake into driving around with me so we can find abandoned street dogs in the mountains, on the minor streets, and in alleys downtown. We end up finding lots of pooches, and soon they find out we have kilos of food bags, water, and medicine in the car. With intense and eager enjoyment, I cook massive bowls of meat, rice, and vegetables for the many mutts.

CHAPTER 21

MY LIFE FULL OF ABANDONED STREET DOGS

He who feeds a hungry animal feeds his own soul.
—Charlie Chaplin

The classy beauty of a lady disappeared when I replaced my high-heeled black Prada shoes with a pair of sneakers or a pair of green rubber boots. I look as a bewildered, terrifying mountain jinx, in blue jeans and a white T-shirt, but I don't care. The street dogs are more important than looking pretty in a classy outfit and being a perfect styled doll.

Drake finds a website about street dogs in the Philippines, because I want to do more charity work for the many helpless, hungry and sick abandoned pooches. I'm always in a hurry, running back and forth, and pushing him, so I can get out in the mountains to feed them. Often, we drive out during the late grim nights, while the breeze is cooler, then most of them appear from their hiding spaces after a tropical day. Several of them, most puppies, I treat for heart- and lungworms, and many get wound care or whatever care they need. I'm not a veterinarian, but I know the essential, necessary skills of proper dog care. With loads of patience to get them closer to me, I rapidly grab them and without fear of getting bitten, I stuff the medication in their throats, gently hold their muzzle while petting and talking to them until they have swallowed the medication. He gets overwhelmed with my fearlessness and believes I'm risking my life—that I might get bitten and infected with rabies. He is not aware of my vaccinations; therefore, I'm sure I won't get any diseases from the dogs. By good luck, my awareness of the danger, possessing patients and having a loving heart, no dog ever has bitten me.

In the pouring chilling rain, one late night, I notice from the flash of the car's light a little puppy sitting on the road, feeling miserable.

'We know her. It's Lucky! But where is her brother Snoopy?' I question.

He promptly stops the car, then I jump out and call for Snoopy, but he has disappeared. Lucky has a best buddy, Anxious a beautiful brown dog, with caring eyes.

'Nor can I find Anxious. They always hang out together.' He has taught Lucky and Snoopy to survive the dangers of the persistent noisy streets and the scruffy hills. Lonely she sits soaking wet, scared and watching our movements.

'Poor little Babe.' Glancing at her, as it breaks my heart. Lucky hurries over to me and clings to my leg, refusing to leave my side.

'Oh, darling, I cry for her loneliness. I can't find Snoopy. What do we do?' Within a split-second and unmotivated I snatch Lucky in the night's darkness, as a sneaky, soaking wet thief I take her to the car and bring her home with me.

'Holy Virgin Mary! I'm petrified. Have I done something illegal by taking the dog?'

'Oh, good Lord! My darling ML, now you are the dogs, Mother Teresa. Mwah!'

'Aww! But I'm scared that someone saw us.' Worried, we drive back home.

'Nothing will happen, Baby; you saved Lucky's life. I love you with my entire heart. You are such a special warm-hearted person. So generous to animals and humans.' He cheers me up.

Lucky has never seen houses inside before, so she behaved and stayed outside, in the rain, while I dry her up. But this time under protecting roof and snuggling in warm blankets. The following day we bring her to the vet, get her vaccinated, buy crackers for her stomach, heart and lungs for them to get healthy too. Also, a treatment for fleas and ticks. After a few days, and several attempts, she finally dared to go inside the house. Lucky is a fast learner and a hilarious dog, and we care so much for her, so she rewards us by looking after our home from the first day. Sneaky and unfriendly, suspicious people and venomous snakes get afraid of her, so neither of those comes ever creeping into the house.

We keep searching for Snoopy and bring Lucky with us every time, let her run in the area for two hours, while we explore in the scruffy hills. A week later, someone tells us they saw a fast driving roaring truck had run over Snoopy. Dead and cruelly ditched in the mountains.

Shortly after, Anxious is back and keeps sneaking, begging and rubbing his body on my legs. Normally he is very timid, but today he with an intense stare glares at me with his loving brown eyes. His behaviour has changed from what he often does when I'm nearby, so I squat and with calmness talk to him. He appears as he is crying, then I can sense he wants my help for his excruciating sufferings. By instinct, I lift this 30-kilo massive dog up, and troubled, I discover something has injured Anxious. I'm upset! It's from a snakebite, as I notice he has a large open wound in his groin—at least six centimetres wide, and vastly infected with running yellow slimy bacteria, and is very swollen.

'We have to hurry to the vet,' I yell to Drake.

Determined, I push the pooch into the car, jump in, having his head on my lap, while speedily drives as a lunatic off to the vet.

'No matter what it costs, you fix Anxious. Please, Doctor Nhung. Do whatever you can.' I sob in front of him.

Three weeks, Anxious sits in solitary confinement at the clinic. Phew, without our help, the poor fella will die in the mountains. We visit the distressed mutt every day, for at least an hour. Distressed, I sit with Anxious in his cage, comforting the wounded fella, next feeling heart broken when I must leave him, as I can hear him sadly cry. It overwhelms my heart with the sorrow of his crying, it's almost too much for me. After a brief time, he gets better and we bring one more doggie to our home.

Step by step, we get familiar with the vet Nhung, because of our daily visits with the pooches, which made us well known at the clinic, as two friendly Scandinavian 'Puti'. Nhung is helpful, discounting the dog supplies and medicines we purchase.

After Anxious is ready to leave the clinic, he too becomes a regular family member, because I got so detached to him, that I couldn't set him on the street again. Believe me, he protects and watch over me as a sharp hawk. When I watch his wrinkly forehead, as a concerned doggy; I smile because he looks so worryingly cute; that's why his name I Anxious. Often Drake has no chance to get near me, without Anxious growls at him. When Lucky finds a snake in the garden, she grumbles fearfully and Anxious barks, so it's wonderful to have two faithful and intelligent snake watchdogs taking care of our safety. They love to play together, sometimes wildly, and sometimes they are very unruly too. We spoil them with excellent and healthy food and loads of lengthy walks, play with them and perform dog training. Quickly they discover how to give high fives, sit behaved before they get their food, or little snacks. Our reward is they take outstanding care of us and become excellent watch dogs.

A Buddhist monk Luang Cha from a nearby temple has heard of the things we do for the canines and needs our help. We get in touch with him and drive to the temple to hear how we can assist him. Luang Cha needs a sponsor for a vaccination program for his little puppy. Aww, what an adorable little 10-week old black feisty furball, whom I christened Lama. We bring him to the animal clinic and the vet Nhung start the heart- and lungworm treatment, and later, the vaccination package over the coming weeks.

Each time we pick up Lama at the temple, we drive him to Doctor Nhung. It makes me proud and ecstatic of sponsoring Luang Cha and Lama. As a surprise, and for their thankfulness, they invite us for a unique Philippine dinner, followed up to watch Muay Thai boxing. A well-known combat sport of The Philippines where kids to older adults take part in the sport. It's known as a discipline as the art of eight limbs, where the boxing combines the use of knees, elbows, fists, and shin. Wauw interesting to watch.

Luang Cha asked us to watch the age-old lucrative frightening and rough cockfighting, but I don't fancy that. Though, it's a massive business in The Philippines, despite complaints from many animal rights groups.

The most exciting thing is we learn of the daily life of being a Buddhist monk and watching how it's a lively and inspiring community for itself. At the temple, the monks grow everything themselves, and are self-sufficient for their meat and vegetables, a different livelihood to watch, noticing that they appear as harmonious, friendly people.

During almost our two years in The Philippines, we saved many dogs' lives, rescued from miserable conditions in many minor cities we drive to, and is my heart's support that I can contribute to something great. It helps me survive my isolation with Drake and takes my mind off his many rollercoaster ride mentality. The animals make me joyful by having a noble purpose to support elephants, street dogs, and buying food for the local dog shelters.

A funny thing happened one day while driving on our way to downtown, when we meet a local Buddhist monk in his orange/yellow clothing walking lonesome at a slow pace. With a bamboo stick in his hand, he guides his seven fascinating animals of gentle giant grey holy cows. The cow is a tribute and celebrates the soulfulness of cattle and the special bond between man and cow.

'Stop the car.' I shout when I spot the monk. Rapid I jump interested out to take pictures. Geez, I'm a geek on every occasion, wanting to take photos. Sweetly the monk smiles at me, and pleasant poses for me, as I nosy, talk to him.

'Hi, may I take pictures of you?' He nods and smiles. 'What's your name?'

'Nihat.' He is smiling, and I like him from the first moment.

'How it's being a Buddhist monk?' As a fast-moving chatterbox, I ask loads of questions.

'Fine.' He has difficulties speaking English.

'Are those holy cow's?' I ask curiously and ask for much more.

'Yes. I like to improve my English.' Nihat says with his broken English. It's amazing how you can communicate with people, just using your hands and say strange noises.

'I can help with some education.' I quickly offer him.

'First, I must ask my Buddhist master. He must give me permission of your donation.' I realise it does not allow them to take a present from others without approval from the top.

In a brief time after, we meet him and his holy cows again.

'Hi Nihat.' I gladly smile. 'Have they accepted my offer?'

'Yes, thanks,' he answers joyfully. 'But you must check me in at the school and pay.'

For three months, we send Nihat to school. We often meet with him, then he tells us a lot of being a Buddhist, about the country and Buddhist fairy tales.

One of my unique adventure I enjoy with the street dogs; they get their unique names—Hyena, Black Spot, Hairless, Scallywag, "Ugly", "Snake Dog", "Gawks", and so on. No dog goes without a name, and they respond to it when we call them. This might sound crazy, but to me, they must have names so they can become their own specific little individuals.

Specs is a long-haired bronzed middle size 20 kilo admirable mutt, with light brown circles around her eyes. I must giggle, because it's hilarious—her eyes look as she is wearing glasses. A little timid and is among one dog; we found at a dangerous region on a mountain road, where many other canines ran. At once, we end up taking one more pooch home with us, so now we have three caring street dogs in our home. But things don't always end up to one's heart contents, while our landlord Nielson discovers the crowd of pooches.

'One must leave.' Nielson, the angry Swede grumbles. 'You may only have two hounds.'

Heartfelt and sad; we drive Specs to the local kennel we support, close by the Buddhist temple, with their many elephants. Though we often visit Specs and bring Lucky and Anxious with us, she misses them, as we miss her. My heart bleeds for Specs every time we must leave her, as I can hear her heartfelt cry.

*   *   *

We did not expect something dreadful happens, but suddenly our local dog friends Waan & Mali call us.

'Something awful has happened to Specs at the shelter. We have in a hurry taken her to the animal hospital,' so with decisive we drive hastily to the veterinary hospital.

'An irresponsible speeding driver causes this horrifying mess.' Mali says. I'm crushed!

'Within a few hours, Specs has lost every sensation—both motor and autonomic nerve function in the lower half of her body and has severe fractures of her front legs.' Gasp! That is Nhung's first reactions while talking to us.

'We have taped her front legs together. She is in a cage for observation.' Whoa! When seeing my poor little pooch in such a miserable and treacherous condition, I'm convinced she will not survive it. She is a sad sight, with hanging sorrowful eyes.

As Specs sees us, she gloomily raises her head, recognising us, but looks awful distressed and despairing.

'We must take new X-rays,' Drake insists and Doctor Nhung and Drake reveal there are several serious fractures on both of her front legs. With great pleasure Specs raises her head, then struggles to get up on her front legs, for her to get closer to us but can't.

'Let's take Specs home with us,' and Drake check her further from top to bottom, for spine and nerve damage.

'Yes! Perfect, darling. Right now?' I am in despair,

'She has a spastic paralysis too on her back, I think.' He concludes, because instantly, she collapses as soon as she tries to move.

'Oh my, darling. You must start on a treatment plan instantly.' I beg and persuade him.

'The accident must have caused damage to her nerves. You see, Mary, it's not just her muscles. It affects her nerves.'

'Without our help, Specs will have no chance to survive. Darling, she will die if nobody takes care of her.'

'I'll start a treatment. Babe, you can follow it up with rehabilitation on the grass.'

'Splendid idea. And daily pool exercise.' This is where I notice some of Drake's fantastic sides, as he steps up the game. 'I'm proud of you, darling. Thanks for helping.'

A few weeks after I must travel for a week to Copenhagen, for an important family event for my son. Drake is suddenly furious with me for leaving him alone with two healthy dogs, and one damaged canine. From being proud of him to getting heartbroken and disappointed in him when he protests of my upcoming trip. He is continuously complaining that he must be alone and take care of the dogs.

'For Christ's sake, darling! How difficult can that task be for you?'

'Why can't you just stay? Forget about this event!' He bad-mannered angers.

'I'm leaving. It's a promise. I know it's a tough job for you. But honestly? It's only for a week,' I stubborn and heated protest.

Miffed over my decision and because of my absence, he almost gives up on the poor dog.

'Specs is shitting and peeing over the entire house.'

'I'm sorry to hear, my love. Please continue the treatment.'

'Bloody hell, it's horrible. Daily I must bathe her.'

'Darling it will get better. Only you can help her. I trust you in your skills.'

'Christ, it's too much. She will not eat.'

'Darling, I'll hurry back.'

'I'm sick and tired of this shitty mess,' and daily he nit-picks over Skype about everything.

'I know it's a tough job, taking care of Specs,' and resolute, I push and inspire him to continue.

'Mary, you must come back now. Otherwise I'll give up on Specs.'

'Darling, as soon as I'm back, I start up the rehabilitation again.' Whoa! I'm frustrated with him—disturbed to see that he can't survive one week without me.

A week has passed, even though I'm supposed to be in Copenhagen for important tests because of a suspected tumour in my breast, I postpone the appointment further five weeks.

I fly about twenty hours each way, and the distance between Denmark and The Philippines, which is roughly 10,000 kilometres. It's not as having a fast run over to my friends for a chit-chat or having a quick coffee with the neighbour.

'I feel we somehow got stuck with the treatment.' He complains when I'm back.

'True, there is not much progress. What do you suggest, honey?'

'We can invite the American doctors I know. I'm sure they can assess Specs. And help us.' We approach it from a fresh angle.

'With our treatment, and their PRP, we can combine it as a complete treatment. That gives us new hope to get Specs fit again.' And he invites John and Christian to help us.

In recent years, doctors have learned that the body can heal itself. PRP (Platelet-rich plasma) is a concentration of the patient's own platelets to speed up the healing of injured ligaments, tendons, muscles, and joints. They take one to a few tubes of the dog's blood, then John and Christian will run it through a centrifuge to concentrate on the activated platelets and inject it directly into the injured body tissue. This releases growth factors that stimulate and increase the number of reparative cells the body produces.

Together with ultrasound imaging to guide the injection, the treatment and the rehabilitation, we steadily understand Specs enhances her functions. Impressively, she improves, and shows speedy and remarkable development with the PRP injections. Soon, she gets full control of her entire system, her front legs heel rapid and her body gets restored. Within short time she can run as any healthy dog again.

I am grateful to the team of doctors who believes in us of getting Specs a good and better life again, as she fully regains her ability to walk and get her normal functions after the fantastic miracle treatment! Without their help, she perhaps never got better, however Drake showed phenomenal qualities, to save her, which makes me love him even more.

Specs is adopted by Waan & Mali, where; she continues to enjoy a healthy and joyful life, as I am full of happy tears and grateful, because she is still healthy and happy.

To make it easy I have arranged my famous envelope solutions, in the dragon boys' lunch box with $5,000, before my eight weeks of hectic and exhausting travelling to Israel for my second Pilgrimage. Next to New York, then Copenhagen for my breast surgery, and the following weeks of rehabilitation before flying back to The Philippines again. I need to get away, but it's hard; I'm always hanging in the air. The most draining thing is; I have little control over what my beloved does in The Philippines—how he spends my dough, or what Drake is doing! I'm way behind with my accounting, and sometimes I downright forget to ask him off, repaying me what he owes.

It's my pleasure to send you on a magical journey to the most stunning Holy land of Israel.

CHAPTER 22

SOLACE AT THE SEA OF GALILEE

The best remedy for those who are afraid, lonely or unhappy
is to go outside, somewhere where they can be quiet, alone
with the heavens, nature and God. Because only then does
one feel that all is as it should be and that God wishes to
see people happy, amidst the simple beauty of nature. As
long as this exists, and it certainly always will, I know that
then there will always be comfort for every sorrow, whatever
the circumstances may be. And I firmly believe that nature
brings solace in all troubles.

—Anne Frank

Why quote Anne Frank? I admire her strength. She is an
important person for us to understand of the cruelty
that happens to a massive group of people during the
Second World War in Europe. She was German and Jewish and had a
relaxed relationship with Judaism, as I have with Catholicism. During
the Second World War, her family went into hiding in the concealed
rooms behind a bookcase at her father's work. For two years, she wrote
a diary—until the feared Gestapo arrested the family with cruelty.
Their first petrifying journey was to the horrifying Auschwitz and next
to Bergen-Belsen, a dreadful concentration camp, where they died, and
only her father survived. Later he found her diary, and his discovery
led to the publication of the journal in 1947. Anne Frank was one of

the most discussed Jewish victims of the dreadful Holocaust, then her book became one of the world's best known and has been the basis for several plays and films. I have great respect for what she wrote of her faith in Judaism, since Jesus was a Jewish preacher and a central figure of Christianity. Having these two religions in mind leads me to, once more, to explore the notion of solace in the magical Holy Land, where it began with God, Virgin Mary, and Jesus.

Travelling from The Philippines to Denmark, I'll the next morning travel for my second pilgrimage to Israel, with the group from the Copenhagen Catholic Church. Oh, my goodness! I need this trip, because I desire for peace in my mind, far away from Drake. I have enough of commanding, disastrous behaviour and business proposals. At a certain point, I'm used to the many bumps in the relationship; so, it's difficult for me to spot the red flags. To be frank, I don't know whether my love life has become unhealthy or toxic, because of too many negative thoughts. Too much complaining and too many hurtful emotions, so I struggle to find out whether I'm happy. At many points, he has problems with supporting my independence and dependence or comfort and encouraging my wishes. My loneliness and isolation make me stay in the relationship, and I'm always hoping he changes his mind of the demons and faults he believes I have. In this is born the urge to make one more emotional trip to Israel, where I must decide if I want to stay with him.

* * *

After twenty hours of exhausting travel, I land in Copenhagen, grab my suitcase and walk the brief stroll to the Airport Hotel. I only want to sleep away my anxiousness, so I slam myself into the double bed and glare at Sherlock Holmes on the TV. Damn it, I have trouble falling asleep, because of jet lag and my upcoming travel fever to Israel.

The calmness falls over my restless and blood-sugar-low body, with tiredness at midnight. It's pitch-dark outside, and the birds have not yet awakened when I wake up at four in the morning. The warm running steamy water gives me a relief for my tired morning eyes and loosens up my stiff bones, though my exhausted body shows to hang tattered as I wash my hair. The morning buffet opens first at five-thirty. Damn! I can only get fruit yoghurt and sip a quick coffee from the temporary small morning buffet at the hall's corner. Fast, I grab two boring sandwiches with cheese, a banana and tuck it into my bag, so I can eat it when I meet with the others at the Airport.

* * *

Many days later and as I get back to my room at the kibbutz in Ein Gev, where we stay, I call Drake on Skype to tell him about the travel from the first day and what we have experienced so far in Israel.

'Hi my precious Baby. I'm looking forward to hear about your travel.' He beams, waiting for me to tell of the last day's adventures and listen with excitement.

'At Terminal 2, the group of thirty-six people had arrived and was ready for check-in. The tour manager Joyce had my practical papers and handed it over to me. I greeted many unknown members. Some I've never seen before. Few I knew from my last trip to Israel.'

'Good for you, Baby. What airline was it?'

'Austrian Airlines. An Airbus A321 from Copenhagen. Arriving sharp at nine AM in Vienna. We had a short stopover before the next flight to Tel Aviv. It joyed us getting on the trip. Many were talking of our earlier trip to Israel. Geez, it was so crammed with Orthodox Jews.'

'How do you know they're Orthodox Jews?' Drake asks.

'I could recognise them from their overlong hair. And corkscrew curls on the side. Also, their long black coats and hats. Did you know, originally, they came from Eastern Europe.'

'No, I didn't know that, Babe.'

'For festive days, they walk around with enormous fur hats, made of reddish fox or dark brown mink. It's somewhat sweet, also exciting to watch them and their dresses.'

'Oh, yea, now I know how they look.' He said.

'One of the 630 commandments say, "you must not cut the beard or the corner on their heads", meaning their sideboards. They spend much of their lives studying the Bible.'

The tzitzit is a knotted ritual fringe worn on their clothes. It's attached to the four corners of the prayer shawl. (Tallit gadol.) Matthew 23 says, "A woman with heavy bleeding runs after Jesus and touches the tassels on his shirt. When she had touched him, she became healed." They use them only when they go to the synagogue and wear their prayer shawls.

'Wow, that's interesting, Baby. How long did you stay in transit?'

'They estimated the flight to departure around ten-thirty AM. We would land at three PM in Tel Aviv. It was full of excited people. Oh, my, it was horrible in the small, noisy, crowded waiting room. You could hear the mumble of the Jews, praying and nodding their heads. My sense of orientation with the time variation was out of rhythm with my inner Meridian clockwork. I was tired and detected the jetlag.'

'Oh, poor Baby. Yea, I can imagine you must have been.'

'There were a few children with us. James, a nine-year-old boy. Poor him, he got sick on the earlier flight. Yuck, and had thrown up. Ha-ha, next he was craving for creamy potatoes. "Do you want chocolate?" I offered him. "No, thank you. I don't like chocolate." He said wrinkling his nose. Instead, I gave him my banana. He was pleased.'

'Oh, Baby, you're always so sweet to others. Mwah!' He smiles content.

'Hmmm, it was buzzing with many languages—Hebrew, German, English, and Danish. I thought intensely of how you were doing in The Philippines. Darling, I wish you one day can travel with me to the Holy Land.'

'Yea, we do that one day, my precious MM. I've not been there in thousands of years. Hi, hi, yea, since my crucifixion.' He grins.

'Ha-ha.' I took it as a joke. 'Well, while we were waiting in this small cramped echoing waiting room without the chance to buy food and drinks, we got a depressing PA announcement. "The airline staff is having a professional meeting." Damn, announced loudly from a high-pitched female voice.'

'Damn! So typical, Babe.'

'Yea! The smaller children grew impatient. I sat on a cracked and horrific hollow blue metal bench. It caused the steel to plunge well into my bum. My back was in agony. Unrest was spreading among people.'

'Why?' He asks.

'Because of hunger and thirst. We had no chance to enter the restaurant on the other side of the massive glass wall. It was getting tedious. Jeez, so humid and gloomy in the room. Phew, a long waiting time.'

'Oh, Baby, you needed my healing hands.' A smirky smile appears on his face.

'Yeah! The echoing buzz of human voices was spreading violently in my ears. It confused my brain. Then I suffered from a beginning anxiety attack. Jeez, I was feeling as my heart was pumping faster. My claustrophobic condition worsens. Of the sudden, oh, my, I miss you. Your comfort.'

'Oh, little girl, I miss you too.'

'You were my only thought passing through my upset mind. My stomach rumbled as a growling grizzly bear. I noticed my blood-sugar was getting low. "Wow! Are you hungry?" Joyce asked and offered me half her sandwich. "I'm starving," I told her, and it helped when I had gulped the sandwich with refreshing water.'

'You must remember to eat, Sweet Pea. I wish I was there for you.'

'Hmm, are you sure, darling? Well, during the waiting time, I checked my emails. Nothing from you. Why? Swiftly there came a new high-pitched PA announcement. "We must announce delaying of the flight to Tel Aviv. The staff is attending a technical meeting. We postpone the departure for two hours." Damn, and it sends a human shockwave through the entire room.'

'Wauw! So, you couldn't get anything to drink or eat?' He stares worried at me.

'The ground floor staff opened for the frustrated passengers for them to go to the restaurants and shops. Together with Jenny, I went outside to buy a sandwich. Finally! We quenched our thirst with a well-deserved excellent Austrian beer.'

'Wow, that was nice for you guys. Great beer, by the way.' He smiles gorgeously.

'Yup! Next, there came a new incoming call for departure. Holy moly, we had once more to check-in and be ready to embark. We boarded an old worn-down plane. A B767-300. Christ, I got worried. Peace was falling over most of the passengers. Though you could hear lots of screams and cries from the less happy younger children when we started at top speed.'

'Oh, I hate these screaming children.' He irritated, complains.

'Ha-ha, not that bad. Few from our group had been fortunate enough to sit in business class. Most of us sat in monkey class. As slaves. Jeez, on the worn-down old horrible green colour seats. Oh my! It reminded me of the good early seventies. After three and a half hours, we arrived in Tel Aviv. "Please be extra polite when going through the passport control." Our priest, Andrew said.'

'Oy, Baby, did you remember not to get your passport stamped?'

'Yep, I asked not to get a stamp—because of our trip to Qatar.'

'They denied Emma from our group entry. Many other younger people too.'

'Huh? Why?' He glared surprised at me.

'It was of an extra security measure. Whoa! It caused loads of unnecessary panic. Andrew got Emma through the administration, and we could continue our voyage. Ahead of us were three hours driving by bus to our last destination. It has been a tough day.'

'Oh, Baby, it sounds as a though day for you.'

'Yea, it was. Our tour guide, Ellen gave us different informs, "You can only use Israeli money. It's not everywhere you can spend dollars. We will drive to Ein Gev." She told us.'

'Where will you stay?'

'At the Sea of Galilee in northern Israel. It's beneath the sea's surface. We can swim in it. We stay in a kibbutz.'

'What is that?'

'A small Jewish agricultural colony. Ellen told us; "We have 270 kibbutzim, meaning group in Israel. The official languages are Hebrew and Arabic. The most influenced religion is by Christians, Jews, and Muslims. Though with 80 percent of Israel's population being Jewish.'"

'It sounds to be a magical place. I can't remember it after being away for so many years.' What is he talking about, I muse and continue to tell my story?

'Holy mother, it was a stunning drive past the Jordan River. I could see many kibbutzim in the region. While arriving, we were getting sizzling garlicky and lemony food. The staff at the kibbutz had kept it warm for us.'

'For how long you will stay there, Baby?'

'For the next four days—exciting! They had arranged the entire tour with all paid visits. Including breakfast and dinner. Lunch is at your own expense. The first magical evening, we were gathering in the great red hall. There we got our special pilgrim blessing.'

'That was nice.'

'Ay. Together with a younger woman, Isabella, I'm sharing room 509. The night falls, the Moon Shines bright. Oh, my, and the glittering stars radiate from the glassy sky.'

'Yep, you love the Moon and the Stars, Sweet Pea.'

'Hi-hi, yea. After my nice bath, I watched Isabella doing her evening prayer. Then it was goodnight. We left the balcony door slightly open for the chilly breeze to enter the warm, humid room. Throughout the night, the cool wind was blowing into the room. So nice.'

'Was that wise, Babe? Is it not dangerous?'

'Hmm? Well rested I wake up to a ravishing morning at six. And I hear a dulcet symphony from the swallows. The essence of a bright, fresh day. Ha-ha, hundreds of fluttering twittering swallows fly fast in and out, as Isabella opened the door completely.'

'Oh, my goodness. What did you do?'

'Embraced it. Stretched my stiff body while I was still resting in my bed. Then inhaled the pleasant fresh air into my lungs. Phew, and I let my lazy body get up. Isabella praised her mellow morning prayer on the bed. Aww, so sweet. As a tiny, fragile angel sent from heaven to watch me.'

'I told you I would send you a guarding Angel.' Oh, my, he smiles so lovely.

'Huh? Oh, okay, thanks. We have a splendid view overlooking Lake of Gennesaret. Wow, it's so scenic and magnificent. I was watching the calm sea. The Sun was shining from a cloudless sky. It was as it sent back to the time of Jesus. With my broken thoughts, and with a glance, I discovered modern laughing people strolling on the crunchy gravelled footpath.'

'I can imagine it looks beautiful.'

'Yep, and next breakfast. First, we start the day's program with a Mass. Then we met by the bus heading north along the lake to the ruins of Capernaum.'

'What are you going to do there?'

'Celebrating another Mass at the Church of Saint Peter in Gallicantu. A fishing village on the northern coastline of the Sea of Galilee. The next drive went to the eastern slope of Mount Zion. To the Roman Catholic church named after Peter's triple rejection of Jesus. "Before the rooster has gone twice, you have denied me three times." Peter said.'

'Oh, yea, I remember that sentence. Peter was such a turncoat.' He smirks strangely. What did he mean?

'Huh? What? We drove on toll road 6. A stunning part of a vigorous green lowland. We passed several towns with lots of olive trees. The synagogue is the best-preserved building. Andrew gave a brief Bible summary of the place. How Jesus had healed people here. We had a stunning one-hour Mass in the scenic church.'

'Oh, yep, I recall the place with the many healing people.'

'Oh, my. Will you believe it? While driving to the next part, our little Mass boy, Tom realises he has forgotten his backpack. The bus rapidly heads back. Mom, Dad, and Tom go outside to search for it. Jeez, they can't find it. Ellen went back to the church. Phew! Luckily, we had arrived at the right time. The church was nearly to shut for today.'

'Oh, no. Did you not get it?'

'Phew! They found the backpack, to his great pleasure. Another tourist had seen it and handed it over to the nuns. A Japanese tourist had photographed Tom and told him to take it off. Aww, everyone showed compassion for him. Ha-ha, so the ending is jolly.'

'Oh, that was great. Where did you then go?'

'We continued to the Church of the Primacy of Saint Peter. Jesus had met with his disciples to teach them to catch fish there. Fishing somewhere else, they would find nothing, and they had followed Jesus' advice where he was pointing. Catching 153 healthy, kicking fish.'

'Oh, my precious Babe. It's so wonderful to sense the Sea of Galilee and Gennesaret Lake. I love your narrative of the fishing.'

'Wow, then while I was standing by the shore, it chills in my body. Brrr, as it's a ghost. I sense "your" breath on my neck. Oh, my goodness, it was as you had put "your" blessed hands on my head. Next, it points towards the tower of the church. A nice but a strange sensation of goosebumps ran over my body. It touched me like being warmed by magical soft angel feathers.'

'Hmmm, alone by the shore; it's amazing. I told you I would be there, my sweet Mary Magdalene. Mwah, mwah.'

'Yea. It felt as Jesus's hand. "I see how you follow me," I whisper to myself. Next I glare at the cooing pigeon on the tower's top glaring at me. *Yes, I see you! I love you. I will be yours forever! You are near me.*'

'You see. I can touch my Mary Magdalene from a far distance.'

'Ha-ha. Though strange tender words ran fast through my mind. Suddenly it disappeared. Weird. An enigmatic experience.'

'Yea, it sounds weird, though not, Sweet Pea.'

'Then I strolled to Saint Peter's fish restaurant. Tasty, we got Saint Peter's fish with head and tail shared among us. Yummy served with fresh dates.'

'Ha-ha, I like your narrative of sharing of meals. I feel I'm eating from the same plate with you—just you and me.' He beams and I'm continuing my story.

'The next day's trip was sailing. One hour across the lake, from Tabgha on the north-western shore and back to Ein Gev. It was calm, floating in the rocking brownish water. Only the stern waves moved at a steady pace along the white boat. It was scenic to watch. Tom was playing "pirate of the Caribbean" when he notices a ship out on the horizon. Ha-ha, the chap delegated me, captain of the boat. Then we positioned the cannon and boom... boom... we shoot. He's a cheerful little fella. He reminds me much of my eager boys at nine years old.'

'Baby, you're so good with children. Tom truly must have enjoyed the game.'

'Ha-ha, yea. Back at the kibbutz, we had three hours at our own disposal. Several of us strolled along the gravelled footpath, crunching under our feet. Then we ended until by the lake to bathe. Tom enjoyed the splashing water. Oh, my, so funny. He tried with eager to catch dangerous crocodiles or sea monsters.'

'Did you tell Tom about the sea monster from Taiwan?'

'Yea, as I was laughing, standing next to Tom as I told him of the sea monster. His imagination was growing. Kapow, tjuh bang, slam and fighting a wild battle with the sea monster. I got soaking wet from Tom's splattering water. The other women were enjoying life in the calm water far away from him. Ha-ha, swimming around as little bathing nymphs of the ancient time of Jesus.'

'Sounds as you had some mesmerising days, Baby.'

'Oh, yea, darling. I grabbed my bag and diary and wrote fantasies from the past. Imagining I've been here with my you. That we hand in hand bathed here. Had the entire lake to ourselves. While daydreaming of you, I pictured us in the lake; me clinging as a monkey to your soft, warm body. In peacefulness. Wow, and in the steady and blissful greenish lake. Oh, my goodness!'

'Oh, I miss when you cling to my body. I love it when we walk naked in the pool.'

'My imagination didn't lack. We were sneaking to the shore to enjoy each other's company. Alone. Before the Sun's glow turned away in the mesmerising horizon.'

'Sounds mesmerising, Baby.'

'It was. I visualised that you could perceive my thoughts. Feel my soul. I sensed the emotion of your warm, gentle breath on my neck. Oh, my, while your hand gently was sliding into my hand. It pained me missing you so much, darling. My thoughts were too often of you.'

'Aww, Baby, you're so sweet. I also think of you all the time.'

'The Sun was still burning from the blue sky and warmed my body. As if it were you embracing me. Hmm, with your magnificent warm rays of the Sun. I meditated over you while sitting by the shore of the lake. In peace, I was watching an elderly couple promenading hand in hand along the shore. In an instant I miss your lovely tender kiss. Mwah! Envision us on foot. Holding each other's sensitive hand in a heated grip.'

'I'll always hold my Baby's hand in a heated grip.'

'I know. This fantasy was my dream medicine. Not to be too afraid. Lonely or unhappy.'

'Afraid? Don't be afraid. I do not leave you alone.'

'Something good happens inside my soul. Having such lovely, dreamy thoughts of us.'

'I'm always there for you, Sweet Pea. Nice dreamy thoughts.' He smiles so gorgeously.

'The girls were no longer bathing. They enjoyed the Sun's warm beams on a turned upside boat. Hi-hi, giggling and buzzing as busy bees. They talked of praying the rosary in silence. The hush had fallen over the shores of the lake. Only birds were singing lovely twittering tunes in the trees. Adults and children had disappeared. I stayed in my daydream, listening to the chirping songs. Wishing you would come and pick me up for a walk. As I walked along the shore, dipping my feet in the lukewarm water, I imagined the day's last swimming with you.'

'I even sense the smell from the saltwater, Baby. And seaweed permeating our nostrils.'

'I dreamed of the bluish moonlight shining on the shiny lake. And the stars were glittering upon us. Wow, then a shooting Star was falling through the universe. Ha-ha, so I made a wish.'

'My precious Mary M, I can imagine us hugging close. Touching the Stars. Breathing their light on us while the waves with lightness sing their smooth splashing song over the beach. Wauw, giving us peace. What did you wish?'

'Something about us.'

'Tell me, Sweet Pea.'

'Nope. Abruptly Isabella interrupts my trance of fairy-tale imagination. "It's dark now, Mary. I can't read anymore in my book. Let's go back." As we got back to the room, I called you immediately on Skype. Here I'm telling you my story of the last day's adventures.'

'You are so poetic!' I'm very pleased to sense and hear Drake's rasping voice, then we say goodnight.

Isabella has finished her prayers and is ready for dinner, and next we will enjoy our evening Mass. The men must sit to the right. The women to the left. It gives several instances of confusion and is very entertaining, so everyone laughs. Tom is busy with his strictly counting people, as if we are a bunch of dangerous criminals standing for man count on the prison corridor.

'It's the day of remembrance and mourning, from 8 p.m. The sirens will sound in commemoration of the fallen soldiers who have fought for their country. Please respect the howls of the sirens. Stand still for one minute to honour the fallen,' Andrew informs us.

Last, we sing, then preview tomorrow's schedule, while enjoying chilly white wine and beers in the tranquil garden. Most of us get tipsy, though during our festive some stewed nonsense comes from the witty and cheerful manager, Joyce, telling cracked anecdotes and hilarious jokes.

CHAPTER 23

MEMORIAL AND INDEPENDENCE DAY

> I've found that there is always some beauty left in nature,
> Sunshine, freedom, in yourself; these can all help you. Look
> at these things, then you find yourself again, and God, and
> then you regain your balance. And whoever is happy will
> make others happy too. He who has courage and faith will
> never perish in misery!
>
> —Anne Frank

The girls chit-chat outside before we settle for the night. I call Drake to tell him about the past exciting event.

'Hi darling. How are you today?'

'I'm okay, Baby. I've waited for your call. Let me hear how it went on you last trip.'

'This morning the flapping, dancing and a soft symphony of the swallows woken me. Despite the tweeting dancing birds, it was a splendid morning to wake up to with a gentle cool breeze. As Isabella and I sat on the balcony, I took in the sunny morning air. Then enjoyed my first hot coffee. In the horizon, I was watching at the peaceful glossy lake. It made me relaxed and cheerful. Next, I jumped into a refreshing shower. Ahhh ... letting the warm, gentle drops soak my body. And washed my hair. Fresh as a chirping bird I got dressed and joined the others for breakfast.'

'Sounds as a lovely morning, Baby. What were the plans for today?'

'It's still Memorial Day before Independence Day. Today the actual celebration will begin.'

'I thought it was only yesterday.'

'Today was Tabor mountain. As an extensive family, the Shibli Bedouin tribe lives at the foot of it. The bus couldn't get the entire way up. Some trip was in abundant taxis. Many other waiting tourists made it as a long waiting time. Ellen talked of the original sources of income in Israel—mainly tourists, agriculture, and diamonds. Israel doesn't have diamonds underground. But raw blocks containing diamonds, which they import. They cut the stones and sell them on the stock exchange.'

'Ha-ha, maybe you should bring some rocks back home with you?' He laughs.

'Ha-ha, hilarious. They buy oil and steel from other countries. They also cultivate their caviar in small fish farms. And sell it to fine restaurants in New York for almost $500. Hmm, it advances Israel within electronics and the medical industry in Israel. Did you know that?'

'No, I didn't, Babe.'

'Now, it's the second harvest time of year. In the old times, they always sacrificed something for the temples. This to ensure a good harvest next time.'

'That's interesting.'

'The Sea of Galilee is three metres below average water level. They have major problems with its water. The country is working on new salting plants. They will use the seawater for drinking water and agriculture.'

'How will they do that?'

'Hmm, I don't know. Wow, from Tabor, we had a stunning view over the Jezreel Valley. There we hold the Mass in an enormous church. A wonderful experience. We passed several mangoes and date plantations as we drove south along the lake towards the Jordan Valley.

Andrew gave a quick speech, praised of the Lord's Prayer and Hail Mary. Same ritual several times a day. From Route 65 through Afula, we drove towards Nazareth. Afula is a city in the Northern District known as the Capital of the Valley.'

'Oh, my god. Good old Nazareth. I miss the place.' What did Drake mean by that? 'Who is Ellen?' he then asks.

'She is a Danish citizen living in Israel. She was born in Denmark the same year Israel got her independence. Zion was the ancient name. A Jewish family in Copenhagen raised her.'

'Interesting.'

Ellen told us she became friends with many Jewish kids, and later many of her friends moved to Israel. When the Six-Day War broke out in 1967, several groups from Denmark and other countries moved here. Shortly after, they went back to Denmark again, and in the late sixties, they moved to Israel with their two small daughters. She worked a lot and learned Hebrew and Arabic, and then she became a guide for Christian groups. In the early seventies, a war began, and the guided tours stopped. Her husband is a pharmacologist and had an important job, so they stayed. He still does lots of medical research here, and she said they will never leave Israel again, because it's their home.

'What did you else do, Sweet Pea?'

'We arrived at the artificially constructed city. An open-air museum in Nazareth Village. It's reconstructed as the daily life of Jesus's era. Known as the Second Temple period. Originally built after the return from Babylon. Then adorned and enlarged by King Herod. It's a city of much biblical history. Museum displays show what agriculture implements, animal enclosures, sheepfolds, vineyards, and threshing rooms looked as. They depict a synagogue. Residential houses and kitchen tents. Weaving areas. The carpentry workshop where Josef worked.'

'My father was a carpenter.'

'I know, darling. It's said that here is the domed Basilica of Annunciation. It's where the angel Gabriel told the Virgin Mary that she would carry a child. We visited the small Orthodox Church with the well named after the Virgin Mary. Here she was always fetching water.'

'Oh, dear Mary Magdalene, was a fantastic mother.' He grins.

'Yea, yea, okay. At lunchtime, they served a biblical meal. It was similar as what they have fed back then—lentil soup. Wow, big green and black olives. Yummy and sweet-smelling naan bread. Several lemony, garlicky and minty sauces. Green crisp salad. Big red crunchy apples. Scrummy and sweet date purée. Delicious. After a half-hour of well-deserved lunch, we prepared to continue for the next agenda.'

'You should try to make these meals when you get back home to me.'

'Ha-ha, yea maybe. Well, next was Migdal, a city from the Second Temple period. "Magdala" in the Northern District. Ending up in the old town of Tiberias on the western side of the Sea of Galilee. This is a fundamental Christian and Jewish district for many pilgrims. With the Tomb of Maimonides and Abulafia Synagogue with its well-known mineral hot springs. Geez, it was a warm and hectic day. On the Armageddon plain is the foot of the Megiddo. The place that, in Christian apocalyptic literature, known as the site of the ending battle between the forces of good and evil—well-known as, Armageddon.'

'Oh, yes, there we will have the ending battle.'

'Huh? What do you mean?'

'Yea, our ending battle.'

'Eh? I don't get it. Anyhow, the Sun had set on the horizon, and the darkness had fallen into a refreshing night. The Moon was a quarter full. Hanging with its cut downwards. My imagination brought a picture of the little man sitting with his fishing rod. Cradling in his boat with one leg hanging over the edge of the Moon. The sky was black, so it was hard to see any sparkling Stars glowing on us.'

'Ha-ha, Babe, I was the man on the Moon. Hi-hi ... and watching you.'

'Aww, so sweet. I was thinking of you, darling. I was having a hard time getting in the right mood. The spiritual contact didn't flow through the atmosphere to me. Then I fantasised of the many places you claim we have wandered in Israel. Then I cast my gaze upon the nightly landscape of the breathtaking country. Wauw, and taking in the many small, enlightened villages we pass.'

'What a wonderful way you tell me of your today's adventure. Oh ... love it, Babe.'

'Thanks, my love. The girls sat chit-chatting before we settle for the night. In the meantime, I wanted to call you, and now I'm telling you about our past event. I know it's late with you, but I saw you were online, darling. It was worth a try if you still were awake.'

'Oh, my sweet eternal love, I'm so happy you called me. I love listening to it. I have a sensation I'm with you in the desert as we were before. It makes me joyful while I can sense your hand as we walk. Then talk philosophy of life—of us and the future of humankind.'

Did he say so, because he knows I'm a great fan of the great Greek philosophers, Plato, Aristotle, and Socrates? Then we say goodnight.

Isabella and I chat on the balcony, enjoying the luminous Moon and shining Stars in the sky's darkness. While staring at these magnificent glittering diamonds, I sense my closeness to Drake after our lovely chat on Skype. My imagination sends a silent message to him that will jump from one Star to the next, wishing they'll reach their goal across the globe. My senses of imagination send him warm kisses, while I daydream, they land on his soft lips that I want to kiss.

As I've finished my tea, I jump into the final refreshing warm bath, get ready for bed and tuck myself hugging the pillow and snuggle the duvet tight around me. Out from my right eye corner, I'm eyeing at Isabella, and see a horrifying ghost—gasp—she has put on her greyish night cream. She shows up as a spine-chilling lifeless person, with her gloomy mask over her face, and before she lays her gentle face on the pillow, she reads from her sacred writings and next tells few witty stories.

'Good night, Isabella. Thanks for a rich and hilarious day,' I mumble, turning out my light and falling fast asleep in solace with my lovely dreams, looking forward to the bright light of tomorrow and wishing Drake can sense my thoughts in his Asian dawn. I'm awful, melancholic! Though, the urge is enormous for me to be here alone. Deep in my soul; I know I need to find my new roots without him.

* * *

The next day and being back at the kibbutz, I'm dwelling in the day's presence of the memories, when swiftly I call Drake, as the other days, to tell of the day's adventures.

'Hi darling, I hope you had a stunning day.' I beam as we get connected.

'Yeah, it's okay. But I miss you, my sweet Babe.' Drake seems sadden.

'Likewise. Do you have time for today's adventure in the Holy Land?'

'I'm ready to listen, sweet little girl.'

I babble as an unstoppable waterfall.

'It was an awful morning. I couldn't get up. Isabella and I came to bed too late. My eyes ache. Ick, sticky red and swollen. I got an eye inflammation. The day before in the bus, I was sitting in a draught. Or am I having an allergic reaction? These days we have much pollen in the air.'

'Oh, Babe, I can see your eyes don't look so good.'

'I couldn't put on make-up. I resembled as a frightening scarecrow of a swollen, sick ghost. With my disoriented, lifeless body, I rushed in the shower. Trying to wake up and get my bones to speed again. I hurried for my breakfast, despite my gruesome appearance. Snatched a chamomile tea. An apple and a banana for the trip. Ellen promised to pass a pharmacy to buy ointment. Bah, everything was closed. Luckily Gladys had antihistamine and some eye drops.'

'What did you see today?'

'Katzrin. An ancient village and synagogue in the Golan Heights. The site is an open-air museum. We went to a silver workshop owned by Eli. He had opened only for us. I bought a bracelet and two rings. One with a Hebrew inscription. As we continue to Bental Mountain, an Israeli settlement established during the Six-Day War. From a cloudless blue sky, the glowing from the Sun shines vividly. Overlooking the incredible green hillier landscape. It's so beautiful on Mount Hermon. We can see snow on its peaks.'

It's a mountain cluster that makes up the southern end of the Anti-Lebanon mountain range, bordering Syria and Lebanon. Along the Golan border, where they have fences, we may not pass. The section is full of landmines, so you can only walk it on the marked trails. Because Syria demands that they want Golan back, the Syrians have no interest in revealing where they have located the mines. Then a tragic accident occurs.

'Ellen got serious and dramatic. Told us that in the winter the year before, when there was still much snow in the mountain, a group overlooked an overturned fence. Ignorant of the risk, they had continued into the dangerous mining territory. With a blast, a ten-year-old boy died after stepping into a snow-hidden landmine. And there went a shockwave through the entire bus of horror.'

'Oh, boy, that's awful. Did you also walk there?'

'No! As we walk by the fortress and catacombs, tiny irritating insects swarmed around my face. Yuck, I tried to blow and wave them away. Despite the insects, it was a breathtaking view. As we got closer to the catacombs, I noticed they were eerily dark. I didn't seem safe. I was not interested in getting in there. Uh-oh, I feared getting lost in the tracks. I went back.'

'Ha-ha, Baby, I can imagine you didn't enter them.'

'No way! During the waiting time, I arranged my practicalities. Toilets. Buying water, fruit, and salty chips. I was not in the mood today. I got sick. Geez, uncomfortable during our non-stop bus drive. The journey continued north to Banias. Through the Drusian region. That's where the Druse wear unique large pants. They would look good on you, darling. Ha-ha.'

'Ha-ha, ha-ha, so funny. Loose-fitting apple-catchers. Enough space for Willy.'

'Hi-hi. We drove at the steep mountain through thousands of hairpin bends—right, left, steep downwards. Yikes, the bus cruised as a ship in a raging, unstoppable storm. Without warning, the driver jammed on the brakes several times. Often he was holding back for other cars. It was a horrifying drive. Narrow gravel roads took us through a zone rich in bird life in a lush green nature. Yikes, dizzy and uncomfortable, I got nausea. It intensified after his horrendous driving to the mountain. But I still had an awareness of spotting many enormous flapping birds of prey. And stunning white storks.'

'Seems to not be your best day, Baby.'

'No, no. Jeez, suddenly Ellen loudly shouted, "Whoa! Watch out!" to the chauffeur. Oh, my, many of us got scared. Out of the blue, a giant turtle appeared. Ha-ha, it wanted to cross our path. The massive creature had calmly parked itself in the middle of the road. Not moving an inch. The chauffeur performed his best driving skills and turned with care around the turtle on the narrow-gravelled road. Brassy it crackled and crunched under the enormous wheels during his manoeuvre.'

'Did he get around the turtle? Without harming it?'

'Yea, and then he drove to the ancient site of Banias. At the foot of Mount Hermon is a huge spring. Once they associated it with the Greek god Pan.'

The archaeologists once uncovered a shrine dedicated to Pan. It's an ancient Roman city. The spring flows the entire way into the Jordan River. Imagine it's starting in Syria and ending in Africa.

'Peter pan. Ha-ha, ha-ha, was he there?' He jokes.

'Come on, darling. Ten kilometres ahead was the Lebanon border. She again shouted to the chauffeur, "Gasp! Watch out!" when another car appeared around the corner from a mountain wall.'

'Jeez, Babe, sounds as it was a dangerous trip you had.'

'Hmm, yea. Out of the blue pops up ten white Danish Vestas wind turbines. Tall and massive, standing on one of the mountain peaks. What a strange sensation, glaring at the modern Danish technology so far from my home country. Anyhow, it was a wonderful day. During our open-air Mass, the bright sunlight catches the babble of a pleasant sound of water from the waterfall in the distance. The radiating glittering colours of the rainbows spread before the water.'

'It must have been a stunning sight?' He glares dreamily at me.

'It was, I tell you. But the humming noise from the people, who didn't respect the Mass, grew louder. Loads of small children enjoyed the natural world around them. I was in a relaxed position, standing behind the others, trying to hear Andrew. Mostly I could only hear the waterfall in the distance.'

'Baby, it's as we whisper sweet words of love to each other during your journey. We feel in every way immersed in and united with all of nature.'

'I loved the experience as a real pilgrimage.' Twittering birds were delightfully chanting and honeybees were buzzing in the many fragrant flowers. In the distance, big and tiny butterflies fluttered in the warm breeze from bush to bush. Instead, I enjoyed the scenic landscape. The chirping birds and the laughing children's lovely playing.

'Did you take some wonderful pictures?'

'Yes, I did. I was unconcentrated. I couldn't hear Andrew. I took pictures instead. I've so many now.'

'I want to see them when you are back home.'

'At lunchtime I munched a pita bread with chicken. And a Coke in a Lebanese restaurant. Ugh, not the most mind-blowing food. It was dirty in there.'

'Oh, Baby, I can imagine you lost your appetite.' Drake pities me.

'Oh, yea. Next, we went for a walk. In the former old Syrian region. Again, Ellen warned of the risk of landmines. Not to walk outside the designated areas. The bus took the poorly walking to the next meeting spot.'

'Do they have landmines everywhere?'

'No, no. During a quick break, Gladys helped me, putting drops in my eyes. Of the sudden, she dropped her backpack into the river. Holy moly! It was floating to the Jordan River. Thank God, there was not much current in the river. Joey turned out to be a quick gazelle. Plunging into the water, with shoes and clothes. Ha-ha, and he fished the backpack out of the water. Gladys flung the bottom of the bag open. Oh, my goodness! Water poured out as a flood. Everything was wet— hymnbook, cash, and phone.'

'Whoa, that was not good. What did you do next?'

'Most of the group was hiking along the marked winding paths to the large waterfall. Darling, the nature was fantastic. We were following one of the three rushing rivers that flows into the Jordan River. Others walked another route. Over a sizeable new suspension bridge. There we met again. Andrew and I enjoyed the natural splendour around us. We talked of burdens weighing with sadness on my heart of my stepfather. It was relieving. Though we couldn't get any concluding on this.'

'We experience God's love seeping into our veins and hearts. You are at peace with me—no anger. No fear. It's replaced by total calm. Little girl, don't think about your stepfather.'

'No, I know. I tell you, darling. It was so magical. At the massive sputtering waterfall, we climbed loads of unreasonable stairs, ending up by the bus again.'

'Oh, your breath appears so sweet, Baby. Each one you take and with each heartbeat, you show me how total love comforts. Thus, we live forever.'

'You're so sweet, my love. As we got back at the kibbutz, I was first dwelling in the day's presence of the memories. Next I called you. I hope you loved my telling of the day's adventures?'

'Yes, Sweet Pea. How do you get such an imagination? It's so well told. It's magnificent!' He overjoys.

We say goodbye, then I ponder; *Why is he only so caring when we are apart?*

After dinner, Andrew and Joyce brief us on tomorrow's program. 'Tonight, you must pack your belongings. We will leave Galilee. The next journey is to the magical and hectic Jerusalem.'

Rapidly we get packed, because Isabella is meeting with Yosef, a sweet young Israeli guy.

She wants me to go with her to a club he knows, so we went to a local bar with him, at the private part of the kibbutz.

CHAPTER 24

JERUSALEM

> I returned to Jerusalem, and it is by virtue of Jerusalem that
> I have written all that God has put into my heart and into
> my pen.
>
> —Shmuel Yosef Agnon

Early in the misty morning, the staff brings our suitcases to the over-packed purple tourist bus. Everyone sits in their seat, and pious as sweet innocent angels we sing, while driving to the Jordan Valley. There we have a temporary break at Qasr Al-Yehud, where Jesus's baptism took place. The calm atmosphere spreads, and Andrew speaks of Emperor Tiberius and the fifteenth year of the reign, while Pontius Pilate was the governor of Judea and Herod being the ruler of Galilee. Famous names we know too well from ancient history. The more we drive south, the more barren the soil turns, from lush greenery to a golden sandy and stony desert landscape.

At the Dead Sea, the Sun gleams peacefully on its unusually salted water, appearing stunningly *dead*. If you get water in your mouth or eyes, rinse at once with clean water, or contact the lifeguards for help. It's that salty!

'Do not drink the water! *Take off* your jewellery; it will become discoloured. Enjoy the black mud.' Ellen told us before people jump into the sea. The mud is perfect for lubricating the skin, muscles, and joints and relieves but does not treat, just at once. The saline is good for psoriasis, though, to be aware, as it burns in wounds, but it cleanses. No danger in it.

Most of the group enjoys the bright blue, turquoise calm water, with the white salt on the shore. I'm not in the mood for a dip, because last time, I had an unpleasant experience with the Dead Sea, where we climbed the scruffy cliffs to get there. Though loads have changed during the last year and a half, as they have rebuilt it and transformed it into an adequate bathing beach. Lots of recent showers, and easy access to the stunning sea, so together with the Dutch priest, Pascal, we enjoy the picturesque view with floating people instead. A sweating hour as we sit watching the others swimming. It is unbearable in this heat, as we cannot find calming shade nor any blowing wind. Next to us is a Qumran (a shop), offering sweet flavouring Dade honey (mashed dates).

'It's good for baked goods. Smear it on bread or stuffing in food.' The lady tells us.

The Qumran offer stunning jewels of Roman glass, embedded in gold or silver. Tons of different t-shirts, caps, pottery, Dead Sea Scrolls Replica, and other tiny, scruffy junks as keyrings, pens and small magnets.

At noon, we arrive at a chaotic restaurant filled with lots of hungry, panicking tourist, behaving as wild non-fed lions. I grab the rice and chicken, then join an awful crowded queue. While waiting an endless time for a salad, I give up and skip the lettuce, heading towards the checkout. Oh, my! Such an ignorant and rude bloke at the checkout.

'We'd like to pay,' Ellen kindly tells him in Hebrew.

'Go to the other queue,' he answers wickedly.

Disappointed, Ellen and I go to the other checkout where Sister Miriam is paying for her food, and at the same instant she turns fast towards me. Oh, my goodness! Sister Miriam gets pushed by another feisty, angry customer. Beetroot salad and hot sizzling falafel with brownish and yellow and reddish-coloured scented spices tumbles over my beige pants and sandals. As a pig, I'm soaked in with old kitchen waste over my entire body, while wandering fuming around in a greasy pigsty, as I get awfully grumpy. Shut up! How embarrassing.

Infuriated, I leave my food on the counter and go for the restroom, taking off my pants, and wash them. Well, I never! A stupid, curious chap stare at me as if he's never seen a half-naked woman. Aw, this suck! I'm growling with Danish swearwords I can find, shouting afterwards in Danish; 'Shoo! What the hell are your stupid goggling eyes looking at? Piss off!' While I'm only standing in a top and thongs.

Blimey! The worst is to come, when I must put back on the dirty soaking wet pants and sandals. With wet splashing footprints, water dripping from my pants, I'm walking through the entire restaurant, while everyone glances at the wet, drowning angry snarling sea monster. Sadly, in the back of the trunk of the bus is my suitcase buried, so I can't grab any dry clothes.

As a lizard, I sit on a big hot stone in the Sun to dry, and take off my pants, then put them on the boiling hot rock. I'm starving and thirsty, though I've no intention of returning to the hopeless chaos of that restaurant. I'm terribly sweating, and the irritating flies clings as sucking slimy mites to my clammy skin. Desperately, I try to wiggle them away, though; I become more stressed by their nasty itchy bites when their vulgar slurping trunks gulp on my sensitive sweaty skin. In the meantime, several boisterously buses with hundreds of laughing and loud chatting tourists arrive for dinner. Wauw, I'm awful embarrassed when people pass me, glaring weird at the half-naked Danish gal.

Thank God! It's not me going into that chaos, I muse getting outrageous frustrated.

'Mary, you have missed nothing as far as the food goes. I'm so sorry of this episode. It wasn't my fault.' Sister Miriam humbly apologises.

'It's okay, Sister Miriam, I know it wasn't your fault.'

'Geez, Mary, the space was so cramped and unreasonable,' Miriam is comforting me.

'No matter how I turn it, Sister Miriam, I'm still hungry and thirsty.' I smile and she helps me to buy a bottle of water and an ice cream, but I don't want the ice cream.

In the bus, Ellen talks of the Dead Sea scrolls (Qumran Caves Scrolls), while the chauffeur takes us off the major road and onto a small zigzagging gravelled road through the desert of Judea, following the original pilgrimage path, Jesus walked on his way to Jerusalem. We reach the Monastery of Saint John and Saint George Monastery, and in the middle of the desert, in the eastern West Bank, is the stunning cliff-hanging complex with chapel and gardens. It's a short stopover, and Tom gets in the meantime a 'free' ride on a lazy camel, guided by a local Bedouin. With a smirky smile, the Bedouin gives him a 'free' juice, pretending he is so delighted with Tom. Ellen out of enjoyment buys the lad a bracelet from the Bedouin, so the boy believes he's getting everything for free. But, but... it's not for free! The local sneaky dude expects more from us. The adults must pay for the camel ride, and we give a penny, including paying for the juice.

The cracked zigzagging narrow gravelled route ends at the major road, inattentive to the driver thinks it's a one-way road. But he gets wiser! Astonishingly, he realises it's a two-lane, when other cars slowly pass by! I'm musing; *how will they ever be able to pass with two busses?*

In Jerusalem, we pass through the primary entrances to the Old City, and through Damascus Gate, arriving by the Syriac Catholic church of Saint Thomas, in the eastern and Arab part of the city. This becomes our accommodation for the next days. The first excursion goes to Catholic, Orthodox, Armenian, and several Christian faiths places of worship.

At the entrance is the anointing stone, and according to the Catholic faith, you must kiss the rock over the rosette at the gravesite. At the tomb of Christ, we walk to the Armenian Chapel, below Golgotha, where they nailed Jesus to the cross and where they buried him.

A long wearying day ended, and finally we get back at the monastery, having dinner. The rest of the evening is for free, but I'm exhausted, and go to bed, forgetting to call Drake.

I'm up early, at the next sunny and cooler day, despite not having slept very well. Outside is an unbearable noise of Muslim praying—chanting to Allah, ringing throughout the city, while the Sabbath began the day before. Many people are partying in the streets, and below the window, the Jews have a party on a patio on the Sabbat day. The small children happily play on the green lawn, playing ball or hiding-and-seek game, and many Orthodox Jews stroll on their way to the synagogue. Schools, businesses, and workplaces are closed, so no bustling heavy traffic during our next trip to the Mount of Olives.

At Pater Noster, the Roman Catholic church, we study the many stunning memorial tablets with the Lord's Prayer, beautifully written in more than a hundred languages. Anna reads it in Serbian, Hannah in Italian, I in Spanish, Ellen in Hebrew, and Andrew in Latin.

Next, we visit the cave where Jesus taught his disciples to pray the Lord's Prayer in the church constructed in 1152. A Danish bishop (Svend of Viborg), donated funds to this spot and when he passed away, they buried him inside the church. Again, a busy day, so I don't have time to call Drake. This is our last day and after Andrew bless our purchased holy effects, before we go to bed. At four AM we must leave the place and fly back to Copenhagen, and I don't have energy to call Drake and go to bed.

I want so much to cry my eyes out until the suffering tears disappear as I write my next chapters. But I can't. It's deep-rooted in my stomach, as the pain crumbles my inner soul with a clenched iron fist, smashing my heart and soul. I cry grieving tears inside but prefer to laugh rather than to weep. It's immensely hard to laugh over something so unmanageable tragical and tear-jerking hurting. I get lost as my agonizing tears get stuck inside my soul. I do not understand it, as the unwise chick runs around in her cage of misery with a ripped-out heart and as a chopped of head.

CHAPTER 25

A TINY CHICKEN BRAIN

> To make extra money, my parents would sell eggs and
> chickens. I was very little. I remember a chicken's head being
> chopped off with the chicken running around. I wasn't sure
> if my imagination was running away with me or if it really
> happened. It really happened.
>
> —Michael Keaton

It's heart-sickening as my frustrated feelings reappear glooming of the time with Drake. While I ponder over the many overheated love letters and next thinking of the devastating correspondences, which gives me a mix of joyful and horrifying flashbacks of the time when I believed he loved me. At first, everything was magical with him, when he was caring and paid much attention to me. Then I got lulled into his more constricting and mentally abusive behaviour—the devaluation phase! During this period, I walked on sharp cutting eggshells with him. Passion turned to emotional suffering, though it was hard not to fancy him. Simultaneous with his madness, he also had compassionate and magical sides. I didn't want him to dislike me, but of a reason things turned in the wrong direction. I went from being magically happy floating on a soft pink cloud, listening to angel music, to a phase where he gets more dominant. He criticises me much, using his massive power as a doctor and systematically to dissuade me from my concerns.

* * *

I'm excitingly glad to be back in The Philippines, after my enchanted event in Israel and after two month's absence, I'm hoping to get travel peace in my exhausted body. I show my radiant smile when Drake picks me up at Manila Airport, and as an overjoyed love bird, I cling to his hand during our two-hour drive back to the house. The atmosphere shows high, and he appears cheerful, while we chitchat of my travel to Denmark and New York. The magical fairy-tale of what I expect is my life's exotic and loving adventure doesn't last. In disgust for my absence, he has arranged something strange with a new investor in Iran—and behind my back. He believes he has made the deal of the year—yea, perhaps of his lifetime, so with proudness he tells me his demands to do business with the Iranian.

'I have splendid news, Baby. We will move to Chalus. Hurrah, I'll set up a five-star clinic.'

'Eh? Huh? Chalus? Where is that?'

'Iran. Yea, Mr Samir loved my thirty-eight years of experience. Oh, my, now I can enclose what we can bring to Iran.'

'Oh! What is going on, darling?'

'Mr Samir will give me total support for the development. We will get official permits.'

'Oh? What are we going to do there?' I'm surprised of Drake's sudden change.

'Woo-hoo, Babe, I can do medical research at the university. I will find talented local doctors from abroad. They will finance for building, equipment, and a start-up running costs.'

'Darling, we don't know Iran.' I protest.

'It doesn't matter. I will be a consultant for the construction of the place. Install all medical equipment. Mary, you will do consulting for marketing plans. Fix décor and dress code for staff.'

'Eh? I'm not sure. It doesn't appeal to me.' I growl.

'Baby, I will perform training courses for staff, therapists and doctors.'

'What about a contract? Better think of that, darling, before we consider of leaving.'

'For me, it is of vital importance to start a neurologic research program. Focusing on the brain dysfunction.'

'Argh! Brain? What do you know about such things? Drake, I'm not interested in moving.'

'Rubbish! My reliable protocol has a marvellous chance of success.'

'It will ruin everything for us in The Philippines.'

'Nonsense! It takes advanced research in this challenging discipline to achieve that. I can involve the medical university in Iran. Baby, this is my ultimate dream for a new success.'

We wind up receiving an official invitation to help Mr Samir to set up a minor hospital in the outskirt of Chalus. I have no urge to leave The Philippines, because I feel more secure and happy here with Drake.

'Mr Samir is a multimillionaire. Babe, this is an excellent opportunity to earn substantial money.' Drake sees only millions of dollar sign in his greedy eyes for leaving The Philippines.

'What do we do with our dogs?' I sob, heartbroken of leaving them behind. 'I'm not the slightest interested in leaving.' I irritated glance at him and found he is staring at me, annoyed.

'Sweet Pea, this is no problem,' he swiftly replies icily. 'We can bring the dogs back to the streets.'

'What? Are you serious?'

'Yea dump them where we found them. It's only street dogs.'

'Oh... my... God... You can't consider that?' But he meant every word. I can't get over my heartbreak—how could he propose such a cruel solution? I am furious. 'We must find somebody who wants to adopt them.'

As we arrive at home, he proudly shows me the business plan. It looks promising, though; I comment on few points of his original method. Basically, I understand only a little of his calculation, and I usually can grasp that many of his ideas in the treatment protocol are reasonable.

'Hmm ... Don't you think it's best first to get a legal contract with Samir? It's vital, darling. Before we move to a new country.' Staring at him, hoping he will agree.

'Don't you worry, Babe. You well know I'm the best in the world. Only I can do this.'

'It's too risky. I don't like it.' I'm suspicious.

'Don't see the daunting writings on the wall. We can trust Samir.' He growls.

'But still it's risky, Drake. I don't want to move. I enjoy it here in The Philippines.'

'Jeez, Mary. It's an obvious chance for me. I can earn lots of money again. I won't need to depend on you.' The dragon growls.

'Eyh? Sincerely!' I caution. 'We have had too many failures.'

'What? I feel utterly screwed and disappointed that you classify it as that, Mary.'

'Okay? then I must trust you.' I glare at him, dumbfounded, when he raises his voice.

'Jeez, Mary, it seems as you only want to hurt me.'

'I'm anxious. Something is not right. I'll be proud of you if it finally will succeed.'

'Argh, Mary! I will not allow you to ruin this for me.' He snaps.

'Oh, my god!' He decides it over my head, then another experience in our life begins.

Thank the stars, both dogs get adopted by a loving family we beforehand knew, and I feel I have a right conscience, so my heart is pleased. Over the last years with him, I realise I've drained almost $300,000 from my savings on his many unsuccessful adventures. I'm exhausted and devastated with the wasted money spent on his many scruffy business proposals and our nerve-racking livelihood. Self-centred, I see Iran as an opportunity for me to be no longer paying for the leech, then in my infatuation and my need to have him beside me, I hope and trust in him and Samir.

The next and unknown journey in Iran can begin. My glorious memories and my loving dogs are now a part of our history—of a dream I believed was real and long-lasting. In my grieving, as we leave The

Philippines, Drake's famous words pops up, 'Baby, everything has a beginning. And everything a natural ending. An end can often be the beginning of something new and exciting.'

Ha-ha, yea, now we can prepare for a new run and our fresh 'Iran crusade', not knowing how the beginning of a new life will turn out there.

*　*　*

Iran is difficult to access, and it's bureaucratic with visa and work permission, but we have after several weeks finally received the official invitations from Samir. This leads us first to travel from The Philippines to Qatar for the first certified procedure—everything paid by Mr Samir.

'We must do every necessary document at the consulate in Qatar,' Drake explains.

'I'm *not* content. I feel unsecured. Yea, scared.' I caution.

He enters the next wicked phase of his pessimistic side—meanness to me; 'What's going on in your tiny chicken brain. You are so dense, Mary.'

'I frankly regret having let you convince me to move,' I say, because he often pops up as a mean jack-in-the-box is unkind and calculating when he doesn't get what he wishes.

'You aren't good enough. Gee, Mary, you're not clever enough.' Apathetic the bastard growls at me.

'What? Honestly? I'm not sure you are honest with me.' Rapid I am near to get broken, and I can't see upside-down anymore, with his callous and scrupulous ugly comments.

'Mary, it's wrong what you accuse me off. But I've learned that's how you are! I'm not lying! *You are!*'

'Huh? What did I lie about?' I'm flabbergasted every time; he turns things around.

'You are utterly mean, Mary. *Not me!*'

'Whatever.'

'You took everything from Paul—it pissed him off as you do me,' out of the blue he roars at me as he is a tiny ill-mannered man-child. 'Your family and friends hate you.'

Might be, it's because Drake divides me even further from my family and removes everything that draws my attention away from him. Then it's easier for him mentally to abuse me when I don't possess the resources of people I trust.

'You need psychological help, Babe.' Was one of many sudden comments from him.

'I've never taken profit of you! But *you* use me!' The gale-forced dog of the sudden accuse me of. That sentence I end up hearing many times.

It goes on and on, and the rambunctious dude has gone utterly mental.

I'm 100 percent dependent on him and I ponder; *Wauw Mary, it must be you who is wrong.* I'm confused to my bones when he is jealous, mainly when I speak to others, particularly when it's men. Intimidating and rude, the feisty inflamed dog barks and accuses me of absurdities.

'You're worthless and stupid. Now I get it why Paul wanted to divorce *you*.'

'Huh? What the hell are you talking about, Drake?'

His behaviour is only to humiliate me in front of others. The man I love becomes brutally aggressive towards me, and swiftly Drake has much more and new strict rules for me but none for himself. It's as if he owns me.

'You steal my knowledge.' The storm-tossing, angry clown suddenly roars.

Well, I will spare you for the endless list of mean sentences, he often shouts in my face. I'm shaken and discover what an impressive matter of pressure he is putting on to me because of his selfish power plays and lies. I always apologise and blame everything on myself. I don't believe in my inner senses of judgement anymore, when he shifts from fluctuating, devilishness and meanness to arousing, dishy sweet tenderness. I'm stuck with him in Iran, so I'm always on eggshells with him, and life becomes a living hell, full of upheavals. It's not the man I fell in love with, so when I try to pull out of the knock-down-and-drag-out relationship, his many excuses of being sorry appear.

'I'm so sorry,' he excuses. 'Baby, I'll do everything to prevent this from happening again. My brain has been working on high pressure for what I did to you.'

'Ahh, it is okay darling, I understand,' and forgive him again.

'Sweet Baby girl, I feel sorry for you.' Tenderly his voice changes and gets more antagonistic. 'I realise how you try to fight your inner demons; they are ready to tear you to pieces.'

'Eh? Darling, why are we talking about demons again?'

'Mary, I have spent years of my life making your miserable life better. Jeez, then I've put my life on hold.' And he gets even more hostile.

'Darling, I know you have been there for me.'

'What I don't understand, Mary, what's in it for me?' And out of nowhere after Drake paused few seconds, shouts as an angry grizzly bear raising furiously his hands in the air. '*Nothing!*'

'Huh? What do you mean?'

'Damnit, Mary! It's only for you outright to deceive me.' He disturbed growls. Shortly after shows his loving *other* part, speaking heartfelt to me with a rasping tender voice.

'Baby, my love is deep and heartfelt for you.' Gently, he takes my hand and fondly kisses me on my forehead. Yak, I dislike those kisses on my forehead and feel so degraded.

'I'm in tears. Darling, I'm massively confused.' And glance at him.

'Sometimes I can't control my thoughts, Baby. I mean nothing by it. I always regret when we talk of it,' squeaks the angry, stirred up paradise bird.

'I forgive you. Let us not talk more of it.' I peep sorrowfully, and then he shifts his cataclysmic mood again.

'Sweet Pea, you shall not constantly prove your love to me. I notice you do,' he grumbles.

'Fear is my doubt. Doubt is my fear. I feel you use me.'

'I notice you love me. I'm the chosen one. That you dare to say I use you is too much. I have started with Iran on my own.'

'Trust is my anxiety. Sometimes I fear you so much.' I can't take his pestilential shift from sweet to angry and reverse.

'I'll be bloody glad if I can do it without you, Mary.'

'Huh? What? Oh, my goodness.'

'I've no place for a sick soul as you. Christ, you're hideous, Mary.' Roaring, he glares crossly at me, convincing me of what he says.

'Now I get nervous when you talk like that.' I'm dumbfounded.

'I'm your life. You are mine. I'm your salvation. Your comfort when you are sad.' Calmly he shifts again and tries to comfort me. 'I'm your soul mate. Baby, you can always lean on me when things are tough.' The rip-roaring dude acts as if he is God.

'Creating confidence is my hopeless fate of never being able to trust anyone.' I glare in sadness and cry.

'Babe, I'm glad you're trying to move towards the core against the demons. We must pull them out of you by the root.' The exorcist growls.

'I don't fancy when you think I'm possessed by demons.'

'You must admit it, Baby. It confirms to me I've not been mistaken of you. I've found my way back to what I'm best at. I did again by myself.'

'When I get confidence in a person, I doubt whether I can trust in that person.' I enter a defence mode.

'Sweet Pea, I'm your best friend. I'll always be there for you. Though, it might be its best we end our bond?' He pats my hair with his fingertips.

'Huh?' I'm in tremor! 'You failed once by not showing confidence in us. Not telling the truth. It nags me.' I counteract, hoping Drake understands I'm talking of the Asian call girls. Then he shifts again to tenderness.

'I'm your lover, Baby. I will never let go of you.' Suddenly he changes his mind.

'I'm full of confusion, darling. You shift all the time.'

'No, I don't. You do. I'll clinch you in my heart and with my body.' Oh, my goodness, it's perplexing.

'I don't get it, Drake. You want me, then you don't want me.'

'I'll give you great satisfaction in every cell of your body with my hands.' He beams lovingly at me, while he is wrinkling his brows, trying to affect my sexuality.

'Being deeply hurt is one thing that brings out the worst fear in me.' My hands reach out to his, and he stares at me.

'Baby, I'm the only one who understands you. I take the good with the evil. Your faulty is temporary. The goodness is everlasting.' His breathing is uneven.

'Eh? Faulty? Darling, broken promises and untruths make it difficult to create serenity. It makes me scared and insecure!'

'My sweet little girl, I sincerely hope that my massive love for you can always overshadow the demons that tear inside you.'

'Eh? I'm sorry. Try to understand me. Not misunderstand.'

'Sweetie, you must trust in me!' His state changes to tenderness.

'I want to believe you, darling.' Then stare at him, disoriented.

'I hope that you will understand with me being there for you. Trust me, Baby.' He grins.

'I trusted when you said, "It will never happen to me again." But it did! That's why I'm afraid it will happen again.' I'm thinking back on his massive hustler lie in Macau.

'I will be to the end and beyond.' He irritated pulls back and irately crosses his arms.

'When we are not together, fear and thoughts of the worst kind go through my head.'

'I hope every day to showing you—I am towards you. Trust me, Babe. I'm there.'

'You say you've always been the only one who understood me. Hmm?'

'Baby, in many other ways of daily life—that my love for you is genuine. It's not pretended. I've no conditions!' His eyes become significant points of persuasion.

'I'm afraid of being used. Why are you mean? Next sweet to me?' His jaw drops in surprise at my question.

'What? Bloody hell, Mary! I deeply wish that you will do everything you can to get in balance.'

'Your often-sweet way of being makes me sometimes think; there might not be a loving man for me.'

'Aw, come on, I'm your mate. Your loved one. Your husband. Your Jesus.' He swings as a wild, uncontrolled pendulum.

'I often try to convince myself of what I have with you does not exist.' I scowl at him.

He leans forward towards me, pulls me in abruptly. 'Babe, I'll give you goose pimples on your arms and back when you climax repeatedly.' Again, he uses the dirty trick. 'I'm the only one who can glance deeply into your eyes. See you—the one who can sense you.'

'I'm scared, Drake. Constantly surrounded by evil. Falsehood. Insecurity and lies.' I sob.

'Argh! Jesus! So, unbelievable mean you are, Mary. I let myself in your horrible life.' He thunderous shouts, continuing his raging speech. 'Are you that angry with me?'

'No, I'm not angry. Confused! Yes.'

'Only I have superb control of what's going on inside you—even when you go nuts. You are so difficult to understand, Baby. Jeez, then hiding in your stupid holster.'

'I'm not sure if I can trust that you love me as you say.' I sorrowfully sob.

'Sure, you can trust me. Sweet Pea, I love you. You're honest and good. You can talk to me of what you're struggling with. Your deepest phobias.'

'Huh? What do you mean?'

'I know you can see when you beat reason and justice. Then you get lost in your mind.'

'Eh? I understand nothing.'

'You understand better than you did before of controlling your thoughts and grasping them. You get a reason out of no reason.'

'I can't follow what you're saying, Drake. Do you mean all is my fault?' I glare at him.

'Damn it! You see ugly motive where there is none. Babe, you see fairness where it's hard for you to see anyone. You do it all the time.'

'I've never known a person as you.' My heart beats faster in the confusion of not knowing if I'm right or wrong.

'You can grasp yourself better—give useful expression in words and actions in the fact "to be sorry". Your enormous heart will always do the best for others. But you expect to get again, Sweetie. You can't always get that. That's why you get disappointed and upset.' He concludes.

'Why can't you just allow me to enjoy and love you? Do you understand what I mean?'

'No! This is how people get upset. You expect those you give to and are good to can grasp.'

'I fear the worst, when you swing so much, darling.'

'Baby, you expect people will give back in the same heartfelt way. It rarely happens. Man is selfish. He will not give. But is very good at receiving.'

Ironically, I sense Drake is only good at receiving, and being selfish. I overrule my concern.

'Forgive my confused mind. My bad thoughts of you. Maybe they are unfounded.' I cry and hear that I'm making a big apology to him.

'Baby, you get disappointed. You expect what you do not recognise well—a reward for being good, fair and giving your heart to others.' Then he hugs me and continues to preach. 'I have learned the art of giving. Not expecting to get anything back—though one always hopes. When that happens—no reward comes—you close off with a smile.' He pushes me aside and glance intensely at me. 'You move on in the path of life. Don't face back. I can still get disappointed.' Again, I'm in his embrace. 'I also get upset having a hard time getting out of it. Then I can sense when someone is possessive of me. Mostly those who are suffocating me.'

'Eh? Am I possessive? Am I suffocating you?'

'Hmm ... Regret is a demon that one must work hard to get rid of, Babe. Being there doesn't mean letting it control one's life. You are sitting in a downward spiral that only makes you unhappy.' Swiftly he pushes me aside again and changes his mind. 'You should not bother me or others by your outrage and negativism. I became much better at finding the right balance within me. And I face forward to getting this last demon out of me.' So, he admits he has demons.

'Forgive my ungratefulness. Okay, perhaps it's my fault,' then I stop sobbing.

Too often, I seek forgiveness from Drake by blaming it on myself.

'Forgiveness is the cornerstone of a balanced life. When you realise that you can never expect goodness from others. What you give, they will never return to you. Babe, then you can live in balance.' He pauses for a minute, thinking and glaring at me, while I sit mute and study him, not understanding anything.

'Babe, I openly try to get everything clarified between us—to see if we are moving closer together. Or are on our way. Or on each way.' His words frighten me.

'Are you afraid I will leave you?' I sincerely try to be a superwoman for our relationship.

'If you won't become hysterical or get crazy and disappointed over people, we get closer. I ask you to think of my words. They are words of lifelong knowledge with people who I have helped. I got "nothing" in return.' And he babbles and babbles as an unstoppable excited parrot, while I'm impatiently listening.

'Baby, only you have given me your heart.' He gives me a tender squeeze in my hand. 'Your joy in return for my love and tenderness for you. Never forget! Sometimes you do. Keep strong, my little girl. Mostly for us! I keep strong for us. You know I love you eternally. Trust me.' And finally, he stops, and we sit in a silent embrace.

I only expect one thing from Drake—that closeness and intimacy will replace the ecstasy of our 'honeymoon phase'. I want steady love. Not nastiness. He can't always give me that love, and he has no decent level of personal responsibility as it relates to his destructive behaviour. Too often he talks of me having a demon. I don't possess such. Is it entirely in his screwed-up head?

I give him what he wants, although it's never enough. His superficial emotional life shows more and more up as emptiness and distance in our relationship—not as the many love declarations he pretends to give me. He shows, instead, that our relationship, for him, is massively tediousness, so he fills it with explosive conflicts or annoying silences towards me. It's always arguments of demons and money, and nothing is ever his fault.

CHAPTER 26

MILLIONS OF DOLLARS IN IRAN

If your only goal is to become rich, you will never achieve it.
—John D. Rockefeller

Mr Samir is of Persian ancestry, known of the imperial Iran and worked himself up from nothing to having many immense companies and is famous and wealthy. Drake fast realises there's easy money to collect, so he will not stop to bring himself into a position to get an affordable deal with Samir. I'm no longer essential for him. The one son and Samir's ex-wife Yazmin, who lives in Qatar pick us up at the airport.

'Everything is ready on express time. Your temporary visa will be available before you travel to Iran. It's complex to get all the permits for the country. Ha-ha, best thing is I have an influential father. You can pay your way through everything.' Abbas laughs.

It's not the first time I've experienced such moral depravity of bribery. Such acquisitions of benefits via payment or the provision of services occurred often in The Philippines. For me, it's a peculiar world I'm living in since I met Drake. Corrupt services are not exactly my style.

After a long, tedious day at the consulate, the family invited us to a Persian dinner, where we meet with Karim, Abbas's sister and other family members. It thrills them of the new initiatives with us, and their hospitality is overwhelming in their lovely home. It's no different from beautiful homes in other countries, except for the extravagant and stunning Persian rugs, many large figurines and statues, and the vast dark wooden kitchen. Their enormous bathroom boasts golden water faucets, a Jacuzzi, and in the garden is a vast swimming pool.

Several business associates, friends including a GP participant. As I greet doctor Mustafa, I get distressed. Something is wrong, I'm feeling uncomfortable with him.

'Nice to meet you, Doctor Mustafa. I'm Doctor Drake, Lucifer Bates.' He proudly greets Mustafa and sits next to him. 'What a splendid chance with the hospital *I will* build for Samir.'

Mustafa is the 35-year-old private family doctor of Arabic ancestry. Handsome dude, with a twist of mystique and slick behaviour.

'Hmm ... Interesting.' Mustafa mumbles, gazing at Drake, while lifting his black bushy eyebrows, and smirks.

'It will be important. We can offer the newest technology—a fantastic investment.'

'What technology? Any special medic's?' Mustafa's eyes are tense as he smirks.

'I'll have special European doctors working for us. I've the best contacts from the world,' Drake slickly brags and shines as a star.

'Oh! Wauw! What is your plan?' Mustafa asks curiously.

'A top-notch clinic—mainly within beauty and cosmetic surgeries; ear, nose, and throat operations; body therapy; injury rehabilitation; and stem cell treatments. Believe me, my business plan is huge.'

Drake's extreme sense of self-importance and pathological grandiosity aren't lacking over the next hour. Oh, my God! He's so in love with himself. I've never heard him boast of himself so much before—how good he is, and his supposed over forty years of medical experience. It's all slick attention-seeking, a play from the gallery, and it's all about him, him, *him*. Oh, jeez, so much he lies!

Mustafa listens intensely, and the competing between the dudes begins. I observe Mustafa's personality and body language, stare at Drake and make my notes. Mustafa appears sneaky, unpleasant, and not content with Drake being number one in control. Something doesn't match the scenario. I've learned there's a considerable difference between Scandinavian, Asian, and Middle Eastern cultures, so as a guest, I try to adapt to the distinct cultures. Whoa! That's harsh for Drake, breaking all the rules. Mustafa's many questions cause them to compete against each other more, and there is an inharmonious atmosphere between them. Who is the best? Each has his own agenda, and things could quickly go the wrong way. *Drake has no chance to become the leader of the pack, I ponder,* and my thoughts frighten me. I'm uncertain whether it's right that we move so hastily to an unknown new culture. I try to take part enthusiastically with my awful English, and sometimes times, I warn Drake in Danish.

'I beg your pardon, Doctor Mustafa, my English is not so good. Doctor Bates will translate my question.' I excuse myself when I interrupt.

The sneaky snake gets annoyed—me as a woman interfering with the men's business.

'Why don't you take part in the *women's* conversations? Then I can talk business with Doctor Bates.' The chauvinist commands several times. It hurts my feelings, leaving me with a numbness.

'I'm sorry. I want to take part here. I'm a partner. Samir invited both of us to prepare the clinic.' I behave politely, though I'm on fire inside.

Cling, an abrupt sound come from a bell. 'Please go to the dining room.' Yazmin says.

The table appears exquisitely decorated with various Persian mild and spicy specialities. Glass noodles, brown and Basmati rice, with vibrant red cranberries and barberries; lamb, fragrant chicken, and garlicky beef kebabs; colourful vegetables and many sorts of nuts; and smoked fish, black caviar, and tiger shrimp. Delightful comforting smells waft through the entire room. Pickles, hot flatbread, and green herbs, along with fruits—apricots, raisins, big red pomegranates, purple plums, and black prunes. The different flavourings along with the dried lime, freshly chopped parsley, and the many sweet, nutty things send delicious lemony, minty and garlicky scents to my nostrils. My eyes shine as I take in the many exciting, colourful dishes. I spy a red and gold eggplant and tomato stew cooked with turmeric and a pomegranate walnut stew with chicken. Cinnamon reaches my senses when I get closer, and I am flash backed to the sweet Danish Christmas aroma. There is a mix of orange saffron and bright yellow turmeric, and they decorated most of everything with deep red tomatoes. Dessert includes unique kinds of cake, along with vanilla- and rosewater-scented ice cream. No alcoholic beverages, but lots of chilled sweet drinks, hot black tea, and icy water.

For a few hours, we enjoy the feast, and of the sudden people say goodbye. We grab a taxi back to our hotel, and exhausted, I smack my bum on the sofa, tired after today's events and new impressions.

'Darling, I don't understand what Mustafa said. To many things don't fit.'

Whoa! The angry bunny jumps loud and screaming out of his rabbit hole and stares fuming at me. 'What a horrible twisted mindset you have. Stop painting the devil on the wall. What does your stupid nonsense mean?'

'Mustafa specifically asked you to teach him in your skills—*for free!*'

'What the hell is happening to you, Mary? Your way of understanding and mistaking has always been difficult for me to understand.'

'Calm now, Drake.'

'*It's tedious!* You're so sceptical of whatever I do.' Yelling, he wrinkles his angry forehead.

'I have a hunch the dude will take over your position.'

'You don't have a damn sense of doing business, Mary. Only I have the knowledge!'

'I don't trust Mustafa. Nor do I feel safe with the snake.'

'Argh, you dislike everyone. Everyone is a mean pig in your eyes.' His roaring continues. 'Don't bother me with your imprudent expressions! The entire plan is mine! *Do you understand?*' And it's obvious to me he doesn't want me involved in the business.

'Darling, why do you react like that?' I dropped the jaw to the floor.

His tirade doesn't stop there. 'You've nothing to say in this matter,' he roars, maddened. 'You follow my rules. You don't have a millimetre

of the skill. I need to channel my entire energy into this clinic. *Alone!'*
His eyes and voice wanted to strangle me.

'Bah, I apologise for my interference,' scared I stammer.

'At last I can make huge cash flow again; it should delight you. Jeez,
I don't believe you love me enough.' Such a reckless excuse he brings to
the table and continues. 'Bloody hell, Mary, Grr, you have no goodness
in you.' Apparently, he wants a fight with me.

I'm utterly speechless and can't follow his sudden aggression and
outburst.

'Why do you criticise me? Christ! You possess an unstable mind.' he
shouts on my way to the bathroom.

'Gah, I give up. I'll bathe now. Will you join me?' asking him to
avoid further discussion.

'*Understand* it Mary, I'm not your enemy. Don't rub in it.' he
grumbles.

'Let's not talk more of it tonight. We sleep on it,' I mumble and close
the bathroom door.

For a while I wait for him to join. Shattered, I sit in the cabin's
corner and let the warm water runs down my body. I want to cry,
because I feel so dejected.

'What are you doing, darling? Why didn't you join me?' I ask upon
entering the room.

'I made some corrections in the business plan,' but he won't tell me
what it's about and goes for his bath.

In bed, I tuck my body into Drakes and grab his hands, then with
cosiness, he wraps his arm around me in a firm hug. Our vow is; never
to go to bed without a kiss and saying goodnight.

'I love when you squeeze me into your body, honey. Then I feel safe
in your arms.'

'Hmm ... grumble ... mumble...'

'Sorry darling, I messed up. It was careless of me. I'm to blame.
Forgive me?' As a begging puppy, I woof and give him one more kiss.

He is lying on my right side, while I'm clenching my ear tightly to
his chest, and listen to his smooth heartbeat.

Bum, bum, *bum*—it's rhythmic and comforting, while he talks about his plans and excitement. His crispy voice has a fantastic soothing influence on me. Then it muffles more out in space until I fall into a deep sleep.

Four days went by in Qatar. Next we went to Iran to prepare the business. None of us have any knowledge of the country, other than he can turn a fast buck.

'Darling, I'm uncertain this is the right thing. It's an unknown adventure. We still haven't any contract.' To me, it's important to know more—to secure our future with a contract.

'Baby, this is my biggest chance to make wealth again—millions!'

'I'm not sure how to describe this. It's a strange experience I'm having with you.'

He spans at me when I worryingly express my doubts. However, staying in Iran is my clear opportunity to get out of the many financial obligations I've taken on with him, so that would be great for me to get rid of the commitments.

'Mary, I can earn like the amount I lost in the States.' He only thinks of dollar signs.

'Too many things have changed harshly in our relationship.' I'm very concerned.

'Babe, it's not so important that you are a part of it. I only want my Babe to be here.' The money has focused him utterly on the wealth he believes Samir can give him.

*   *   *

Iran is officially the Islamic Republic of Iran a country in Western Asia in the south-eastern Caucasus, and bordering Iraq, Azerbaijan, Armenia, Pakistan, Turkmenistan and Afghanistan. It has a coastline on the Caspian Sea; and boasts 83 million inhabitants. It is home to one of the world's oldest civilizations and Arab Muslims conquered the empire in the seventh century AD. The Iranian government is widely considered to be authoritarian. The country is rich in oil, natural gas and fossil fuels. Iran has 22 UNESCO World Heritage Sites, being the 10th largest in the world. Historically, Iran has been referred to as Persia, though the country changed its name requested by Reza Shar in 1935 to Iran. In 1979 Iran had a revolution and hereafter Iran, officially became an Islamic republic. As many perhaps remember, the Iraqi army invaded the western Iran in 1980 launching the Iran-Iraq War.

Iran has a rich wildlife, including panthers, grey wolves, the Eurasian lynx, foxes, wild pigs, gazelles, Eagles and falcons. Domestic the use donkeys, camels, cattle, buffaloes, goats, sheep and the horse.

Samir sponsor our accommodation in a hotel apartment in Chalus residing one million people, and a stunning city, with several renovated old buildings in beige limestone. The Daryadar Alican Centre, with its distinctive architecture and curved flowing style, is one of the modern buildings, a stylish cultural centre, and a famous venue for international events. There are some few modern skyscrapers in town, The Gilaneha Tower (under construction at the time), the five Flame Towers (Hotel Rouhani), Khamenei Hotel, and the Hassan Tower,.

Some places of Iran are barren, and walking along the harbour promenade in downtown, you can smell a somewhat sweetness and see the crude oil—black gold, seen in potholes on fields or floating in massive oil clots in the Caspian Sea.

The national Eastern cuisine culture taste fantastic, with lots of fresh organic herbs, greens, and vegetables, and most of the national dishes they prepare with organic lamb, poultry, and beef.

Iran has tons of lakes, seas, and rivers, abundant with white sturgeon, salmon, grey mullet, and sardines, and the country's best-known delicacy *black caviar* from the Caspian Sea, well sought after in other parts of the world.

With great joy, Samir and his staff welcomed us as we arrive at the vast hotel. Mr Arman, a fantastic guy, has the primary responsibility for our safety and comfort, helping us with everything. Samir has a surprise for us, so our next experience is a weekend in the beautiful Mountains, to a tiny village four hundred kilometres north of Chalus. A week after on an early morning, Arman picks us up, waiting for us in front of the reception, while our eyes get gigantic as we notice the white Rolls Royce. That's our ride. It's the first time I've driven in a Rolls Royce.

We enjoy the next many hours, driving from a barren area to a stunning productive mesmerising uncultivated green farmland.

'Why have they not cultivated such a perfect productive area? This could be a superb opportunity to do some farming.' As I'm eyeing gladly between Drake and the stunning views, reflecting my idea is amazing.

After five hours of driving on small unmaintained roads facing the snowy mountains, we arrive as kings and queens, at a lush, elegant five-star winter sports resort up in the mountains. Samir arrived in his private jet the day before, and his family and business associates arrive in their Ferraris, Lamborghinis, and expensive Porsche's. They friendly welcomes us, and Samir greets us before the staff shows us to a bright large double room with white and beige furniture, and a pleasant smell of fresh flowers filling the space. Fresh fruit stands on the small table and chocolate on our nightstand, and at once we feel comfortable, as I'm looking forward to a romantic weekend with my beloved, who is in an excellent mood.

Samir's intention for the extended weekend is for us to get more acquainted with everyone. Karim, Abbas, and his wife, Laura, along with their sweet 3-year-old daughter, Minu arrived a few hours before us. Karim and Abbas have a hilarious sister, Jasmine; she's full of life and loves to party, and she has brought her 7-year-old son, Omid, with her. Light music plays in the background and the kids squealing as we sit and chitchat. I sense it will be a stunning cheerful weekend, though I'm not counting off what will happen between Drake and me. Samir has arranged plenty of dinners and outdoor experiences in the lovely garden-fresh scenery. Lunches at unknown restaurants in the adorned vigorous mountains listening to birds chirping as glasses clinks during the cheers. An adorned scenery with splashing waterfalls in a green forest, as a few of the guests and I go for horseback riding, while the horses eagerly snorts, as we guide the animal to exploring the gorgeous location. Samir also takes us to another special spot, a magical hidden restaurant deep in the forest, tucked away as a small secret temple. You can literally taste the forest, surrounded with plenty of chestnut trees, their most magnificent symbol of their country. Crickets chirp, crows cawing in the threes, everyone laughs, and Samir's phone vibrates constantly. It's a one in a lifetime experience, of how the locals enjoy the vast rough nature, having dinner in a special forest restaurant. As we stroll around, we pass the spot where we can enjoy the chef chops meat on a massive tree trunk.

'This is the chef's signature kebab.' Samir smiles as we watch them preparing another dish—the famous shepherd's meal known as Dasharasi—between two stone slabs.

We taste the many fantastic regional flavoured dishes, and joins it with superb full-bodied red wine, with a delicious bouquet of exquisite grapes tasting of darker flavours such as plum or chocolate.

CHAPTER 27

ANGEL AND DEMON BATTLE IN THE MOUNTAINS

> I cut myself because you wouldn't let me cry. I cried because
> you wouldn't let me speak.
> I spoke because you wouldn't let me shine. I shone because I
> thought you loved me.
> —Emilie Autumn, *The Asylum for Wayward Victorian Girls*

D rake and Samir get time in between to talk business, though I'm confused, because they appear sneaky and do it behind my back.

'Why am I not allowed to take part, darling?' I frustrated dare. 'Will you tell me of the agreement?' Yet, I want to trust Drake and hope they will do the arrangements wisely, when I ask him on the second night.

Whoa? Heavy and angry thunder falls straight to my head, when *Thor's hammer* at full blast hits the ground. As a blast of a fire spiting volcano erupts, things between us go haywire. I understand nothing of his eruption coming out of the blue.

'Grr, bloody hell, Mary. Yesterday, you started the worst crisis in our unique relationship. We experienced it before. Hmm, but survived in love and understanding.' His reaction is fuming as an uncontrolled spread of wildfire.

'I don't understand.'

'This is the worst to date. Argh, again, the root of evil is money.' He exhales deeply.

Strangely, Drake aggressively starts a tremendous fight, and rages as a feisty bull, breathing deeply. Oh, dear, I fear what comes out of his mouth, because his anger is gigantic. I stare nervously and dumbfounded at him.

'Whoa, Drake, I don't understand why you reason it's of money.'

'Last night, I went for a walk in the raw surroundings.'

'Huh? Why? You think it's a shit crisis that *I've* put us into? Why do you expect it's me?' I'm sad and tired of his horrendous accusations. 'It's not my intent to create crises. I'm not alone in this shifty wealth disaster.'

'I had to figure out about us. I didn't come to a nicely decision.' He turns off the light music.

'Okay. And?'

'Dear me, my thoughts went through many loopholes and chambers. I can't find reason in what happens.'

'Holly molly!' I exclaim.

'I will start from the brief conversation that this time started *your* anger, Mary.'

'I'm sorry if your conclusion was dreadful. It scares me when you begin as this.'

'I can see that Copenhagen *always* gives you the most negative ugly feelings—mainly because of anger!' Growling at me.

'Eh? What does Copenhagen have to do with this?' I realise he's hugely pissed over my straightforward question.

'There are loads of details in our life that I don't bother to talk of. Instead, I'd want to turn the time forward to last night.' His blabber become a massive confusion in my head.

'I gladly tell you that the farming project **I** spoke with Samir of might give *me* worthy cash on *my* account. In that spirit, I'm glad. Me solving the farming issue in Iran.'

'Darling, it was *not* Samir, who started talking of this farming issue.'

'Wauw! The train went completely off the track with you, Mary.' He is fuming fire.

'As we drove up here, I asked you; what of the vast uncultivated landscape. Then I suggested the many farming projects they could create. At once, we're in the same spirit.' I protest.

'Baloney! You tell me it's fine if I can make a profit on the prospect. I didn't ponder more of it. It's fateful that I didn't reflect of it thoroughly.' Wrinkling his angry forehead.

'We talked of extensive projects and brilliant solutions. Of Danida in in Europe. We talked to Samir, and *suddenly* it's only a *Drake* project?' Staring flabbergasted at him.

'Suddenly you say, "Well, then you should doubtless get half of what I could earn?" Crikey! That's with both trades. Including my salary in the hospital,' he wraths and gets copper red in his face.

'Frankly, the idea was not yours, Drake. Again, you take over my ideas!' I furiously protest.

'Cuffing hell! Are you completely out of your obnoxious mind, Mary?' The dragon roars.

'Excuse me! You arranged a conversation on the topic with Mr Fabulous. This chap is in a similar project in another country, you tell me. *Wow! Great,* I say.' Honestly, I don't get it why Drake so often acts so imprudently.

'Butter my butt and call me a biscuit! You're such a stupid woman! I responded as a joke, "Only if I likewise get half of your income and alimony." I didn't mean it.' The notes of our conflict get high. 'Then you replied, "You can't get that; it's my money." Flipping heck, you exploded in the usual way, "Forget it! I need not to hear of it."' His rude, sarcastic manner is unbearable.

'Yea! Ha-ha! As usual, the little chick in your Pinocchio strings shut up during the debate with Samir. For pity's sake! I made a few comments in Danish. You solved it in English for me.' I want to scream the entire hotel into tiny fragments.

'Blimey! I tell Samir I got contacts to create a solution. If a trade can set me up as a broker. Get outta town, Mary. Then you decide you want to get half.' The roaring bull sees red.

'You grab the chance to do something here. Sneaky as you are, you do it without me.'

'Argh, what the hell is wrong with you, Mary? Cripes! You're so ugly to me.'

'*Ugly?* You consider it's your sole project. Yikes! That's how you are! Suddenly you tell me not to interfere?' I have no more words for him.

'The stupid little chicken brain of yours doesn't get it, Mary!' How disrespectful of him!

'No! I don't get it, Drake! I give you great comments and ideas for solutions. I said to you; not both of us can talk to the guy on the phone at the same time. Can we? Meaning, you do the talking. Christ, then you run the race alone.'

'I got a once-in-a-lifetime chance to get serious money back into my account.' He yells.

'Whoa! I'm disappointed! That's where the entire trust between us explodes—hence my outburst. Then you tell me you won't share.' *Fine with me*, I ponder. I'm utterly numb in the face of his rage.

'For heaven's sake, Mary. I want my financial self-esteem back.' He can *only* talk of coinage.

'On top of it, you get the backbiting boldness to say that I don't share my alimony with you. Holy crap! Ouch, that's a venomous bite, Drake.'

'Flipping hell, you will get more income through our clinic activity.'

'Jeez, then you complain that you won't get access to my pension if I die. Well, I never! That's a ghastly move of yours.'

'Christ! You don't need this farming project. I do! Besides, you will get from the bedding sales.' His greedy boisterous voice is not to be mistaken of.

'Don't you get it, there is a reason for my outburst? And watching and listening to your many wrong moves? Darling, no matter how hard you try, with your many proposals, you will never get the pension.'

'Good gracious, Mary. You already own a vast income.' *Is he envious?* I muse.

'Gee! Shut up, Drake! I'm incredibly disappointed—not to mention furious at you.'

'For God's sake. You possess significant assets because of your deal with Flopper.'

'Yeah, nicely observed. It's my wealth. I always share with you. I find it awfully absurd that I must always transfer half of my money to your account.'

'You should give me much more. I educated you for free.'

'*What?* I got nothing for free. It's no longer for discussion, and so, my comment, "Forget it." You always think and talk of *money, money, money.* You did so, from the first day I met you.'

'Heck, no! I'm not always talking of money. But you don't want to share with me.'

'Ouch, what a mean blow from you, Drake. It's not about money, it's the principals of sharing of what we do together.' I try to appeal to his common senses.

'But it is!'

'Huh, what are you talking about?'

'Bloody hell, no! I don't want to share this project with you.' He is firm in his conclusion.

'You will not share with me if we get an income?' I grasp the greedy bastard is in deep denial.

'Hell no!'

'We agreed that, whatever we do together, we share. You were wrathful of Flopper not sharing with me. You are becoming an even nastier Flopper. I trusted us as a team. Obviously, I was wrong.' I'm jabbering as an unstoppable out-of-control water tap.

'Don't you dare to compare me with that fool.' He screams.

'You'll be able to get your financial self-esteem back—even if you share with me.' I can sense my anger is hitting the ceiling, then my blood pressure rises to heights I don't appreciate.

'I'll not share with you, Mary. Period!'

'Shucks! You can keep your *damn* project and money to yourself. I'm no longer able to trust you in whatever the future will bring.' I am shattered, even though I'm firm in my outburst. 'Do it without my help. Good luck, Drake. I hope you will get your financial recovery. I understand it's more important to you than I am.' Grief-stricken, I cry inside of the pain he causes me.

'Babe, you told me if something happened to you, your funds will be out of reach of your children. You promised I'll get everything.' Suddenly he changes the topic.

'Oh, my God! You hugely enjoyed from it previously—for years.'

'You haven't prepared for that. If you die today, your kids and Flopper will get it.'

'Eh? I never promised you that.' *Is he planning to kill me? To get everything!*

'Flopper and the kids can open a bottle or two of champagne and celebrate. Including the bastard will be off the hook. Get free of his damn wife support.' Drake self-assured and grudging shouts.

'Oh, boy! I wonder if that's a "neglectful" recall on your part. My motive is pure! You cannot access my funds.' At that instant, I was afraid of what happens if I give in to his commands.

'Baby, we talked of securing what comes out of creating business together.' He gets slick.

'We can talk of this issue if you ever get divorced. My children get it!' It outraged me.

'The income can't reach your children.'

'I'm distressed that you bring it up, Drake. Just the conclusion of it is petrifying!' Whoa! I'm traumatised and worried.

'If you die before me, it must go back to me, Mary. If I die before you, it goes to you.'

'Huh? You talk so much of death that I become petrified. Are you planning to kill me?'

'Jeez! Ultimately, the funds must go to a charity fund. Only a minor part. We will decide how much can go to our family heirs.' His blabbering of money, death, and inheriting issues is a never-ending story.

'So far, we created nothing together. It has only been expenses coming out of my account.'

'I did never ask to get any of your income.' He lyingly smirks.

'We can talk of what to do with our income. If it ever happens. And if any actual business turns a profit.' I pause for a second, rolling my eyes.

'You allowed me to use your account in The Philippines during your travelling. I was glad, Babe. I could pay wages to our staff.'

'If business ever becomes a reality, then we can fix these issues. It's difficult to create a fund when we get no profit. Honestly! Be reasonable, Drake,' I snap and get exhausted with his *ping-pong money game* and his massive greed.

'I never asked for anything, Mary. I have gladly received when you have given. Thank you.' With the words *gladly received*, he boldly smirks, and must have forgotten the *lunch box* envelopes!

'Honestly? I'm drained by your remarks. I don't want to comment on that.' I sneer.

'But your blast last night came as a blow to me. We can't talk of things wisely. Instead, I'm suddenly the worst person on earth—a charlatan—as every man who promises you a lot.' Though, Drake doesn't produce a shit of it.

'I didn't call you a charlatan. That comes from my dream story.' I growl, feeling he's stepping over the line. 'Cruel and unreasoning! Yes, you are. You promise much, but don't comply, Drake. I don't mention the many promises you did not fulfil.' I take a deep inhale and exhale despairing.

'Oh, boy, then your sour muzzle came on when you said; *Forget it!*' He rustles with some papers on the table.

'Why do you guess I said that? It causes sometimes anger— something I've parked on the shelf for the sake of peace.'

'Christ almighty, Mary! I cannot catch up with your anger in these debates,' it annoys him.

'Argh, I can't catch up with you in these tedious discussions either. For me, it's better to forget than to let you push me into a corner. You're so dominant, Drake. I better throw the towel in the ring.' Pausing for a minute to think, what's next?

'But this time, it is to be different.' He roars.

'Drake, I can't handle a war with you. I'd willingly let it pass. Hoping you'll calm again.'

'Mary, you rudely called me a charlatan. It comes from your nasty demons in you.'

'Stop it, Drake! I get upset.'

'Argh, it's as if something crazy is happening inside you, Mary. I can't get in touch with you. That's why I keep to myself.' He is searching for reasons for a fight.

'I only wish is to live happily with you.' I'm trying to cool the conversation.

'I tried to approach you this morning twice. You didn't take it.' And he calms a little.

'You always say I'm not taking your help or love. I hugged you. Is that not to receive?'

'I don't know how to break the ice, Mary. I dare not talk of the subject; out of fear it will be worse between us. That money has such power over our relationship wasn't something I imagined.' Does he want me to feel pity for him?

'What?'

'Yeah, you are the one with the money. I only receive alms from you.' He gets up on high-pitched notes again.

'God Almighty,' I exclaim. 'I can't understand that you can get this across your lips—*alms?*' I'm disappointed.

'It's different for a man to have it that way than it's for a woman.'

'That's a mean blow in my face. Shit, it hurts, Drake. I have never given you *alms*! Willingly, I've given and shared from my good heart.'

'What if the characters were the opposite? I was the one with the money, as I've always been before. Then it is a natural thing to be with you. Then I'd be the one who paid and gave of my heart.'

'Holy mackerel! You are an awful old-fashioned man.'

'Why is it different with a man?' He frets.

'You live in the spirit that the man is the hunter. Christ, and the woman is the babysitter.'

'Doubtless because the man has traditionally been the one who brought the money home for both parties. And not the other way.' Smirking, stupid dude.

'The case is not so, Drake. You must understand that.'

'When a woman does it, I can see it as more than a loan. Mainly for a nonmarital relationship. He must repay.' Again, he's whining of capital!

'Oh, gosh, if it wasn't for the great love, I bear for you, I will never do what I do for you. I will live under the same philosophy as Kate— meaning *you pay, Drake*! Is that what you want?'

'I don't know. Last night I became afraid of the power of money,' he grumbles.

'Time is not as it has been for you earlier. You cannot do that until our projects come to fruition. Now we own *nothing*—no income! Only my alimony, which I share with you. We don't live as a married couple. There are reasons for that. Your marriage!'

'We talked of this earlier. I'll get a divorce.'

'According to Danish law, if I remarry, you must take care of me. Can you do that? *No!*'

'I can't.' The greedy dragon roars.

'You are causing the issues yourself. It's always of the power of money! You don't admit you are *not* the provider,' I'm forcefully.

'I want to change that, if it's possible for me.' He becomes as a meagre whining child.

'Don't promise something that might not last. You promise so much and fulfilled none.'

'So how do we resolve the case? Babe, I cannot speak sensibly to you.'

'You don't own the order until you deliver, and the money is in our account. You didn't deliver nothing! We got no dough.'

'We haven't any agreement between us on our financial circumstances, Mary. We must avoid such discussions if we are to stay together in peace.'

'Bah, yeah, we should. We can't trust each other.' It's obvious to me he's worried that I might not give him what he wants.

'We must base our financial agreements on the fact that we are still a loving couple, living together. If it allows us to marry one another, we must make a deal worthy of a married couple.' I hear in between the lines he wants to secure himself, no matter how.

'What are you talking of?' I don't want to comment on it. It will not be from my funds!

'We make a deal. Sharing fifty-fifty of what we create together. This will regard clinics, because that's what we do together.' He's slick. 'I took your advice on my bedding products. You invested $5,000 to renew my patent. Plus, wages to the staff. You will get half of the earnings.' Well, I still get no *half earnings*.

'It was a long time ago that we made the deal. I get it, Drake. I need not to pay for our joint costs anymore. Is that what you are telling me?' Then feeling relieved.

'I'm okay with you keeping the Flopper income. And the pension for yourself. I've never dreamed of having it.'

That's a massive lie, and Drake tries to be easy going in his explanation. 'Oh, yea, because it's mine. Why do you mention such stupid things?'

'Samir offered us a salary for our work. Though, we won't get the same. What we earn, we can save in our own accounts. We will not share it between us afterwards. Not as long as we are not married.'

'Well, neither of us is being offered any payment.' The dandy is tedious to me.

'We may take your wage as candy money.' He is always making himself better than others.

'Might be it's so little that I don't even want to bother working for lousy coinage.' I yap.

'Mary, for me, it's the beginning of restoring my financial life.'

'Keep your dough, clinic, or whatever for yourself.' *Go for it, buddy boy!* 'If I must live with you in such petty-bourgeois conditions, now that things are changing for you. Hmm, be my guest. It's okay for me. Keep it!'

'Baby, I hope you grasp it's important to me. I need to make *my* capital, so I can spoil you.'

'Maybe we have nothing more in common. I can leave—keep my wealth for myself! You can keep whatever you earn.' What a lame excuse he brings up and I realise his only goal is to become rich. 'Afterwards, I can ponder on how wrong I was trusting you and your promises. I don't need you under such conditions. Nor do I need you falsely to spoil me.' Ironically, I pat him on his shoulder.

It shows Drake doesn't listen to me, diving into the next point he wants to make. 'In addition, we must divide the profit paid each year from the clinic deal in half. That will be an equal 25 percent to us each. Baby, it's not that awful, though.'

He will never achieve it. 'Do as you like. It doesn't match your promises. Be my guest!' My negative attitude continues.

'This is what I need for me to get to the top again. That's my goal!' The fella cheers.

'We'll keep our funds separate. Do what you want, Drake. I don't see that it's needed any more for me to cover our costs. You can survive yourself. Get on your vast feet again.'

'I will, Mary. It must allow me to make a personal income from other activities that may be available to me—and then *not* share with you,' he dictates, speaks only of *him, dough,* and how much *he* wants.

'I understand your complete context of the financial arrangements. My bank is closed. I'm frustrated with your comments. They verify that my grim feelings of you were right.' I want desperately to leave him. *Shit! What do I do? I'm staying at a mountain resort and can't go.*

'Come on, stop it! It's of unique kinds of seminars. Or whatever may come. I can come up with what I was worth before. I hope.'

'I'm disappointed in myself for having allowed things to go this far. Sadly, I didn't stop the relationship when these fears came to my mind.' *How can I get away from here?*

'Mary, I hope that you can see the gain in it. And will welcome my skill to raise myself.'

'Darling, it's obvious you no longer need me. I'm only your girlfriend on your terms. Now you can live in solitude,' I mutter and want desperately to pack my bags.

'I don't know what to do or say to you. What's going on in your hateful head right now?'

'What? It sounds as greediness to me. I must pay. You won't give back.' Gazing at the suitcase in the corner, I'm ready to pack.

'Um-hmm, are you not willing to continue with me?' It scares him.

'I am seriously considering not continuing!' I genuinely want to end the relationship.

'Whoa! We must get control of such idiotic things. So, we can live in peace and patience again.' He glares surprised at me.

I'm dejected and wretched. I can't work under such mental pressure from him. The hurtful things he did can't get me to cry. Instead, I sit numb.

'If you got any other thoughts, come out with them now. Let's get back on track. It's not bearable this way. I don't want you to leave.' He turns to begging now.

'I can get angry, when I've been in Denmark—I hoped, being able to cope with my frustrations.'

'That awful anger you possess is not good, Baby.'

'I cling to the family I believe I have. I'm to blame for letting it affect you. I'm sorry; it's not fair.' Heedless, I take the burden on my shoulders, forgetting *he* started the fight.

'It's okay, the action of your family can sadden you. But it's tough that I must carry the bumps every time.'

'The case has nothing to do with Copenhagen.'

'You have no one left who is brave enough to talk to you. Nor be your friend.'

'Darling, the anger is of us! It makes me sad!' I glance at him sadly.

'Baby, I'm your best and only friend—the only one who has given you respect. Honour, and joy.' Cunningly, he is trying to direct me to his advantage.

'Yes, darling. I'm glad you understand me. It's a mistake I told you of my glum life. That and money made awful problems for us. You're a problem-solver. Then you go into my brain to crack my problems. It's a terrible idea.'

'I'm the only one who has understood you and what splits you.' He smirks, staring at me.

'It will be better if I continued being the cheerful woman you met that summer—without me telling you anything. And not created problems for you. I regret I didn't keep it behind my solid iron armour. Stayed in Spain. Then stayed long-distance lovers and visited each other instead. But we couldn't stand that! Am I right, darling?'

'Figuring you out has been difficult and often hard.' Glaring and grinning at me.

'I chose, without understanding properly, to fall into your arms—to move around with you.

Was that wise?' I'm on the edge of breaking.

'Baby, I realise now what's wrong with you.'

'Oh, shut up. You keep telling you know what's wrong.'

'Um-hmm, after yesterday, I'm afraid that I cannot solve or cure you. Though I hoped.'

'Don't say that. I'm unhappy.'

'Dealing with the mind game is better with expert forces.' Staring reproachfully at me.

'Hmm, yeah, we have fought many battles together. For that I'm forever grateful to you.' Sniffing sadly, and once more, he has broken me. Every time I felt safe, he said something that changed everything.

'Baby, you're mentally ill. You're possessed by too many evil demons.' His changes are sudden, often, and extreme.

I'm dumbfounded, sorrowful to hear such accusations. 'I'm sorry, no one else is going into my brain anymore. I've had enough of your mind-twisting help.'

'Oh, boy, yesterday was crazy,' he growls.

'I've run from one shrink to another ever since my son died, and my husband betrayed me. I've analysed myself from head to toe. No shrink or other people diagnosed me mentally ill. I'm unfortunate, given the things that have happened to me.' I'm focusing on my suitcase again, ready to pack and run away.

'I'm a doctor of solutions. Jeez, but I can't find the solution for the one I love.'

'Darling, I only need your love and understanding. If I can't get that, I surrender.' It's hard for me to keep my head clear—to keep track of what he says between the lines.

'Baby, I'm crushed. And was sure you didn't want me and my intrusion with your soul. You wanted to handle it yourself. I didn't dare. Just as I don't dare to speak with you now.'

'Ahh, Ohhh, a lifetime of sorrow and distress is difficult to resolve in a brief period. I apologise—for telling you my defeats.' I'm increasingly troubled, feeling more and more discarded by Drake.

'Gah, I can't deal with you in a discussion. It always has to be your way or the highway,' he growls scornfully, trying to bring everything to ahead. The fast-adrenaline-charged ride spins up and down with him.

'Pardon me! I often notice that you don't see or hear when I put the blame on myself and not you. You have trouble accepting when I'm right on topics we discuss. You often say you can easily remember things. Darling, you can't! Then you twist things to your favour. I give up the fights against you. I agree with you instead. I'm sure you can't see it.'

Drake often shows how firm and forceful he is, but he is basically a patronising bastard.

'Bullshit! It's not quiet and sensible chats. It can't give us peace. Nor fit solutions when you show your damn *anger*,' he hisses, stirring himself up again.

'Oh, my, this is precisely why I'm scared to help. Even comment on your choices of your projects. Gee, you always tell me you know better. And that only you have experience, darling. Do you assume I'm stupid? I've done many interior designs. And with success.'

'I felt as I couldn't so much as pack a box right in The Philippines.'

'Eh? What do boxes have to do with this argument? I watched you make plans.'

'There was nothing I could do that was good enough for you, Mary. I didn't worry.'

'A few times I come up with a comment. You admit I'm right in my review.'

'Argh! There is no reason for me to stir things up. You don't get it, Mary.'

'Well, the next minute, I'm stupid to you. I recognise this syndrome too well. Darling, I don't want to take part in it anymore.'

'Oh, my, you rapidly cut through where you should not cut. Babe, it makes it impossible to find proper results for both of us.'

It may well be Drake believes he's doing the right for me, and he may assume he can save me. Instead, he makes things much worse.

'Oh, my darling. When I come up with ideas, at once you toss them away. Later, the same ideas pop up in *your mind*. Yea, as if every idea is *only yours*! In your head, you are the only ultimate super brain in this relationship.'

'Aha, I see it as you believe it's only what *you* consider that's worth something—be it small practical things to gigantic things alike. You're not clever, Mary.'

'Gah, I'm used to put myself in the background—as your cute little housewife being pulled by your strings.'

'Christ, you must learn to listen.'

'Jeez, I don't need lengthy debates when you beforehand have all the answers yourself. That's why we can't talk quietly.' I'm steadfast on this point.

'Baby, you must bite things in you which you do not agree.' He is growing angrier.

'Hmm, I find this wrong. Yea, I'm a perfectionist. You are too! To you, all must fit in every detail for both of us. This can create problems. I'm good at packing, stacking, and organising things. Everything must fit into the smallest box.' *I don't understand why we have such a stupid conversation.*

'Aha, bah, I've been putting up with your criticism, Mary.'

'Eh? Criticism? Gee, you are obsessive within the medical arena. But you're not good at everything. And neither am I. But endlessly you correct me.'

'Your reproach is most often irrational and being corrected.'

'Things are not good enough for you when I'm training with my therapist skills. You expect you are the only and best leader in this matter. You can't accept if I study outside of the box. Or do different from you. Having an unusual tactic is okay.' I do my best to be calm with my opinion.

'My little darling, worse luck, I'm in my sixties. I have lived with solutions my entire life.'

Poor little man-child! I muse. 'Jeez, did you literally play the "old dude" card? I could have opted out. But I love you. Love holding your hand. Listening to your voice. I'm not taking any notice of your age.'

'Aww!' He smiles, and his eyes suddenly shine. 'Other times, often related to trivial things, you give advice or lectures for a child.'

'Huh? I have never considered you as a child, darling.'

'Ha-ha, I can only smile and cling to what you say, Baby. It's sort of sweet. Though sometimes annoying.'

'Oh, God! I never saw you as old! Nor do I want to control you as a child.'

'There are more important things to focus at. Life should not stress pointless things. Baby, it's not been a problem for me to adapt. That I'm grateful to have had you with me is an understatement.'

'No problems for me to adjust to our relationship. I definitely do.'

'Mmm... I've been in love with you since we met. It's been an honour for me to give you my entire time. And my energy to help you with your divorce.'

'Darling, why do we then have this stupid discussion?'

'The research needed to win the glorious victory over Flopper. Oh, my, it was a superb team job. It was hard to get through emotionally.' Drake is suddenly caring again, and it frustrates me with his constant shifts.

'You held me by the hand day and night. Thanks.' I mostly enjoy being with Drake, because he is an unbelievably charismatic person, though I can't take these up-and-downs.

'Argh, you were definitely not "a walk in the park". But we made it. We had the energy to stay in business together. It did not prove easy-going where we were.' He smiles sarcastically.

'Our lives are hard. Many of your plans constantly fall to the ground, Drake.'

'Only our love held us together. Despite your frustrating Denmark travels. You keep giving your children whatever they ask for.' He sounds jealous, as he wants another discussion.

'Jeez, don't go there, Drake. For Christ's sake! I'm a mother!'

'Each time you come back to me as a winged bird. Then you need love and care. Only I give it to you in full measure. You calmed with me after a brief time. Came back to balance. Ouch, and what's the angry reward I get back from you?' I don't need such a discussion with him.

'Why are we having this stupid discussion?'

'Your kids beg for money, iPhones, iPads or PlayStations. You give them whatever they ask for at once. Baby, you possess such a good heart.'

Now he's cranky over my generosity! I don't get it. 'Blood ties are hard to cut, darling.'

'It is heart-breaking to see your "sadness" when they are backstabbing you.'

'Christ! You're a father yourself! Your children backstabbed you. You whined as a baby about your kid's wedding. You were for the rats. I supported you. I bought a wedding gift. Did you ever send them?'

'Baby, your heart is enormous.'

'I gave you money you could send to your wife. Did you ever do that?' He doesn't answer.

'What happened to your children? And your kindness to them? Babe, they abandon you. You stand back and can't understand what happens.'

'Darling, *thanks*, it is only a modest word. Thank you! I'm at least overjoyed to get your help. It's heart-breaking for me to see your sadness.'

'Relating to money. Yea, it's true, Mary, you are one of the most rewarding people I know. You are never afraid to "spit in the box". Or to help someone in need.'

'Oh, finally, you say something right. I often feel ill-used.'

'Ahh, yea, you have been very generous with me.'

'None of what you said and planned turned into something, Drake. I surrender. Here, "money" comes back into the game.'

'I know, Mary. You gladly invested in equipment.'

'It's here where the entire *money* issue began. I have only outgoings on my accounts! This was not part of my plan with you.'

'You get it back as soon. When I can repay. It stands by power.' *Will he keep that promise?*

'I frankly hoped, because of your age, to enjoy life with you at a secluded island in the Caribbean. You are a stubborn bull in the ring. You only want to do your own thing.'

'Ahh, yea, it's time to get things settled.'

'You only want to recollect millions on your account. You are not *realistic*, Drake! I've backed you with everything—sadly, for one failure after another. The mistake is doubtless for both of us.'

'Soon it will turn into the last payment for you, Babe. I will invoice Chalus.'

'We are not good enough to investigate. The failed business was far too costly for my lessons.' Though, it's not boring to be with Drake, but it makes it more complicated.

'Baby, you'll get your costs refunded. We must get them completed.' He smiles cunningly, with more assurances. *I wonder if he can keep his promise.*

'Nice! I'd rather spend it on something good for the two of us— as a pleasant home. But you are a stubborn adventurer. Thinking the entire world needs "only you". You waste valuable years of your life. This confuses me.' Sensing my answer is honest.

'I will close the company in Sweden. Hopefully, I'm getting some money to pay back Betty's $15,000 investment in my company.'

'Huh? Betty? Who is Betty?'

'If it leaves some, then it goes to me. Then I can breathe again.'

'Who is Betty?'

'Babe now is the chance. I received it with a kissing hand, because of Samir.'

I gaze at him in amazement. 'We have no agreements with Samir. No legal contract to protect ourselves. We've shipped our stuff to foreign countries. I've spent oceans of time and dough on it.'

'Grrr, Babe. You'll get every penny back as soon as Samir pays the bill.'

'I sense as I'm being tricked one time after the other. Who pays? *Me!* So, money becomes a problem—*my money!*' Pinpointing the issue. I can see Drake is about to explode.

'The equipment will belong to our new joint company. You'll get 25 percent back for *free!*' He angers, flapping with his hands up in the air.

'Um-hmm, is that a promise? Darling, this idea is an enigma to me. *Free?* You will sell the equipment to Samir? We agreed to share equally. Please explain the word *free!*'

'Well, I hope there will be profit from the trade. I want some back from my investment.'

'For years, you have promised to repay for the machine. The loans and the deposit. Then you pay Betty first? Who is she?'

'It's difficult to sell used equipment at a new price. There will not be much of leftovers.'

'By now it's over $45,000, for the machinery alone.' I'm annoyed and angry with him.

'You are the "breadwinner". I enjoy your *generosity* and *understanding.*' He smirks.

'I understand how hard and humiliating it must be for a woman to support you. But if so, you should not have begun a relationship with me. You could have done it yourself with what you had.' I suspect he has been with me only for my wealth.

'I wanted to change that relationship as soon I could get work.' He grins.

'I did never look down on you for the lack of income. Nor been unkind to you. And always supported you.' I try to get self-righteousness.

'I promise what we do together, you will get half of it, Baby. Even if you get your investment back in the equipment.' This sounds as a sour burp from him.

'Hopefully, we can be successful, Drake. Um-hmm, not least for your own sake.' Thinking; *I can always own the dream.*

'Sweetie, we share because you invested in my knowledge. And my skills—fifty-fifty share.' More sour burbs float out of his mouth.

'Your sour burps don't fit you. If the repayment is a problem for you, then we must talk of another solution—one that sticks to the promises you gave me.' I imagine my entire investment draining out into the dirty sewer.

'When I'm divorced, I must become your partner in the company in Hong Kong.' He hopes.

Will it ever happen? Damn, I'm having a non-profit company in Hong Kong and The Philippines.

Only by marriage does he suppose he can secure my funds.

'I love you. Not because I need a man to cuddle me. Or give me finger orgasms. I trusted your word. I can't take more discussion now. I'm cooked,' ending the conversation.

At least we go to bed holding hands and share a goodnight kiss, speaking no more of it and enjoy the rest of the weekend in peace.

For the first time, I dared to stand up, but in my soul, Drake broke me. How can he treat me so awful? I'm affected in my soul by more psychological traumas than ever, and there's so much damage in our relationship, that I lose trust in him. My normal functioning is brutally affected, and I see the world as chaotic.

CHAPTER 28

THE BURNING DESIRE FADES

> However, many holy words you read, however many you
> speak, what good will they do you if you do not act on upon
> them?
>
> —Buddha (Siddhārtha Gautama)

No one can sense my grief as the pain pops up again during this process. It's the worst pain I've experienced in a long time, Millions of words don't take me back to happiness—no matter how much I try. My stuck tears and the clenching iron fist in my belly need to get out. They cannot. Then I want him. The next moment I don't, as I know it's not healthy, because everything seems to be a lie with him.

Life is too short to waste on grudges, thinking of how our relationship was so wonderful in the beginning, as I never saw the storm on the horizon. I must ask myself and reflect on Drake's many dissatisfactions with me, or it will nag me for a long time. I must step forward, so I'm not stuck in the same situation with unhappiness.

Drake always knows what he is doing, and nothing can confuse him. In his mind, he truly trusts in his own many deceitful lies, although, in his brain, he does nothing wrong, so he considers himself as supreme!

Mentally, I try to laugh off the horrible fight. Next I apologise of everything because I wanted to get back to the man I fell in love with. From being admired by Drake in the beginning plunges me into denial. Next, he cruelly despises me. That makes me dislike him. One moment I can't see the wicked in our situation, then the second instant I'm clear in my head and see too many faults. Though, I have no intention of angering him, because I only want to give him my love, and to be in a decent space; otherwise, I will never get what I desire the most. He gets one more chance on top of the many earlier opportunities, so I forgive him, though I'm drained by his mental abuse. I want not to forget any of the mistakes, but I wish to learn from my flaws and not have regrets, and hopefully, he will change his mind about me. Am I wrong?

The weekend ends peacefully, and together with Samir we fly back to Chalus in his vast private jet. As a royal queen, sitting in comfy beige leather seats, I enjoy the view over the snowy mountains, and listen to light music playing. The bottles clink when the flight attendant is pouring icy bubbly champagne in our glasses while we laugh and enjoy the glorious experience.

Being back in Chalus, Samir looks at a suitable five-storey building nearby the city centre and decides for the five-story newly renovated building for the project. Hectic we plan for a grand clinic, with unique kinds of medical specialities. Drake and I only need to provide the drawings for the interior space and next working solidly on the plan, as Samir has set our timeframe to completion to be four to six months.

At our next meeting with Samir we receive our first salary—US$10,000 in cash, proudly it got stored it in our safety box. Surprise! After two days, Drake gives me the next invoice, with the note, 'Darling love, terms of payment, *use* of equipment, monthly, $1,600. This could be the last payment you need to make. Love, Drake.'

'What is this, Drake?' I'm staggered and equally disappointed, because it's difficult for me to imagine he is squeezing the last dollar out of me after our earlier discussion. It's a moment in my life when I want to give up on him. I can't take him anymore, and my burning desire for him vastly fades. I don't want him to make me bitter over his greediness, and I will not allow him to turn me cold inside because of his hurting.

'It's your monthly payment to me.' He seriously smirks, content.

'Can't we take the payment out of the money we got from Samir?' It's a gentle suggestion, from the way I phrase the sentence—which means he gives me a big fat *no*! It's my naïve mistake.

'Babe, I know you're generous to me. And equally invested in the equipment. When it's possible to repay you, I will. It stands by the power of our agreement. You'll get every penny back. ASAP as Samir has paid his bill. Then the equipment will belong to our new joint company. It's not a fit idea to pay the last invoice from the cash.'

I felt a chilling pressure from Drake to pay. I didn't dare say no or stop! Not that I minded helping or lending him money—it was okay to a certain point.

'Baby, you know I'm not earning any money. You promised me to support me all the way and pay it all.' He keeps telling me. The same phrase comes repeatedly: 'Sweetie, you tell me you will live on a remote island with me. Yea, and I need not to work.' Such a *bloodsucker*! He gets outrageously furious at me. Greedy! Parasite! It angers me.

'Holy moly!' I'm miffed over his stinginess.

Don't let this make you unkind, Mary. Be calm and possess self-control, I tell myself and pay the damn bill, hoping it's the last one. *Luckily, it is*, I convince myself. But… but… Will I ever get the dough back?

Our relationship creaks, and Drake gets nasty, aggressive, and negative towards me, and the stress he puts on me has disastrous effects on my health. My body frequently goes into a hyper-alertness mode—more often than I want it to. My nervous system responded by releasing a flood of stress hormones, including adrenaline and cortisol, which roused my body for emergency action. It's as my 'fight-or-flight' reaction is on high alert, and my heart pounds faster, my blood pressure rises, my breath quickens, and my senses become sharper. I try not to let my mood shift based on his wicked actions, though I'm immensely exhausted mentally, emotionally, and physically. Damnit! I feel so dependent on Drake. Unwise woman! Why can't I see or learn from his constant betrayal? It frustrates me of being so irresponsible. I am helplessly trapped in what I believe is love, and I don't know how to get out of it. Are there too many red flags I can't see? I can only blame myself for being caged in the madness of love with my captor. He had arms made of steel, and impossible to escape from.

I knew everything must be too good to be true. Despite my awareness and warnings from others, I want to believe the best in Drake. I can't deny he has also some good and loving parts. I thought I'd found a man I could trust, someone who could love me. I assumed he was a person who respected me. From the depths of my good, warm, Christian heart, and I forgive him for all his sins. I trust he can change for the better.

I didn't increase my strength and stamina to speed up and enhance my focus—preparing myself to either fight or flee from the danger at hand. Bodily and mentally, I'm feeling changed from what I'm used to be, and have no longer control over myself. It's as I don't fit in my body or in the world anymore, therefor the passionate love fire inside me is rapidly being extinguished more and more with each passing day.

As I notice warning signs, I feel I need to gather evidence; I keep in secret on a memory stick. *It can be useful someday*, I thought, and get obsessed with my research, with finding the truth. Why? I don't know!

Much has happened since we left The Philippines, and simultaneously as we prepare the building in Chalus, we continue working on our bedding business with China and The Philippines. We arrange with Samir that we need to travel to London and China for the upcoming two medical expo's, equally to handle my legal papers in Hong Kong. For the first five days, we stay in London for the expo, and then we travel back to Chalus again.

Three weeks later, we travel to Hong Kong, and both events are a part of my venture for our private business. As an investment, Samir pays for our flight from Hong Kong to China, and generously gives us furthermore US$10,000 *in cash* for hotel and daily needs. Everything gets prepared, and we meet with our partner in Hong Kong, and next with the largest bedding manufactory before we'll take part in the China expo. The size of the Chinese manufacturer Xing and Jang Smart Living Group is in an enormous building complex, in an impressive zone that's a city within the city—with over one million people and just under 3 million more in Shanghai.

We experience a good understanding with Xing and Jang Smart Living Group, and we want to take on the world market with our products. Xing and Jang Smart Living Group gets excited about Drake's background, so we only need a website and movie clips to tell our story. As we set the agreement, they produce the first prototypes. I will do the professional photographing and prepare for YouTube, with him as a spokesperson.

Is the market ready for novel ideas? There lie still many challenges for us—among them store displays, explanations, videos, and sales portals to visualise on a TV screen. Drake's plans get massive and longer than a short story. I don't understand half of his delusions of grandeur.

Once it's completed, he wants to finish the website together with our IT guy in The Philippines. I can't wait and am brimming with excitement for it to happen, so it means our business venture has officially started. I'm impressed, but I didn't notice the pros and cons. While doing both jobs I realise, it's a tough task, when he wants simultaneously to promote Samir's clinic and our products on our website within the next four to six months.

'It will focus our goals. We will open the clinic complex. Then we can launch our own products simultaneously.' Drake proudly brags, and I jump right into his trap of megalomania.

Come on, dear reader, everything sounds amazing!

The revelation of this prime point of a fantastic freaking fraud show continues.

*   *   *

The fanatic show is not over yet, and it's not done in China, while we must attend the enormous medical Expo in Bao'an District. That's for this purpose Samir generously gave us further US$10,000 in cash, since the Expo is about finding medical supplies for him.

A major city in Guangdong Province, bordering Hong Kong, and a global technology hub. It's one of the fastest-growing cities in the world since the nineties, and home to almost 20 million people, and host to multinational companies. It's *massive*, and so are the expo.

Oh, my God! I hardly dare to tell the next scandalous story. As we arrive at The Ritz-Carlton, Bao'an District, we want to keep our $10,000 in the room's safe-deposit box. Clever! Blink… blink. Unfortunately, the box doesn't work, and the hotel staff can't fix it immediately, so shit happens! Right? What do we do?

The following day we prepare to go to the expo, so cleverly ;-) we split the money between us. Drake has $5,000, and I keep the other $5,000 securely tucked away in my bag. I watch my bag as fiercely as a growling pit bull terrier. During the expo, the sack is never unattended and securely wrapped around my leg or across my neck and shoulder as I sit with exhibitors or walk around. As anyone else, the chick needs to pee.

'Can you hold my bag?' I ask Drake while he's waiting outside the restroom.

There is a lengthy queue, so it takes a while until I'm back. Not pondering of my bag, *since he holds it*, I go unwavering hand in hand with him to the restaurant.

'Please give me my sack, darling.' As I turn around facing him when I want to pay. Beforehand, I hadn't noticed if he still had the bag, since I took it for granted, he still had it.

'Eh? I don't have it, Baby.' He smirks and waves his arms in circles.

'What? But you hold it for me while I was in the restroom.' Panicking, I scowl around as a headless confused chicken.

'No, you didn't, Sweet Pea,' he retorts. 'You took it with you. Um-hmm, you must have forgotten it in the restroom. No, wait. I'm not even sure you had the bag with you. Someone has stolen it while somebody was sneaking around during our visits at the last stall.' He grins.

I run as a panicking chased rabbit back to the restroom. Nothing! I'm burning inside, and sense the start of an anxiety attack, as my blood pressure gets higher, and my heart pounds faster. Next, I head to the stall. No bag! Now I'm scared shitless and want to cry. No $5,000! I lost my passport, Chinese exit and entrance visa, and my credit cards, my new iPhone and a new camera. I can't get out of China now. I'm trapped! The mystery is immense! My brain speeds two hundred miles an hour as I backtrack, going over every minute of my day. I'm frustrated but also confident I gave the handbag to Drake. *Gosh!* He had responsibility for it for less than ten to fifteen minutes, and I don't dare to go against him and accuse him of losing it.

At the expo police station, we report the loss, also as when we get back to the hotel. Next, we call the Danish embassy to request a new urgent passport, and I also need a new entrance and exit visa, but I don't know from were. The frustration gets enormous, and no matter how much I retrace my steps, every time it goes back to me handing over the bag to Drake.

Well, surprising news comes the next morning.

'Good morning, my love.' He smiles over his entire face. 'I have glorious news for you.' Raising his hands and claps. 'I went to the police station in the early morning hours while you still were sleeping. Woo-hoo! Smile, baby. They found your handbag in a bin near the restroom.'

'Huh? Really?'

'Yeeeaaah! Sadly, without the cash. No iPhone, nor the pocket camera.' He leers proudly.

It seems bizarre the Police suddenly had found the bag, and the first thing I do is to empty the entire sack to check what contents are still there.

'Strange, how come my credit cards, visa, passport, and other valuable things are still in the sack?' Gazing dumbfounded at Drake in confusion. 'These are documents of prime interest on the black market.' He just smirks strangely, lifts his shoulder as he knows nothing. 'Darling, why didn't you take me with you? Shouldn't I sign for something at the police station?'

'No, no!' He smirks, clapping in his hands.

'Let's go back there. I want to know where the police found it.' I glance at him worriedly.

I'm glad my passport and visa are there, but I must block six of my seven credit cards, and keep one so far. Most annoying is, that will cost me a costly trip to Denmark to get seven new credit cards again.

'Baby, you need not to go back. I fixed it. I signed for the papers. I told you the Police found it in a bin.' He doesn't comment on the weirdness of him having done so on my behalf, without my knowledge.

The next action Drake performs is to write to Samir, telling him of my stolen handbag and credit cards—including *"all our money!"* Meaning, that Drake included the $5,000 he still has, and wants Samir to pay for our hotel and food. Do I need to tell you more?

Well, I will, anyway. Samir transferred the funds for the payment of the hotel, and the sneaky Drake became $10,000 richer, without my knowledge.

I dislike suspecting a person I love. But damn! My sensation was always right. For many years, this matter haunted me—whether I was right or wrong on that point.

After our China travel, we spend two weeks in The Philippines— first for the final closing of the office in Manila. Next, travel to Batangas to finish the last pickup for shipping our belongings to Iran. We say goodbye to Kris, Lindy and Leo who adopted Lucky and Anxious and lastly we do the last check-up on Specs and say goodbye to Waan and Mali.

She is in superb condition and runs around as though nothing happened to her many months before. I am thrilled and makes me be okeydokey of leaving her as we travel back to Iran for the next four weeks, before I go back to Copenhagen. Oh, my goodness, it's one travel after another.

Coming back to Iran, Drake receives his visa but has not yet gained his work permit.

'Why did I not get my visa when you got yours?' I disappointed ask. 'It's mysterious! I am not happy!'

'Oh my God, Babe, you are absolutely too much. Don't be gloomy. Samir demanded a psychological evaluation of you first. He thinks you are not normal—that you are mentally ill. Baby, he is right. You possess too many demons swirling in your head.' Loudly, he laughs mockingly at me.

'What? Mentally ill? Are you nutty?' Traumatised, I stare intensely at him, while my jaw drops to the floor.

'Remember, we are guests. We're invited by a prominent person. Samir has lots of contacts with the higher court. And the president, too.'

'*Are you serious?*' glaring flabbergasted at him, then gaze the other way.

'We can't let you run around as a mentally ill person. Can we, Babe?' He sure got the nerve.

'We still have no signed agreement from Samir. That worries me. I get a weird gut feeling that something is not right here. And now this *psych* test?' I anger, while Drake blabbers of strange things—a discussion I don't need.

'Baby, you came into my life when yours looked the worst. I was facing a new phase of mine. There's nothing I *wanted* more than to be with you. You *meant* much to me. I *loved* taking you into my arms and giving you love.'

'Eh? Wanted? Meant? Loved?' Dumbfounded, I gaze questioning at him.

'Later, I supported you through your difficult divorce. And your vicious demons, since you needed *my* help. You needed someone you could *trust*—someone to *help* you for your sake.'

'Why are we having this weird talk?'

'You found that in *me*. I have spent *my entire time* trying to find solutions for you. For you to win. To get the most out of your divorce. I absolutely didn't do it for the sake of *my* win.'

'Oh, my Drake, you make yourself sound as the fantastic saviour of the entire world.'

'Baby, you were alone against a force that was greater than you can imagine. But we tackled it just right—with *me* taking a vast amount of time and energy. I gladly gave my share.'

'Darling, you sound atrocious arrogant. Yea, like the slick Mr Collins from Jane Austen's book "Pride and Prejudice". Geez!'

'With joy in my heart, our relationship *had* a wonderful beginning, Mary. Though, this here is tough—it's too much for me.'

'Eh, had? Tough? It sounds as a massive *goodbye!*'

'Your lawyer could never achieve such an excellent result as I did for you.' He keeps on blabbering like a self-assured, stunning, prize-winning wild parrot, saving me as he came from out of the glorious blue.

'Drake, I do not understand why you are saying these things.'

'I never asked for your financial help just for my sake. I always sought balance in my life with those I've dealt with. Though, I could not get it. Or find it.'

'The confusion in my head is massive.' Instead, I imagine that I possess those vicious demons—that I'm not normal.

'Baby, when we met, I understood your background for a while. I saw someone who needed me.' Yeah, I bet! The prince on the white rescue horse.

'Eh? I don't understand what you are talking about, Drake.' Shaking my head in frustration.

'Baby, you needed balance in your life. Only I could give it to you. But only at the expense of my life and sacrifice.' God has spoken.

'Darling, I'm grateful for your help. But, eh? Why this discussion?'

'You must understand, I devoted my time, Babe. Every resource I had to help you with your fears. Bit by bit, I came to understand you—your complexity. Your shadowy demons. Mostly, your remorse.' *Yeah, I did my absolution in front of him,* sarcastically I ponder.

'What? Remorse? And you keep on talking of demons.'

'Yes, because that's the last part you need to find peace and balance with, Babe. This is something that drives you and me as a nightmare in our lives. This is the last thing that we need to find a solution to—your rash, hysterical attacks. Your struggles that come to life.'

'Ahh, okay, I see. What does that have to do with a test and Samir?'

'Samir has seen such wobbly conduct with you. He asked me; "what is wrong with Mary."'

'How dare you to discuss such private things with Samir?' I'm traumatised to my inner bones.

'Oh, boy, Mary. When you pop up as a jack-in-the-box, wrong and unfounded, I've learned to keep quiet. If I single-handedly go against you, you get even angrier. Argh! Then you come to stupid conclusions.'

'A-ha, ok, fine. When *you* wanted to go to Iran, I have had a mighty gut sensation that it will end soon between us. For that, my heart and soul get sorrowful.'

'Babe, in your mind, it's always the fault of someone else when something goes wrong. I understand. Only I know you better than anyone.' He acts as the glorious, mighty God.

'So, you suppose everything is my fault?' Though, I can't recognise any of his accusations against me, and imagine it's a description of himself.

'I think it's your defence mechanism. A survival mechanism that makes you react as that. You are alone, Babe. Your temper makes you even more alone. You are in a vicious cycle that you can't fight your way out of. It's pursuing you, although you are struggling to get out of it. I think we came a long way on that front too.' He grins while pointing the finger at me.

'Then you should do the test too, Drake. Not only me.'

'You can't be more wrong in your conclusions. I don't need such a test. I'm too clever. I'm not sick in my head as you are,' The bastard is smirking as a stupid red ass baboon.

'I sense you're tiring of me. You don't need me anymore. Now you have Samir and his wealth.' Shouting, angry and sarcastic.

'I know you have been a lever for me, Baby.' He clears his throat and grabs his water. 'That's something I have been afraid of. And feared that you would see it as dishonest if something went wrong in our relationship.'

'My sensation is something I sensed for a long time.' I sigh and sniff.

'It's a conclusion you could easily come to. But that is wrong.' Now, he's fuming fire out of his mouth and nose, as the ludicrous dragon he is.

'You know you can be on your own feet again by staying here. You have no more debt. And I've paid the last payment for the equipment.'

'Oh, my God! You still got demons that control the grim part of your mind. Does it never stop? I thought we had overcome them. Argh, they keep on popping up from time to time, Mary. Damn it, yeah, as a mean jack-in-the-box.' He is angry and almost suffocating in his loud fit of coughing, so I get a shudder.

'I conclude that you no longer need my support. I sense that you reached your goal. A goal that my heartfelt love has helped you achieve.'

'Jeez, I experience it as your rage that you take out on me. It makes me sad. And it gets me completely out of balance myself.'

'Honestly, Drake, I sense that you no longer appreciate me. That's why you are moving away from me.' It saddens me. I realise we get closer to the discarding phase.

'Oh, boy, I must take great care with what I say so you don't misunderstand. Sometimes I can take it. Other times, it's hard. Especially when I notice you're unreasonable in what you say and accuse me of.' He yells and gets a fit of coughing again, and I wish he will choke.

'Lately, you have shown a coldness to me—something you never showed before. That makes me sorrowful. And frustrated.' I sniff and want to cry.

'Jesus Christ, Mary, I prefer to keep quiet. When I say something, you respond with even more rage that makes me collapse.' He pauses and blows his nose and clears his throat. 'I have never done that before in my life. I even got wiser over the years. I'd want peace.'

'I honestly sense I'm losing you. That's what I want to tell you. You blame everything on me and my non-existent demons.' I'm making excuses and get more distressed.

'I don't want to fight with you, Babe.'

'Who is fighting who? The wrath is not on me, Drake. You exploded with a wild rage.'

'Grr, you dare to judge, it's only you who have helped me financially. To get on my feet again! That I want to get rid of you. This is wide of the mark. I hoped to find my Mary Magdalene.

To live happily ever after with her.'

'I have no more words. I'm empty. Unable to go through such suffering again.'

'I can turn it around and ask you; "Is it you who wants to get rid of me, Mary? Now that you are in a fantastic condition to survive financially?"'

'Whoa! You suppose you have done so much. Shared so many unique things with me. Are you that special?' I'm sure that's how he built up my trust, for me to get faith in him.

'Gah, I can obviously no longer live up to your hopes as your partner and life mate. Both paths are disturbing thoughts.' The jack-in-the-box gets angrier at me and uses his weakness to make himself as the victim, so I should feel sorry for him.

'If you don't want or need me anymore, finish it now. I'll leave you and move back to Copenhagen.' I'm determined, even in sadness.

'For goodness' sake! I believe Flopper had a hard time understanding you. He couldn't see you as you are—a sweet and warm woman with plenty of courage in life. But also, out of balance with herself. A woman who sought security and faithfulness.'

'Eh?' Scratching my forehead. 'I don't get why Paul suddenly is a part of this discussion.'

'Baby, I grasp the most essential thing in you—the desire for someone to give you happiness. Genuine love and care. Flopper didn't bring you comfort. Did not hold your hand in his. Did not say he loved you. He took your nasty urges and needs as a burden. Then he came up with this extreme sex. Even if you didn't desire or needed it. But he could then satisfy *his* desires.'

I'm listening and listening to the fast splattering waterfall.

'Flopper thought he could start dirty relations with other women. Then he found out, in his perverted mind, that watching his wife being nasty abused by others excited him. He would only hurt you by slaughtering you. Deep in Flopper's gloomy mind, he became more malicious with you. Do you imagine he wants you back?'

Drake's vulgar way of nagging me with his endless rude waffling is impossible to interrupt.

'You are getting too personally and hurtful, Drake.' I don't get a decent chance to answer.

'We fought a fierce fight for your rights. You came out of it better financially than most women do. Flopper will gladly trick you into not having nothing.'

'I know you fought much for me. I truly appreciate that.'

'Who will trust you? No one will think it's something *he* invented. You will be the witch.

Flopper will emerge as the "poor" husband.'

'Why do you think so? Paul will not do that.'

'What was next for us? Our crush grew day by day. You know I'm the only one who loves you. Yeah, even cares for you. Being together, we could concentrate on our future and work. You wanted to live on a deserted island. Us living off *your* money. But I want to take part financially. As I always have done before, Babe. I can't! I must start over again. We tried our luck in Asia.'

Drake's fierceness and anger run as an unstoppable broiling water tap, and he is hardly breathing or pausing, while he jabbers as a fast-running out-of-controlled steaming locomotive.

'We couldn't find what we were looking for. Then came Iran on the radar. It's a great happiness to end my career on a top note. I will take that opportunity with or without you.' He smirks.

'Then do it. I don't care.'

I'm shattered. Drake broke me with his criticism. Mostly, I want to go to bed, then scream my heart out and speedily leave him. Anybody can be a victim of abuse; however, there are specific contexts and individual characteristics that can make a person vulnerable. Among these are unequal power dynamics, as it is with Drake. When I entered this relationship, it was because I intensely wanted it. He must have thought I wanted him so desperately, that he abused my burning desire by telling me I should do this and that for him. And ever since, his behaviour and exploitation escalate more and more.

'What an offensive way to treat me,' I peep.

'It affects our life negatively, Mary. All the damn demons you have. Demons possess your family. I saved you from the evil devil.' (Meaning Paul).

'It only confirms my opinions of you. Only a troubled and upset man will say such things—only someone who has no sense of right and wrong.'

'Baby, I'm the only person who can help you get rid of all your devilish demons. I'm your resurrected Jesus. You are my Mary

Magdalene. We walked the Jesus Trail together in Israel back then.' That is a harsh misuse of my strong Catholic faith. I am about to lose all my faith in Christ. I am shaken and devastated. I still have a hard time getting back to my faith.

'To ease you, darling, I will do the test for Samir's satisfaction.' I am forced to undergo the unnecessary psychological evaluation, so in protest, I'm accepting it.

He glares wicked and victorious at me with a skewed smirk. Satisfactory he is rubbing his hands, while he seems to think highly of his cruel judgements of me—so high as to make everyone in our surroundings get the opinion that I'm mentally sick.

'I have nothing more to say. Except for this—everything has a beginning, and everything has an end; such is life. Hi-hi.' The steaming locomotive stops with a satisfying low giggle.

Drake believes I depend on him, and on the wealth he can get with Samir or his non-existent love for me. Considering how narrow-minded Drake's conclusions are, the fella should know he's not the only person in the world who can do what he brags about. The smartest move he can make will be to realise that he will not be here if I had not supported him, and his many wild stories and me being cornered.

The psychological test finds me healthy, and I believe Drake ought to do the test instead of me. I'm confident the testers will find what a narcissist he is. A sociopath!

After that, I go silent. No arguments with him. I only observe and consider my future *without* Drake, even I from the beginning believed in the shared future. Next to trusting the glittering beauty of our mutual dream while floating on pink clouds—till I gave him the non-poisoned red apple—for next I trusted his tender embrace and passionate kiss; till his soft red lips became the snake's poison—and until I realise, I've kissed the devious devil; with his fatal kiss. That's the day I emotionally died.

CHAPTER 29

DEMON ESCAPES THE
SHADY ANGEL

She kissed me. She kissed the devil. Only a beautiful soul
like hers would kiss the damned.

—Daniel Saint

So far, we celebrated our first Christmas, enjoyed a stunning New Year's together and travelled to London, China, Qatar, and many other countries. Basically, we've only been in Chalus for ten weeks during the six months since we arrived. And we still miss the signed contract between Samir and us.

'Soon, Mary.' Drake says hundreds of times. I no longer believe in it.

Though, I sincerely try to trust Samir. The lovely soft pink clouds no longer float smoothly into my life. Instead, we replace the stunning colours of my entrancing dreamy sunrise and the sunsets with daily heavy rain and thunderous blasting storms. My beloved, with whom I used to watch every morning until the stunning sunset on the horizon, mentally disappeared. I'm often in solitude when I watch the Sun from our vast balcony, while distressing times get to daily stormy winds of massive struggles. Fussing, he brings up another discussion to the surface.

'I do not understand of what your weird silent punishment is of, which you subject me to, Mary.' He barks loudly.

Half-asleep on my way to dreamland, I get a blow to receive his sudden angry outburst in the middle of the night.

'Huh? What? This is not a punishment to you,' I grumble, rubbing my eyes and sitting up with a start, and turn on my bedside lamp.

'I know for sure that if it was me who did this to you, you will launch a hysterical attack.'

'Jeez, Drake. My silence is because I don't need ugly discussions with you every time we try to do something about the clinic. My review doesn't count anyhow. You want it only your way. You get it without me interfering.'

'If I only knew what I'm doing wrong. Then I can correct my mistakes.'

'Christ! You consider it a penalty of silence. Okay, that's your interpretation. You think I'm vindictive. I'm not spiteful. Nor do I punish you. Goodnight Drake. I want to sleep. Not argue.'

'Babe, I do not understand what's wrong.' Oh, my, and he wants to continue arguing.

'Nothing! Go to sleep!' I answer, insensitive.

'I want to know it now!' The man-child is roaring, and he will not give up the fight.

'Argh, I'm tacitly watching what you're doing. If I shut up and keep my opinion in my pocket, then I will not go wrong. And your doubtless right. Yeah, I will launch a hysterical attack. Honestly? It will help nothing!' I turn around and want to sleep.

'So, I must just go on with what I need to do?' Strange question he asks, and I turn towards him and stare confused into his eyes.

'Huh?'

'Well, all alone you want me to get the clinic up and running. Okay, then I must bury myself with work!' He sounds as a scorned little man-child.

'Darling, no matter what I say, whether you are wrong, I always get cannon balled by you; "Such nonsense, you say, Mary!" Christ! So many times, I heard this sentence?'

'Okay, I see! You are no longer interested in me.'

'Ugh, you can't understand it when I say something that doesn't fit in your head. I grasp it as you do not understand what's wrong.' The conversation is tedious to me.

'If I'm not good enough and cannot fulfil your dreams, then it's better for you to find your happiness with someone else.' The little preschool child growls.

'Darling, just keep up your work! I too want to get the clinic up and running. But I don't want you to treat me with ugliness. And offensiveness when I come up with ideas or comments.' *Is he breaking up with me in the middle of the night?* I ponder and continue.

'Baloney! You talk rubbish.'

'Ha-ha, yea, whatever I say or do, you misunderstand it, Drake. It's not appreciated by you. You take the entire credit for the work. Be my guest! We will see if you can use me later.'

'You are amazing financially, because of me. I healed you.' Again, he talks of pennies.

'You upset me every time. Love obviously must hurt. It does now.' He surely does what he can to hurt me.

'Babe, you're able to get a carefree life without wealth concerns. I'm not. I think you should go back to Denmark.' He wrinkles his brows in anger.

'Huh? Eh, Denmark has no more meaning for me. It died when I moved in with you. Just as it did when my son died. There is only one burial ground to remember the dead.' What a prick.

I'm dazed and can't believe that he is ditching me. 'If I no longer had an interest in you, do you think I would squeeze your hand as you never would allow me to squeeze it again?' I grab his hand to cuddle it with love and continue blabbering.

'You are better off in Copenhagen.'

'You want to work on what you always wanted. Okay, I accept that. It's not optimal for me. We waste too much of our love on something else we honestly don't need. Now I only get a limited love from you, darling. In the beginning, I got much more.'

I get the sensation of a hurting pinch in my heart from the idea that he will break with me.

'If you want me to go to hell, then tell me, Mary.' I don't understand his feisty angriness.

'Darling, as a Christian believing in Jesus and the Virgin Mary, you can't get it past your lips wishing you to hell. If I'm losing you, I don't need another man to ruin my life. I will opt-out of love. Live with myself. You're healed. I'm not. There are still lots of things that hurt my soul and cause me despair.'

'I have before been able to endure problems. I can't help you. Find another man.' *Why is he talking of me finding another man?* I ponder.

'Find another man? What? We lived off my funds. You enjoyed it, darling. You used it to launch your many failed projects.'

'I'm not ready to die now. Especially where I can finally achieve the greatest I can in my profession.' He whimpers as a baby. *Why is he again talking of being dead?* I muse.

'You flip a sudden switch in your head. Jeez, then you think I can just "find someone else and find happiness again." Isn't that more an excuse on your part to get rid of me?'

'You know it will give me satisfaction, Baby. And knowledge that I reached the goal of my work if I stay.'

'Yeah, it is the only project that can yield a return for you. Maybe you no longer need me.'

'If you don't want to take the last trip with me, I understand that too.'

'God damn it, Drake. I see you with me. Not without me. We managed many problems. Went through hell. None of us are ready to die.' I try to be calm and comfort him.

'If we part, let's do it kindly. Let's find a solution that's good for both of us.' I can't follow his nebulous talk. What does he mean?

'Do you think after the massive energy we spend on this business; I'd then give up on you? Your words hurt! Darling, I get it more than it's *you* who wants to be free from me.'

'Baby, I'd prefer not to lose you as a friend.' What a strange remark of his.

'Not lose me as a friend! Oh, my goodness! These are doubtless the words that hurt the most. It sounds as a massive goodbye. Then we can always be friends?' Frustrated, I gaze at him.

'Perhaps it is.'

'Oh, then what? "By the way, Mary, thanks for your financial help. I can survive by my own now"?' I burst out ironically. Incredibly, Drake means so much to me, and though, being with him is as fighting a hopeless battle in a blasting war zone.

'I can help you with something else. Do it in Denmark. You're too complex, Mary.'

'Huh? Complex? A person you no longer want to be with,' I pause and stare at him. 'It will give you the peace you need. Then you can satisfy the last thing that's in your head. You can reach the goal you missed in your younger days at any cost! It can be a hard price to pay.'

'Baby, I will help you get a clinic put together somewhere else. If that's what you want.'

'Huh, a clinic somewhere else?' I baulk and sense; it's best I'm clearing out. 'So, I don't get in your way here in Chalus?' It's obvious to me he will be without me.

'You had ambitions to show what you can do. Do it in Copenhagen.'

'Forget it. Not interested! I'll manage without you.' I get distressed.

'You possess talents far beyond those that Flopper believed you had.'

'What talents are you talking of? You knocked many of them to the floor. You made it clear to me. Only your work matters.'

'Or you can do great in Sweden.' He's steadfast that I should get the hell out of his sight.

'Losing you it means you will lose me as a friend. My love is unlimited for you. I don't want to be in pain; I've lost my greatest love. Being "friends" with an old flame I cannot keep. I'll be to the rats in my spirit.' I mourn for the loss that has begun. Have we reached the discharging phase? Is he in his right senses?

'But you need not to work. You can afford to lie on a beach, Baby. Enjoy reading books, with a colourful icy pink cocktail in your other hand. You hold the world in your hands. Go to Caribbean. Hold on to it as you've held mine,' He loudly laughs, trying to cheer me up again.

Drake mentally leaves me alone on a brisk deserted sinking ice floe in the Antarctic and not on a sunny white beach with palms, turquoise sea and an icy cocktail.

'I want to work. But not from early morning until I go half dead back to bed. Then I will never get the time to lie on the sunny beach and read an enticing book. What is the beach worth without being there with you? We don't spend time on it anymore. Why? Only work 24/7. What can I use "the world's hand" for when it's not yours? I can only hold two hands. Yours.' It's as if he's completely changed. I sob.

'Okay, but please let me know what you want, Babe.' His response is freezing cold.

'What I want? I want our life back. Your love—not just watching you work and complain of me and others. That's why I'm grumpy. Silent and hiding inside my shield. That's why you think you're losing me. I'm not happy as I used to be.'

'Were you ever happy with me? Ha-ha, I doubt.'

'Jeez, darling. I seek the happiness I thought I had found in you. Do I have it? If so, you know what I want.' Tired, I'm ending the tedious conversation, turn off the light and try to cuddle next to him.

Drake goes silent and turns his back on me and falls asleep. I'm turning restlessly around in my bed, as my brain ponders the hopeless situation. We walked into this project blindfolded. Okay, they provided us with suitable housing and a car. We worked hard day and night for Samir, despite our many travels. What do I do? Honestly, I've had enough of his cruel, intoxicating games.

*   *   *

I'm packing my suitcase and travel to Hong Kong. I must ponder of my destiny, and the relationship with him, as I shake my head in confusion and don't know what to make of his sudden change. A week after my arrival, Skype jingles, while I'm reading mails on my computer.

'Hi, my darling eternal love. I miss you so much.'

'Good morning, darling.'

'It's painful to be without you, Baby—and especially on a day as this. I was thinking careful of the best course of action for us.'

'What do you mean? Are you okay?'

'It's now five o'clock in the morning. It does not entice me to lie alone in my bed. I am and have on every occasion depended on you by my side. I love you forever, Baby.'

'I miss you too and being next to me in my cold bed.'

'It gives me time to reflect on things that are more important—how lucky I am that we had found each other. I'm lucky.'

'I'm glad to know, darling.'

'You are a gem of which there is only one in the world. It complicates you with the way your life has formed for you. Though, without ever slowing your depression.'

'Huh? Depression? What do you refer to?' We have talked so little since I left Chalus.

'It's not what you needed. It can only give you violent reactions in your soul. I know it takes you. It has not left you yet. But we tore few ugly demons out of your soul.'

'Hmm, why do you say this?' I'm confused.

'You dealt with your destiny. You failed to put up any defence to lessen the pain.' I sense he is sorrowful being alone there.

'Eh? What shall I do?'

'I'm happy—because you let me get deep into your soul and heart. You allowed me to show my feelings to you. To show you that love is not just a fiction. Or a Fata Morgana that you could not capture.'

'Well, I'm glad I could give you that joy, darling.'

'When you went on your Jesus trail and saw an oasis in front of you that just kept getting further away from you.' He talks gibberish. 'It would never stand still long enough for you to throw yourself into its chilly water. Then soothe your sore and burned feet.'

'Eh, I'm not sure I can follow what you are saying. Are you drunk?'

'I know we again will find the balance. Calm air. So, we feel most comfy within our relationship when you can find peace in yourself.'

'Have you smoked pot?'

'Stop it, Mary. If you won't let the anger rise to your head, then we can embrace and love each other. Be in love with each other in total happiness.' *Cocaine blabber.*

'Darling, I hope for a better solution for us. Despite our disagreements.'

'We will sleep with the comfort of knowing that the next morning, we will be with each other. Then our love will become more significant.' Suddenly he is so much in love with me.

'Okay. Fine. I've sent you a picture of me standing in the big mall. Did you get it?'

'Yeah! I hope you will come home again, Baby. I genuinely love you. No one should take your love from me.'

'Nice to know. No one does.'

'If I had a private jet, I would rapidly take it and pick you up in Hong Kong.'

'Well, I hope I'm leaving soon.'

'You're my forever lasting love, Baby. The one my heart has a burning desire for.'

'Darling, the thought of coming home to you makes me happy.'

'Sweet Pea, I'm glad you're approaching again. I can almost feel you. I hope you will soon be back in my arms. I must go now.'

'Take care, darling.'

'I love you, Baby. I miss you. Get home to me *now*! See you soon.'

* * *

On average, a woman will leave an abusive relationship seven times before she leaves for good. How is it possible for survivors to return to their abusers? Many factors play into going permanently, so if you are one of those people who responded to your abuser, understand that leaving is a complicated process. Don't feel shame about having gone back. Some survivors have grown up in abusive households or only ever been in abusive relationships. When this happens, those who have been ill-treated don't always recognise that barbaric behaviour is destructive.

They might just think it's normal, according to the National Domestic Violence Hotline 2017.

* * *

In good faith, I return to Chalus, but only to realise none of Drake's promises ever come to fruition. Quickly, he gets one of his 'out-of-the-blue' weird ideas again, and things go blasting haywire. Unexpectedly, he sees and hears ghosts in our apartment, and convinces me that Samir is bugging it. Several times, unexpected security people visit us and ask strange questions, and by Samir, we are told; its future patients. But it's as if we are under suspicion and continually being questioned. Things turn bizarre between us, the staff at the clinic plus Doctor Mustafa.

We have an upcoming trip to Singapore scheduled for a week-long education, followed by a week in Qatar. Goodness gracious, that gives us peace of mind. We plan to investigate if we can set up a clinic in Qatar instead, and our contacts will help us.

As we return to Chalus, they finally hand over my visa, which has taken eight months; however, at least both of us have now received our work permits.

Alas, something weird happens, since Samir and Doctor Mustafa have heard of our latest Qatar trip. Drake gets franticly agitated and panicking, so it ends with a vast argument with Doctor Mustafa.

I get heated. 'We need a meeting with Samir,' I tell Drake. 'There've been too many obstacles with Mustafa lately.'

Drake arranges it, and his smirking blabbering begins at Samir's office. 'I hope your treatment is getting a healthy and vibrant Samir back to Chalus. We have prayed for your recovery.'

I wanted to vomit over his obsequiousness, and Samir only nod with his head.

'Let's talk about the present status of the project. I feel obligated to present my view with a positive update. Yea, to encourage you of the situation in a fair light. The clinic is near finished. Most of the equipment has arrived. We only need to assemble it. Preferably by a technician.'

'Hmm… good.' Samir nods.

'After you told me you wanted to proceed, I understood it to mean with the full clinic. Right? As previously agreed. Then Doctor Mustafa sent me an email. Hmm, stating you have hired him to take over the project?'

'Hmm… I see!' Samir mumbles.

'I'm disappointed in the lack of trust in me. Though, I acknowledge your decision. What we still need to complete, Mustafa can do without my help.'

I notice that Drake is trying politely to argue against Samir's strange decision. But I can feel Drake's anger is close to burst out when he continues the fast blabbering. I remain quiet.

'I have handed everything to Mustafa. All my files. Brochures and vendor contacts,' he agitated continues. 'Mustafa can complete the buys of vital gear to get the clinic operational. I've told him of what we need. Which items are vital for the clinic to become active.' Someone knocks on the door and he pauses.

The secretary enters the room with a large tray, comprising three glasses, a teapot, sugar and cookies. She pours in the hot tea and put three small plates with cookies on the shiny mahogany desk, then leaves the room.

'Be aware there is a delivery time for some key equipment. Six to eight weeks. One major item is the X-ray machine. The one I advise is top of the line.'

'Take a glass of tea.' Samir hands over the sugar and divide the three plates between us.

Drake continues his fast-running blabbering. 'The delivery time could postpone the opening if we don't order it soon. I've surveyed the unit. I feel it's the right one. I've prepared education programs for medical and technical personnel. With that, I'll be ready to offer my know-how. And the latest technologies, as you firstly requested. When are you ready to hire the personnel?' He's talking complex, trying to be a smart-ass.

Samir scowls at him and says nothing. The Dragon parrot is jabbering without pausing or breathing air into his lungs, and I sit still and listen to his massive update.

'For me to run this program, we must agree on the financial terms of such an elaborate educational program. I've trained medics and therapists before. I *always* get a *vast* fee for each educated person. I'll give an exam at the end of the program. I'll require two top scientists or specialists as external examiners to assist me in the evaluation. It will cause a passing or failing grade for each course participant. We will certify the individual "student" in the respective discipline.'

Drake pauses for some seconds, slurps from his hot tea glass, grab a cookie and munch on it, while he thinks of how to approach the next agenda.

'I offer my clinical expertise and services for special and difficult cases on the same basis as the visiting clinicians and experts. I *want* you decently to compensate me. According to an agreed amount as related to the income produced for the clinic. The same goes for every other on the visiting medic program. The clinic needs medical candidates trained in *my* specialities.'

Samir stares wearisome at him, sitting relaxed in his black office chair, and swallows the rest of his tea. Irritated, he's gazing at his big Rolex, studded with diamonds in the watch case, and only asking; 'Do you have more to say?'

'I've made an outline of specialists needed for the clinic. I gave it to Dr Mustafa. I'm willing to offer my services to take part in the evaluation and selection of the candidates. They must possess certain basic skills for me to build them into top medics and therapists.'

Oh, boy! Drake has prepared an entire essay on his many requirements. Not only that, but he sounds as a God—as if he is the only one capable of the entire tasks.

'I'm willing to entertain an agreement to get top surgeons and other specialists to Chalus. I have a sizable network. I can find such doctors. I can offer specialists in the right environment in which to work. This is of great importance if the clinic is to become a quality clinic.'

Samir glimmers again at his watch, as if he is in a hurry.

'In that respect, I received the consent of the absolutely best and most experienced cardiologist in the world. We will be the only clinic that has this special equipment in the Middle East and Eastern Caucasus.'

Aggravated Samir pushes his office chair back, puts his right leg over the left knee, and glares at his watch again, but Drake continues as a non-stoppable waterfall.

'We must get a cardiologist on staff. I will train them to provide this service daily. I'm in contact with the Swedish Doctor Johannsson for the neuro-spinal department. The British Doctor Jones will come as an intern. But under my guidance, in the neuro-spinal department. We must offer Jones a reasonable compensation package. The Norwegian ENT surgeon Doctor Berg will take part, subject to the clinic having the OR facility I have outlined.' Drake observes Samir to see how he will respond, while he continues to boast of himself as a bloated walrus.

'I have done my job for now! Doctor Mustafa has taken over the project as per your instructions. I've prepared him for completing the interior and equipment for the clinic. He has the info he needs to buy the remaining gear and expendables. I can, in good faith, take a little time off from the project until all is ready for business.' And Drake leans his body provocatively forward, resting with his arms on Samir's desk, as he is nearly to threaten with his next agenda.

'Mainly, I must make up for what Mary and I lost in personal income during the past eight months. We must get our own business running. We closed our clinic in The Philippines. Opted out on other clinic options. We have put our bedding business on hold, because we believed in Chalus. It was a vast project. We planned to get a profit from our work here. So far, we *only* gained a little alms. I hope you understand our dilemma, Samir. Please understand that we did not lose faith in Chalus. We believe it can become a great clinic if you implement the original concepts.' He leans back in normal position on his chair, takes a deep breath and snatches the last cookie on the plate.

I'm surprised over Drake's last comment.

'For our circumstances, there is one item that we want to resolve. We were told before we came that you would reimburse every of our expenses for our moving.' Samir's eyes are wide open, and I'm in distress that Drake brings this to the surface at this point.

'Abbas got our receipts a long time ago. We updated the refunds to include the latest costs.

I gave a copy to Karim last week. The amount is US$15,000. It will be helpful if we can get the money today. If all you asked me to do in Chalus, and if you still want it, we can take time to discuss how we can move on from here.' He appears exhausted as his speech ends.

I'm flabbergasted, and Samir says nothing, gets up and walks towards his safe, and takes the cash and hands $15,000 over to Drake, then politely says, 'Goodbye!' pointing at the door.

We continue the work in cooperation with the team at the clinic, though it's difficult.

Before long, the next exhausting outburst comes from Drake. 'Babe, I don't know what is going on. This I weird.' He seems outraged. 'Samir has sent me a message saying; you are no longer welcome to join meetings with us. After our last meeting, he wrote that you are an interference in the meetings.'

'What? I didn't say a word.' Momentarily, I think this is a joke.

'Yea, that's why Samir was angry during our last gathering.'

'Only you were blabbering as a fast rapping parrot. You demanded several things from Samir.' I am outraged!

'Samir has forbidden you to be a part of the project.' Drake devilishly smirks.

It's spine chilling and utterly weird to get such a message. 'You must joke!' I exasperate. 'What did I wrong?' I shout, then lower my voice to a disappointing level. 'I'm worried, Drake,' and then he hands over the phone, so I can read the message. *Strange! It's not the same phone number I have for Samir.* I muse.

'Why did Samir not tell me this face to face instead? It's not even his phone number.'

'He has several numbers. I don't know why he used this one.'

I'm wondering if it's Drake who wants to get rid of me and not Samir. *Does Drake possess a special sacrificial demon for his obsession?*

Is his world fertilised with inner anger, with no sense of other people's perspectives? I muse suspiciously.

In my perspective, Drake suddenly possesses his own greedy agenda—to keep the entire business for himself. I have spent a substantial amount of time and effort in helping to put everything together within the timeframe we've proposed. Suddenly, I'm 'disposable'? I'm very disappointed and can't understand what's happening. I have been the lifeblood of his livelihood for the past three years, while I've supported him! Without my support, he would never have been in Chalus, nor met our friends from Qatar, Mufasa and Arshia, while they were in The Philippines. They were the reason we ended up in Iran.

'You must tell me why the sudden has this vast surprise popped up?' I ask, disappointed.

'I'm sure we are being monitored in the apartment. That's how Samir found out.'

'Found out what?'

'Your intentions to go behind his back with the clinic in Qatar.'

'Huh? Um-hmm, but it's not the case that we'll start anything in there.'

'Yea, we talked of it; therefore, I'm certain Samir bug us. How come he knows of Qatar? I didn't tell him, Babe. Did you?'

'Ha-ha!' I'm shaking my head and don't want to think of being bugged. 'Come on, Drake! We only explored the possibilities. It was in line with our future partnership with Samir. How come this is such a surprise for him?' And I gaze at him in amazement and don't want to talk of it, because Qatar will never become a reality.

'The most alarming thing is that Samir says he knows you went up to Abbas's room again, after the latest party.'

'*What?*' I bellow and my wobbling jelly legs nearly collapse under me. Drake lies.

'Samir is angry that you made a pass at Abbas.'

'*Holy crap!* Where does such nonsense come from? Abbas could be my son. Are you insane? You know well that Abbas called me. He was sorrowful. He wanted guidance regarding his marriage. I told you! You knew I went up there.'

'I didn't know! You sneaked up there while I was at sleep.'

'Oh, my God! When I came back, I told you the entire story. You didn't sleep.'

'No, I woke up, because you were not in bed.'

'Get out! Such crap! Abbas was drunk. He flirted with me. I left when he made a pass at me. Why would I tell you that, if I was the culprit? Christ! The story upset you deeply.' Angry, I defend myself, I'm silently reflecting; *he must be mentally ill, since he brings up such ridiculous stories.*

I no longer feel welcome, but as a nuisance—an interference to Drake. Under such circumstances, I realise the end is near for me in Chalus. I'm worn out, exhausted! Whatever I do or say is wrong in his mind, and the relationship with him becomes a greater disaster. My burning desire for Drake totally fades, and in disappointment and anger, I pack my suitcase. The devilish demon escapes the shady angel, being on my way to visit my friends in Singapore.

CHAPTER 30

A Country-To-Country Refugee

> Not necessity, not desire—no, the love of power is the demon of men. Let them have everything—health, food, a place to live, entertainment—they are and remain unhappy and low-spirited: for the demon waits and waits and will be satisfied.
>
> —Friedrich Nietzsche

I transformed from possessing a burning desire to getting the sensation of being sent to hell by Drake's maliciousness. It feels unimaginable to me and being a country-to-country refugee—that must escape and hide, only to find myself again. Over the course of a year, I've travelled to forty distinct places around the globe. Now it's Singapore, to visit friends who own clinics in Singapore and New Zealand, because they have put an idea up of collaborating with them.

In the meantime, Drake's panic spreads, because he hates that I am no longer attending to him. He has not gotten his divorce with any of the authorities in the countries we've lived in, not succeeded with anything, and he's losing everything, including me. Every time I try to leave him, he changes—again becoming the loving Dragon boy, so I give in, chatting with him over Skype.

'Hi, my love. Finally, she's on the chat. I miss you, Baby. I love you crazily,' he is trying to sweeten me up.

'Hi, darling. Likewise,' I try to be optimistic, yet also frosty.

'It's so empty here without you. Glancing around, I see only emptiness. Your trip went ok?'

'Yea, it did. Can you call me later? I first need my coffee.'

'Fine. Get your coffee. I just drank one. It was so hard to say goodbye to you at the Airport. You were incredibly beautiful. I wanted to go with you. I don't enjoy being without you.'

'I'll call you later.' Then I'm getting up to make my coffee and enjoy a ten-minute break.

The keys are banging on my keyboard, clicking on my mouse, and I have contact with him on Skype. 'I'm back. The coffee is excellent.' I chuckle. 'Why didn't you come with me?'

'I didn't get a ticket or any clothes with me.'

'My suitcase is full of clothes. Ha-ha, you can always borrow a pair of my thongs,' I joke.

'My bum will appear weird in them. Willy will be beside himself. Poor him,' he clowns.

'OMG! Will you believe it. The fat Mamuska sitting behind the security screen at the transit searched my entire stuff in the trolley. Not only that. Jeez, she also searched my entire body. Holy moly! She looked offensive when I pulled up my electronic stuff. How can I get dangerous stuff going from one flight to the next? I don't get it,' I joke, worried.

'I don't want them to grope my darling,' he chuckles.

'No, but the fat Mamuska did! She could hardly wait until I'd packed everything back into my trolley again. It took a while before I finished. Ha-ha, I had plenty of time. Who cares when a star goes through?'

'You are my only star, Baby. I miss you.'

'Aww ... It feels as I'm letting you down. I had a wonderful dream of you last night. You kissed me passionately. Then loved me as you loved me before.'

'Aww ... Oh, sweet Babe! That's so sweet of you.' M-wah, he sends an air kiss.

'It was so nice to kiss you like that—to sense your soft lips touch mine again. M-wah.'

'I love you greatly too. It's getting late. I need to go to bed. Goodnight, sweet Baby.'

'I can still feel your lovely passion and warm kisses. Thank you. M-wah.' I'm glad and warm inside my soul.

'God will be with you. I'm directed by God to protect you. Jesus is there for you.' So sweet he is, and he waves.

'I know you'll protect me. You told me. Is that why I survived?' I'm calm, headless, and believe in every word from him.

'I will be. Sending my love and affection. Goodnight, my precious darling.' He ends the conversation and has again controlled everything—including the unwise chicken who is hiding in her cage with a chopped off head.

The ping-pong game begins entirely over again.

A few days after, he calls me again. There are problems in his Chalus paradise.

'Hi, my precious little Baby. It's not so much fun here.'

'Hi, darling. Why not?'

'Samir sacked me *without* me ever being hired.'

'Oh! I feel sorry for you. Samir never hired you. So, you can't see yourself as being fired without pay. Darling, I feared it to happen one day.'

'Damn! Especially after doing everything that's possible under such limitations here.'

'Darling, make decent choices, which are also in my favour.'

'I'm robust enough with vast shoulders to take such a blow. But it still hurts me. Samir replaced me because Mustafa wanted and knew everything. Then he got cold feet.'

'In Qatar, Mustafa doubted you. Remember? I had a bad feeling. You trusted him. Not me.

I couldn't stand listening to the self-important competing between you two. Mustafa only wanted your know-how—make quick money if you for free taught him your skills.'

'So, let him! I'm leaving!'

'Yea, now Mustafa runs off again as a cowardly dog. As he said, "I stay only one year." *Good luck!* I pondered, *then the clinic probably will run itself into the ground over the long haul!*'

'Damn bastards! Samir relied more on an inexperienced little itch mite.'

'Ha-ha, yea, Mustafa has no more in between the ears than a flea with no ears or brain. So, he will have nothing to do well with! Didn't that tell you something?'

'Um-hmm ... Baby, I'll come Singapore. To visit you! If you don't mind.'

'Meh, eyh? It's best you try to find a solution before you come to Singapore. I gave in for you to get the chance for a fresh life in Chalus. I wanted to be with you and hoped I was wrong of my frightening suspicions.'

'Samir never understood what I could do as a doctor—what I, as someone who has helped over forty thousand patients to find a better life, can offer.'

'Fast, I knew it would not bear the fruit you wanted. But you dazzled me with it. Samir gave us an apartment. A slight lump of money. They promised their asses of the shifty fourth division.'

'Samir doesn't possess the patience to give me the understanding and confidence I expect, being an unpaid giver to a new era for Iran.'

'Samir should not exploit us. You treated a few people for free. If the big boss was so keen on getting a seven-star clinic, why didn't he put the formalities in proper order? If you want to stay, Samir must pay.'

'I'll not stay in Chalus. It's sad that such a superb project must die for the wrong reasons. I'll leave the country with my head high.'

'Mustafa don't have the knowledge as you. Don't give it away for free. Mustafa and Samir don't deserve it! Let Samir pay for everything! You need to save up for your old age.'

'Samir doesn't understand what I can give him. He believes more in an inexperienced little desert man from Qatar.'

'Samir doesn't understand what you can do. That's why Karim, Samir, or any other patients never came for treatments. You got no patients. The few who were there have checked us out. The "Russian snoops", as you called them.'

'We were also double-crossed by Mufasa and Arshia.'

'What? How? No, Arshia would never do that.'

'Yeah, friends we trusted we had. Arshia told Samir we went behind his back.'

'Darling, put an end to this gross exploitation. I don't want to take part in it anymore.'

'I get it, Baby. We talked of it many times. I made my choice.'

'Iran is not ready. You will get more problems. Entry, visa and payment. Everyone with a brain will quickly figure out that the project can't pay off without a high payment for them. Otherwise, Samir had paid us a long time ago.'

'I will ask for severance pay and more free time to reorganise our lives.'

'I don't know what's wrong with your plan. Figure out what to do for yourself. I got other plans for myself.'

'Huh? It's important Samir can look up to me when I leave. Later, Mustafa and Samir will understand they made a vast mistake by not treating us properly. I ponder on another plan I want to implement.'

'Okay. When I get back to Chalus, I'll pack everything and leave for good.'

'I want my bedding out in the entire world. It will take hard work. It's more fun than what we have been doing for the last seven-eight months. I want to work hard for the next four years to save for my old age. I must focus on our lives and not on others.'

'Sounds good for you, darling.'

'I want to go with Chang Ho in China. With clinics—or with him as the primary engine. I will hold medical seminars. I want to write scientific documents for the medical online portals.'

'Interesting. Will you move to China?'

'I'll write to Michael and Morgan in Singapore. I want to spend time on the vitamins. We can sell via the internet.'

'Fine. Oi, hey, wait, coming to Singapore. I don't think it's such a good idea.'

'I'll investigate in the medical things Michael is doing. See if there's anything for us in it.'

'Before you leave, make sure I get the bills refunded.'

'Okay. It takes a lot of money to push. We can't do more than sell it through our website.'

'Eh? I don't want you to spend more money, Drake. My wallet is closed.'

'What do you mean? Anyhow, I want to work as an external consultant.'

'Fine. Oh, and what Samir paid you for the machines you must repay me.'

'Argh, yea, yea. Might be best under a two-year contract for my business partners. I can help to make improvements.'

'Impressive! You will be very busy, darling. Sounds as you are changing to the better.'

'I want sales commission for the machines sold through the seminars I hold. And develop the entire background of facial treatment. And helping to find the solutions to brain disease.'

'Great ideas, darling.'

'That's where I need Michael's knowledge. I'm sure we can solve this Gordian knot.'

'Sounds interesting.'

'I want to stay active. Keep myself *young* for you. We need to have fun again, Baby. Take control of our lives in our own hands.' Drake's plan seems off track to me.

'Before my summer holiday, I come to Chalus and pack. Things are going in the right direction again with my family. I need peace for my family. Without them, I cannot function.'

'I'll cc you the e-mail to Michael and Morgan. Talk to you late. Bye my forever lasting love. Mwah, I love you. Thank you for being mine.'

Then Drake influences our mutual contacts in Singapore, with proposals and several over-the-head cracked ideas.

Subject: Consider our business

Dear Michael and Morgan,

Mary and I like to thank you for welcoming us to your facility last time we were there and for taking time to consider our business. If you are interested in becoming our distributor for our products in Singapore and you feel you would enhance your market share, we'd like to discuss an agreement with you.

Mary is in Singapore now, and I'll join her early next month. Please let us know and we will meet with you.

Sincerely,
Dr Drake Lucifer Bates

After a week, Drake calls me again.

'Darling, my forever lasting love. I miss you dreadfully. It's over three weeks without you. I hope you received the mail to Michael and Morgan.'

'Yes, I did.'

'Okay, Sweet Pea, I'm coming to Singapore.'

'What a surprise! I didn't expect such a visit.' I'm not sure I want Drake here.

'Babe, we can do business with Michael and Morgan. Also, with Doctor Peter and Madelaine in Downtown.'

'Stay in Chalus! Start a fresh life there. I have split my life into millions of tiny crystals because of you. I can't take anymore.'

'But I've tried to apply for the divorce again. This time in Sweden. Because I live in Iran, they can't handle the case. I must prove that I can't bring a case in the country where I live. I can't prove it.'

'That's not good. Go to US and get it done.'

'No, are you crazy? I can't travel to US. I aim to come to Singapore. I so much want to marry you. Singapore is a part of the British Commonwealth; there I can apply. Baby, I'm desperate that you have left me.'

'Hmm, when do you plan to come?' I trust all will be better and want to help him.

'I have no money to travel. If you want to see me, can I loan money for a ticket? We can then settle our disagreements between us. I love you desperately.'

With my head under my arm, I fall for Drake's desperate trick and buy him a ticket on economy class and call him the next day.

'Did you get the ticket?' I'm frosty towards him.

'My sweet, beautiful Babe, I'm looking forward to coming visiting you. I can travel in business class and get lounge access.' Blink... blink... and he's smiling gorgeously.

'What do you mean? It's not business class. I can't afford it.'

'Hi-hi, Babe. You probably haven't searched thoroughly enough. Look at the price you found compared to the one I'm attaching here.' And he sends a link. 'Can you change the ticket to the one I found? It doesn't cost that much extra.'

'Fine, yea, yea, I'll look at it. Talk to you later. Bye.' *Oh my!* So ungrateful he is. I change it to business class, and forward it by e-mail, with no comments.

Days pass by and a lengthy e-mail from Drake pop up. Oh, my goodness, what now?

Subject: No words from you

Good morning, Baby,

I haven't heard from you for many days. Thanks for the flight upgrade. Here, it's filled every day with deep frustration over my *paralysis and pain*. It's difficult for me to live with the thought of having become disabled. I lost what, for a lifetime, I have been able to say with pride I was perfect at. In the evening, when the pain comes, I go to bed and try to sleep without taking medication. The pain can become so intolerable that I must take it to sleep. I exercise every day, and I take it to my current limit and more.

If I go too far over the line, the punishment comes in the form of pain when I lie down. I work with my damaged fine motor skills; however, I don't have the full delicacy I always have had. My handwriting has never been perfect, and now I find it even more difficult to move the pen. It's far harder than I imagined anything could be. I don't think Doctor Hagen understood sympathetic pain or traumatic post-surgical neuropathy.

I don't understand how it happened—what happened in the nervous system and exactly where. It's a mystery, but I'm working diligently to solve it. In the meantime, I do what I can to of not being depressed of my horrible fate. I try to let my normal positive mind be my mantra that will guide me if I don't regain my full mobility.

I'm not giving up. I'm working on a solution throughout the day and achieved results with my efforts. My deltoid, teres minor, and subscapularis are still not cooperative. Yesterday, I woke up and saw that my usually good and strong biceps are shrinking worryingly. To my surprise, I got a little infraspinatus and teres minor left. I have trouble doing anything myself. I need you here to help, to treat me.

I should write no more of my physical problems. It must bore you. I'll do everything I can to get a wonderful time with you and not spend too much time on my *ill health*. I will and must recover, except I've not found the wise stones yet.

I love and miss you. I'm glad that you don't experience the problems of my illness. It has brought me into a *psychological imbalance*. Damn! It's not uplifting!

Can I also ask you to transfer $2,500 from the enclosed invoice from Xing and Jang Smart Living Group in China? Then we can get ready for the next step without stress over a bill, because I won't dispute it. I can give you money later when we meet. I promise! As you know it's not transferable from the internet bank here, nor can I pay from the Asian account, as the recipient must first register—troublesome! I keep my Swedish bank account on a low flare, so I can't transfer from there either. Hope you will do it for *us*?

Yours forever,
Drake

Whoa! He is playing the "sick card" and complaining of having trouble transferring money, which doesn't make me as suspicious as it should. I felt sorry for his illness, though, it's a very bold move from his part. I pick Drake up at Singapore Changi Airport. He will stay with me for the next five weeks, in my rented apartment by Marina Bay Sands.

While we are in Singapore, it turns out Doctor Michael and Morgan are not ready to do business with us, nor are Doctor Peter and Madelaine. We must give up our hopes, while the entire projects fall to the ground. Drake has changed for the better again, and I consider continuing a future for us, but what will come next?

CHAPTER 31

THE COFFIN NAIL DEMON!

> When someone lies to you, it's because they don't respect
> you enough to be honest, and they think you're too stupid to
> not know the difference.
>
> —Unknown

Iran is history, I imagine. But suddenly Samir urgently asked Drake back again to finish the job. Oh, my goodness! This is a never-ending 'jingle jangle' melody. Singapore went to the trash, where should I go? I follow Drake back to Iran, hoping it will go smoother this time.

Will I ever get wiser? Yes! No! We travel back to Iran and Drake's problems with Doctor Mustafa get worse, then things between Drake and me go off track, so he blames me. I'm afraid of him. Every other business goes erratic and comes not to completion. It's a disaster! I smoke in between when Drake can't see it and once again; I find myself on a horrifying stressful spine-tingling ride, where he decides the speed. It's too much with him, and he often gets furious!

'Bloody hell, Babe, you need a wake-up call. We must talk! This is hard to struggle with.'

'Christ! Is there anyone here who needs a wake-up call, then it's you, Drake!'

'I'm devastated of your sadness. The swinging emotions and anger. I miss you, Sweet Pea.'

'Miss me? Ha! I'm sorry for getting into your life and supporting you.'

'Yuck, Mary, you replaced me by your other passion—cigarettes! When you get a brief break, a fag takes your free time. Not me!'

'For three years I've not smoked. Now you're on a suffering trip.' Jeez, he always grumbles about cigarettes. I sense a great unease that something is wrong in our relationship.

'Before you had time and love for me. You kissed me lovingly.' He growls.

'Jeez! You are sending me to hell because I smoke now and then. They soothe me. They relieve my stress.'

'Argh, you're so far on a side-track, Mary. Yuck! Yuck! Yuck! You don't love me.'

'It scares me you even believe what you say. It's appalling!'

'You cared for me. Now you avoid me.' Again, he puts out sensors to see whether I'm willing to allow him to cross my boundaries.

'Such bunk, Drake. I never regret my love for you.' Though, the criticism from him steadily lurks beneath the surface.

'Oh, boy, seek help, Mary. Your once fresh aura now smells and tastes cruel. An arrow goes through my heart.'

'Argy-bargy! How can you say so? Things must spin in your head as a cuckoo clock!'

'I miss your kisses and cuddles. Holding your hand, Baby, while we sleep.'

'Darling, you never kiss or cuddle with me. How can you then miss it?'

'I miss hugging you. Yikes, you smell so ugly. You are a fool.' He shifts from nice to nasty.

'Whatever! Just treat me meanly. I can handle it. I'm so used to it.'

'Willy misses getting eager. Especially when we kissed passionately. Now you smoke.'

'Ha-ha, oh, my, what a lame excuse.' It's horrible to use my smoking for his failure to perform. Can't he see how much Chalus is splitting us apart? Something that was so striking between us, it's ruined. I'm trying to get him to understand.

'Well, Willy needs kissing as part of his libido. That's how he is.'

'Whoa! Now I'm the culprit? I'm the reason your love pistol doesn't work.'

'Willy can't get to Minnie's mum. She's fighting with another passion.' He talks rudely.

'It sounds like some kindergarten talk.' It has been so in most of our relationship. Am I that horrible to Drake? *This is not a healthy relationship.*

'Willy asks you to tell your Minnie that he misses her.'

'Stop that baby talk. We all have our problems to deal with. Jeez! Having a smoke now and then?' I don't understand his worry, nor that he keeps on blaming me. I take a sharp tone with him.

'That's why Willy's daddy rejects her.'

'What? Hogwash!' We are fighting over the injustice being done to us, instead of sticking together. It's devilish. It's succeeding well. The balance of power is unequal when he speaks as I'm a child.

'Better I crawl back to my cross. No one wants me here. And you refuse me, Mary.'

'Such twaddle! But be my guest. Get crucified. This time I can't save you.' Our story is fit for a comic book!

'Huh? What does that supposed to mean?'

'I'm upset. It's obvious that your first crush on me has gone away. I take the blame for your failures.'

'Yuck, Mary. It's because you are too busy with your smokes!' he nit-picks, as if he were the God of hotness and performed for years.

'Damn, Drake! You're no brain. Troll!' Using my smoking as the reason for him not having intercourse with me? *Oh, my God!* I never smoke near him. I brush my teeth. Wash my face and hands afterwards. And I chew gum. I must not forget, according to him, it's always the other's fault!

Drake is suddenly jumping into another topic, of how tough the phase is we're going through to get our income and business up and running. There is nothing strange with that, and I'm stressed. Nervous.

Everything scares me. I shiver nervously at his threatening signals that I'm not good enough for him. He thinks he has proven again that he can make his work operate. It's happening on that front for the time being, but he believes it is difficult because they put me aside for the wrong reasons and says it is because of cultural differences. He is so difficult to figure out, and every time I trust him, he changes to his *devilishness*. As a jack-in-the-box.

'I don't want us to get separated for lack of understanding. Baby, I love you.' He smirks.

'But, that's what we are. You break my heart deeply. Loads of wealth has more power than an insignificant sum of it!' *I miss the man I fell in love with.* I'm in so much pain, because he constantly complains of me. I still imagine that our relationship is possible.

'Bloody hell, Mary, you are so wrong! Samir can't buy me off. I too must have an income.'

'Sure! I know. I can't compete against Samir.'

'I must play my cards wisely. You should understand it.'

'You are too much, Drake.'

'You're a giant fool. How can you be so evil?'

'Your passion for money is greater than they are for me.' I'm afraid of losing him.

'Why do you always run things the unpleasant way?'

This has to do with economic reasons, and Drake doesn't want to fail. He failed. Even he believes he can set up the world's best clinic once again. I don't want to partner up with the fiend. He shows that part too often, and then he starts on his dead speech that his knowledge must continue after he leave the country, or he is dead. Such a massive God complex. Ha-ha, he will become a good-looking corpse, however, I prefer him alive. Stupidly, I still imagine he is the perfect man for me.

'I want to be the conductor who puts this grand game together and makes it work.'

'Find the stop button, Drake. I can't handle it anymore. Be a laughingstock.'

'I will be sorry to skip it right in front of the finish line.' Jeez, the dude has finished nothing.

'You're gradually killing me with your nagging.' In his mind, I don't do as he wants.

'Baby, our personal problems are as mosquito bites on the back of an elephant.' He laughs.

'Yea, yea, whatever. I told you that Chalus will be our downfall. I throw the towel in the ring. I give up!' But I still want a wonderful future with him, if he wants to pursue it too.

'We are moving forward step by step. Damn you, Babe! You sound as Satan's offspring.'

'Woah! Those are your words. Not mine!' I thought he had driven the demons out of me. Damn, I'm craving desperately for a smoke now.

'It will look good on you, if I'm not replaced by your other passion. Damn them. Your demonically fags!' He gets angry.

'Woah! I must disappoint you. One *coffin nail demon* stayed!' I felt resigned and turn my attention away from his narcissistic behaviour. He believes the devil rules over me and he wants with his entire heart to get me back as his beloved Mary Magdalene and talks about how God will intervene on Judgment Day.

'God will take away the devil and all evil people. Only good people will resurrect. Like me!' He preaches as Drake is the Holiness himself.

'Holy mother. Whoa! That's creepy talk. Such a rash, manipulating lie. What is the name of the sect you are a member of?'

'Argh! You're damn sick, Mary! It's your coffin nail demon.'

'Ha-ha, yea! Your ugly hair-raising tendency kept one alive.' The smokes help myself release me from Drake's devilishness.

'Gee, you are damn brainwashed, Mary, into believing that you are always right.'

'Whoa! It's an intelligent way to comment on. Drake, enjoy Lalaland.'

'What shall I do?' Then he changes for few minutes to be in pleasant mood. There is nothing else he wants more than to be with me. To support me and be there for me. The condition makes it a little difficult for me, as he starts his next complain.

'Baby, when you throw yourself on the bed with your clothes on, I can't get in touch with you.'

'Ey? Holy crap! Sometimes I'm so worn out that I fall asleep on the bed with clothes on.'

'When I try to help you get your clothes off, you get mad at me. You speak like a slave and a stupid sheep.'

'Argh, come on! What the hell are you talking of now? Seems as you feel yourself on the top of the game.'

'You lie your head at the foot end. Why?' OMG! There he goes, acting as a sufferer as had I abandon, and ignored him.

'Might be my head is at the wrong end. Don't misunderstand it. There's nothing wrong with it.' I don't understand this tedious discussion.

'It's sad that I must go to sleep without kissing my beloved with the passion that is sacred to us.' Falsely and deeply the poor dragon sighs.

'Kissing? Huh? You frustrate me too much.' Too often I sit scared in the shower's corner, while the water is running over my body. It's as Drake is punishing me and gets angrier with me.

'What can I do to be better than your smokes?'

'I'm devastated by your hatred of me. You don't bathe with me anymore.' I want to cry.

'It's scary and sad. I hope you get wiser?' The sucker apparently believes that I don't love him enough. That he allows and tricks me to fall in love with him, made me not aware of the horrifying agenda he was planning. It's gross! The worst part is that he crushes me completely. I can't stop the smoking out of frustration and fear. Why is Drake treating me like that? I love him, though the storming crush has settled. He can't even give me a bit of intimacy, closeness, or love. He is only complaining and must suffer from a lack of emotional life. He tells me only pleasant things in his love letters or when he needs something from me.

'Soon you will travel far away for a long time. Baby, I will fade inside.' He plays sad.

'Argh! Come on. I'm only away for a short time.' I truly need to get away from him. 'It's my dream to visit Athens and the Greek islands.'

'Well, I've my enchanting kissing pictures of you. I must live from them.' He mourns.

'You will join me later.' The trip is part of my repair list of what to do, and my break with my family in Italy, because I need to reunite with them. I've failed them too much, and that's not my style, so I'm sad.

'It's okay! Fine, you go if you must, Babe. I'm not happy with it. Maybe don't come back.'

'Woah! It can't be that bad for you.'

'I will try to keep you in my mind during your absence.' Such a selfish, jealous fop!

I perceive Drake can't love me in the same way as I love him. I think it's more of him being afraid of being alone, so he needs me with him.

'I must work the ass out of my pants until I fall asleep exhausted.' He whimpers.

'What is it you want from me?' Ruminating *he's bored, and he fills the space with conflicts.*

'I want to be with you, Baby. But if I can't, I can easily be with no other women.' He simpers falsely.

'Eyh? Every time I've left you, you're sweet-talking me. Then I come back!'

'If you don't, you will be the last woman in my life. I'd rather live alone.' I gaze at him curiously, trying to understand where this is coming from.

'Ha-ha, ha-ha, do you want me to believe that?'

'Maybe you should find your way home to Denmark again. Stay there. I don't need you.'

Snarling at me, he's not willing to give me space in my own private sphere.

'Geez, have you taken something you can't stand? Are you drunk?' Glaring weird at him.

'I am fine, Mary. I'm living in the realm of reality. You may also come to that soon when you wake up from your selfish intoxication.'

'Oh, jeez, Drake, you sound as you know if it's God's own truth. Amazing!'

'Argh! You portray yourself as someone who is not very intelligent. Jeez, your way of arguing is sick and negative.'

Swiftly, he changes the dialogue. 'Samir is ill and drained. He'll make no further venture.'

'As long as you hold on to the lies and the belief in this, it will not get any better.'

'Samir wants me out. I promised to take care of business. I need his approval to proceed.'

'You run yourself down, darling.'

Drake feels it forces him to give Samir an understanding between them up front, and Samir should allow him to complete the task—give him the power and funds to do so.

Our relationship is on a horrifying slope because of Chalus, and I can't take it anymore. Of the sudden, the clinic project has suffered vastly because of lack of communication, because Samir is not comfy in their understanding. We don't have a normal life. I have no comments. It's his choice. We came to Chalus because of his skills and know-how, and instead of hiring professional staff, Samir asked *us* to do everything. Shit, almost a year now, and nothing has happened! I don't trust we will get it together properly between any of us, though Drake can finish his project—or stop it completely. There's no room for two independent people, and Drake hates when I criticise this point.

'It's frustrating, Babe. Don't you see the pressure I'm under? We were expecting to have an agreement between us and Samir. It's still missing.'

'Ha-ha, we will never get it. Sadly, I can't help you.'

'Samir wanted a seven-star facility. Top medics from around the world.'

'Yea! And have you found any doctors?' It's only fake news!

We still don't have the equipment necessary to operate. Drake believes he sacrificed his scientific work, because Samir has put his work on heart, and cellular physiology and brain disease on hold. Nothing is good enough for Drake, so now he acts as a victim vis-à-vis Samir. I'm afraid we cannot live together in Chalus, and I'm not sure Samir wants Drake there anymore. Doesn't he get it?

'Baby, I can't do such work after working ten hours a day. Then you complain I don't love you. I have no creative energies left.' And he believes only *he* has fought hard to make it all work.

'Poor you. Why comment when I'm not allowed, anyway.' I find myself forced to consider a fresh life, then he must tell me when he is ready for us to live together again.

'Samir promised me I could research here.' I speculate if that will ever become a reality. Drake had no budget—only Samir's explicit statements of space and quality to go by. It's now clear to Drake it was a mistake, what we did, and I'm glad he's finally realising it. We should have agreed a budget for it to be precisely how much Samir wanted to invest, but we didn't.

'It has caused a major problem of understanding. And hopes between you and me, Baby.' He goes to the fridge and grabs a bear.

'I consider if I shall take your statement as an expression of regret, Drake.'

'I told Samir I needed an agreement.' He comes back to the living room, and slurps from his bottle. 'Baby, we need to agree on what the future relationship will be. I wrote a proposal. I'll take time off.'

'Thanks for the beer!' I glare ironically at him in surprise of his selfishness. It's struck me he or Samir cannot use me for zero positive here. And I get up to snatch a beer from the fridge.

'I see now that we should have done it from the beginning. I did not listen to you, Babe.'

'Cheers!' I take a sip from the bottle. 'Yet, we're always squabbling over stupid things—whatever my ideas are to you or if I smoke.'

'Baby, at no time has no one said critical things about you— nothing! On the contrary!' He gets up again, enters the kitchen and pours himself half a glass of Jack Daniels. 'Babe, they prepared for you to work with the clinic's functions. But not for direct treatment of patients.'

'You told me not to deal with that business anymore. So why do I need to stay? I've no trust in it anymore.'

'We must prove to Samir you have an official education. Trust me, don't give up.'

'I no longer trust in "possibly this or maybe that". It's only getting it the way *you want it*.' Now, when I want to leave, he realises things are wrong. My sense of justice has come to the test as I've discovered the quantity of pressure I'm facing, given his selfish power plays and many lies.

'Babe, I didn't know any of it. Sadly, a diploma from me doesn't apply. First when I can get it accepted by medical experts here.' More lies on top of the massive over-flooding cup of lies.

'Well, well. Interesting!' I exclaim. 'The diploma you gave me is not worth a damn shit!' Ahh! *The gigantic monster got me.* Shit, it's so much money I've trashed because of Drake. Next realising that no classified organisations, privately or publicly ever has verified any of his diplomas. They are worthless! Crap! Fraud alert! And I cannot use them anywhere other than to dry my ass with them. Shit! I have wasted all my investments to toilet paper. Payment thrown straight into the toilet, flushed down the shitty drain. Such a devious shit for brains!

'It's my intent to get that through,' he protests. And hey presto! Now Drake wants a real educational platform, where he will train the doctors we hire, and with an examiner for exams and as an affiliate of their medical university. There will be a formal credit of what he does, and he will get it pushed forward. *What does that help me? Does he believe that himself? Hmm ...* It will for sure never happen.

'Holy crap! I'm mad. Disappointed to learn that the diploma is worthless.'

'Why are you being like this, Mary? That's not nice to say of me!'

'Vast blow.'

'It's not worthless. I know that my diplomas at this point have no value anywhere. Consider it as a beginning for the purpose of trying to exchange it for an official one.'

'Fantastic!' I retort, *it will never come to reality*. No matter what he does, Drake's education and diplomas will remain worthless scruffy shit.

'You need not to go through an entire training with an exam. I'll fix it for you, Baby.' He knows it will drive me crazy, because I fear exams.

'No, thank you. You have shown what it makes you of as a fraud.' Not something that has my interest anymore. What a waste of time and money! I should never have trusted him.

'It will take a year to get everything ready here. I couldn't do it in any other country. You must wait.' Geez, it's so messed up with him.

'I will consider where else I can do it. I can't trust you.' I'm tired of his lame excuses.

Drake believes we must show 'transparency' if the authorities are widely accepting such education. Then it will be a platform for similar education in other countries. His upcoming textbook is far from being finished, but he believes it will be the first foundation for the education, and that will be his gain. So far he has not even begun on his textbook.

'It will be to your advantage having a formal education from a university. Baby, I can help you with your paper.'

'Yea, yea ... Well, you don't have a protocol for the university.' Rubbish goutweed.

'I must examine you before they start the official training. You must go to school at the university here. They will teach in my treatment protocol in English.' What delusions of grandeur!

'We'll see whether I can learn your subject well enough! I need motivation again.' The mood between us gets characterised by frustration, confusion, uncertainty, and fear. It's emotionally turbulent.

Next Drake wants us to learn Persian, so he can understand more of what is going on around him. According to him, if I take this training, no one will go against my education, and Samir will allow me to work at the clinic. Yeah, sure, fantastic! Language school is interesting, though the problem is that nobody can speak English here. How in heaven's name will we be able to learn Persian, except of us going to language school in Denmark? I am becoming increasingly irked with the way he constantly switches between his two personalities, when he laughs at me, during his massive megalomania, and that I will need a piece of paper saying I'm not a crazy nutcase. Oh yeah! The idea is stupid. Because Drake could never think of me as an amazing woman. I've lost the desire for Iran, because of the circumstances. I mostly want to scream.

'We must figure out what will happen when I'm back from holiday.'
I say.

'I get it. We can make deals with other clinics. So, we don't have fixed expenses. Only revenue. We won't bother to lean on one place.'

'I won't stay anymore,' I anger and again he changes the topic.

'We can come and offer treatments in other people's clinics. That set-up is better. I've done it well earlier. Patients can make an appointment, but Samir can't stop me from doing it. You must be the *star* as I am. That's what the patients are asking for.'

'I do not understand what you are talking about.'

'You can never have or get everything. You take and give. If a clinic you work in cheats, then there are always others who will steal from them, meaning I'll steal patients from the cheater.'

'What? I'm depressed and upset. I haven't been as miserable as I am now.'

'Babe don't be that dramatic. Do as I do. When I miss you the most and think everything is hopeless, I work.'

'See if you can pull me up. What do you want me to do? Trusting you blindly?'

'Yea trust me. I look optimistic at everything again. You are in a rage.'

'I have my opinion. You have yours. None of you want me here. I don't trust any of you.' My anger spreads inside me.

'I don't trust you either. You feel wrecked by Samir. You think I have chosen his side.'

'Because you have. The truth about your entire fake world will come to light one day.'

'Take a pill for depression. Christ, Mary! Give me something concrete and provable that I'm fake.' Then he tries to be sweet and seductive, and acts as the man I fell in love with. 'Baby, you're lonely.' He pities me. 'You don't believe you can be with me here in Chalus. You feel you need to hide if you are here.' The next moment, Drake talks of Sandra. 'Then there are my relationships with your daughter.' A drastic change in his speech happens. 'Sandra wrecked me right from the start.'

'How do you know? And why of the sudden does Sandra come into the picture?'

'I can't show up with you if Sandra is there. I understand it with Flopper. With your daughter, I don't get it. She has distrust. Sandra hates me. She prefers that I not exist.' He shows his powerful side.

'Sandra has nothing to do with Samir and us. I don't get it.'

'Samir does not possess such strong unpleasant opinions towards you. These are cultural differences that we must overcome. With Sandra, there are no cultural differences. Only a deep hatred for me.'

'Come on. Sandra hardly doesn't know you. Can't you manage without always talking badly about other people?'

'Rubbish! These are other powerful, unpleasant opinions from her I must live with. Is it reasonable? I feel wrecked too—not by you, but by Sandra.'

And suddenly a fresh idea pops up in his mind. 'Prepare a fresh start for us in Sweden if you don't want to stay here. We can figure something out,' he suggests.

I cannot understand Drake's changeability. It's hard for me to tackle. He seems rootless and has many problems in Chalus, yea, with everyone. I have no decent life, as everything always goes from A to Z and back again. His devaluing personality is the opposite of the charming man he was at the beginning of our relationship.

I never comprehend what Drake wants—except for wealth! Then he shows his sweet side, deliberating it can benefit him. He's suggested twenty dissimilar business proposals to me that year alone—a secret clinical trial in Singapore, building a clinic in Qatar Healthcare City, yea, you name it. He's as an unstoppable tornado and a turncoat—constantly coming up with innovative ideas and turning on or abandoning old ones and those involved!

During the fall, enough is enough for me, so I leave Iran permanently. In my frustration over not feeling welcomed and being accused of so many unpleasant things, I write a letter to Samir—without Drake having any awareness of it:

Dear Mr Samir,

Dr Drake has many times said to me, 'Everything has a beginning, and everything a natural ending. An end can often be the beginning of something new and exciting.'

Why do I write this? I'm frustrated with the outcome and think they have taken an unfair action against me. I'm a person who is loyal, honest, and truthful, so what went off track between with us? With grief, I think you never took enough time to know me better.

Drake told me you excluded me from taking part in future meetings and working with patients. I wonder if it's a misunderstanding between us. I can't tell.

With an open mind, lots of effort, and over an extensive number of times, I've worked hard for your project, when you welcomed us to your wonderful country in good faith. Thank you. We came to make this clinic work for you and the people of Iran, though we had no legal contract, which you promised. Yet, we kept on working hard.

You have rewarded us with what *you* called 'pocket money' and sent us for expos and education opportunities around the world, so we could do our best for your clinic. Thank you so much, it's much appreciated.

Drake said you have severe issues with me and my lack of English skills. I'm deeply sorry, Mr Samir. When I tried to express myself, I could not find the words, therefore I needed help from Drake to translate, and I apologised to you. Your response was, 'It's okay and accepted.' I trust your good intention in this matter.

Drake tells me you requested a psychological evaluation of me, because you thought I was mentally ill. I don't know if he speaks the truth. Though, the evaluation showed I was normal. Then he told me you stated I'm an interference, and a nuisance at the meetings because Drake always changes his mind on settled arrangements with you. I don't understand this point! I have no influence on his decisions, and now I'm kept from being a part of things, despite my partnership with him.

I understand from Drake; you assumed I went behind your back to start a clinic in Qatar. This is not *true*! I'm sorrowful deep in my heart over such allegations. There must be a misunderstanding, because I've only true intentions of Chalus.

Qatar was only a feasibility research we did for the future with you and us. There was much pressure from Arshia and Mufasa, who wanted a clinic in Qatar ASAP. They have many acquaintances and business associates who needed treatment; they told us, but we said we can't create anything if it will become a conflict with you. Arshia told us you would not have any issues if we began, but we wanted to discuss it with you first.

While in Qatar, Drake told me I couldn't get a work permit in Chalus, but when we came back, they handed it over to me. Beforehand, we explored alternative options for me, because I needed future business options if I could not work in Iran. I don't consider that as going behind your back. Before we left Qatar, I decided *not* to start a clinic there but to go back to Europe or Hong Kong.

I too must earn money, because Drake has not earned money over the last three years. He got his work permit in Chalus, but I didn't. But unfortunately, no income was in our pocket, and I can't continue to pay for the expenses.

I chose with optimism and refreshed spirit to come back to Chalus after my business trips and to support Drake.

To my surprise, he told me I was no longer in the partnership with him or you. I wonder if that was a mistake. There will be no sharing with Drake future wise because his earnings will only be his, as he said.

I'm sorry for these misunderstandings, Mr Samir, and I'm split open by everything. It breaks my heart in thousands of pieces, so I've packed my belongings, and they're ready for shipment to Scandinavia. I'm in a development with a fresh clinic there, where patients will wait for treatment. As I told you earlier, they mean much to me, and my intention is to help them, either here or in other countries.

This is my life. I'm only human, but I have my heart in the right place. I wish you the best and thank you for the understanding.

Sincerely,
Mary

On a cold and windy late Autumn day in Chalus, I shattered, pack a suitcase for my travel to Hong Kong. Drake's idea of that my company should run small clinics in Sweden is splendid, so I consider the thought. It gives me the chance to be closer to my family, and a perfect excuse to get out of my bond with him. So many times, I have tried to escape his brutal games with me, because it has scarred and bruised me too much. I'm lost within myself and do not know of the extent of my damage.

Will I ever be the same person again? Drake has broken me, and no words can describe it, and I'll never be able to fit into the world again. I'm destroyed, though I still love him, because the adventure could have been so beautiful, but now it's over.

Yet we keep in touch and it makes the parting even worse for me. I must stop my burning desire for him and let everything fade. This is where the million-dollar question comes in!

CHAPTER 32

GET YOUR HANDS OFF 'SUGAR MAMA'S' COOKIE JAR

Instead of loving people and using money, people often love money and use people.

—Wayne Gerard Trotman

D rake's performance is immensely disappointing for me. During my stay in Hong Kong while finishing my business, I use time off to think. I'm still hoping for the best, but he doesn't understand the serious issue. My common sense tells me to stay away, though my burning heart craves living with him. He has lured me, using both my weaknesses and my strengths, and knows when to put me down and push me, when to blur reality, and when to speak words from my mouth. He has complete control over when to bombard me with flattery and honey talk. I can't find my way, given his constant change— one moment a tyrant, and the next the seductive dream man.

From Hong Kong Airport, I grab a taxi to my rented penthouse with a compact kitchen and a living room with a sofa and a vast TV. Cleverly they have tucked the bathroom in the back of the long hall, while my bed is in front of the large panoramic windows, offering a stunning view from thirty-second floor over Victoria Harbour in this popular area outside Central Hong Kong.

I meet with Candy from the real estate agency, in my search of a new apartment on the Kowloon side. A tiny sweet woman, coming towards me wearing a pair of three-sizes-too-gigantic men's shoes, so I laugh silently in my mind. It's difficult to find a decent apartment in this overcrowded part of the world, and the prices are drastically increasing for small apartments, so we don't succeed today.

After getting back to the flat, I smoke in front of the building, and the concierge fella comes outside, lights a cigarette and stares intensely at me.

'Where is that stink coming from?' I ask the concierge fella, sniffing the awful fishy smell which hits my nostrils, and I want to puke.

'Ohhh,' he replies. 'It's the dry fish sector, where the Chinese buy their fish. Don't worry, the stench doesn't go up to your apartment.'

How does he know that? 'But it does!' I reply. 'I'm get sick. I get nauseous because the stink comes through the ventilation pipes. The AC spreads the sour pussy smell even more. It disturbs my sleep. Yuck, I dream of sour fish and mermaids.' I laugh.

The following bright Autumn sunny morning, I'm sitting at the waterfront, observing people and the traffic by Victoria Harbour. One ferry after another pass in the canal—turbojets, Cotai, Ferries freighters, and slight tugs. I'm reminded of my first time in Asia. Shit! I miss him.

People wade past me, with their feet dragging in their oversized shoes, then I recall the visit from the shoe store from yesterday.

'Can you bring me a size six?' I asked the shop assistant.

She gazed at me. 'What?' Then she came back with a size eight and nine instead. 'These fit you!' The assistant claimed. 'Size six is too small for you. They will not sit loosely enough.'

'Huh?' I was an enormous question mark, then she laughed, and I noticed her shoes were gigantic. 'Ohhh. Is it normal to walk around in oversized shoes? It's not healthy for knees and joints.' I grinned, trying to convince her.

The funny episode makes me giggle as I watch the lumbering people. *Well, this is how they do in Hong Kong,* I conclude.

I spot a fisherman swiftly catching a fish, fighting a fierce battle to haul the beast ashore. Locals photograph and admiring the wonder. *Is this something they've never seen?* As I gaze at the white monster with yellow fins.

A guy proudly shows his image to the fisherman, but basically, the fisherman doesn't care, and throws the fish into his bucket, and quickly I seize a fantastic snapshot of him with Kowloon and the massive skyscrapers in the distance.

Strolling further along the promenade, I find a peaceful area where I slap my bum onto a black metal bench, then a fishing cutter disturbs the silence, docking and unloading boxes. Next to me stands a goofy guy. Christ! The goofy stares intensely at me, so I get scared. *Will he steal my bag?* I muse. Yikes! He's strolling too close to my private sphere, but finally, he leaves.

Minutes later, the next suspicious bloke appears, and stares fixedly at me, so I clutch my sack more tightly to myself. Two young Asian guys walk by hand in hand, staring in our way, and the suspicious guy quickly disappears.

A sweet older couple are slogging hand in hand, so I imagine the picture of Drake and me. Young happy lovers pass by, and then a cheerful Dutch couple at my age strolls and stops in front of me. The handsome bloke is having a hard time taking his eyes off me, then I smile.

My phone rings, it's Drake calling via Skype.

'My darling love, my thoughts are with you constantly.' He smiles content.

'Can I call you later?'

'Why? I miss you. I fill my thoughts with emotions of love and caring. I wanted to tell you; all I want is you.'

'Okay, fine darling. Let's talk when I'm back at the apartment. Call me in one hour.'

'Love you forever, Baby.'

My heart turns passionate, sensing angel feathers stroking pleasantly along my neck. And my feelings of missing Drake get even worse. He's emotionally destroying me, while I unaware put my hand into his recent flaming pot and burn my heart on his sweet loving words.

I cannot concentrate, so I'm getting up from the bench. As a zombie I stroll back to my apartment, enter the hall, push the switch, stare ghostly, then the lift dings and opens the door. After a brief minute, the lift dings again as I arrive on thirty-second floor and stand in front of my door. Nervously I'm jingling with my keys, open the door and slam it after me. The first thing I do is sitting on my sofa, turn on my Mac and check my mailbox, and up pops his mail while he in the same moment calls me on Skype.

'Hi my lovely baby. Have you read my mail?'

'Not yet, I just opened my Mac.' Clicking on my mouse, browsing other mails.

'When you talk to the lawyer, show him my suggestions. By now you have a company, and we can invest in offices and facilities.'

'Okay, hmm … what is it about?'

'We prove that the company will bring employment to HK residents. We'll set up a clinic. Eventually by a joint venture with a local company interested in getting my technology.'

'Let me look at the mail. Just a sec,' then open it, reading his distinct suggestions.

'Our contacts can find a solution with their business friends in Hong Kong. They can give you an employment contract under the table.' He glares at me while I'm reading.

Subject: Clinics in Hong Kong

I can get a license in Hong Kong, so we must build another clinic. I think we are looking at a start-up investment of $100,000 to $150,000. We'll advertise, lecture, and have open houses. If we're alone and maximum hire, the number of employees required to be 'legal', then we ourselves will be masters of what we do, and we won't lose our residency card. We'll buy into an existing clinic, based on my knowledge and expertise.

Love you passionately,
Drake

'Okay, I've read it.'

'I've prepared another alternative plan. I'll write more later. I don't know if I told you this, but I suffer from what they call post-operative neuropathy. Google it.'

Ahhh... Again, fresh ideas, and more often Drake plays the sick card.

'Why? I thought you were a healthy man.' But he doesn't respond on my question.

'How are you and your non-smoking doing? Are you being persistent?'

'I guess so.' And lie straight to his face.

'I'm going to a meeting. Wish you a delightful day. Cheerio Baby.'

The next morning, he calls on Skype again.

'Good morning, my forever lasting love. I hope you get a grand day. I miss you and wish I could be there for you.'

'Good morning.' I quiet murmur, slurping my first cup of coffee.

'I have heard no reply on the mail, so you must be busy. Hope you are well?'

'I understand the mail slightly. I don't want to spend more money. I don't know what good it will bring.'

'I hope you don't miss me as much as I miss you. It's bad. Baby, I'm not sleeping well at night. I don't get enough hours. I read and write on my projects until I get sore in the ass from sitting.' He glares content at me, having his face close to the camera.

'Sure, I miss you too.' I'm not so talkative.

'It's a great relief that my PSA looks good. It minimised the cancer risk in my scrotum.'

'Nice to hear.' Am I too frosty?

'But it's crazy with Mr Willy. He has failed me for a long time. I'm working to fix it.'

'What's wrong with Willy?' But Drake talks of other things, that he is finding solutions. And about Samir was nervous that I had left.

'Samir comes from one angle. I come from another. He's disappointed. Said we never asked for money.' Drake pauses a second and slurps his coffee.

'Things got freaked out. "We are not to be the ones asking for money. This is not something we do," I told Samir.'

Samir and Drake had gotten on offensive terms with each other. And Drake had overseen the construction and procurement. It would have been better if Samir had waited until they completed everything before we came to Chalus. Then, we could have had income for the past year, as he told Samir that now we lack a revenue.

'Does Samir know I have left?'

'I told him you had to leave. To set up distributors elsewhere to earn money.'

'But I can't afford more investments. Nor buying something new. I cannot cope anymore.'

'Samir wants me to concentrate on finding doctors.' Though Drake can't get any, if Samir doesn't get something attractive to look towards to, so Drake will find locals. Samir also told him they will not allow Drake to perform stem cell and PRP because a licensed medic must give the injections. Samir has found out Drake doesn't have a medical education. I don't understand why Drake wants to stay. The truth always comes to the surface.

'Whoa! That surprised me, because I thought I had free hands. Oh, yea, and get this. Samir knows of Qatar! He was furious. "Mary can never do that without a medical license," Samir told me.'

'Okay, awful luck then. Well, darling, Qatar is no longer an option.' I ponder if Samir has told Drake about my letter.

'Samir appeared curious, "Where is Mary? Doesn't she want to be here anymore?" when he realised you had left. I told him; for private reasons. You're in Hong Kong. I was frosty with my answer. Samir acted weird. Suddenly he wants everything done. So, he gets it. But it gets expensive. How do you like them apples?'

'Too many terrible things happen between us.' I scowl irritated at him.

'Samir got upset. I didn't want to go into it.' Drake plays the massive 'in control card' by telling me he has put Samir in his place, and that he will not put himself under his administration.

'Gosh! Samir is so controlling. "Have you changed your mind for the project?" Samir asked me. "I have gone frosty on the way you treat us," I said. Samir didn't understand. He felt his investment was more than agreed. "With whom?" I asked. No answer!' Drake's voice is ironically deep and bitter.

'Might be Samir is angry with you. As I'm angry with both of you.'

'Why are you angry at me? Baby, you are going through a phase of your life that involves doubt and safety at the same time.' And he slickly praises me of how kind and the most stunning woman I am. Simultaneously, I'm told I'm arrogant and hysterically mad—so much that my anger seems to get no boundaries. Apparently, no superlatives can describe my rage in Drake's view.

'I don't feel safe. "Everything we do, we do together. Nothing shall separate us—nothing!" you once said.' But we got separated and don't do things together. Drake wanted everything for himself.

'What a pity you feel such a basic wrath. You cannot see the wood for the trees. Mary, you are a stubborn beast!' the feisty dog growls.

'Hm-mmm. Thanks for the *stubborn beast* compliment. I'm determined, not unfair!'

'You will not listen to other than yourself.' He wraths.

'When one finger points at me, three will always point back! You are a *stubborn beast* too—one who will only listen to and look at himself.'

'Sadly, you take everything in and let your resentment rattle on without delay. They've grown every day since you left.' He wants a fight.

'Yea, it began in Copenhagen! The night where you told me you will not share.' Since then, everything went wrong. Are that what Drake calls *a lovely relationship*?

'I sense how you become more difficult with yourself. Babe, you're tormenting yourself. You possess so much anger.'

'Might be. You have so many times played on my emotions?'

'*What!* If it isn't Samir who is the scapegoat, it's someone else.'

'I don't see Samir as the scapegoat; you are! I'm tormented. Not the other way around.' The situation created that doubt in me. What was his actual plan with me?

'It's not a walk in the park with you.'

'I never promised it to be. You always accuse me of being possessed by demons. Drake, it's fatiguing! I've lost some and kept few.'

'*Bullshit!*'

'Huh? It's not bullshits! I moved on with my personal growth, with thousands of scars on my soul. And my heart.'

'Don't say I can thank myself for you not being here.'

'You create more wounds in me. I get more scars in my soul.'

'*Bullshit Mary!*. You're an adult. You can stay here with me. If you want.'

'What do you mean that I can stay with you? I don't need that. Chalus is no longer my home.'

'You got a residence. And work permit.'

'Yea? And? I don't need it any longer.'

'Baby, this is your home. Even if you don't think Chalus is the navel of the world.'

'You're right. Chalus is not the *navel of the world*.'

'We haven't given it a chance.'

'I've tried. And given you so many chances.' And he doesn't act on my sadness. I want to find a place where I can live in peace. Alone!

Drake talks about his suggestion that Dr Mustafa should leave voluntarily, because the two fighting dogs can't cooperate. They have no mutual respect, and Drake thinks Mustafa is a stuck-up and spoiled asshole. Drake doesn't want to use his gunpowder on such a spoiled brat. If, for any reasons of friendship with Samir, Mustafa absolutely needs to stay there, then Drake's interest in finishing the project there is equal to zero.

'What do you mean by playing on your emotions, Babe?'

'So often you told me everything and anything you believe I want to hear—only for me to give you another chance.'

'What rubbish are you talking about? I saw your anger after you escaped from Flopper. You travelled with a huge ballast of tremendous bitterness and insecurity.'

'Every time, you make me feel as a fool. Then you suddenly change to your mean side again. I don't regret my sincere love for you.'

'Baby, slowly, you calmed. You rejoiced when I gave you security. I gave you love in significant quantities. Let me give you the warmth and love I still got in me. Hold you in my arms. Give you security again. You're vulnerable.'

'I'm glad I could give you some love and got a little in return. Was your love ever sincere?'

'Rubbish, Babe! The *Denmark syndrome* is in you again. You can't live with or visit your family. You get disappointed and that eat you up inside.'

'Why should I stay? I'm up against too much. What do you not fancy with me? Is that a development of the good kind? I should have run off before I fell in love with you. Enough, Drake!'

'You don't want to admit your faults. That's why you have mended fences!'

'When I'm not with you, you want me back. When I'm there, it's better I disappear. I doubt we can find each other again in harmony. And that's not because of my stubbornness.'

'Baby, you talk nonsense. You boil inside. You get still disappointed in them.'

Drake forgets my anger began in Chalus, and it grew with the many evil things he said of me. I'm not unreasonable with myself, though I believe the surroundings are. That he believes the boom of my anger since I left Chalus has something to do with my pains in Denmark, I find it as an easy excuse on his part. There is no Denmark syndrome. I've a hard time seeing a future and finding trust again, so what fun is there for me in Chalus? Only a lost, glad life I once had with him.

'You're so dramatic, Mary. You want to find a scapegoat. You are not patient. You might not want to look fairly at what is going on in our lives. You don't want to give it a chance, as before.'

'The disappointments are merely of everything that has happened. It has nothing to do with my family. Nor anger, scapegoating, or lack of patience. That's bullshit, Drake!'

'You overreact! You are unreasonable with Samir. That situation will resolve itself.'

'BS! Asses are constantly being licked, "Mr Collins". I saw it last time when you not backed me up in the argument with Mustafa.' If I go crazy, my rage comes from not being treated well.

'Don't compare me with that fool Mr Collins. You've not realised that you're welcome in Chalus.'

'You don't understand. This project meant much to me. I've put so much into it, for you.'

'Baby calm now. I'm sorry you can't work as a therapist in the clinic. I can't do anything about it. You can be my lovely assistant.'

'Are you selfish? I invested in you! You nicked the project alone. Shame on you! I'm not your assistant.' Yea, that's the reward I get. What a strange partnership, and I'm wasting my time with Drake.

'Compromising is often necessary. You did it during your marriage. Sometimes you must bite things in yourself to get things running. You used to live in a strange relationship with Flopper, where sharing of you with others was okay.'

'Hogwash! My greatest mistake was telling you my tragic story.' I should never have told Drake. It failed me—if there was a shabbiness; he used the horrors of my past against me. It's unbelievable that someone I believed loved me used something so disgusting against me.

'I wanted to know your story. I didn't use nothing against you.'

'Humbug. I got drained before. You swore that I will never experience such tragedy again.'

'Babe, you had to bargain with yourself. I'm sure you allowed others to hurt you by what they did.'

'Oh?'

'Compromising is not unfamiliar to you.'

'Umm... I didn't compromise with Paul. I did it so much with you.'

'Gibberish! You got disappointed and hurt by Floppers affairs and behaviours.'

I was a fool to believe in Drake's love and stayed, maybe even too long. He proved that he was smarter than me. Maybe because I'm such an honourable person and have a great heart. I can't see nothing wrong in others—until it's too late. On that account, I lost my children. The rest of the story he knows too well.

'That you stayed, Babe, I'm delighted. You couldn't understand what Paul was doing.'

'Hmm? My mistake was not to stay in Spain. Or Denmark. Senselessly, I threw myself into a passion with you.'

'Flopper fooled you into believing him. You saw the matter and your married life from two other viewpoints. He put something in the scene to get what he thought was a legitimate excuse to screw around. You didn't understand. That is why you get deeply hurt and angry.'

'The last of my self-confidence has disappeared lately. That has made me negative and angry. Even before I left Chalus.'

'I must leave for now. I've much to do. Talk to you tomorrow.'

'Drake, is it hard for you to manage the warmth and love I desire? Is everything only about you? We should have thought of it, before getting involved. You have shattered me into small crystallised fragments as tiny crushed snowflakes.' I want to cry.

'Baby, we will talk when I come to Hong Kong next week. Take care.' And he disconnected the conversation.

Basically, I believe Drake is an intelligent man, and he'll probably solve everything. So, I'm not ready to discard him, but I must find out what I want with him, before he arrives.

We have been decent at supporting each other in the past, and good at adjusting to each other's peculiarities. Where has the goodness gone? What has happened to our warm hearts and what we promised each other to become? All disappeared when we couldn't fulfil our promises.

I have known for a long time that Drake chose Samir's and his money over me, and Samir has power over him. That's what Drake needs and not me. Wealth!

Do I lack immense patience? Yes! But he doesn't listen to me, so he often contradicts himself, when we talk of the many failures and mistakes we made. I understand better now why we have had so many. Once, Drake said; *Mary, you are the reason I went back to my old profession.* That's why I supported and trusted him, though I couldn't see through his behaviour. Was I wrong with everything? Did I not support the greed enough? Its better if Drake spends his time wisely, rather than spending it on strange behaviour. Congratulations! He is a winner in the lottery. He made it! I didn't! Considering, I will let him go his own way so he can pair up with Samir. Next I can congratulate him on his recent marriage, and I remember the words of Diana, Princess of Wales, 'Well there were three of us in this marriage, so, it was a bit crowded.' Which also reminded me of my past marriage and how the ambiance in my relationship is with Drake.

* * *

The following week, Drake arrives in Hong Kong, and I'm excitingly waiting for him.

'Sweet Baby, I'm so pleased today.' And he appears ecstatic to see me.

'Fantastic!' I cheerfully answer while hugging him.

'Before I left, my relationship with Mustafa has gone into a useful phase.' Hand in hand we walk outside to grab a taxi.

'Great. Let's see how long it lasts.' My unhelpful ironic answer doesn't please him.

'Mustafa has gained an impressive deal of respect for my knowledge. He knows who the boss is!' He proudly cheers.

'Wow! I'm happy for you.' Pondering the next. *What a sudden change!* 'Have fun with him. Enjoy and be happy together. You deserve each other.' Oddly, he scowls at my spitefulness.

'Now the networking phase begins. I will enjoy having you with me, with your catching lovely smile; people fall for you straight away.'

'Drake, you talk gibberish. Obviously, you enjoy it.'

'Rubbish! Baby, with your ability, I can proudly hold you on my arm. Yee-haw, we will meet with the high court.' He grins. 'And talking with ex-pats from many countries.'

'Networking phase? Um-hmm, interesting!'

'It's a shame if my brilliant idea cannot run. It will break my dream. I will feel as if I failed. Don't give up on our dream. I'm at the finish line here.' He seems proud to succeed.

'With my negative attitude, it's probably a terrible idea for me to take part.' I sulk.

'I'm sure the spirit I put into setting up my last clinic will reach the utmost heights.'

'I'm happy for you. You've achieved what's needed.' But I'm not happy.

'It will give me great joy and professional satisfaction. I made it again!' Then he cheered loudly, waiving high with his arms in the air.

'I'm proud of being a part of your success. Rejoice! Get your satisfaction that you can't ever seem to get.' I'm not in the mood for his shit.

At last we arrive at the apartment. First, I make us coffee and take out two bottles of chill water from the fridge. Silently we enjoy the view over Victoria Harbour while I cling to him.

'Stunning view, Babe.' He abruptly continues. 'We will come together with every embassies and consulate. Joining their parties and other networking roles.'

'I don't think this will excite me.' I will start my life again without being shown off as a circus bear caught up in someone else's strings.

'Such baloney. We will get contracts to treat staff and families. From every country.'

'You were always wanting such a clinic. Hmm, that was not in the cards for us in the beginning. Did you lie?'

'I never lie. I did the entire hard work.'

'Wow! I'm happy on your behalf.' Answering angry and ironic.

'It's time to do what I do the best—*working a miracle a day.*' Yeah, believing he's a genius.

Hmm. Drake thinks he made it again. Though, at the expense of our relationship and my funds. He believes we're facing a point where we'll get chances to know people from embassies, consulates, and giant companies alike. According to him, things will turn around. Incredible! What *delusions of grandeur*!

'Babe, I can't run from my destiny! When I tried, God pulled me back.'

'I never asked you to run away.' But he never gave me any help. I'm disappointed that I can't be part of the team. I seriously thought I could. Only he thinks he can finish this! I wish with my heart that he could welcome my desire. Jeez, he sounds as God almighty himself. As he is one of the few in the world who can do this. What makes him sure of that?

'I want you there with me as I finish my career with dignity.'

'Why do you want me there? Is it of being admired? For you to brag of your stylish wife. One who takes excellent care of you?' Angering very distrustful.

'I want to see your lovely smile. Hold your hand every day and every night.' He grins.

'Be thankful if you ever see my "lovely smile" or hold my hand again.' I felt stupid saying this to him, when I in the same second reach out for his hand. 'I'm sure you got no time left for me, anyway. What is there for me to get up for when I wake up alone?'

'Gibberish! I'm there every morning. Few people experience such love as I have received from you. Sweet Pea. I'm glad I could experience it.' Then he lovingly squeezes my hand.

'But you no longer hug and kiss me for the first fifteen minutes to wake up the sleeping beauty.' Blink... blink as I was Bambi.

'I'm up many hours before you. I'm working on the project.'

'No kisses or saying goodnight. You turn your head to the side when I want to kiss you.' Mwah. I send him an air-kiss. 'I see only a neck. At eight PM I skim a sleeping *dead* man on the couch.' Sucks!

'I promise everything will be much better.' Mwah. He returns the air-kiss. 'Let's try to find each other again. Pick up every good quality in us. Move on.'

Our shower time and walking around in the pool has disappeared. I'm not allowed to see him naked anymore. Not to touch his body, as he always removes my hands. I'm pushed away when I want a hug, as it fears him I might want to shag? I'm in misery.

'You *have* been a grand life partner.' His cheerfulness turns to be bitter.

'*Have?* Sounds as your quote. "Everything has a beginning and a natural ending."'

'I prefer it not to end. I can't say enough of our divine relationship.'

'Divine? I gave you a fresh beginning of the natural ending of our life. Grab the beginning with your new sugary Chalus life.'

'Running from what I'm so passionate of will mean ending my career unworthily.'

'I'm not demanding you to run from everything. I believe you should have stopped a long time ago. I would have liked that. Stay in Chalus.'

'It's not always been easy. But we've adapted well.'

'Bah, whatever. Don't stick your tail between your non-existent balls as a cowardly dog. I'll do it for both of us. I got the "balls".'

'Oh fuff, what are you talking about? We grew according to each other's habits and flaws.' Pointing his finger in my direction, as I'm the one to blame.

'Drake! Things have only turned out for *you*. Not for us.'

'Samir sees only me as his partner. We have not settled everything. But we will now.'

'Great. Woo-hoo!' Strangely, Samir invited both of us for the business, and now Drake believes Samir can buy him out when he retires—as a retirement savings for him. It can't be a surprise to anyone that we were together on this project. But only he will gain a profit from the project! Then he believes I can attend parties, functions, and take part in promoting the clinic. Jesus Christ, I have been a *figurehead* before. Apparently, I must continue to be one. Considering of the Denmark syndrome or my demons and my devilish horns. Muahaha, there could be too much devilish sausages and smutty ketchup in this game.

'Nonsense. We'll be getting everyone to gather around what I stand for. In terms of treatment—my philosophy! With you by my side.' Proud and bragging.

'Who do you think I am? A sweet little cookie you can pick up from the jar. Take what *you* want?' As a predator, he will eat me! That's how I feel—consumed by others! And he believes only he holds the power to direct the rotten medical treatment method into his principles.

'Baby, it's huge! Hold it tight in your hand, darling, and next I protest.

'I'll not be attending parties where I only appear as Mrs Doctor Bates.' Does he think I'm such a stupid goose who lives only on her fake husband's success. Come on! Is this a joke? Imagine how embarrassing I will be for him. Uh-oh! He will present an uneducated wife. A *nobody!* I don't want to look dumb, because I'm not a medic or a professor. It's basically the only thing that counts for him.

'Baby, don't you understand how gigantic it is?'

'Eh? No! Listen to yourself! I'm only a woman in your man's world!' I'm sure he forgets to tell them of the domestic duties I perform and shut up when he asks me of something.

Perhaps Drake can show me off on special occasions, when we dance at the ball at the mighty embassies polished floors. *For the safety of everybody, I'd better stay away.*

He is so confident and spins off massive grandness when he believes he will be the first clinic in the world run on healthy principles that govern the body's well-being—a clinic where the neurology and movement apparatuses are the focus.

'I will stand with the baton in my hand, la ... la ... la ...' He waves with his hand pretending he holds a baton and as the famous Austrian conductor Herbert von Karajan conducts the famous Berliner Philharmonic.

'Congratulations! I'm not sure how damaged your megalomania is. Umm... it's massive. As God or Jesus Christ.' Fumbling noisily with my water bottle.

'I'll make all sing from the same notes in harmony.' His head and thoughts spin strangely.

'Great! Then your baton can swing and make all sing and play from the same notes in harmony. You have always been very good at it.' I growl sarcastically.

'How can I run away from what I'm passionate of? I'm one of the few in the world who can do this! I have only a few years left as an active doctor.'

'Yay! People listen until they find out you lack a clear conscience. Keep in mind that there will always be a "missing node" in the tune.'

'Think of what I've done for the clinic. My textbooks. My scientific articles.' So far Drake has done no textbooks or any medical articles. 'I will look back on my life, knowing I "made it".'

'Eh? Listen to yourself.'

'I need that. Not just because my leaps were not always successful. I am put into the world to take advantage of human bodily problems.' He imagines he will leave an important legacy of events unlike anyone else in this profession.

'They put no one into the world to heal people. Hah! You are not God! Nor Jesus!' Even he often believes he is Jesus.

'It's my destiny!'

'Huh? It's not your destiny.'

'My mistakes pushed me back to my reality—to deal with and get results with everything else I couldn't before. I dedicated my life to human health and science.'

'Hmm ... You have a strange psychopathic behaviour. You must suffer from delusions of grandeur. Enjoy your new dancing partner on the polished floors.'

'If it won't be Chalus for you, because you are stubborn, Mary, then I have another solution.'

'Please darling. Imagine bloody ketchup sprayed over the fine diplomatic wives? Yuck!' I laugh and picture the bloody drama.

'Baby, goodness and genuine warmth of heart are our mantras.'

'No thanks! I need not for you to show me off as a *pretty housewife.* Nah!' And not as a *delicious cookie,* or any other uneducated *figurehead.*

'You've been able to throw many of your demons off your shoulders. But today they pop up in your head.'

'Ha-ha. Well observed, my red devil is pushing me to speak.'

Drake takes on the slicker voice comparable as the pompous slick Mr Collins from 'Pride and Prejudice' that I suddenly have come a long way in my personal growth.

'It should not stop before you die. You always improve, Babe. I love you.'

The fresh team is the harvest of the baby seed I helped Drake to sow. So too with the joy he now possesses—a product of the support I have given him. Great for everyone! Or not? He got the power! That's what men love to possess. He can keep all the damn pleasure for himself.

'Enjoy! If it lasts. More and more I see a wicked self-centred behaviour in you.'

'So awful you are.' And he gets angry at me and leave the sofa.

'Greed saddens me. Grrr ... Please, I need for you to climb down and out of my arse!' I shout after him. Gah, I give up.

Breathing deeply, I suggest we go for a walk. My temper has made me react anxiously; I'm angry and frustrated and feel I've been ill-treated and with great unfairness.

I can't believe how Drake belittles me to keep me under his control. He talks so highly of himself, though I know he doesn't possess those many skills he imagines he has. He's not a medical doctor. He's a control freak, and everything is a well-acted farce! His life is full of drama—a theatrical play he drags me into.

When we get such discussions, I have often noticed his little satisfied smirking smiles, when I respond as today with his manipulative modes of communication. Again, he is sitting with a victorious smirk across his face, and feels superior after my angry attention directed at him?

Have I not realised I perhaps was living with a self-absorbed sociopath? Naive—that's what many will properly say about me. No! I'm a vulnerable, trusting woman who loves too much. Drake knows I have a heart of goodness and possess unlimited trust in him. He utterly uses this, then controls and psychologically abuses people. One thing I have noticed is; everything he does is only for his own benefit—to get as much as he can get.

CHAPTER 33

THE ROOT OF EVIL IS MONEY

> For the love of money is a root of all kinds of evil, and by craving it, some have wandered away from the faith and pierced themselves with pains.
>
> —1 Timothy 6.10

Greed is an excessive or ravenous longing for material gain, be it status, power, food or money. I am referring to that wickedness of Drake's only thoughts in his head. Money is neither good nor evil, so the problem is not with wealth itself. The problem is with the excessive desire and lust for it that constantly was the only thing he desired. Satan, also created as Lucifer, had beauty, wisdom and power. Drake's position in our paradise could not satisfy him, though I used to believe we lived in bliss together. He wanted a glorious throne of his own and was not content with what I gave him because he had a lust for more and wanted more glory and be in control. His love of power and wealth is fanaticism, which resulted in many evils. His desire of being rich and powerful resulted in our destruction because he couldn't serve both me, his power wish and his love of money.

* * *

'Sweet troubled Mary. I'm devastated by your response from yesterday. I've been thinking the entire night. I'm sorry we can't talk nicely to give an understanding of our misunderstandings. I'm having a hard time getting mad, because I care for you.'

'I'm disappointed that you believe I cause our problems.'

'You cannot be more far away from the realities of me and us. I'm dumbfounded and saddened. I don't know what to do about yesterday's talk. I want everyone to see you as I do—a sweet and nice person.'

'Darling, you have created success for yourself and a hell for me. Don't talk about being *troubled* and *devastated*.'

'Whatever I do or say, I will lose again.' And his destiny is set once again, as he believes he cannot win no matter what, and thinks he will lose everything. Even his sanity, as he supposes that he is really no good for anybody.

'Darling, I also feel devastated and sad over the split between us. But it's simple Drake. I sense you are sleazy, narcissistic and licking everyone's ass.'

'I cannot live with your inflammatory comments about me. You went too far over the line.

You make yourself ridiculous, Mary. I'm not smutty. People can be kind without being sleazy.'

'Whatever I write or say, it's always wrong in your perspective. It's sociopathic.'

'What? Sociopathic? I know what a sociopath is. Take it back. How did you arrive at your "diagnosis". Is that not taking your hatred towards me a step too far? Everyone considers *you* as a psychopath.'

'I don't like being treated unfairly. It's only about you, Drake.'

'Tell me how I fit your understanding of what a sociopath is. Your evaluation is very much contradictory to what I have heard from others throughout my life.'

'I'm upset by what's said. Also, the lies from Mustafa. It's not okay, you believe more in him than in me. It made me angry.'

'Thousands of patients always liked me.' And here goes the famous violin playing the tune of how many patients Drake gave a fresh life. 'You must retreat from your "diagnosis" as being wrong. I will gladly let them examine me by a competent psychiatrist. Nobody deserves such a harsh diagnosis. Unless it is right.'

'It's so many lies and promises.' I'm not in the mood for another discussion.

'You have the obligation to tell me when and about what did I ever lied to you about. I lost my children too. I'm no good. And my son calls me a narcissistic psychopath. I have nothing left. I'm paralyzed and sad. I'm not meant for anybody.'

'I love you, darling, but I lost you to the *power, greed* and *money*. Can we stop this talk?'

'No! You must stop your demeaning behaviour! You confirmed with your actions you are a very cruel person! Everyone wonders about your Dr Jekyll and Mr Hyde manner. Stop all your lying shit. You seem so flooded by hate. Negative notions, which shows how troubled you are.'

'I only ask for the same affection that you gave me in Spain—your hands holding mine. Your arms wrapped around my torn soul. Your kisses on my lips. It was the best love of my life.'

'I realise that it was just a luminous dream I dreamt, having you in my heart and soul.'

'I sense you're saying that it's finally over between us. Is that correct? Drake, do you understand how indifferent I am to the greed of money? And the power you seek?'

'Oh, boy! I'm a no-good asshole. I deserve nothing better.' He whines.

'I don't care about the glory. *I only want you*! I see you not as a failure. I support you. And look up to your knowledge and skills.'

'Baloney. Babe, you tore yourself out of me.'

'God joined us, but the devil won. We feared it so many times before.'

'Babe, I hope we will see each other again on the same track.'

'I hope too. Chalus ruined our relationship because of power, money, greed and the glory of destroying the world. They created a war and conflict.'

'Oh ... uh-oh ... I must lie down.'

'Are you okay?' And I continue talking. 'I want you while you still are healthy.'

I want us to do grand things together. Life is like a Japanese cherry blossom tree in full bloom. The flower falls off the tree to the ground at the slightest breeze. Then life is over, for this symbolic delicate blossom, and Drake's age is against our love. It's delicate like the flower on the tree. When he has withered and fallen off the tree's crown, it will be too late. What is wrong with my wish? From where I stand, it's love. I can only live and love in peace and harmony—not in war. If his subject dies, when he dies, he can't see it die. He will not enjoy it after his death. Being in love continues in the afterlife, and I believe we will live together forever in heaven. And go there in the significant aspect of love, and in eternal harmony under the paradisal elysian pink flowering trees. There we can find eternal life, with us sitting under the blooming tree, kissing and holding hands.

'Babe, I'm not feeling well.' He has never complained about being ill.

'Is it jetlag?'

'Hm-mmm' He mumbles taking his hands to his head.

'I only want to enjoy you, while you still can. Is that a wrong wish?' I get up to grab a bottle of chill water from the fridge and hand it over to him.

'Aww, my arm and chest act up with pain.' I wonder why this self-pity sickness pops up.

'Are you okay, darling?' I pause and glance at him.

'I'll see if I can get some rest.' And he slaps his corpus on the sofa, pretending he is ill, and falls asleep.

Constantly, he is coming with new symptoms of illness. Does he want me to pity him?

After an hour rest he gets up consuming a slice of bread, drink a large Hendrick's gin, and eat a cute little baby cucumber. Suddenly, he turns everything upside down. He loves me. Then he criticises and demeans me. Next he is sorry for his behaviour, but he does not intend to change. It always goes in the same direction—up and down! *Do we have communication problems?*

'Babe, let's go for a walk.' We stroll along the promenade, enjoying the lovely weather.

'Are you better now? I was worried for you.'

'Sweetie, I could never cause a break between us—not now and *never*.' He suddenly says.

'But we don't make love anymore. You use your age or sickness as senseless excuses?'

'I'm old. And sick. You are the only one I really want and am passionate about.'

'Darling, you're not old or sick. I accepted the age different between us. My love is great for you too. But I didn't expect to be your sugar mama! So far, it's been for over three years.'

'When you are in the best corner, you give me soul and joy. When you are in the opposite corner, you can drive me mad.'

'Yea, yea! A monastery for me will be the best. Yea, rather than being in love with you.'

'Ha-ha, ha-ha … Babe I don't think you're suitable for a monastery.'

'Yea, yea, well, if a monastery becomes necessary for me, then I'll go. I'm not given any satisfaction on Minnie anymore. Only if I beg you like a little child.'

'Ha-ha, your wicked little girl. There may be some bumps on the road. They are not so bad as to be lasting.'

'You can't only satisfy me just with holding your hand. Being embraced in your firm arms. And rarely kissed gently on my lips.'

'What to do about it?' He smirks.

'Gah, none of it happens anymore. It's tough competing for the favour of your love.'

'Baby, I can never leave you. You're my destiny.' He smiles so sweet.

'I wish of living the rest of our lives together—not of living in solitude. I feel lonely. Let down. Abandoned by you.'

'I don't want to lose you. But it seems you are choosing to get rid of me, Babe.'

The end on our disagreements is simple. I didn't listen to the advice I got a long time ago. We talk no more then he suddenly turned around and walked back to the apartment.

The last day, Drake sits with his calculations on his massive spreadsheet, with millions of strange numbers, as he suddenly freaks out on me as I kindly ask him, 'What are you calculating?'

'Argh, I can't help but thinking of a discussion from our last serious trouble.'

'Oh, I see. And?'

'From the weekend with Samir. From the day you started the worst crisis in our special relationship—the worst to date. *The root of evil is money!* I said to you.' And he begins to quibble about an old discussion.

'Hmm ... darling you are by now well established. You don't need my support anymore.'

Drake can earn his own millions. Make a living on it, as I'm sure Samir will pay him plenty when the clinic and Drake's bedding business gets up and running. Within a few years, he will have regained his lost millions.

'Christ! You own no good in you! You are intolerable, Mary! You always told me you did what you did *for us. From your heart.* You lied!'

'I'm not so fixated on wealth. I can't do more for you. Why this sudden outburst?'

'You're so coloured by your egotistic self! You shout so loudly, that it's hard to think.'

'Holly moly.' It's too bad, I didn't listen to my divorce lawyer, when she warned me about him. Love makes blind. Jeez, I've been sightless.

'It's been a pleasure to see you blossom from the new financial freedom you got.' And he believes he always supported me in everything. Had helped me with advice, guidance and his hard work to get my wishes fulfilled.'

'Well, well! Although the impression given to the outside world was that only *you* made and owned the dough.' Meaning, those *I* had. Samir and others had the same impression.

'Let's talk about the accounts you don't believe I've handled correctly.'

'Why? I can't even borrow at the bank for housing in Hong Kong.'

'Huh? I understand you were hoping for a better handling. But it's only a matter of looking through the posts.' His eyes are blinking red with the anger travelling from his brain to his mouth.

'I must consider something else. Perhaps Sweden.' *Oh, boy! I am tired of his never-ending story about what he owes me.*

'You put *your saved money* into my account, as agreed. I didn't take a penny. I paid bills as shown in the bank statements. I've posted every payment and withdrawals from my account.'

'The numbers don't match on the statements, darling.'

'Argh! Jeez, if they don't match your statements, then there is an explanation. I did nothing deliberately of bad will.' What surprises me the most is he often told me; he had no access to his internet banking. Suddenly he has statements for three years back! And I've not received them all, but the bastard has also 'forgotten to deposit' every penny from the envelopes in The Philippines.

'Only payments of rent, car, and utilities show up for those specific months.'

'If the postings are not correct of what I used the money for, then we must look at each post and clarify. Without quarrelling.'

'Fine!' That's what I got out for not calculating when I paid for everything. I trusted him. Even asked countless times for him to repay me. He always said he had no access to his internet banking, or made other lame excuse, which complicated it. 'Darling, after three years nothing is repaid. That stink!'

'I'm sorry that you don't trust me anymore as a financial partner. That's a serious matter. Then we cannot do business. Nor create a financial life together.'

'The math is not right.' He very well knows I spent little money in Asia.

The cash he redrew for me from our first meeting in Hong Kong came from his Bank of China account.

'All cash you redrew is deducted from my accounting. The rest I used from my own MasterCard.' Luckily I have saved the bills and statements in my files. 'Everywhere else, I paid. Any payment you made I promptly transferred back to you.' I said.

'True, you paid me back. It's deducted.'

'All else, I transferred to your bank, under the heading, "education money". Rent, car, leases, your loans, the debt to your accountant, trips, and much more I paid. That's why your math is off track. I'm sure you forgot some zeros behind the shabby numbers. For what you owe me is far more than your suggested petty amount.'

'What? Missing some zeros is way too wrong. Are you stupid? How did you get to that number? I didn't take cash from those accounts for myself.' Her screams my head off. 'So, there should then be a lot of money. But it's not there. Christ, your imprudent woman, look at the bank statements. I never cheat. I never stole your money. That's all!'

'Apparently, neither you nor I can calculate.'

'I see. Oh, boy! You are too much. Shite. So that's how it is? Mary, you are full of it!'

'Darn, oh, my! I only asked you to repay me for "the deposit" three years back. "Equipment", "accountant debt", and your bank loan.'

'Are you so *stupid* Mary, that you don't understand that I see you are harassing me with your false bullshit? Bollocks to it, I'm deeply traumatised!'

'I'll send it to the accountant. With our living costs, to figure out how much you borrowed.'

'Bloody norah (read Mary), I'm wretched by your speech. I don't know what to do. You're so *impudent* to me. As someone who doesn't know a holy shit about anything. Darn! Shame on you. Mary!'

'Maybe we also should look at sharing housing. Car, hotel, and travel expenses as well. That can cost you dearly, Drake. You love to take from me. Damnit! You find it hard to give back.'

'Grrr, you are the lowest person anyone can imagine. You just keep going. Everyone is damn tired of you. And your BS. Holy crap, then you decide I'm not worthy of you anymore.'

'Gee ... You put the equipment money from Samir on your account. Is it yours? That's a gross breach of trust. Then strange arguments pop up for discussions.' For all the world, he wants to win, and in his eyes it's always me who is *wrong*. It's never his fault and he is always blaming it on me or others.'

'Christ, you don't think you're fixated on coinage. But I am? Money broke our bond.'

'One day, you can repay what I paid. I've done what you needed. It's best I start anew.'

'Our agreement was that you should get your investment back. When I can repay you!' He shouts. 'I'm ready to pay and settled. *But I can't!*' Next he screams angry. 'Shite, you can only see everyone cheating on you. You feel shabby and persecuted. Jeez, these are choices you make. That sucks. You got *nothing* to do with our bedding business anymore. *I owe you nothing!* Got it?'

'Don't bother of paying back the flight and hotel bills, Drake. I've managed it.'

'Bollocks to it. *I always supported you!* We needed each other. Now you want to break our relationship into nothing but *money?*'

'If you mean there is any unfair distribution in the bills, let me know. We can settle it once and for all.'

'Bloody hell! Then you will find out what our relationship has cost you? You always said the opposite. How can you settle it in money, Mary?' His wrath makes me flabbergasted, when I sense his heated aura. The furious rage in his head runs down his neck to his shoulders, through his boiling blood in his veins, waving his arms high and back into his filthy mouth when he continues.

'You were the breadwinner. Oh shit, then suddenly you turn on a dime because you don't agree with the calculation. Damn you, Mary, now you make it up in expenses. And I must pay? Because I lived with you? It's incredible! Grungy bitch!' I see his frantic head become copper red with insanity as he, in madness, paces his furious walk.

'You're such a *stingy little man!* You can keep the damn dough. I genuinely don't care.'

'It's so loathsome that you absolutely must crush me for wanting to complete my career with dignity.' And his crappy speech of what he can do for a lot for many people begins. That's his motivation—not the money, he believes. How he can leave something valuable for the future. That's what he wants. And he thinks he got a lot more in him that needs to go out to the world.

'I'm sorry you want to prevent me from my goal. And call it fixation on money. That's a low-down down. *Stupid goose!*'

'Thanks for what you gave of no good to me. And what I paid for you. It seems you don't trust my accounting. And I don't trust yours.'

'You feel lonely and abandoned. You regret having done what you said you would—namely supporting me. I supported you too. In *every* way. Totally *unselfishly*. I never asked for your wealth. Grubby woman.'

'Live your life. I'll live mine. Then you are rid of me.'

'Jesus, Christ, you are so paranoid about wealth that it takes the best of you, Mary. It's so gloomy to realise you got such a foul evil part. It comes out sometimes. It destroys you. And your surroundings. *Shitheads* like you absolutely must clap your grimy hands for no reason.'

'You are never happy on my behalf anyway. Even if I achieve something good in my life.'

'You slut! You can't see it. You are so *assuming and stupid* in the way you view our relationship. Everyone is not after you and will not cheat you. There are many who might like to.'

'I wasted my life on something I thought was real and heavenly.'

'Damn you, I'm not among them, Mary. But when you settle everything according to the money you have spent on our lives, then it becomes something murky. I took part with my heart in the right place—always! It wasn't enough. I'm sorry.'

'I'll never get wise about men. They all seem to be of the same kind.'

'Shitheads like you are only hoping I'm the problem. Then you can say what you want about me. I'm not what you say. If it makes you happy, I'll take it in. That's how you stupidly think of our unique, relationship. I'm sorry you end it. It breaks my heart. Prick! I knew I had found the right one.'

'I can always sell our $23,000 mega "rocks" I bought. Then I won't lose on that account.'

'What? Jerk! Did you steal my ring? How dare you! It's not yours! Even if you paid for it.'

'Jeez, apparently you have forgotten they are at the goldsmith for repair.'

'Thank you for allowing me to be with you during our *good* time together. I want to look back on that time with joy. *You're sick in the head. You are full of no good!*' He shouts. 'Thank you for our time together. Thanks for nothing. Jeez, such a hell cat!'

Drake's sense of reality is weak. Is he bipolar? He seems manic! What planet is he living on? And he thinks I have thrown him on the street. That he hopes it will be my best decision as it applies to my life. It seems as his son had hit the right spot when he spotted him as a psychopath. I'm sure his neck hairs got raised as a crazy wrathful pit bull terrier who wanted to attack me—to bite my throat or twist my neck until I lay dead in the gutter.

He puts pressure on me so he can get rid of his debt. He succeeds! I'm muddled and angry. Drake can bring out the worst in me. Do I react too fiercely and out of proportion to the topic? It's not the subject of money, it's more that I'm not being heard. Then accusing me of stealing the ring, that's too much for me. He constantly rejects me and makes tons of excuses, so he lay the blame on my shoulders. Am I that bad? Why did he then stay with me?

From his point of view, it is banned from breaking things off with him. It's a terrible defeat for his self-esteem to find that he lacks control of me. It's too much for him, and for a psychopath, only he may end things. He is toxic!

My spirit is low when I consider doing future business with Drake. I know that every relationship has its problems, and we have ours too. My love and care are not enough for his greediness, then he wants the last *cookie* in the jar, and consume me with what he says and do. Sugar Mama closed the cookie jar, barring access for the man I thought was the love of my life. I've never felt so controlled by a man, yet I can't see through him, and he always gets away with what he does.

In the beginning, he made me shine as a bright twinkling star in a clear night sky. Now, he turned off the light on the sparkling star to something shady—took me to the darkest night of my life. He tore me into thousands of shattered pieces, because he skinned away my happiness, leaving bare something gloomy. The woman in black Prada shoes ended up in his black hole of meanness, when the man she loved revealed his genuine character—the shadowy, hidden darkness of Drake Lucifer Bates.

CHAPTER 34

AN ICY SWEDISH ADVENTURE

His heart wasn't as beautiful as his smile.

—Warsan Shire

O n the south coast of Sweden, a few hundred metres from the white sandy beach, I rented a three-bedroom house and nicely decorated the home, with newly purchased white furniture's, including a sofa with big pastel blue and rose flowers. I have unpacked everything and it's wildly snowing outside. Christmas gets closer, though we will each celebrate it alone—Drake in Chalus and me in Sweden.

Every day I stroll to the beach to enjoy the impressive bridge between Denmark and Sweden, knowing I have only an hour's drive to Copenhagen and my family. The sea calms me and I notice the many massive white turbines on the horizon, and as I reach the harbour promenade I enjoy its many small stalls, though most of them are closed. As I sit on a bench and drink my takeaway coffee I watch the many sailboats and yachts in the still water, then I stroll back, and pass the many tiny canals with small boats, while everything appears idyllic and calm.

In front of my doorstep I have the green surroundings, and watch the children playing on the playgrounds, all seems perfect, and I feel happy again. I've researched business options and studied physiological topics and feel relieved for the first time in a long time to be without Drake. I'm on my way back to myself again and can breathe normal again!

Then comes a dire need, when it hurts my soul as I feel lonely and can't handle to live alone. Sometimes I want to cry in my loneliness, though I can't cry out the unhappiness, and I can't stand it. I'm still in contact with Drake as a long-distance relationship, and lately, he has bombarded me with hundreds of e-cards. I miss him, so I gladly lick his loving words into my broken soul, with his smattering of messages from him:

+ My dearest and best love,

  Here is a special love note for you. My thoughts are with you constantly. I fill them with emotions of love and caring. Everything I want is you.

  Love you forever. D.

+ My sweet, dazzling love,

  Merry Christmas, my precious, the one my heart burns for. I hope you have a lovely Christmas, and everything goes well for you every Christmas. I'm excited to see you again, but you must do what you think is best for you. I'm eager to hear if we again can celebrate our own Christmas and New Year's.

  Love hugs and kisses. J.

+ My beautiful Sweet Pea,

  I wish you a cheerful New Year and a tiny Chinese cracker greeting for you this morning. Now you know I have you always in my mind and miss you immensely.

  Your Drake.

+ *Happy New Year!* Thanks for everything in the old. It has been a year of trials, with many challenges that we and you should not repeat in our lives. Our lives are far too important for something as the strife we have had. We did our best, but for others who couldn't care less. Now we must do it for us. I'm full of confidence of what will happen during next year. I will be the only one who is solving the riddle of dementia. I didn't get a greeting this morning from you. I'm saddened.

I got an enjoyable sleep. I thought through everything and concluded that the best thing for us is to concentrate on running clinics in Scandinavia. I've got cold feet with Chalus. I hope to have this business plan done soon. Maybe we can meet with your bank. I look forward to seeing how you can flourish during this progression. Then your family can wonder where your strength and initiative come from. They don't know that behind a solid woman stands a marvellous man—*me*! Let them think you did it alone, so you can get the approval you deserve. It will be good for your soul. Now we must get our clinics up and running in Scandinavia. Let's take the right steps calmly, and then the world will open for us.

One thing is sure—I love you more and more, my dear Mary. I dearly miss you.

You are my dream woman, and I knew this from the first time I saw and touched your little foot. I love you with my entire heart.

Love and kisses,
Your forever loyal Drake.

He sweet-talks me. And in between his words of love, he sends me tasks related to different business proposals for Scandinavia—as this one:

Subject: Vast cities in Scandinavia.
My beautiful Baby,

I've investigated several vast cities. I found a few clinic communities with many compact rooms. It's not relevant.

We need to set up at bigger private hospitals, and this will need many calls to open doors at each of them. We need, at least, treatment rooms with bathrooms, a waiting room with a reception, IT equipment, and internet. Our start-up budget per clinic will be $50,000 per unit. We'll need one receptionist and one marketing person, and two nurses and assistants and one physiotherapist, who I can train. I've arranged meetings for you in several of the vast cities.

Remember to continue working at our bedding company, and I've written letters to the Chinese manufacturer Xing and Jang Smart Living Group. In addition, you need to continue working on our clinic project. Remember to tell your bank of the loan budget they received with our business cooperation. If the mini hospital in Stockholm can become a reality, you must borrow minimum $250,000.

Drake

I don't answer, because I've hardly done shit of his demands. Then he calls me on Skype:

'Hi, my precious Baby. I cannot take the pain anymore.' He whines. 'I'm in agony and will see Doctor Berg tomorrow. I'm sure there is something severely wrong with my scrotum.'

'I'm sad your health is poor.'

'You don't care if I die of cancer. Besides, I also have insane pain in my neck, shoulder, and arm. It drives me furious.'

'Hmm, your conclusion is so wrong.' Answering frosty.

'I'm glad you're not here to experience it with me. You will get annoyed with me. It's hard for me to be at reduced strength. I usually find solutions, but I haven't found one this time.'

'Well, I hope you get better.'

'I've been thinking of how I got that subluxation. I did that during our last trip from a mix of an awful bed and brisk coughing. I subluxated my chest and neck. Shit, I have a stuck vertebra.'

'Oh, my! Not good! Did you get someone to examine you?'

'Yea, I went to a colleague from Germany. I thought Doctor Mayer was good. He couldn't release it.'

'Why not?'

'Mayer's cervical technique wasn't good enough for a difficult case as mine. It takes incredible skill to adjust those vertebrae. A general release of the neck and chest does not help.'

'What do you mean?'

'Mayer needed to adjust three vertebrae precisely. Atlas, C5 and C6. They are difficult to adjust. He next loosened everything above and below. He couldn't set my atlas. He tried several times.'

'Has Mayer left again? Was it the guy you wanted to use, in Chalus?'

'Yes. I hoped Mayer could have done it. At least for him to be a star here. He isn't good enough. I can't use him. Enough of that. I must fight this pain until I get it resolved—even if it turns into an operation.'

'I hope you will find a solution.'

'I don't hear that much from you, Babe. I felt awful for you dating a stranger. I have slept little tonight. I've thought of it throughout again.

'Huh? A stranger? That I'm dinning with my friend Liam has nothing to do with a date.'

'Your date might be a step of letting go of me. Liam may not be a possible new partner.'

'Eh? I'm not searching for someone else. Nut-head.'

'My conclusion is—right or wrong—that you are moving away from me.'

'Doh!! I'm not interested in Liam. Only you are my love. Don't you get that? Your obdurate fool?'

'Hmm ... Liam may not be a possible new partner. But maybe he's a remedy in your process. Your rage is incredibly powerful. It destroys both of us.'

'Gee! I'm not searching any. Ha-ha, I teased you. Ooh, my, you got soooo ... jealous.'

'Baby, you know you are my eternal love. I have no more energy. But I care for you.'

'I think you understand how hard it is for both of us to be apart. I love you too, darling.'

And so, have gone most of our conversations between us for the last months, when a whopping surprise appears as Drake calls me.

'My loving Baby. It's the worst news in my life. Today, Samir threw me out immediately.'

'What? Really? Why?'

'Yeah. Without warning. I've one week to pack my stuff. Damn, I've no place else to go.'

'What will you do?'

'Samir is threatening to toss me in prison. I'll come and stay with you.'

'What? No, I'm not prepared for that.'

'I've brilliant plans for us. We will unite our bond in understanding in relaxed love.'

And he gave me new tasks to prepare clinics in Scandinavia and find nurses and therapists.

He will handle management, banking, accountant and lectures at every global trade show in the coming year. Yea, and I can take care of marketing, and a website for our bedding in the Orient. Then he wants us to move to Andorra, to meet with other members of the 'brain science trust' and he will write the dermatology section in his book. What book? There is no book. He wants to prepare lectures and create a training program for staff, then work as a consultant for Sonic-wave Medical in Germany. That sounds as a lot, as Drake wishes to do this within a few months.

'Baby, we'll talk of the details when I see you.' He looks drained and eager at the same time.

What do I do? What is wrong with me? I only want to be friends. But I'm still in love with Drake, and on my way to again overriding my own needs and values, while I have lost my independence and dignity again, as he is once more holding me in his hollow hand.

I allow him to come to me, excusing myself I owe him the help, and pleased when he finally leaves Iran. I miss his presence, after these many months of being apart, which has done something good for us.

I genuinely believe we love each other, so we try not to take up old discussions again.

Late in the evening on a freezing winters day I'm to pick him up at the train station, when a sudden wicked, anxious emotion runs through my mind. My iPad, which he used before, is in my possession, and without thinking of what I'm doing, I charge it for him.

I'm traumatised, when I on the front screen see many notifications—alarming mail. I open the messages, then scream; 'such a son of a bitch!' reading the damning horrifying emails, written the same morning to and from another woman as messages he sent before he left Iran.

Shaken, I search further in the mailbox. Shit! Screw him! I'm shaking and dizzy. My heated blood speeds as if fuming fire ants crawls through my narrow veins, and before I faint, I slam my body onto the bed. What a damned cursed Casanova!

Distressing, I find several love exchanges going months back. Casanova is riding two horses—her and me, by dating Mitzie behind my back. What a prick! I don't understand how Drake can be such a douchebag. How can he keep Mitzie warm behind my back? It tears apart my heart. What a crazy sociopath, when I with anger read their exchanges:

Dear Drake

How are you Mr Peaiman? When do you come to the cold North again? Let's meet. Where have you celebrated New Year? Don't freak out when you see my picture. ;-)

Love,
Mitzie Babe

My smashing little Sweet Pea, finally you answered me. Thanks for the picture of you. ;-)) You are an adorable little precious girl. <3. What a glorious eye-catcher you are. You go right into my <3 heart. You were so divine when I first met you. ;-)) *Wauw*! I must tell you; I have had so much on my <3 heart for many years. I must talk to you under the gaze of :-) (-; four eyes—just the two of us—and over two chilly beers. I don't care of the roll of fat on your stomach.

I will stay with a friend in Sweden for a month and work on a project. Then I will move from hers. Give me your lovely time. Let's meet and talk and enjoy ourselves. I would love to see you again, Sweet Pea.

I had a lonesome time in Chalus. :-(

I'm leaving Chalus in a few days, so give me your phone number. I'll call you.

I'm looking forward to staring into your lovely stunning blue eyes again. ;-)) I am madly in love with you also back then. Only I was a clown :-(and a wimp. I wasn't strong enough to split myself from my wife. I could have had gorgeous children with you instead. I should never have let go of you.

Finally! I said it! I'm sorry little girl it took so long.

Love and miss you, ;-)
Drake 'Peaiman'

Good morning, Peaiman

Damn! You woke me up from my old love realities. :-)) Oh, my goodness! Wildly in <3 love? I hadn't seen that coming. ;-) But we reciprocated it. You were my first genuine <3 love of good :-)) and :-(evil! I'm Looking forward to meeting you again. It makes me a little nervous, because I have a burning desire for you.

Here is my phone number. +4526421655. Call me.

Mitzie Babe

Good morning, desirable little girl.

Don't be nervous. ;-)) I just tumbled with this inside me for too long. I kicked myself in the ass many times. I was too weak. I didn't expect to get those tinkling nice chilling goosebumps for you again. My heart is burning for you. It's a nice feeling to love you, my sweet little girl.

I'll call you now. I need to talk to you, my sweet litlle girl.

Love and miss you, Sweetie,
Peaiman

Subject: Spirits for you
Hi, gorgeous Peaiman

I must write even we just spoke. It's not you I'm nervous of. Old love never rusts. You just made a massive earthquake in my otherwise safe life. It gives me fluttering butterflies in my stomach and sends a flaming arrow through my heart. I am excited as I'm a twenty-five-year-old woman again. I'm nervous I cannot cover my emotions for you. You have me in your hollow hand, 'J'. You are touching something hot inside me. <3 It warms my heart. 'J' :-)) It's not good, sometimes, it hurts so damn much.

You showed me another fresh life. The man who I am so deeply in love <3 with—suddenly announces that he still has grand emotions for me.

I'm glad we found each other again. It means much to me! 'J'. I'm reliving the hours of waiting for your visits, and our stolen moments. Everything turns me towards more gleaming moments of laughter and adventures with you. You make me the happiest woman in the world. *I want only you*—the man of my dreams.

Love, <3 and kiss, kiss. :-))
Mitzie Babe

Yuck, such a dirty love rat. My entire world collapses. I'm angry! Argh! Pickup artist! I print the letters, then flash back to the time when I found love letters between my husband and his mistress. No one wants to discover something that is so hurtful or bothersome, and it is an utter lack of respect for me. Every relationship has basic ground rules, and Drake doesn't follow any to support a healthy bond and doesn't value the rules or me.

In my anger, I drive to the station when he arrives on the last train, having the letters in the back pocket of my jeans. As a fuming black panther, I walk back and forth on the platform, then the train arrives, and I see him standing in the door. I don't smile when he beams at me and happily steps out and wants to embrace me. Normally I fly into his embrace and not let go of him. Not going to happen today! Furious, I turn my body and cheek to the side, refusing him!

'What is wrong with you? Are you not happy to see me, Baby?'

I stare anxiously at him, ready to attack. Ready to pull out my razor-sharp claws to slaughter his flesh. 'I have only one question. Is there something you need to tell me before we leave?' I ask calmly, shaking and glaring harshly into his eyes.

'Huh? What the hell are you talking about?' I wait for him—wait to find out whether he will answer honestly. Nothing!

'Who is Mitzie Babe?' I stare heated at him and wanted to kick him in his ugly balls. And who is Drake "Peaiman"?' (Peaiman = A traditional (prescientific) faith healer.) No answer is forthcoming. My body shakes with resentment, and my knees wobbles as jelly, while the heart pumps rapidly and I'm close to faint in fury. I want to puke! I want to spit at him! I want to … I want to … I want to slaughter him!

'Eh? I don't know anyone by these names. Oh, boy, it sounds as a porn movie,' he grins, gazing downwards to the left and next over my head as the lying bastard he is.

Heated, I grab the printouts from my back pocket and throw them in his face. 'Can you explain these letters?'

'What the hell is wrong with you? Nitwit!' Then he picks up the letters.

'I found them on my iPad, when I charged it for you.' I'm mad and frosty towards him.

'What the hell are you dimwit doing gazing at my email?'

'Enough is enough, Drake. Screw you! I don't want to go through the same shit again. Get lost! Jump into the sea. Drown yourself!' I turn around and march away, leaving him alone at the train station, with his lies and pile of luggage on the platform.

'Baby come back. I only want you,' he shouts. 'It's only an old friend. It's nothing!'

Standing on the escalator, I turn around and giving him both of my middle fingers to his ugly lying face, turning my back again before sinking from his view.

Over the following weeks, Drake calls many times. I don't pick up the phone, but finally I give in and we discuss the matter.

'Babe, it really bothers me. It's sad you keep bringing "Mitzie" into it. I'm not two-timing.' He harshly is trying to assure me.

'Ohhh, I see. I don't trust you. You're cuckolding!'

'You're so stupid, Mary! It's unbelievable my words are not enough to pull you away from your obsession. A secret relationship! Argh! Pull yourself together! Such a blockhead you are.'

'I'm trying. But you lied.'

'Nothing is going on between Mitzie and me. Understood? Doofus! She's only an old flame. We are only talking about past times.'

'Yeah? You don't write such letters to another woman if there is nothing between you.'

'There was once. Not anymore. Neither of us wants to relive the past or make it our future. It's only a friendship with her.'

'What if I wrote such letters to Paul?'

'I know you say that you know men too well to know that is not true. I'm not as other men. I demand that you listen to me. Then understand it is as I say. It's a demolished chapter!'

'I don't trust you, Drake.'

'Stop these accusations. It will not endure. Get it out of your head. Stay positive instead.'

'I stop fighting over it; you will never admit to the affair. Such a cuckolding person you're.'

'Let's meet tomorrow. I'm writing for a lecture and need positive thoughts. If you have any, I'd love to hear them. The negatives I can't handle right now.'

'This is a rotten sign. You try to blame me for all and wants to be right no matter what.'

'I don't have time for marathon discussions. See you tomorrow, Mary.'

I give in, and we meet many times at his hotel. Then I feel I'm wrong and the disagreements aren't allowing us to decent decision. He refuses to see things in any other way but his, and then he is angry with me because he doesn't have anywhere to be.

Abruptly, I feel sorry for him, and may God know why I once more believed him, so I forgive him after one month. However, I have a hard time because I keep remembering his foul stuff, although, I rather want to remember the shimmering events.

I let him move in with me and shortly after, his stuff arrives from Chalus.

That's where I answered the million-dollar question of my senselessness. I don't regret my action, because at this point it's where I put many missing pieces of the puzzle together, and I realise his grim scheme. As Paul often told, 'Keep your friends close but your enemy closer!' I take the old advice and use it to research Drake's past and present thoroughly.

The following month goes by, and he has arranged meetings with Steven Jansen, who he calls 'Nombnots', a nickname given to him because Steven never thinks before he speaks. Drake calls Alan Hansen for 'Mr Fabulous', so I laugh at their silly nicknames and invent a new nickname for Drake, from being 'Bambi' to 'Captain Awesome' because Mr Fabulous and Captain Awesome are thick as thieves. They do and have done everything together for many years and they believe they are super cool heroes when they defraud people. It's at this point where the many extra weird projects pop up, which Mr Fabulous and Captain Awesome presents to me. They range from buying ten large cottages and a vast plot, then to build mini hospitals or clinics in different locations from the north and to the southern part of Sweden.

I am extremely cautious, and every time I take advice from the bank's financial advisors, who give me several warnings about Drake's many projects. Being cautious, I invent excuses. 'I can't pay,' I tell him.

'The bank won't loan me the money.' Or I'll say, 'The bank is still doing their considerations.'

So, it went on for the following years, where I lived with the best liar in the world and learned valuable tricks from him.

Drake constantly brings up past issues, and he doesn't hesitate to cut me off then often walks away from the discussion. He bullies me with my beliefs, and more problems arise, when I sense he does not value my thoughts and opinions.

CHAPTER 35

FOURTEEN HOT AND COLD

Oh don't cry, I'm sorry I cheated so much, but that's the way things are.

—Vladimir Nabokov

I believe things can get better, so I try to make Drake be okay with me. Viewing at the bark is the same as glancing at the trees in the forest, which you can only see from far. While walking in the forest, I sense him in every tree—on the bark, in the soil, and on the stones, while I carefully step around. Then glance to the east, west, north, and south, and glare above and below. I never find my answers—never discover what I'm searching for. I find only hopelessness and lack of air, then I need to breathe deeply into my lungs and thus cleanse my heart of unhappiness. It poisons the air and the water in the river, watching the trees die, and the leaves fall from the crown, as black dead spots on the forest ground. I no longer sense his heart knocking with the same love for me, when it's often expressed in his responses and comments to me. I send him tiny hints of how I miss and love him, but he never tells me he misses or loves me. It's okay! I'm used to it, because his affection only comes when he needs something, then he sees me from a unique angle. I try my best and it senses great when I'm trying or hoping he can find love again.

As I am gazing at the drawing hanging on my wall of the man with the heart in the boat, I realise I can perceive it from several angles. Maybe the man in the boat sails alone to the open sea and drowns the heart resting in the boat. I see it as it's Drake sailing his love life, taking it out to a deserted island, to live in everlasting peace, love and harmony—him and me. That's why it's hanging on my wall.

But this is not the boat trip we take together. I try not to cry over him—in the same way I learned not to cry when they beat me as a child in the orphanage. Instead, I ponder of my life—the dreams I once had when I was having an ablaze time with him. I don't want to play with the madness and hope endlessly of a love game that I know I can't win, knowing that love requires two people to love each other, two to dance the tango.

It does not comfort love in my troubled heart, craving for Drake, so I ease myself with a teddy bear sitting on my bed, but it cannot reciprocate or give me love. There's no reason to worry if I'm good enough, but it gives me warmth in my cold bed and consolation in moments of depression as I cradle its paw, pretending it's his hand. It's soft and pushing the cuddle toy close to my shaking body, I pretend its him lying there. Stupid and childish?

Drake does not meet my need when he is near, and he is not emotionally present. I try to look forward to our few stolen perfect moments together, because he still lives deep under my skin, and is still close to my senses and my heart, which can be nice or sad. Feelings are hard to control, and I'm out of control, wishing in time the Sun will shine over us again. To have lost him emotionally is a tuff medicine to swallow.

I perceive the Sun and stars shining on me again, though—having cleared my mind that he can at least be my friend, then let the Lord shine on my path. Let my life rise to new heights, where I may not have to crave his love and acceptance so much. It can be a frustration in my mind, because I can't get the one, I want, wishing only time will show me the way.

I promised Drake five years to see what he wanted to accomplish with his life. Time is running fast, and four have gone by run. Will I fit into his life? Maybe not, so I follow him as far as he allows me to follow and keep giving him every opportunity—as two people who love each other should! I don't want to give up on him, and I don't want to tie him.

He should not expect me to put myself in chains, because I won't wait forever, even I miss him by heart, and I miss us, but everything is a hopeless dream. I unwisely hold on to him. Sense him, kiss him, and feel the heat from his body and hands, though it becomes more seldom.

It is just the 'girl in her black shoes' with hopeless and unattainable dreams. Once upon a time, we were as two people in one person—two souls in one unified soul. What I smiled at in the past was nothing to smile at now, because it wasn't reality. My smile is partially on track again, though it's not a cheerful smile. Drake loved my smiles, but I have lost the gleam in it, because there is nothing more to smile at. His smile is drop-dead-gorgeous.

It's not a perfect boyfriend I'm seeking, but somebody I can act silly with, someone who loves being with me and treats me well. That's enough. Is that too much to ask?

The constant criticism of me under the surface, and the discarding phase is on its peak when he sends threatening signals. I'm not good enough, though he thinks I can't live without him. His Yo-Yo performance continues. Up and down he goes—a grim mood one moment and a superb humour the next.

'Sweet Pea, you have amazing drive and courage,' he says to me one day. 'You use your head wisely. I'm proud of what you are doing. I look forward to seeing your results. You get better and better—and fast. I love it!'

'Thanks, darling. I only want to make you proud and happy.' I love when he cheers me up.

'I love your professional description of what you do. It's perfect. You show a qualified side in your knowledge of anatomy. I'm glad of what you have achieved through your hard work and studies. You have had great attention.'

*   *   *

And then up pops a new-fangled idea in his mind. Croatia! I have a major weakness. Shit! I'm too impulsive. *The future is now*; I muse. Insight and awareness of the future should become an inspiring and innovative force in my life—dramatically expanding my horizons through travel to distant destinations or exotic lands. Progress in my career depends on my ability to think in brand-new trajectories. It may again be the time be for exciting innovative opportunities, then I have a great desire to expand my consciousness and seek further boundaries with him.

First we spend one week in Dubrovnik, Croatia, in Southeast Europe. It's a part of the former Yugoslavia and has a population of over six hundred thousand. With its tall peaks along its borders with Serbia, Bosnia and Herzegovina, Montenegro, and Hungary and comprise, the most stunning and rugged black mountains terrain in Europe.

As we drive from Dubrovnik Airport, we arrive at a stunning spot tucked away in beauty, close to the Montenegrin border at the coastline on the waterfront of the Adriatic Sea, in a small village. Next we had one weeks' vacation in Montenegro where we stayed for few days at a lush small boutique five-star hotel. And authentic Mediterranean hideout and the heaven of serenity where Tom Cruise had his gourmet food a seafood feast—delivered to his luxury yacht Lady S., during his visit to Montenegro. It is a perfect retreat of choice for us, a true escapism, accentuated with comfort and luxury, intertwining a sense of privacy and a friendly openhearted atmosphere in this family-owned unique site.

As we stroll along the sea front promenade to Kotor, a fortified town close by, characterized by winding streets and squares in the medieval old town, we find The Roman Catholic Cathedral of Saint Tryphon from 1166 in a small square of Kotor old town.

It's a masterpiece of Romanesque architecture, with slender Corinthian columns alternate with pillars of pink stone to support a series of vaulted roofs. In the arches are remains of Byzantine-style frescoes, and the gilded silver bas-relief altar screen, is considered as Kotor's most valuable treasure.

That day, I have a peculiar religious experience with Drake inside the church. Mystically and strangely, he stops up. I gaze at him in surprise, wondering what is wrong.

'What are you doing, darling?' I ask, watching him closely.

'Ohhh.' He pauses. 'I'm musing about the cross with Jesus.' He pauses and then brings his right hand up and nuzzles his chin. He tilts his head slightly, observing as if he's questioning something, then he tilts to one side and next to the other and walks closer to the cross to study it, staring and investigating at Jesus's hands and feet.

'What are you thinking of?' I ask, gawking at him curiously. 'Is there anything wrong?'

'Hmm… that's weird,' he starts, pausing before he adds, 'Oh … Right now, I just feel the pain Jesus went through, when the Romans nailed him to the cross.'

'Huh? Come on, that's blasphemy! Where has that come from?'

'Yea, I sense the pain through my hands and feet right now. I can't make the pain go away.'

I panic. 'Are you having a heart attack? Why are you hurt?' I'm sure I didn't hear him correctly. 'Is this a joke?'

'No … No … It's as if it's me who hangs there. As the Romans crucified me in the past life,' he finishes, eyeing at me as he's in pain.

'What? Eyh, doh … Frankly, Drake,' I say awed, 'let's move on!'

But he keeps gazing at the cross, while I continue exploring the church, fascinated in the many stunning frescos.

As I go back to the fake Jesus, to my grand surprise, Drake reaches out to me. 'Try touching inside my hands,' he tells me. 'Don't you notice I have got underlying scars inside my palms?'

'Ohhh! What now?' Then I take his warm hands in mine, viewing at them and palpate his palms. 'I notice nothing!' While I push calmly inside the palms and on the back of his hand, then he moans several times.

'Aw … Aw,' he whines. 'There, Babe—exactly where you press! It's where the Romans fastened the spikes into my hand. Can't you massage it a little? Then the pain will go away?'

Playing his Jesus card! Yikes! He mimics as he wants to cry. As I massage his hands lightly with my fingers, I wish his illusory pain will disappear—not because I believe a damn bit of his so-called 'Jesus pain'. At least I enjoy rubbing his lovely warm hands, while I ponder, *does he want me to massage and kiss his feet as well?*

I can't forget this ludicrous experience and find it ridiculous and hypocritical. It's as if he wants me to feel his alleged pain—as if he wants to convince me he is more 'holy' than he is. This makes me lose the last part of my faith in Christ.

On our last day we drive to Perast an old town few kilometres northwest on the Bay of Kotor a picturesque gratification for the soul. It's one of the most out-of-the-world unique countries I ever have seen, with its dramatic natural contrasts and colourful rains. The coast is bursting with stunning scenery, mirrored in the crystal-clear waters of the Adriatic Sea. Along the stone and pebble coastline, pops up stunning picturesque islands in the horizon—perfect for serenity or romance. It gives you the impression of being at the edge of the world and in Perast, we enjoy our coffee break and later have a lovely dinner, as we enjoy our last day here watching the sight of the Islets of St. George and Our Lady of the Rocks, while the Sun sets behind the massive mountains.

The first weeks is over, and our next destination is Croatia again, at Zjarko's Spa resort in Dubrovnik, with its big swimming pool and many elegant apartments.

The friendly local businessman Zjarko welcomes us and accommodates us, in our vast apartment comprising living and dining area, kitchen, bedrooms and a large terrace with sea-view.

The next day, we talk to Zjarko. Guess what? Drake is on the spot again, and tries to do clinic business with the man, while he is bragging with his expertise. Zjarko listens interested and recalls an old closed private hospital for sale, which amazes Drake.

Immediately, they arrange several options, with us as the primary investor, though I'm sceptical as Drake demands 75 percent of the income.

Zjarko is exceptionally helpful and invites us for a drive to a quarry and to visit a massive goat farm in the mountains. It's a stunning trip driving on small gravelled narrow roads, ending up at the farm tucked away in beauty of the rough Dinaric Alps in the North-eastern Croatia. The farmers show us their livestock of over 400 goats, the exotic Alpine breed, which there are only 10-12 percent of in the country. The farmers tell us about the vast milk production of around 140 kg/doe, with 3,4 percent fat and 3,3 percent protein; average meat production is about 15 kilo/animal and then with pride they show us the many different types of delicious goat cheese they produce.

During the lunch, promptly, Drake wants to do business with the farmers. My God! Now it's an idea of selling goat's cheese to Europe and Scandinavia, similar as if you remember from the agriculture project he failed at in Iran? He tries to sell the idea to Zjarko and the farmers instead. Will it fall to the ground because of his greediness?

* * *

After the vacation ended we travel back to Sweden, but Drake seriously talks of moving to Croatia. I agree! We have fallen in love with the country and then we make fresh alternative plans. So far, no business has succeeded in Scandinavia, so he is furious, and sits every day with his calculator and spreadsheets, trying to figure it out. For too long he has not worked, has no clinic and has not worked or treated any patients in four years by now.

Then he receives an invitation for a seminar in the Caribbean, and a novel idea is once more born in his imaginative wild west world.

'My darling love let's go to this seminar in the Bahamas. I want to relax in the Sun with you. To love you more and more each day. I want to cuddle with you at night. To make love to you. I want to treasure every part of your precious body.' The Paradise Bird has suddenly transformed into the slickest Mr Collins in his slimy world.

'We must have a splendid time again, Baby. Be with each other,' he massively presses. 'Otherwise, we aren't whole and cannot be happy. God put us together. That is the way it should be. I want only you.'

'Huh? What Mr Collins?' It is sweet—almost too much! And I'm impulsive, when he convinces me to travel to the Bahamas. *Great, why not?* And at once I'm surfing on the internet, buy tickets, rent a car, a villa, and pay for the seminar.

'I can't have a stopover in Miami. You must find a flight that doesn't connect in the United States.' It vastly worries him.

'Why not?' I ask, getting irritated at such nonsense. 'This is what I can get.'

'You must change the ticket,' he growls demanding. 'British Airways flies directly to Nassau.'

'Okay, easy now.' Luckily I have bought on business class. 'I'll change the damn tickets.'

The Bahamas consists of a chain of islands in the Atlantic Ocean and used to be a British overseas territory. On the first day after our arrival, the owner, Janich Waite hold the seminar on the picturesque north side of the island—with its white sandy beach and shallow clear waters.

For the second day, Janich Waite take us on a private charter cruise, swimming in the turquoise gleaming water with stingrays floating close on the white sandy bottom. I'm afraid of them and jump scared around when they get close to me. Every time I see one, I think of the Australian 'Crocodile hunter', Steve Irwin, who got stabbed by a stingray. Drake adores them and kisses one of them, while the guide holds the giant stingray. Then we sail to the secluded Starfish Beach, where we can see colourful starfish, and for the last tour, we snorkel in a coral reef.

What a glowing day, lazing on the boat or the finely powdered white sands, with my beloved, hand in hand. The seminar ends with a barbecue—beach hammocks, picnic tables, and delicious food served on the white powdery beach under shady green swinging palm trees, before the participants say goodbye.

Two days vanished and now we will spend two more weeks on the Bahamas, as it's as a honeymoon that ends up in hell.

As we meet Megan and James, a local businessman, we find out how friendly the locals are. Enjoying the calm surroundings on the beach, having chill beers with them, then on the spot, Drake talks of setting up clinics here. He is all over the world with his many plans every time we meet the couple, and finally, I have enough of listening to his severe big-headedness. It's too much for me, so I leave the conversation with a stupid excuse—I have a headache.

We explore Cable Beach on the western side of the islands, one of the ultimate beaches in the region, and in the most luxurious zone, with expensive villas, glittering turquoise waters, and coral sands. During our stroll, we stumble on many restaurants and beach bars, so we have every chance to enjoy Bahamas. Including a daytrip to the capital, Nassau, a financial hub and a port for cruise ships, and boasts lots of buildings in old colonial style. We visit a Turtle Farm and Copper's Castle, one of the oldest buildings, formerly the home of a well-known plantation owner Eden Williamson and serving as a rendezvous point for the first elected parliament, known as the birthplace of democracy in the Bahamas.

During one of our many explorations of the island, I get a massive surprise, and get overwhelmed when we randomly pass a specific house.

'This is where I want to live for the rest of my life. Oh, my goodness, darling. That's the house from my dream four years ago,' I shout, ecstatic in joy.

Drake stops the car in front of it and it's ten feet from a white sandy beach and close to the entrancing turquoise blue sea. It looks the same as the small white wooden house from my dream, painted in soft pastel blue and rose colours around the window frames and the shutters. It decorates white columns with small light blue and rose rings, then keeps the terrace and stairs in proper position and go to the neatly trimmed soft green lawn. Light blue eaves line the roof's edge, then the white fence, a blue hanging swing, and white wooden outdoor furniture.

Back at the hotel, I double-check my old notes. 'Unbelievable! Darling, it fits!'

Suddenly, he places me in the 'psychotic personality' category. Usually, it's people much older than me who can become psychotic. Or it might happen if you're single and living in isolation or having a poor quality of life, and these are not criteria I recognise in myself. I don't suffer from hallucinations or mood swings, nor do I try to convince other people that I'm right in every thoughts and ideas I hold. You can have a psychotic break if it subjects you to mental strain, such as death or severe conflicts or if you suspect that there is something in yeast that does not match reality.

If I am mentally ill, then I don't understand what Drake wants with me. Maybe he is 'The Saviour salvaging me from my hell or my psychosis. Or is Drake searching for something different?

CHAPTER 36

THE VILLAIN, AND A FRAGILE GIRL'S MIND

Life is hard. Losing someone you really loved is harder. But having your heart ripped out by the One person you really cared about and trusted unconditionally, slowly kills you inside. Therefore, I do not trust anyone anymore.

—Unknown

Damn! When Drake's unpleasant sides show up, he is *not* funny or nice to listen to.

'Mary, your delusion complicates your flimsy gloomy nature.' He spins angrily.

Often, he blames me, saying that I suffer from delusions and that I accuse him or others constantly, especially when I protest in discussions. Dumbfounded, I take in his alleged *delusions*.

'Argh! Babe get control of your dark inner demons. It makes the devil upset your flimsy petty girl's mind.' He smirks and laughs.

I stare curiously at him. '*What?* God damn it, Drake. We are packing. What's wrong now? Have you infected me with a psychotic devil disease during our time together? Perhaps it has increased in recent years.'

It bothers me we've decided to move to Croatia. I have bought new and the latest equipment, done agreements with Zjarko, applied visas, and set up a fresh venture with a new clinic, which is close to be born within one month.

'I'm helping you to get your wicked demons off your shoulders.' He smirks.

'Idiot! Geez! Demons! Devil, and fragile girl's mind? What the hell, Darke?' Throwing my neck slightly back, wrinkle my eyebrows, and pinch my lips together with exasperation. I'm frustrated. The imbecile sits with his spreadsheets and keys in numbers on his calculator. What is he planning?

'Jeez! Grab yourself, man. And your own stupid chaotic delusions? It's jaw-dropping. I'm worn out. Why are you like this?' I slap my bum on the floor and lean up against the wall, gawking at the sucker who wants to discuss these things.

Sometimes, I am disgusted with the madness and irritation at his way of treating me. I love him, simultaneously; I possess an unspeakable aversion to him. My thoughts drive me crazy. Why do I keep loving him? I can't get reality to fit with his promises. His negativity upsets me, and the joy of life gets taken from me when he hurts my heart, and when I'm broken, he becomes kind again.

Things get hectic while we pack, and he boxes his cartons and then runs to put his shit in storage. We decided I'll travel in advance and he'll follow in a few weeks.

On a nice early morning, the Croatian driver arrives, standing outside my front door with his gigantic lorry, with a forty-foot container attached to it. He smirks at us, dingy, smelly, and appears unpleasant, while we alone load furniture and boxes into his cargo space.

When we're finally done, the chauffeur bangs the tailgate and punches his fat ass in the driver's seat, and the smelly dude struggles to get the lorry out of the narrow area. Ultimately, he turns the truck and heads south towards the Croatian Mountains.

'I will love, honour and respect you for the rest of my life. Baby, I'll take care of you with every care I can give you. I will never leave you!'

Naively, I believe in his sudden promise. We hug and kiss outside the empty house, talking about when he will arrive. I'm close to crying because of the parting, as I can't handle it. In the same sweet manner, he's newly adopted, and takes my hand, walking with me to the basement to pick up my car, then he drives it up to the front door and parks.

'Babe don't worry now,' he says gentle and loving. 'I'll get there within the next few weeks. I promise you.'

Drake gets out of the car, walks towards the front door, and picks something up in the hallway. Sticking his head in my side window, he keeps talking. 'Baby, I need to attend other plans in Holland.'

Wondering what he's talking of, I glance at him with bloodshot eyes. 'What? In Holland!' Turncoat! In my wildest imagination, I don't understand he's breaking his promises.

He appears weird, as he's hiding something from me. My stomach rumbles nervously with tons of frightened butterflies, having no clue of which direction to fly, and floats frenetically inside me. Are they close to death? Their wings get hurt by the massive congestion along with my anxiety inside my belly, as I die gradually inside. He doesn't answer the question—pretends not to hear it.

Instead, he stares nervously at the car and then directs his gaze towards the front door and down the road as if to see if the lorry has disappeared.

We stand alone in the street on this transcendent summer day. The birds sing a lovely tune in the trees, and the flowers are still in full bloom. I can faintly hear the splashing of ocean waves in the background, while the Sun's reflection through the windshield of my car blinds me. The sky is blue with puffy white clouds that soon will turn grey, when soon God turn to cry dismal rain, asking Thor to hit the hammer hard over my head. It will send blasting thunder and lightning through my inner world, when the atmosphere will turn black with desperate pouring clouds through my eyes.

Drake pulls something out of his pocket and gazes fretfully at me, while he in an uneasy move, gives me a closed envelope.

'Goodbye, Baby,' he says. 'See you soon in Croatia.'

I can sense there is something utterly wrong, though I try to ignore my gut feelings as I glance around, confused. It's as a permanent parting with Drake—as if he had only been here to help me pack and otherwise get rid of me. It's as he wants to make sure I will travel as far away as possible, and as a cowardly dog, he sticks his nasty tail between his crooked legs. Suddenly, the seat belt feels as it's strangling me, and I can't get out of the car, getting completely petrified.

Because it's a rental car, I must hand it over at the Airport today. I panic and reach out the rolled-down window, searching frantically for his hand—grasping it one last time in mine.

He glares relieved at me; with a stare I've never seen in his eyes earlier. As he releases my hand, he rushes to tell me, 'remember not to read the letter before you arrive in Croatia.' Then he squeezes my hand lovingly, for one last time, and waves.

Confused, I drive south until I arrive at the majestic bridge between Sweden and Denmark. Exquisitely, it stands high against the breathtaking blue summer sky, while a few white clouds swim away from me in the gentle breeze and appear as puffy pillows you want to lie on. I dream of slowly floating away on them to a delicious and serene galaxy in the universe; the vision fills my mind.

The drive across the bridge and through the artificial dark yellow light of the tunnel appears infinitely long. For the first time, I get anxious driving through this tunnel, then the panic spreads inside my body, and I scowl at the letter. I think of accidents, sense the fear of being caught in a tunnel, fire and horrific scenarios appear in my mind. What if I can't get out soon enough if an accident happens? I don't know where I have taken myself, I've never been afraid of tunnels before. Strange, sad sensations swirl rebelliously inside me, while I feel more dead than alive. My thoughts spin around as wild ions inside my confused and broken brain, and I scowl again at the letter lying on the seat next to me. *Why is it so secretive?* I muse.

Arriving at the Airports car park in Copenhagen, I park the car in one of the designated spots for the rental company. Nervously I grab my suitcases from the trunk and load them onto a trolley. I've arrived too many hours before my departure, so I have more than enough time, and I cannot control my curiosity. As I open the envelope, I imagine it's a loving letter, and don't yet know that reading it if it will be the best or the scariest experience of my life. Curious I read his first lines (in part) in the letter:

> Letter: Relationship
> Dear Mary,
>
> We have reached the end of our 'secret' relationship. From the beginning it has never been easy, so the circumstances speak their sharp language, as in our case. We cannot stay in the same housing, because of your legal relationship with Flopper. We met when you were having a hard time in life, and then you wanted us to be together on a deserted island. You had the money to maintain our lives, so I didn't need to earn anything. Now I must make money again so I can continue to afford to take part in our life together. It has nothing to do with male pride but a practical and necessary move to get enough of everything.
>
> It will be best to pay separately for the rest of our lives. Without income, I cannot be part of it for the rest of my life, because I intend to live long enough.
>
> It's simple and you know it, but we drove each other off the track mentally. We need to find inner peace again, but we can't find that together. That's become especially true in the last few months when everything went awry in our minds. We need to find strength and joy in life again. We are demanding in every way. Unfortunately, we were not good at finding the common denominators that could push us forward in harmony, joy, and strength without each of us losing our identities.
>
> It has been too hard for both of us, especially lately, because the way we've lived has been hopelessly difficult. What drove me further away from you was the last month as we slaved away to get *your* stuff collected in boxes and crates. It was hard to see myself as being a 'woman' who had moved in with a 'man' for his money. I was always afraid that a bill landed in my hands ...

Thor's hammer hits my face and the sky turns eerie dark, when God sends a flood of rain through my eyes. With a horrifying surprise, I read one evil phrase after another, and filled with complaints, though it's a simple attempt to justify Drake's actions throughout our life together. Calculating and harsh, his words paint me as the culprit behind the failures of our entire shared life and wants me to appear as the great *Ugly Bastian*.

I don't know if the reader recognises the German children's book from 1845, which rhymes mostly of the wicked children. The moral of the story is flawless—a demonstration of the consequences of misbehaviour, when Bastian first dip the children in ink and then he smears them into tar. In conclusion, the child is rolled in feathers, to punish it. Christ! He wants to appear as a naïve and innocent little sweet lamb.

I stop reading momentarily, thinking; *what does he mean by that?* We hardly talked together, because he only listened to his own ideas and not to me. Basically, I think he has been away from me since he came to Sweden, then I recall his love letters to Mischa. If he loves me, he wouldn't write such things to others, however he might have hoped to get her.

Drake embraced me during the tough period of my divorce, I can't deny that. I think of the alimony, which I should be able to live off for the rest of my life, though I paid for every of his hopeless projects, which all ended in chaotic mess. With a grizzly bear's paw, he stood every month, begging with his brown eyes, when the little boy wanted his pocket money. Did I not immediately give it? If I didn't sponsor his fictional projects, hell took hold of his fiery mind, and I would see the wrong side of his Jekyll and Hyde personality, when he threatened to leave me when I doubted his fancy words and business affairs. He punished me with his posh words and hateful letters, like the letter I'm reading now. It was my biggest fear, him leaving.

How ungrateful of him!

I'm uncomprehending, shattered, and I cry as I stand alone in the dark, smelly, dirty parking lot, and feel as the loneliest, most abandoned person in the universe. It feels as the parked cars disappeared into the shadowy, gloomy universe, and the cheerful people vanished as dew in the sunshine, while my innermost thoughts turn to Armageddon. The building crashes over my broken body, and petrified, I stand shaking in the middle of a sinister thunder of a twisting cloud. Sky and ocean get into a crashing revolt, at the same time my head produces a throbbing migraine. Damn! It will never stop. I'm standing in the ruins of a war. He has blasted everything to pieces with his nuclear bomb and has blasted my inner world into thousands of fragmenting particles.

> Through the tears, I'm nearly unable to read (in part) the next part of his daunting letter:

> I got exhausted mentally and physically. But as I always am, I'm awakened by everything that happens in my doctoring world, which gives me strength and courage, something I felt I lost more and more.

> Iran could not work as we planned, because there was no contract with Samir before we left The Philippines. Maybe we were unprepared for that adventure, but Samir paid for this venture, so you did not spend money on me. Despite Samir paid our costs, housing and travel associated with the job, so, you must say, I incurred no expenses in this context. I always wanted to treat patients and be making an income again but haven't been for the last four years.

> It always scared me when I had naively entered a relationship with you, because I was just a pendant who enjoyed living with you. I thought Chalus would give me the income I had been missing.

> It's humiliating and disappointing that you put me in a box, framing me as a man who gains from you—a Casanova and a sociopath! I had to start over from the bottom step again—something I didn't expect to do at my late age, but the development has been that it was my lot.

> It's okay! I manage it with smiles and good courage, so I don't glance back and ask why. I don't place blame on

anyone, because if you always do your best, it will work out. You should take that knowledge and watch ahead. I've spent much in time finding solutions to make money.

You paid our expenses while I was living with you, because you had every means to do so. You can't take them with you the day you die. That's why I thought you would enjoy life and spending time and your money with me.

I took nothing with me from my time with you. Instead, it has cost me an old age in financial uncertainty, and *you* didn't allow me to make a saving, because everything was *yours!* Don't start saying that I got a share in your fortune, because I never demanded a divorce settlement from you. Instead, you have *robbed me* and taken your entire home. Shame on you! You are so evil! I gave you my knowledge in the barter deal for housing.

It's a shame that you ruined a beneficial relationship for selfish reasons and to keep your money for yourself. You don't understand or see the goodness in me ...

Whoa! Oh ... my ... God! I take my eyes from the page and sigh in tremor. His fixation on money is intense. Jeez, the few times he earned a little, he kept it to himself. Fat ass! Without sharing, paying any of our costs, or paying back his debt. It's always a never-ending money story with him!

Chalus! Whoa! He overlooked my many protests and went completely behind my back. Red warning lights flashed strongly, but only dollar signs were in his eyes. He also overlooked the full perspective of life in Iran and forgets that Samir did not pay for his clothes, food, expos and travel expenses when visiting friends or family or taking vacations. Those were costs borne by me.

It's about time he realises he needs to earn money. Damn! Four years without income! And it's true he's a pendant, though he has enjoyed life, getting everything served to him on a gold platter. Being in love, I allowed it, but I never imagined that I was living with a calculating mean person. Regretfully I must admit to myself and I too late saw he was a liar, a cheat, and a fraud. But I adored him so much in the beginning, that I didn't see all the flaws, I excuse myself to rectify my mistake with him. I'm angry.

Drake naïve? I don't think he is. No. He is a cunning puppeteer with no means to get people to submit to him and do what he wants when he pulls the 'lovely' strings.

I still hope in that moment that he will repay what I've lent him, but I bet I will never see a penny of it though. His rudeness never ends, and I don't have the remotest idea where this is coming from. I never called him a Casanova, except for I told him of my previous dream of being exploited by a man and it turned into an actual event. Was it a warning? I'm surprised at his self-centred sense of justice and mistaken memories. He never contributed to my life, so today I feel totally taken advantage of by a quirky gigolo, who deceived and exploited me-

Shaking, I peek at the three-page A 4 letter, thinking it can hardly get any worse. I still have the last ugly hateful words to read, while I take a deep breath, and dive back (in part) on the taunting letter:

> Together, we travelled widely, and I have been in tow for your bill every time. Alas, we could not hold a reasonable discussion, because it always ended up concerning wealth. While visiting a mutual friend, Kermit told me he'd heard you had sponsored me throughout our time together—that I only lived with you for your money.
>
> Sure, I admitted to enjoying your goodness, but with Chalus, I expected I could make money on my abilities. And then you as a half-wit moron think you should get half of what we earned from the unfinished pact we had with Samir? Are you a crazy bonehead?

Yea, our discussions often ended up concerning money, when he constantly brought it to orbit. In this letter, 90 percent of the contents refer to money—money, money, money. It resembles the Abba song from the seventies. Is it a scare tactic?

Kermit indirect and sneakily confronted me with the question and thought it was Drake who paid for everything and possessed the millions. 'This has to be a misunderstanding. It's not the truth if you've gotten the impression Drake has become a multimillionaire,' I said, politely clearing up Kermit's misconception.

Many times, I spotted Drake enjoyed saying he had lots of capital on foreign accounts, though he did not own a coin. When Kermit asked, I confessed, 'Drake has earned nothing yet. Hopefully, it will happen soon.'

Kermit and I hadn't talked of it anymore.

I thought it was fair that I should get half of what we earned, so what was wrong with dividing the spoils? In his perspective, I should get *nothing*.

'From the goodness of my heart, Baby, you can get 10 percent of what we earn,' he'd said once with a smirk.

'Bullshit! I equally divided every task between us,' I'd answered.

I continue (in part) reading:

> However, you have not talked of me having half of your alimony—although I mentioned to you several times I'm entitled to. So how come it turns into a 'fifty-fifty deal' when we do the hospital project in Chalus?

> It's best that I make my money. That way, I won't be indebted to anyone and especially *not to you*. I have always served my bread and helped those who needed my financial help.

> You don't want to be the 'bread giver' anyway—even though you have always been generous with me, because you got an amazing income. I hope you find a new home and they don't take it away from you, as you believe I took everything from you.

> God damnit, Mary! I'm always here with you. Argh, and I have never peace from your imbecilic demons. To regain my

strength and confidence, I need to be myself and *far away*
from your meanness ...

His bilious comment in the letter is difficult for me to understand.
He is losing his marbles in his inner rotten closet of a mind. The closet
door must have banged hard into his nut, then got damaged when he
wrote this letter. What in heaven's name does Drake mean? Take my
home away from me? He gave no context for that statement. I put
it together that he must refer to when he lost his own home in his
bankruptcy declaration in the United States.

In the Philippines, he often exposed me to his sudden embarrassing
episodes in a public forum and got frequently verbally mad at me.
When I withdraw the Peso's from the bank, he unexpectedly and out
of the blue, raised his voice at me, demanding, 'Why don't I get at least
half of what you just withdrew?' while we were still standing in front of
the entrance.

I recall one particularly frightening scene. 'I never have an earthly
chance of paying in a supermarket or in café's,' Drake yelled. 'It's
always you who slips your damn overheated golden credit card onto
the counter.' The fierceness shone in his eyes as he let his anger fly at
me, and glared at me critically, with his negative energy directed at me.
Something as this happened every time we went to the bank. It terrified
me every time, so frightened and nervous, I gave in to his wish, giving
him half of the nasty smelling dirty stack of peso's.

Then I recall us packing things together in Sweden, while he one
moment, was excited and happily talking of the additional challenges
facing us. The next moment, he was completely in the opposite ditch,
and shouted at me. 'It is grotesque and unflattering of you that I don't
get half of your alimony while we live together.' The dunce was off his
rocker!

It was just as bad as we packed the boxes, carefully labelling them
with mine or his. He'd been so barefaced as to steal of my belongings
and stored them in his storage unit.

Constantly he let out of several of his sour, foul-smelling burps, 'You
are not fair!' or 'You are not generous.' Next he shouted. 'I want half

of everything in the house's interior. I have nothing for myself.' He got more and more inconsiderate and seemed convinced half of the contents belonged to him, so I answer kindly to Drake. 'Darling, you haven't even contributed a single dollar. I purchased everything for my business. And privately.'

'You take it all. Greedy bitch!'

'Darling I don't. The case is obviously! You will join me in Croatia within a few weeks. Why do you think I should share the estate equally between us?'

What did Drake relate to? There was no point in dividing the estate. It was a complete unsolved mystery to me. He feared I had more than him—that I allowed myself more than him.

He kept saying in anger. 'Only you have financial success. You can do as you desire.' I feared him! I never knew when we'd be out of one of the dummy's terrifying unkind spells or when the bonehead hated me the most! I didn't understand his unreasonable questions. Was the imbecile in panic? Sometimes, I wanted to send the nitwit where the pepper grew so I could pack in peace. But I could never get out of his disgusting cobweb.

I'm trapped in my inner prison, which the ugly lizard rules with a hard claw, and continues his controlling movements of my unmoving body on the dirty soil. I gawk at the massive hell; he's sent falling over me in the daunting letter. It was dead frustrating. I never knew where the devil was mentally—when I would trigger his red switch over something, he thought I was doing wrong.

Stifling my sobs, I (in part) continue reading:

> I want the best for you and hope you can find peace with what seems to give you the biggest problems, namely the belief that 'everyone will cheat on you and take your money'. I'd want to forget that you mean I'm cheating on you. It's untrustworthy! You say that I've taken benefit from you. Obviously, I've been a burden for you! Such a mongrel bitch!

> Don't ask for more from my side anymore. I will not allow you to ruin my kind-hearted life. I know you have

given to me from your heart when you wanted to, so I naively followed you and what *you* wanted. You paid for an education with me, and we travelled around the world, where you for *free* learned many things of treating people and animals.

But *I'm* the only one who treated your dog—even if you were present and training with Specs in the pool. Ha-ha, and you helping with various things in collaboration with the rest of the doctor team in The Philippines? Ha! Jerk off! You don't get that credit! Don't think you can 'sell that journey' to your family and friends. It's *not you* who treated Specs and helped little Rajah to get on the right path. You were *only* in the pool with both kids and Specs. You were nothing else—*a zero and a nothing!* Only some rich bitch wearing a million-dollar blindfold ...

Whoa! I'm speechless, and stagger, hardly able to remain on my feet! My eyes nearly fall out of their sockets. For years, the oaf has been a spiteful parasite, feeding on my goodness. He can never give me good credit, and the few projects we had were always only his projects, he claimed. Although I'm reasonably new to my profession, I know how to perform the treatments. The street dogs I adopted into our homes, the elephants, and the Buddhist monks in The Philippines were my heart cause.

I didn't see Drake ever as a burden, but as a man I genuinely loved. But within time he became a burden, when one mental insult or threat after another from him ended up filling my head and I tried to escape the unhealthy relationship. Then he came to the horse's crib again, asking for forgiveness when I was gone, and he was out of money.

I've heard too many times the masterful distortions he makes in disputing the words between us, and now I own it in writing as well. I turn back (in part) to the horrid pages:

I've made a financial statement, because I'm sure I've repaid every penny I *initially* understood you would pay for. I've learned once again that there is obviously no 'free lunch' and

I was apparently naïve in my belief in us together in a bond, where only *you* had an income.

I know you've learned much about treatment, although not enough! But you got the flair for it, so you could do well in Croatia.

I can offer something great for you. Although I paid $12,000 to 'fix' Becca's machine by eliminating it, when I 'removed' it from her insurance company, who paid her for the stolen machine. It's now in no-man's-land, and she does not need the machine and will not pay me $12,000 to get it back. If she wants to pay you this money to get it back, you can sell *my machine* I brought with me. But you only get the top part, not the compressor, which I paid rough $18,000 for that.

As a farewell and final financial offering for what I owe you, you can then keep the machine you buy, including an extra treatment head that's worth $4,000. Will you accept it? Then we can close the book on us without you believing that I took advantage of you.

I take my personal clothes with me. You can keep the rest ...

Whoa! I can't believe he has the audacity to write that he owes me nothing! Is he out of his stupid mind? What boldness he presents, describing me with such nasty criticism. The dunderhead has just lovingly kissed me goodbye, knowing he has planned the letter a long time before my departure. How could he play this corrupt fake play right until the last day? And now I learn the dummy has exposed me to legal problems by suggesting I buy stolen equipment from someone I don't know. Mysteriously! Puff! Then it's *gone* from Becca's clinic. What the heck! That's the damn machine I've paid for already. In addition, it's part of an insurance fraud it involved him before I got to know Drake, and is the same equipment he alleged he leased, which I, in good faith, had paid leases for $70,000. Then he wants me to pay further $12,000. I can't even use the machine without the compressor *he* wants to keep.

Such a moron! When I had required my instalments back, I get my biggest surprise from him when he told me, 'You only paid 'rent' for it. You were *never* a partner. I don't owe you any money.'

My English back then wasn't as good as it is now, so I overlook some important things on the invoices: 'Use of Equipment' and 'Service Charge'.

I wonder, how can I have been a *user* of the equipment, when I never used it. I didn't even know how the equipment worked. I had no clinical experience or education in the treatment protocol. I was just about to begin the education, and besides, the equipment was not even in my possession. *It was in Asia!* And what is the service charge about? I don't understand it. We had a handshake arrangement between us, so I considered myself as a business partner.

I grasp now, you can't make a reliable handshake with him, because it's necessary to sign a legal contract with him. Realising it too late is my colossal mistake, because I now discover that I can't trust him, when he, cruelly denied our verbal arrangement. The dimwit has taken me by the nose. Shit, in fact it was a theft! Am I then considered a fence?

Drake's long lying Pinocchio nose gets longer and uglier. Fiddle dude! I'm merely a trusting Danish housewife, with less knowledge of English, so thoughtless I never questioned his tricky usage of the word "use".

I understand nothing. It has come to a terrible end, so I realise who it is who's been naïve. Me! He has ruined more in my life than the good he's done me.

> In distress, I read every single line to the end:
>
> You told me I couldn't see my mistakes; said I had become a grouch. Nobody ever said that to me before, so I glanced at myself, then I got the smile back. There are many exciting things ahead that I must do for myself, to help me find the best solution for both of us.
>
> Don't be so reluctant and negative. Watch the blue sky and let's move forward in the awareness that we are two

honourable people who want the best for everyone, mainly for each other. I'm just the soldier sent to the front to make the world a better place, and he returns home, for he's sturdy enough to survive whatever they throw at his head.

When I've grown strong, I look forward to being together with you again. Then I hope to revive the Mary I knew—the sweet Mary Magdalene that I still love. Baby be patience! Be tolerant! See inside to find strength with positivity and joy! Be happy. Don't be self-pity! Build your positive strength! Smile to the world, and it will smile for you!

I'm always there for you, though right now, I can do nothing but regain my psyche and strength, and then I'll get profits for everything.

I'm happy to get the help of my friends and family, so I must take care of every coin I own. Then I can build clinics and create growth, because I could not continue as it was with you. So, I'll 'sponge' on my family and friends right now, and I'll return their generosity in the form of my positive mind and treatments that everyone needs. There will come a time after this where I can give much more again, as I always have done.

Trust me! I only want for you the best. Give me space to find myself! Give yourself space to find your inner self. Take care, Mary. Let's end our lovely relationship.

Do not speak negatively of me. Don't say that I deceived you or in any way took benefit from you. I've allowed *you to use* the knowledge I had, so it would be sad if we were to part as enemies, just because *I'm* not good enough for *you*. It's best I live my life alone. I close with ciao from *the chosen one* who I believe was *the best friend you've ever had.*

Your once Drake

Whoa! I can't get it over my thoughts that we shouldn't be together, yet I also could. While standing in a callous parking lot, I read Drake's

424 | *M. L. Stark*

mean sarcastic letter to the end, and taking in the words coming from his awful world, written from his tactless brain cells. I sense his angry blood flowing in his insane labyrinth of vicious words, when he is sacking me on a piece of smutty white paper.

As we prepared for this next stage of our life together, not once did he lead me to believe that we would not continue our relationship, or I was that horrible as he describes. While packing, he was cynically planning a fresh future for himself, and was filling me with lies—with fraudulent and manipulative promises! That hurts immensely. I have no idea of how horrifying he could be. It's gross! The worst part is that he crushes me completely. He swirls with grandiose greatness and madness. It's awful! He believes he is the most important person, in the centre of the universe. Why didn't I listen to my gut feelings? Why did I overlook all the red flags.

In the back of my mind, I must admit Drake lies often, and is so good at it, so he believes confident in his own deceits that they are the truth. I'm grasping he is a superb pathological handsome and charming storyteller, and it terrifies me, to find out of his hidden agenda. He kept it until he could stick his shifty tail between his crooked legs, as the cowardly dog he is. The sucker hadn't even had enough courage to arrange the conversation with me under four eyes.

As a scared soundly thrashed dog, I sit shivering, pressed in a corner of the garage. The douchebag has left me to my miserable fate in a sinking old tub, crying as I've never cried before. It's warm outside, but I'm crazy freezing, and cannot gather myself or think sharply, while my head explodes with massive pain. My heart pounds, as if the warm blood is being pumped roughly into my veins, then ready to explode when the blood oozed from every pore. It's difficult to draw air to my lungs, and I'm nearby to faint, as everything is spinning in my head.

Desperately, I try to gather myself and wipe the tears from my cheeks. My make-up got smudged, the eyes are bloodshot and with shaking hands; I call Sandra. Crushed, I tell her the truth of the deceitful life I once led with Drake. She is content with my honesty but sorry to hear of my fate, and sad that I never showed her confidence before.

Our hour-lengthy conversation ends, and people pass me by, eyeing me with puzzlement resembling a madwoman, and I look like something the cat has dragged in from the gutter. Nobody asks me if I'm okay, then I rush to the terminals and check in.

'Are you okay?' the woman at the counter asks.

I sense as if she is throwing suspicion on me as I'm a high-priority terrorist, because my body can't stop shaking. I rush to the security zone, though I'm near to vomit as I scan my boarding pass. I throw my water in the bin, and suddenly I'm thirsty. Finally, I'm through security and run speedily to the passport control. The officer in the glass cage gawks suspiciously at me, and can see I'm sweaty, have bloodshot eyes and smudged make-up. I realise I forgot to hand in the car key and ask them at the gate if they will hand it over to Europcar.

With difficulty, I barely reach the aircraft before the staff lock the door to the plane. Exhausted, I slap my bum on 2A, when thoughts of my life, a failed business partner, a deceitful lover, and a lost love affair trouble my mind. I understand nothing. What has happened in my life today?

Although sad, I'm also satisfied, when joy and sorrow both fill me, thinking of the unreasonable things in my life and of Drake. The emotion that he is flying with me pops up, while glaring at the seat next to me, which is empty. The sweet and friendly flight attendant appears eye-catching, tall, and well groomed, wearing presentable make-up and having stunning bright red full lips. They have styled their hair in buns at the back of their necks and secured with nice black leather buckles, and they embellished their dark blue uniforms with a stunning red scarf. On the opposite side of me sits a big fat older guy, talking with a blond woman, though her broken English is hard to understand. Behind me sits an overweight guy who kicks me in the back constantly.

The food is not encouraging—*shopska* salad; turkey with gorgonzola sauce and tortillas; and plum dumplings with cinnamon, vanilla sauce, and blue grapes. It's horrible! I don't eat it. Thoughts concerning life with Drake spin in my head, when my eyes are closed, and I flash back to my many travels with him. I enjoyed every of my travels with him, even they often were stressful, but it was great to hold his hand as we flew around the world.

What thoughts does he have of me? I regret knowing him. Did he take advantage of me? I get sad. I must be crazy in my head, thinking how much I miss Drake, wanting to hold him in his hand, because I felt so much through our hands. Was it his hands or my own hands that sent magical reaction into my heart? Now I sit alone, without his company, while I imagine holding his hand in mine, and that he sits by my side. I buy a bottle of water and take pills for my headache.

How am I going to handle the company and my loneliness without him now? I muse.

In a split second, I lost everything—Drake, my life, my self-esteem, and my dreams. Shut up! It was so tasteless of him to sack his fiancée by letter.

What do I do now? I ask myself, thinking of how I have wasted four years. *Everything is just a misunderstanding,* I tell myself, *a ghastly joke!*

But it's not, it's a nightmare, because here I sit with a single ticket in my hand and a four-foot container on its way to Croatia. Goodness gracious me! I had not kept my brain in the right place living together with Captain Awesome, grasping today I saw the hidden, shady, dark side of Drake coming to the surface. I have been living with a devious person suffering from narcissistic personality disorder. I grasp he doesn't care or understand my mind-sets, because I've only been a tool for Captain Awesome to get what he wants. What a careless, blind fool he is, not seeing how hurtful he is and how much the pain he doles out affects me. I have let a cruel and unfeeling person belittle, demean, and intimidate me for a long time. None of what we did together ever happened and was never launched! Whatever ideas he had, I see it as *fraud*, pondering back on our trip to Asia. Faced with such an impolite subject, Drake was more interested in displaying his own knowledge. It may happen that his intention was good, even if they have criticized the action.

None of the investors were the slightest bit interested in his knowledge—or his massive *delusions of grandeur*. His praise and promises of future business went totally to the ground, when I grasp he is lacking etiquette, with an extreme emphasis on politeness. From the Taiwanese perspective, they must have seen his behaviour as unimaginably rude, in the same way it also must have happened in Macau, Hong Kong, The Philippines and Iran.

I knew I needed to be strong enough to forget him. I needed to leave the relationship behind before I lost myself to insanity. I needed to prove to myself that Captain Awesome was the wicked person, not me! But it's hard and would I be able to do so?

I cry softly as I turn my head to the window and watch Copenhagen from above as we take off, watching the majestic bridge in the still blue water beneath me, while the windmills appear on the bright horizon. Copenhagen and Sweden, goodbye!

CHAPTER 37

ARMAGEDDON IN MY HEAD

People put you down and you start believing what they say
about you is true. The bad stuff is always easier for people
to believe in.

—Julia Roberts

Zjarko picks me up at Dubrovnik Airport. 'Where is Drake?' he asks, eyeing around.

'He has something else to attend to first. He will come later.' Damn it! I hate lying, but I don't want to bother defending him anymore.

Together with Zjarko, the owner of Zjarko's Spa Resort, we stand in front of the huge panoramic windows in the rented 300 m² open-plan penthouse, with the living area opening out to a spacious terrace, enjoying the stunning view. It's searing hot, with the Sun shining from a clear sky over the marvellous dark blue Adriatic Sea with its sandy pink beach. Below I notice two pools, and in the garden furniture sits lots of cheerful guests chatting under the shade of parasols. Behind me, I glare at the rugged gigantic black mountains 'What is this on the left? The small island there. With its stone houses and bright red roofs?'

Zjarko points at the island, 'Oh, it's Otok Lokrum. A famed place.'

On the Adriatic coast, you can also find a famous island-hotel and a deluxe resort, situated to the south. With its pink sandy beaches and one of the most iconic and famous spots in the world, the islet encompasses an area of 12.400 m² for a secluded holiday in a beautiful corner of the nature. During the Venetian Republic, Svelte Basil was an important trade centre. In the nineteen fifties, the authorities decided to rebuild the island to create a unique natural complex of the Adriatic and the Balkans, with its stunning Church of the Transfiguration of the Lord, located on the most elevated part of the island.

Ever since, its guests have been the world stars of actors and other famous people from all over the world, as: Sofia Loren, The English Queen Elizabeth II, David Beckham, Elizabeth Taylor, Indus Ira Gandhi and many more including that Robert De Niro has the restaurant Nobu on the resort.

Zjarko interrupts my thought. 'On the right, you can see Tri Cavala peninsula. It's the new trendy Hotel Dunley complex at the Riviera. Next week the famous martial arts and Hollywood star Steven Seagal is visiting the place. He owns a lux apartment there.'

'Wauw, Steven is one of my favourite actors.'

'Over there is Dubrovnik Old Town. Maybe you remember from last time you were here.'

It is a historic district with rough 40.000 inhabitants and 2,500 years old, which makes it one of the oldest urban settlements on the Adriatic coast and the centre of Croatian tourism. It's known for its well-preserved medieval massive stone walls around the narrow streets, great nightlife and its many remote beaches along the entire Riviera. The historical references date it back to the 5th century BC, also used to be a part of the Roman Empire in the 2nd century. In the 6th century it was part of the Byzantine Empire, and from 1200 until 1828 it was a Roman Catholic Diocese of Dubrovnik. In 1944 it was incorporated in the Socialist Republic of Croatia (A part of Yugoslavia).

Much of the old town was devastated during a catastrophic earthquake in 1970. Since the many buildings were restored to original form, and today the city is a tourist destination.

'How far is there to the beach, Zjarko?'

'600 meters away. Can you see the buildings by the pink beach?'

'Yea, is that a hotel?'

'Yes, Mary. It's famous now. They filmed Casino Royale her. With Daniel Craig as James Bond and the Danish actor Mads Mikkelsen, as La Chiffre.'

'Really? Wow, I know Mads Mikkelsen from Copenhagen. Sexy guy. Yummy!'

'Well, I leave you for now. See you later, Mary.'

Finally, I'm alone and turn on my computer and call Drake over Skype.

'Hi, darling, how are you?' I try to smile.

'Not so good Mary, because our relationship is on a break. The way you have treated me bothers me. You are far from the sweet woman you once were. I felt relief when I was alone.'

'I can understand it from your letter.' I'm trying to be brave.

'Mary, you should not hold me accountable. I can't take being scolded and blamed for things that are unreasonable.' He barks as he wants a discussion.

'I wish you the best of luck in your future life.'

'Mary, you need to know the truth about why I didn't want to be with you. Nor want to kiss you.'

'Why, darling?'

'I can't stand the taste and smell of tobacco. In the beginning, you could restrain yourself. You kept your mouth clean. My feelings don't matter anymore. I loved kissing you back then. It made me want more of you.'

'I don't suppose we'll ever be together again.'

'Being together has left its mark on both of us. The respect that once existed disappeared.

I don't want to hear explanations every time that everyone else is to blame. You can't see the truth, Mary. You can't take responsibility for your own actions. Your unhappy childhood is still hanging heavy on you. This badly and negatively affects our lives, All the damn depressing demons you have. That means you always must find a scapegoat.'

'Oh, is that why the prince in shining armour was so determined to rescue me?'

'I'm the only one who can help you. To get rid of your demons,' Prince Drake says. 'Crazed and nasty demons run in your family. I saved you from the evil devil,' (meaning Paul). 'I'm your resurrected Jesus. You are my Mary *Magdalene*.' That's a harsh misuse of my solid Catholic faith.

'I don't want to give up, darling. I use structure to tackle my struggles.' I'm close to cry.

'It's only you who's blaming. I had visions of helping you out of your demon circus. But you will not receive help, Mary. You know everything best. You don't need my help, you believe. When you ask for advice and I tell you what to do, you seem annoyed at me—because you know everything better. Never forget, we walked the Jesus Trail together in Israel back then,' the bogus Jesus enjoys saying that. At one point, Drake already had made me lose all my good faith in Christ, and it traumatised and devastated me. I still have a hard time getting back to my faith.

'I do not understand what you're saying, Drake.' I got petrified and insecure, so I didn't dare leave him, so maybe it was good I left alone, because his upsetting stuff scared me.

'When I gave my suggestions on how to run the cottage project with Nombnots and Mr Fabulous, you took over and pushed me aside. There was no need for me. Because of respectful manners and kindness, I remained quiet. Your behaviour did not pass them.' I sense it was embarrassing for Captain Awesome.

Personally, I had seen Drake furious but never violent. He could be quick-tempered if something didn't work, often concerning business. The fella never physically harmed me and gave me also many caring and stunning days in between the madness. But he is extraordinarily manipulative—a psychologically violent person, which is worse for me than if he was beating me up. The beating I can handle one time and leave a man promptly, but I couldn't escape his psychic terror. It was like living with a disturbed, handsome, and charming lunatic, like Ted Bundy or John Meehan. They used people—victims who couldn't figure out what was happening to them before it was too late. The problem must be you, Mary, I often thought. Am I the 'demonic psychopath and not Drake? A hairy thought! How frightening.

'Why are we having this discussion, darling?'

'I've been your best friend—I dare say. Your only actual friend.'

'My opinion also counts. It was my money you gambled with.'

'I'm not the ugly person you want to make me out to be when you think mean thoughts about me.' I grasp I was living with a self-absorbed sociopath.

Naive—that's what people say about me. No! I'm a vulnerable, trusting woman who loves too much. A sociopath uses this, and controls and abuses people. Everything is for his advantage—to get as much as he can. The charming prince Drake knows I have a heart of goodness and have unlimited trust in him. Even when he came up with the many disturbing grim stories about my family, when he with drama told me or others how horrible my childhood was. How horrifying and painful as the living at the German orphanage was; *well chap, I know, I was there!* I knew only a little of such people as Drake. Will I find out, what I further can expect from him?

'Is that why you dumped me. Drake, honestly? On a piece of paper?'

'I wanted to start my clinic project quickly. Frankly, I'm fallen way behind financially for the last four years.'

'Why did you then stay with me? You should have told me what your desire were?'

'You cannot say that my saving has grown thru our time. I saved a little. I will start a company in Holland, together with Nombnots.'

'You wanted to have a lucky life in Asia with me.' I grasp that this fatal decision isolated me from family and friends and was far away from my secure haven.

The hidden, cynical side of the shadowy part slowly came to the surface. Drake had managed me by fear, and knew it scared me, so I didn't dare to tell him the truth of his behaviour. Instead, I kept all this fear-based performance and his rotten fraudulent secrets to myself. One day I'll have all the ultimate pieces of evidence I needed to prove to myself that he is the wicked person, not me! I need to be strong enough to forget him before I lose myself to insanity. But it's hard. Will I be able to do so?

'Mary, you needed my hands to help you. I became steadfast by your side to the last. I devoted my time to you. I never understood the rule for getting our bond in balance where we were equally worthy.'

'Yea, yea, whatever, darling. Will you come to Croatia later or what?'

'Let's see. You brought *everything* with you—paintings, furniture, and valuable jewellery. It must make you happy, Mary. You got a clinic that must give you a satisfaction. You reached the shelf where you have never been. You are the monarch in your own Mary paradise.'

I don't grasp what you're talking about.'

'You don't have financial problems. You can relax in your lovely palace on the mountain with the pretty views.'

'You sound jealous.' And he forgets that from the beginning it was a never-ending money story with him. I always gave him whatever he wanted and as the unwise girl I paid for our entire lifestyle—business and private trips and vacations at exclusive hotels. Nothing under five stars was good enough for the chap. All flights were at least business class—even better if he could fly first class. Did he have money for such an extravagant lifestyle? No, no, no! The dude was totally broke! He needed my money and now he sounds massively jealous.

'What about the arrangement with Zjarko?'

'I pass the Farming project with Zjarko on to Nombnots. I feel that the goat people in the mountains should not think I'm untrustworthy because nothing happens.'

'Whoa! Okay, meaning you step out of the project?'

'Yes, Mary! I'm free to build clinics. I can't build my business when I'm being blamed. I can't concentrate. I can't flourish as I used to. Therefore, it's best that I build this alone. It will be good. I expect a lot. I hope you know I'm doing this to succeed. I need to focus on myself.'

'I will always miss you. Feel pain in my heart over losing what I loved most in the world—you!' Grasping everything always has been too good to be true. Despite the awareness and warnings from others, I wanted to believe the best in him. I can't deny Drake had wonderful and caring parts behind his many lies and mean unscrupulous behaviour.

I believed I'd found someone to trust, someone who could love me and who respected me for whom I was. From the depths of my kind, Christian heart, I forgave him many times for his sins, believing he could change for the better. Even when I the first time noticed warning signs in our relationship and got the feeling to gather evidence which I kept in secret on a memory stick. *This could be useful someday,* I thought. Why? I didn't know! But now I'm obsessed with the research of finding the truth, hoping that the suspicious findings can make many things clearer.

'Mary, I can't give you everything, so it must be nothing. Let what we have done for each other be the proof we carry on in friendly spirit. There is no need to crush each other. Nor use sneering and ugly remarks. It only hurts worse. I hope that we can be friends.'

'Fine. Take care, Drake. Live a carefree life. Good luck.' I slam the lid on my Mac and cry.

*　　*　　*

I'll not give up on my fresh life in Croatia, so I accept doing it without Drake. I get more knowledge and spend oceans of time on courses, congresses, and conferences worldwide. I gain skills in specialties and my clinic works because Zjarko helps to find patients and he has a lot of contacts in Croatia, Serbia and Montenegro. My confidence gets partially restored, but it's sometimes difficult to maintain morale. Though I get much support from many new friends, Helena and Maki assistance wherever they can help. Maki is a local tour guide and Helena often assists me with translation when I have patients.

Numerous times they've taken me on stunning tours in Croatia and Montenegro. In September when the weather was perfect, as the sun shines, the flowers bloom, we went to the Ostrog Monastery, to enjoy the fresh mountain air. 200 kilometres from the Croatian border, passing the Capital Podgorica ending up close by Nikšić and enjoy the Serbian Orthodox Church from the 17th century, situated against an almost vertical background high up in the mountains Ostroška Greda.

The most popular pilgrimage region in Montenegro, a picturesque Church with its many frescoes, painted at the end of the 17ᵗʰ Century. Ostrog is one of the most revered religious sites in all the former Yugoslav states and visited by up to a million tourists and pilgrims every year. It's built right into a sheer cliff face way above the plains below, where you can see the white building shining as a beacon against the dark rock, having the upper monastery in the cliff and the lower monastery 3 kilometres below. It's a site of worship founded by St Basil, or Vasilije as he's known here, born in 1610 in Herzegovina which was then part of the Muslim Turkish Ottoman Empire. Later St Basil reluctantly accepted the position of Bishop of Zahumlje and Skenderija, until the Turks attacked and destroyed it, then he moved to Ostrog.

St Basil started with three caves in the rock face, then decided to build the Church of the Presentation in the first cave and added a house for monks and wheat milling in the lower monastery. At the age of 61 he died, and 7 years later the abbot of St Luke Monastery had a dream about St Basil. They open his grave and St Basil body was perfectly preserved and smelled of basil. They took him to the upper monastery, to the Church of the Presentation, where St Basil still lies to this day. You'll be ushered into a very small room where the relics are watched over by a monk, who almost looked as a waxwork of a famous and historical figure from Madame Tussaud in London. As we passed by the relics and kissed the cross (only if you wish), I went backwards out, and noticed the monk was blinking. It's common here to see people get out backwards, clearly instructed by Helena and Maki how to do everything.

'Jeez, Maki, I got spoked. He looks like a wax from Madame Tussauds. Is the monk really alive?'

'Yes, Mary, he is.' Maki laughs at me and we continue to the next destination.

On our way back we pass the manmade Slano Lake (Salt Lake), from 1950 near Nikšić. The lake covers an area of nine square kilometres, surrounded by up to 200 meters high black mountains with the result of the Perućica hydroelectric power plant from 1960. Three big lakes emerged in the result of the flooding of several small ponds connected by channels with its numerous small islands. It's as the Caribbean clear blue to turquoise bright waters, with a spectacular sight you will never forget.

During the heavy autumn rains, large amounts of water flows from the surrounding mountain slopes and then it is possible to watch the beautiful smaller or larger waterfalls, creating surrealistic picturesque images with its wild beauty, a multitude of plant and animal species, in an unspoilt nature with a lake rich in fish.

During my many trips with Helena and Maki I realise how this Adriatic gem, is one of the most scenic countries I ever have seen in my life, and its heartfelt natives.

For six months, Drake and I don't talk, and unexpectedly it dings on my computer, a Skype call from him seeking to make amends.

'I've been thinking a lot about how we can move forward.'

'Okay?' I say frosty.

'I thought of this opportunity. Let's wash the blackboard clean. Start a new beginning.'

'What do you mean, Drake?'

'Let's pretend we don't know each other—or that we only know each other's good, wise, and loving sides. Let's have no past. No cruel baggage. No skeletons in the cupboards.'

'I thought we had tried several times before, Drake. And without being good enough to forget old muck and skeletons.'

'We'll build a new relationship. Of confidence leading to positive love.'

'Hmm ... It will also require you to reset yourself.' Damn, my heart begins to beat fast.

'You are such a gorgeous, loyal, and lovely woman. I miss your lovely warm smile, Baby. You only want the best for those you love. Including me.' Then his Bambi trick, blinks and smiles.

'I often tried to forgive, you Drake. And be kind towards you. We must be two people doing the same. It goes both ways.'

'I want you to take a coach training. Baby, to give you the tools to get rid of your self-effacing manners. It will give you strength. Bring out your rare facts. To feel good. To be in balance must be the goal of a long-life effort.'

'Hm-mmm...' I mumble, am I about to fall for his charm again?

'Babe, I worked hard through a long life with lots of success. I've made terrible decisions, through which I lost not only money but also my children. If you do your best, then you can find your way back to me. Do you think you can do this?' His voice sounds mild.

'I know I can do it, Drake. But why is it me who must find the way back to *you*?'

'If you can do this yourself, I'm willing to do my part. We could meet at the conference in Vienna. I'd want to meet you.'

'Okay, fine. I'd want to meet you there.' Happily, we disconnect— unwisely, I let him come into my life again. I plunged flat into his trap again, having an on-and-off long-distance relationship, which lasted too long. During many days in Vienna, he is kind, and then the million-dollar question lands as lightning from a clear sky during a romantic dinner on the table.

'Hey, sweet Baby.' First chitchatting a little, then he drops the question. 'Can you lend me $65,000 for my project in Holland?' Has he dropped his head in the sea?

'Sorry darling, I'm broke.' Smiling, I glance at Drake, waiting for his reaction.

'You lie! I know how much money you have, Mary. What a peculiar way of loving me.' My jaw drops to the floor.

'I know it annoys you,' I smile.

'You only take advantage of me to get knowledge,' he shouts, furious at my flat-out refusal.

'You're forgiven for your outburst.' I meet his gaze and hold on to my no. My red wine glass is half full, then I lift it up for a cheer.

'You can't spend your wealth before you die anyway,' he protests. 'You might as well help me, Mary. I've helped you with an education. You didn't pay a damn for it.' He angers. That's Drake's opinion! Whoa! He is so wrong.

As a trusting woman I had often felt a chilling pressure from him to pay, and before I didn't dare say no or stop! Not that I minded helping or lending him money—it was okay *to a point*. But the snake scrupulously had dumped me, so I ended up saying cheerio to every loan I gave him. Bye-bye, baby; to money I'd never see again!

Headless, I had invested in too many fraudulent projects, so I could only blame myself for not taking proper precautions. I had realised too late that the shifty handsome dandy boy had tricked me big time! The snake saved the money for himself, including a lot of what he had received from my divorce settlement. When I found out he also stole half of the cash, in Iran and those from Samir; I became suspicious. We kept everything in a safe-deposit box, which made it easy for him to steal, because only he knew the code. He became furious with me when I wanted half of the dough, because the bloke believed all the smelly, dirty cash belonged to him.

Then the dragon boy threatened to leave me when the princess doubted his fancy words and business affairs. The punishment fell over me with posh words and hateful letters, as the latest on I still have in my memory. It was my biggest fear; Drake leaving me.

Despite the dude ruins the rest of the evening, again, I forgive him.

* * *

We are not living together, but we meet around the world, including Drake visits me in Croatia. We meet few times in Holland, in London and spend a romantic holiday in the Caribbean, then travel to South Asia and the United Arab Emirates. Every time, he is charming. I trust him and get gripped by him again, without seeing the wolf in sheep's clothing.

During our trip to Qatar we get a perfect offer to buy a treatment machine, though Drake has no money.

'Can't you pay the $15,000 for the machine,' he asks, 'as a loan to me? When I get the money, I'll pay you back.' He smiles lovingly.

'Um-hmm ... I don't know. Only if we accredit the equipment in my name.'

'No problem.' He agrees 'We can store it with Arshia and Mufasa in Qatar. I will use it to treat them. Also, their family and friends.'

I accept the deal, because I want to help Arshia and Mufasa with treatment, so I transfer the money and get my paper, saying Mary owns the equipment. After we left, Drake returns to Qatar.

'Mary, we want you to know, that Drake has removed the machine several times from our home.' Arshia and Mufasa tell me.

'Huh? Why?'

'He tried to sell it behind your back.'

'Best to send the device to Sweden. I need it there to treat some of his family.' And Arshia helps me to ship the equipment. Shortly after I visit the family one week together with Drake and of the sudden he starts a massive fight.

'Bloody hell, Mary. The machine doesn't belong to you?' He shouts.

'What? Oh, boy! It's not yours, Drake. I paid for it. The invoice is in my name.' But he keeps on yelling at me, so I give up the fight.

Everything dies, I died emotionally and in the middle of the night I load the gear in my car, drive off in the darkness through pouring rain at 3 a.m. as a run-away, until I end up at my storage in Copenhagen, five hours later. Exhausted, the unit gets unloaded, I drive to the Airport Hotel, book a room, and sleep for the rest of the day. Not one moment I feel bad and fly back to Croatia and cold as an ice queen I cut off the contact with Drake.

CHAPTER 38

NOMBNOTS, CAPTAIN AWESOME AND MARY IN COURT

> In matters if conscience the law of majority has no effect.
> —Mahatma Gandhi

Unexpectedly, many months later, I get unwillingly dragged into a lawsuit between Drake and Nombnots (Steven Jansen). I never get peace as the dude is a constant nuisance ghost on my back.

Which of them has stolen the equipment I paid for? This is the question at hand and the case ends in massive chaos, when I claim to the court that the equipment belongs to me.

As the case emerges, it comes clear that both Drake and Steven want me to take their side. I'm trapped in the middle. First, I help Steven. Next, Drake denies everything Steven said. Suddenly in court it comes to the surface of an arrest warrant for Drake in the United States.

Everything goes haywire and Drake denies my claim. The guy lied about everything, and it was always someone else's fault, or they lied. He had denied his married life, and later he *confirmed* his married life and wanted a divorce! The situation was confusing. Now he lied about the Arrest Warrant, and it was still valid because Detectives were searching for Drake in the States! I'm sure that was what the Detectives were doing in The Philippines as well! That's where I grasp why Drake couldn't fly over Miami, during our trip to The Bahamas.

Let me tell you some small fragments of his massive fraud and nasty behaviour, about what he has told Steven of scandalous false stories about me.

'Do I understand correctly that Drake flirted with Casandra?' I ask Steven, surprised.

'Not by touching my wife. But verbally. He always brought sex into the equation.'

'So, he has been trying on Casandra?' losing my courage over the revolting answers.

'Drake was in-appropriate excited about his idea of treating vulvodynia,' (chronic pain or discomfort around the opening of a vagina).

'Oh, my God. He was so fixated of studying pussy's while we were in The Philippines.

'Drake pressed hard to get Casandra to accept it as a treatment idea. But she refused. He also said you were his little whore.'

'What?'

My feelings for the devious rat burst into a thousand pieces. I can no longer cope with Drake, and it's hard to imagine a human can be so evil, and tell smutty lies, and brew stories of tragic experiences in my life.

'At the London expo, Drake explained that your aggressive reaction was because you were jealous of Casandra.'

'Huh? What rubbish is that? The person you love most will hurt you most. He has shown with sickening statements that he is not who I really thought he was.'

'He claimed you were mentally unstable. That you had not taken your medicine that day.

'Oh my God! I'm slowly learning that Drake is not good for me.'

'He said you were on many psychotic medications. You smoked hash with him.'

'Huh? How can he smoke hash with me? He doesn't smoke. It must blob in his head.'

'Drake couldn't stand the thought of always smoking that shit. That's why, he would not be with you. He claimed you became as a zombie taking psychotic pills together with the pot.'

'Eh? Has Drake been smoking pot? Gee ... Such crazy stories popping up in his stupid mind.'

'Mary, I don't know, with him. You also wanted to force him into bizarre sex.'

'I'm traumatised, Steven! What an imagination.'

'It was the only thing that could turn you on. Someone has to be harsh and abuse you—bondage and that kind of stuff.'

'Oh, my! Sick idiot!' Our relationship got killed by Drake's hidden benefits. Inappropriate behaviour. Ego, attitude, and ignorance. Then he spiced it up with some extra salt and pepper to make the story more interesting. How would Steven otherwise know about it?

'Drake claimed your bizarre sex dreams were why he didn't want to screw you. He wasn't that type. His fantasy was to get into your daughter's pants. Sandra, is it? Right?' It tremors Steven when he tells me the narrative.

'Yuck! How sickening! An evil shadow lies over Drake's false smile. Nobody is real in this world.' I'm furious as an unstoppable hurricane.

'The condition for screwing Sandra, was that she was not as destroyed as her mother.'

'Drake is not right in his head. Yikes, it's revolting.'

'At least Sandra's husband didn't use her as a sex slave for his business relations. Well, that's what Drake alleges Paul did to you.'

I wanted to throw up! 'Huh? Such a thing can only come from an injured, weak, and sick person as Drake. What did I do wrong to him?' There will always be people who mistreat you. Drake did so to me. I better thank him for making me strong enough to get rid of him.

'Oh, yea, he said you were a broken woman with too much money. And being with you was convenient for him. Although, you were a disgusting woman. The easiest victim to lure money from. "It's as stealing lollipops from a stupid little child called *Mary*," he said.' To describe letting me pay for everything. I realised I had paid for my birthday present in The Philippines, because I *never* saw the money again.

'What? I was weak. And hurt when I put my love in his hands. Now I'm extra hurt by his evil words. But I'm no longer weak. I've grown strong again.'

'Drake has no qualms about it. He said, "Mary is a miserable little child. I must help; she needs me. Only I can save her from evil. Man, then it's so easy to cheat and steal from her." Mary, I tell you, it outraged me! He told, "Mary only wants to hurt me by any means." Jeez, the dude couldn't get enough of hearing himself talk. It was sickening listening to him.'

'My realisation of his sick imagination made me strong. You cannot trust him.'

'According to Drake, you profile yourself as knowledgeable in his subject. "Mary has no education. She uses quotes from others outside context without she can understand them." He told me.'

'I can only blame myself for being trapped in the madness of love. He had arms made of rugged solid steel. Damn, it was impossible to escape out of his firm grip.'

'He said. "Mary desperately followed me to learn my subjects." With pity, he allowed you to attend courses where he taught others. But you were so stupid that you couldn't understand anything. Even at the lowest level.'

'Whoa! Stupid perhaps. I should never have sacrificed my family, heart and dignity for him. Such a sociopathic deceitful sleazeball. There were too many red flags I didn't see.'

'Drake told me, "Jeez, that bitch has been pursuing me since I wanted to let go of her." However, you insisted in being a part of his business. All of him. He got totally worn out.'

'What? You gotta be kidding?'

'No! Drake said. "Finally, I got rid of the nitwit. Now I can start over again." Yea, you know, Mary, here in Holland with me. But you continued to harass him, he claimed. It was a big distraction that he would like to be besides.'

'This is crazy ... crazy ... Steven. I'm dumbfounded.'

'There's not much more. Yea, well the rest you know. The machine you paid for, yea, puff! Gone! Into outer space! Strange! Biggest mystery in my life.'

'Oh, my goodness. Let's keep in contact. I must leave. Bye Steven.'

Drake's negativity shows the story between the lines—that he wanted to take everything from me and was only for him to gain. Deep inside, he's not interested in me but in the *funds*. That it took me too many years to see through his entire scary scenarios—that I was not wiser back then—makes me sad. What was behind the gloomy shadow of Doctor Bates?

I side with Steven and confront Drake. He has a damaged mind and is weak, as a fragile clay pot that needs riveted together by a psychologist. In his case, though, I think it's hard to fix something that's as sick as him. I call him on Skype.

'Hi Drake. We must talk. I hear you're spreading lies about me. And my marriage.'

'Such accusation is the most incredible thing coming from you. You are out of control, Mary. Unruly and tell that everyone is saying terrible things about you.' He angers. 'You broke my spirit. I try to get on. Then you reappear as a jack-in-the-box.'

'It's not okay, Drake. I hear awful stuff from Steven—what you proudly tell about me.'

'I have heard nothing like it. Everything instantly turns to something nasty.'

'Huh? Idiot!'

'You show every sign of being a psychopath. You need help, Mary. You are at risk of hurting yourself. And others.'

'How can you tell Steven, that Paul has sold me as a prostitute to his business associates.' I get pissed when he accuses me of being a psychopath.

'Such things can only come from your new best friend Nombnots (Steven), so he has some juicy gossip about me. You are preposterous! It's hard to understand that there is such a nasty human being on earth. You were also the same with Paul. That's obviously your style, Mary.' His eyes are on fire.

'Honestly, Drake? Telling Steven, I was taking narcotics to endure Paul's beatings and sexual penalties? You're not right in your head.'

'Nombnots speaks untruths. He commits perjury to the court. And you. Suddenly, he pulls out a lot of papers in court, he got from you. The majority was about downgrading me.'

'Bullshit. Steven said I asked you to give me bizarre sexual escapades in our relationship.'

'This is a case of fraud you are committing against me. It's beyond imagination that I should listen to these accusations coming from you—that I'm not right in the head. You will do anything to destroy me, Mary. Come up with imprudent fictions. I was trying to be good and help you. You're lying! Not me! It's too much.'

'You told I exploited and harassed you. That I paid nothing for your living?'

'Bloody hell, Mary! You mean you own *my* machine because you paid few of the leasing's. I paid every penny back to you—even though you promised to pay. I helped you with the divorce. You fully forgot of that. Argh, you're so fixated on money.' He growls.

'I claimed the equipment I paid for. Now that it's come to a court case between you and Nombnots. Then you accuse each other of theft of the device.'

'Why must I still face claims I owe you money? And the device? I thought we had forgotten of it. Instead, you talk to Nombnots about it. In your endless evil, you send in a bunch of wild reports. Then side with Nombnots. And lie about me.'

'What? I don't get it, Drake.'

'I lent you some equipment. You're a thief, Mary. You will not give it back. I imagine you use it in your clinic.' He rages.

'Huh? I've stolen noting from you. You lent it to me. Why do you proudly share with Steven that you only wanted to use me financially?'

'I have a hard time swallowing your lies. I'm afraid that you have told your fraudulent stories to the rest of my family. You're guilty of ruining my relationship with them.' Lines of anger puckered his forehead.

'Come on. Baloney! Proudly you told Steven that I was an easy victim.'

'Bullshit! If for once you realise that you are not right to be hurting me. If you have any respect for yourself, Mary, and others, then deny what you said about me, to Nombnots. Say, that you wrote everything in a fit of bad temper. Withdraw your claim. Say that your claim is flawed. Not true. I demand you.' His tone is very strict.

'About what?' I just sit and stare at him, dumbfounded.

'Say that Steven used it as a strategy to steal the equipment from me. That Steven stole the device. That you don't make any claim on *my* machine. That I have long since repaid you. Therefore, no case on your part against me. That the case does not concern you. Tell Steven Jansen all has been erroneous and taken out of context. That it was him who contacted you to get information. That everything he has told you has turned out to be falsehood and lies. Only for him to make incoherent statements. And for the purpose of degrading me. The consequence of violating your desire, Mary would then cause a lawsuit for defamation under both Scandinavian and international law.'

My intuitive tells me it's wrong if I give in to his command.

'Huh? Why so dramatic, Drake? Where the hell does these ideas come from?'

'It could hurt me using your lies out of context. I bet you don't want to do it. It will probably be a hard pill for you to swallow, Mary. You are so afraid to admit when you speak untruth.'

'I will consider it—if we can agree on things wisely. Not keep throwing mud at each other. In peace and tolerance. Do you get it Drake? I'm unhappy with everything that has happened.'

'No one should be able to use the info you have provided. There can be no mix-up if they misuse your information.'

'You must live the rest of your life knowing that you deceived me worse than anyone does to an enemy. Don't threaten me, Mary. Don't go on with your attacks on me. I don't care about your lawsuits. And give me back my things.'

'Yea, yea, fine.' Deep down I knew that it's wrong of me.

'I want us to draw a line in the sand. I want to come to an understanding of respect for each other.'

'I'll soon be in Holland for few days. Then you can get back the wanted effects.'

'Don't contact me or my family again. We want to get rid of you. None of us got ever treated so cruelly by anyone before. We want it to end now, Mary! I'll delete every future email. And deny calls from you! I will never contact you again! I can't trust you. Signing *out*!'

'Don't you want your things? We can meet alone on a neutral ground in Amsterdam. I don't want any disagreements with you.' I hurry to say in panic.

'I want a clarification between us. Once and for all.' He smirks.

'We'll close this issue about your treatment head. Jeez, which you believe I've kept. Then I will no longer contact you, Drake. At your own choice.' I wanted to disconnect but stayed calm.

'Your handling of my case against Nombnots has made my life difficult.'

'I did not ask for any additional negative allegations from you. It disappoints me. I tried to reach out a hand towards settlement and exchange. As for you and Nombnots, I don't want to get bothered hearing more from you or him about the case. Handle it yourself. I believe it's sad our relationship ended in such a dull way. I need peace, Drake. I wish you the best of luck.'

'Okay. I want to meet you. Bring the jewels I gave you too. I want them back.'

'What? Oh, my God! Maybe you think it's normal to return gifts. Drake, I don't think it's normal. Had I known you would reclaim it; I would never have spent thousands of dollars to repair the one piece of defective jewellery you gave me. You will get your effects. Don't bother to repay me. I did it in good faith because you promised to give it to Rosalyn later.'

'I can also bring my swim shorts, underwear, T-shirts, and shirts you bought for me. You'll get them back too, Mary.' He ridiculously says.

'Geez! Throw them out! Give them to the Red Cross or Salvation Army. Do you imagine I should walk around in your worn-out underwear? This must be a joke!'

'The bathing suits I'll leave, since you do not want them back. Underwear and shirts are approaching retirement. I must buy new ones. However, they must last if they can.'

'You sound as a poor church rat, Drake.' I smile.

'Where is the neutral spot we should meet? And when? It must be a civilised meeting. Without bad temper or intrigue, Mary. I want to live in peace—without chest pressure or stress.'

'I'll let you know. I need peace so I can smooth my bumpy heartbeats and chest pain. Don't worry about that. I wanted not to tell you. Now you know.'

'I got enough pressure to absorb. I was stupid to invest in Nombnots and Holland. More holes in the cheese have shown themselves. It's not so hard to see through it and understand what the truth looks like. I have done everything with such an investment to protect myself.'

'I'm sad that I've apparently only been one of the women in the line. And you feel that I have ill-used you, Drake.'

'You can't protect yourself from psychopaths and pathological liars. You must look at them completely before engaging with them. Do you get it, Mary? I must leave now.'

'Take care of yourself.'

I'm speechless. It must be a joke! He has lost his marbles. Meanwhile, the case drags on, and suddenly he contacts me again.

'Baby, I have thought about everything.'

'Yea. What?'

'If you make the claim on the machine, you can give it back to me afterwards. Baby, it's a splendid idea.'

'I have no interest in the device, Drake.' However, he sways me to be on his side.

We met four days before the upcoming court case, to look through all the documents. It's the worst decision I made.

A weird question pops up from Drake, while we were in bed after he has played the violin on my pussy and before we will go to court the day after.

'Baby, do you feel like I'm taking advantage of you?'

'Huh? It's a weird question to ask, seconds after you've given me an orgasm. Are you? Is that the case? I hope you're not!'

His silence confirms that he is more than words.

After the trial, I scold Steven and leave Drake alone in front of the courthouse. I am mentally exhausted from fighting the parties in a case I didn't want. I give up and withdraw from everything. Drake can keep the entire pile of shit for himself.

Things didn't turn out as Drake wanted in Holland, because the authorities were after him for his illegal practices. Suddenly he wanted to move to Croatia. I didn't want him there. It must be as a whirlwind spinning in his reckless head, when he is on one of his storm-tossed rides while he smokes pot. One moment, the dragon boy can use me and the next moment, I'm a hopelessly selfish person in his eyes. He loves me, then he hates me. Then I'm the best and most skilled therapist he has known and the week after, I never learned or understood a damn thing.

The nincompoop accused me of being a stupid and hateful thief— said that I was a lying, selfish, and a mentally unstable person who needed psychological help. I was only good enough when jerk needed borrowing money or wanted me to pay his invoices.

Gradually it became a grim task for me to trust him. I found that arguing with a liar was impossible, because he sincerely believed in his own lies. I would never win a discussion with such a moron, because he's a factual Jekyll and Hyde, and he did not stop accusing me of grim things.

'Why the hell did you report me to the taxman for fraud?' the chump screams on Skype.

'I do not understand what you are talking of,' I assure him.

His unscrupulous behaviour continues as the retard smears me further. 'The taxman contacted me. You are a damn cursed bitch. An evil manipulative lying person. You have a one-track mind, Mary. Now

I understand why your family doesn't want to have anything to do with you.' He snarls.

I'm dumbfounded. Oddly enough, the peabrain doesn't accuse me of being an unfaithful and slovenly *old* bitch or say that I had thighs full of cellulite. Got flappy grandmother's arms, and disgusting wrinkles on my face—of which Drake said about Kate. Otherwise, he gives me the entire negative language register he can come up with. He uses the same phrases when I heard the jackass talk of Kate, Maria, Laila, or other acquaintances, with his ugliness and negativity. I could vomit.

'You will be the last woman I ever will be together with, Mary.'

'Ha-ha, you live alone.'

'I'd rather live alone than with a hysterical chick.' I gaze at the meathead curiously, trying to understand where this is coming from.

'Do you want me to believe that?' I am right to question him. I can't count on one hand how many other women there came after me. Busy *poor lonely* chap.

The scumbag is out of his senses and not normal! I'd hope Drake will never speak like this of me. But the muttonhead did!

I'm lying broken in the gutter, as a wounded animal, as if Drake shot me with evilness many times in my heart. Yet, I keep crying and weeping inside my soul for his love in my loneliness. I must be crazy. What is it I miss about him?

I make a list of two columns—*evil* and *great* things about him. The list is massive on the *evil* side. Only few things stand in the *great* column—his tender hands on my body and his fingers on my delicate flower to give me multiple orgasms. That's it!

*   *   *

I hire two private detectives for the case and spend oceans of time on research into Drake.

A sudden warning comes to my attention during my detailed research, as the findings related to the dishonest business. One clue that tipped me off was the dishonest business schemes. Was it a lie about the arrest warrant and his professional experience? Was he an inveterate liar, a perfect predator? Was I the prey. My suspicious findings made many things clearer to me. The truth is gruesome! It was always someone else's fault; however, it was Drake who was Wanted in USA, not me.

At first, I didn't know much of psychopaths but figured out what I could expect from such people. I thought such people never showed empathy for others, and it was all a game them, when people fall victim to such horrifying psychological abuse. It's as being a chased Hitchcock character in a horrifying movie. They are that talented and memorise all their lines, so they can win awards for their incredible performances.

Am I having a shabby diploma from a crock of doo-doo? Not valid! Worthless garbage! So why have I wasted my time being his student? The alleged education was worth nothing—never recognised in any public health organisation. I was fooled, and it's upsetting with these lies. I might as well have continued my education elsewhere then used the energy and efforts for something more serious, instead of such motley worthless crap, I can't use for nothing.

With this too-late knowledge, I began to get more suspicious and continued researching.

I begin to grasp how the puzzle pieces of his sick dreams and manipulation fit, when Drake's falsely sweet, and next, he's evil in between. Then he wants to make me feel as a cool woman, and I give *him* what *he* wants, and he's happy again. During my time with him, I'm "lucky", ironically, to receive over thirty abnormal types of his murky scamming projects.

I find, he was earlier charged with quackery at his clinic. That he owes lots of money to the taxman in the United States and has committed fraud against several business associates, women, and banks, as using the names of others, to set up his shady business. I found some of the judgements from many years back. Here is two of them:

> It is adjudged that Plaintiff Kate West shall recover from
> Defendant, Drake Lucifer Bates, the sum of $300,000 as
> damage for fraud, conversion, and breach of contract that
> shall bear interest at the rate of 10 percent per year, for all of

which let execution issue forthwith. Ordered in Washington County.

Defendant Drake Lucifer Bates is now in default, it is hereby ordered, adjudged, and decreed that the plaintiff City Bank shall have judgement against defendant Drake Lucifer Bates by default in the amount of $300,000, plus attorney's fee of $25,000, plus per diem interest at a rate of $20 since February 1996 through the date hereof. It is so ordered in Los Angeles County.

It is one horrendous discovery after the next. I can't believe the United States has an arrest warrant out on him, a detail that has come to my attention too late. I realise it was the police who tried to find him while we were in The Philippines. But he smartly covered up by telling me several lies, explaining it was because of others, who'd stolen his patents on several inventions, (he didn't have) so they had defrauded Drake.

'The case is important, so I must help them.' He said, and I believed him but discovered too late it was one more *lie on top of the massive pot of lies.* He was always the *victim.* It was always others who stole from him and not the reverse.

After the arrest warrant came to surface in the recent court case, the villain Doctor Drake Lucifer Bates changed his name to Doctor Luke Samael Schmidt.

CHAPTER 39

Sixteen, Soft Clay Moulded To Broken Pottery

And once the storm is over, you won't remember how you
made it through, how you managed to survive. You won't
even be sure, whether the storm is really over. But one thing
is certain. When you come out of the storm, you won't be
the same person who walked in. That's what this storm's all
about.

—Haruki Murakami

The storm of the horizon has worn out, and the end of the
beginning becomes an end. It's a scorching summer morning
on the southern coast of England, when I wake up in my new
apartment, I realise the past is a simple illusion. The past is getting to
an end, then live in the present and enjoy what the future will bring.

I gaze in the mirror, then spot many worried wrinkles around my
eyes that make them look sad. My appearance is that of a hung cat
and my lips hang as a sour mule on a donkey, lacking a radiant smile.
My hair is unkempt, and I lack nice make-up on my face, because
vulnerability and self-pity have ruled my life. The nights feel endlessly
gloomy in my mind, so I can't sleep.

Get control of your life again, Mary. Damn! It so awfully difficult. I'm filled with pain and my heart pounds as wild bongo drums, day and night, while the tinnitus rings maddeningly in my ears. I'm a mess.

There stand moving boxes abound in every room and I mostly wish to throw the entire pile of shit into the sea. But I will not let Drake steer me to a downfall.

Through the weeks, I unpack most of it. Oh, my goodness! I empty over two hundred boxes.

A picture of Drake appears. *What did I find out about the past with him?* I philosophies, gazing at it.

I took this in the beginning, when I was as a soft crying lump of clay in his hand. He moulded me only to end up as a piece of fragile pottery shattered to pieces in his hands. In and out of shape, he moulded me, a soft delicate lump of clay in his tender hands. He found the clay when it was most unhappy.'

I imagine it in my head, that the excited ceramicist sits at the turning lathe, thinking, *how should he shape the soft lump of clay in my favour?* Quietly, he sits with his magic hands on the soft lump and builds it up, and when viewing at the creation. He decides, *Hm-mmm. No, it's not good enough!* Hard he punches the lump to a flat mass and starts all over again, this time making a unique creation. *Damn*, he reflects. *It's still not good enough!* He bangs harder on the clay and starts over again, and does it repeatedly, then gets furious, grinds the clay, and rebuilds it.

Ultimately, he becomes satisfied, but the lump of crying clay gets confused, believing the ceramicist wants what's best. He has created and shaped the clay according to his will, so it can decorate his pedestal perfectly. When he thinks the creation is a perfect bowl, he puts it in the oven and burns a *Burning Desire* into it. The blaze between them is flaming, so he gets to know everything about his recent creation. The ceramist guards and encloses it with tenderness, love, and understanding in the beginning, then gazes lovingly at the stunning pottery.

The ceramist finds the faint cracks in the burned bowl and the strong edges that hold it all together. Then he sees the sickness and the healthy part, and finds the love in his clay lump, now a ravishing bowl, and the weak pottery becomes a reality. She finds a total immersion in her creator, as his hands continue trying to shape the soft lump of clay. He finds out that the pottery gets obsessed with a passionate desire for him and the soft clay has full confidence in his tender hands. Before he has fully formed the clay, he knows all about the awful cuts that lay in his hands.

I was as a soft lump of clay in his hands and was ready for him to shape me in the hope of a better life. I surrendered to his gentle hands, for so long indulgent towards my dear ceramicist. He could mould me according to his desire to have a perfect woman, without my fears and reservations. I would fill him with love, warmth, and care and give him a financially secured life. I only wanted him to fill me with everything good from him—with honest love, because I praised his wisdom, goodness, and love. I worshiped him because he listened to me, and I was thankful for his understanding. For my God. And for my Catholic faith.'

Something didn't add up though! Was it for me or only for himself that he moulded me? For a brief time, it created peace and security around me, when he took everything into his embrace—the hurting and weakened part of me. Surrendering, I lay down in the fragile bowl of pottery. In his eyes, though, it wasn't yet proper shaped into what he wanted me to become. I wasn't proper moulded according to his imagination. As the creator, he told the outside world he had scored a big win, when I had put everything in his trusting hands.

Now the fragile pottery no longer embellishes the pedestal. He crushed it into a thousand pieces and threw it in the trash. Crushed, it lies with all the other drop-dead-gorgeous, broken pottery he created, because none of them was good enough for the desire he possessed. He only wants a perfect bowl, filled with gold and diamonds.

*   *   *

It began in Spain, when we entered the honeymoon phase, before the love story ended with a tumultuous bang of a break-up. The past life with Drake began in good and evil, and it was doomed to be the end before it began. Four years after, he dumped me with his spiteful letter before I left for Croatia. You might think; *Oh, my God! She must be naïve and unwise.* That's okay. Despite everything, you don't know me, but I hope you will understand more after you have read both parts of the story. At the end of our relationship, he has another woman, though he denies it, and lovingly, he keeps on telling me I'm his chosen one, so why is he not done with me? I still have something he wants from me, so he tries to squeeze the last drop of blood from my veins, after I've moved to England during that summer. He wants my equipment and realises I've put it for sale, so he is interested, and announces he is coming to England for another business matter, arriving at my place.

In good faith, I think it's okay if Drake buys the equipment, but he will only get it when all the money is in my bank account. Out of the goodness of my heart, I let him stay with me when he kindly asks for few days of accommodation, because he wants to review what I have. As he gets out of the car, my heart pounds fast in eager for me to embrace him. He glares lovingly at me with his enchanting glittering eyes, so I can barely keep myself upright. He embraces me and with his arm around my waist, we grab the elevator to fourth floor and enter my apartment then proudly; I show him my new home.

'Look, Drake. I finally have a home close to the beach. Like we dreamed of,' I exclaim with pleasure.

'Well, well! Lucky you, Mary. The rich have a lot of joys.' He glares enviously at me, his tone equally jealous voice.

The next day, he offers to assemble some of my heavy shelves and drill holes in the wall for my larger paintings.

On the second day, all hell breaks loose again. The jerk is on a massive knock-down-and-drag-out ride again.

'I'm telling you, Mary!' The angry Grizzly Bear roars at me. 'You're bloody hell too much! Knucklehead!'

I glare at the roaring crazy Grizzly Bear in amazement with lifted eyebrows.

'You God damn stole this machine from me. It's not your machine, Mary. Only I made sure that deal ever came to fruition.' He screams while repairing the castor.

Out of the blue, he is standing next to me, ear-splitting at me and completely out of context. I'm about to fall hard on my rump out of astonishment.

'You know what, you halfwit?' I peep calmly. 'I don't want to have this discussion with you again. I've offered you several times to buy it.'

The bonehead yells, and his fiercely glaring evil eyes will not stop, as his face gets copper red with resentment.

Out of respect for Drake, I had chosen not to smoke while he was there. But I am traumatised that I take my hidden ciggy's and go out on the patio. Shivering, I gaze at the waves of the sea, shaking in my bones. The Sun is shining from a clear sky on this summer day and peak time for tourists on the south coast. On the golden beach it crowded with bathing happy summer guests and people sit on the balconies and enjoy life, with glasses of wine in their hands. I enjoy my smoke, which settles my nerves after his massive rage.

All at once, he angrily rips my door open, so I get a shudder. 'God damn it! Now the dimwit bloody well sits and smokes out here. What the hell is the matter with you, Mary? How can you do such filth? It's disgusting!' The birdbrain screams in English, so I get speechless.

My jaw drops to the ground over his outburst that everyone nearby could hear. 'I smoke when it suits me and as many as I like,' I boldly answer.

The moron slams the door, and lock it, so I can't enter my home. Five minutes pass, so I grab another cigarette, then the door opens with another violent spasm of his insanity.

'God help me! Now the moron sits and smokes another of these hopeless poison sticks. How many more is the goofy going to smoke? You are disgusting, Mary' the retard screams loudly in English as he furiously stares at me while I'm dealing with his lunacy, though I'm staying strong.

I smile and act as nothing is wrong while I notice my neighbour is staring at me. It's embarrassing!

'I'll smoke as many as suits me.' Good gracious me! I should have thrown the fathead out of my home. I deeply regret that I have allowed him to visit me.

After two days Drake travelled back home. Next the peabrain comes up with countless solutions to get the equipment from me. 'Rent it to me,' he suggests or, 'I'll pay it off in instalments.' Then he says, 'Sweet Mary, you should donate it to me for research. My clinic is almost ready.' Other suggestions lands on my table, 'I'll only buy if you send the equipment before receiving my payment.' Yea, you name it! He has plenty of solutions, and every time I give him a flat *no*! Eventually, I withdraw the offer altogether, because the goofy won't comply with the contract.

'The equipment is no longer for sale!' I lastly tell him, and he gets furious at me.

* * *

Drake is a pathological liar. Yet, with his charm, he wiggles into people's lives, and such a person is awful to have around. His speech is full of demeaning statements, so I can only shake my head in disgust. The world is full of BS people you cannot trust, and he is one of them. Stay true to your philosophy of life. Don't get swayed by people who are you to deviate from who you are, usually for their own selfish reasons.

When I talk to others about what happened, there's always some blowbacks. Few people are disbelieving and think I was the hateful person. 'You're jealous!' they say. 'You're stalking him!' Others claim that I'm lying or that I only want to ruin his business. 'You're a scorned woman!' is another one I've heard. And some say, 'You are talking out of turn'. Shut up! The donkey misuses information about fragile women to trick them into his arms and has ended up with his newest secretary. Congratulations to both! Cadance might believe she has won the lottery with the dummy. She will make the same mistakes as me and fall into Drake's creepy dark shadow of his burning fire, in his eerie underworld. I genuinely feel sorry for her. The ignoramus has convinced few people and Cadance I was the demon—that *he* was the victim of a lying behaviour pattern.

When Drake and Cadance found out, they threaten and harass me, tell lying stories about me and so it went on for years. I'm not afraid of him, and I never answer them. He's on a self-destructive path, either too lazy, too stupid and a confused simpleton to work honourably. He has repaid none of his debts to me, so I've lost it all, and it dooms such a chump as him to failure, so I hope others will see his shortcomings.

Many believe me and others have experienced the jerk and stay far away from his influence. I walked away from the imbecile, because I didn't want to be a victim anymore and didn't want what happened. Drake stole my life and family from me, and I don't think he understands what he has done to me—how traumatic it is and has been for me. What I didn't want to be, I became, so the experience has changed me forever and I realise it won't get better with such a nincompoop. He will never stop! He'll only get worse. I've been in love with a fake charmer, a fake Jesus, then slowly he let his disturbing personality traits sneak into our relationship, like a control freak—a psychologically, abusive mean person. I figured it out, what I could expect from him. Such chumps are dangerous to their surroundings, and it's dreadful getting out of their muggy, creepy spiderwebs when you first are trapped as a fly in their foul snare. It's all a play to them. You are the victim.

That makes me disrespect such a person, and I feel sorry for those who end up in his web after me. Hopefully, one day, others will understand the warnings, although, I never became the same, but learned the lesson.

When I stopped having self-doubt and realised I had made a gigantic mistake by loving Drake, my life turned to the better, but I never came to understand why he exposed me to all this. My biggest question was, Why?

Money! Through his actions, his motive became apparent to me, because he wanted *wealth*, power and glory! He has a severe *God complex*!

When my sanity came back to me, I researched the jerk further, and it took ages before I found the many pieces. Next I could put most of it together—our relationship, our families, and our surroundings. I was finally aware of the many red flags I'd overlooked, but I got the final puzzle together, however, it was too late for me, because I was already in the middle of a big breakdown. Slowly, I got back on my feet again, because the research took me back to many hard circumstances, realising that many of his actions during our relationship didn't add up.

That's when I wrote the first line, and my pen eagerly continued scribbling across the paper. The only wrong thing to say is to say nothing! I had to speak out, and it wasn't about being a scorned woman, but about observing it all from a healthy perspective. It was important for me to understand what I had put myself through—being swept up in a scary affair and psychologically abused by a harmful psychopath.

Years after our break, I believed it was the ending of this poignant chapter of the past nearly seven years of a haunted life with a narcissistic psychopath. But it was not, because Drake continued to be mean, as he found out I told my experience to other people. Studies have shown that 4 percent of males are psychopath, which means women are victims of such men, and as Bob Marley said; The biggest coward is a man who awakens a woman's love without the intention of loving her.

The storyline is told as an insight of what to expect from psychopaths. And how the emotions and feelings got a massive crack in my life. Listen to the warning signs. Take them seriously. I didn't, and that was fatal. Living with such a wolf in sheepskin is not a love game nor a walk on rose paddles nor floating on a soft pink cloud. It's catastrophic. I turned every part of my dreams to shame, because the man I had loved had killed the dream I dreamt. The bruises after the physical violence fade away after a short time—but the feeling of the psychological abuse doesn't disappear—because it keeps haunting and following you for the rest of your life. But as Gautama Buddha said; Three things cannot hide for long, the Moon, the Sun and the Truth.

CHAPTER 40

ME TOO, ME TOO, ME TOO!

> I could never get excited about games you play with other
> people. I can't get into them. I lose interest.
>   —Haruki Murakami, *Norwegian Wood*

Doctor Bates is back in another country, under his new name; Doctor Luke Samael Schmidt and running new scams in United Kingdom where he's played his seduction game with several female patients and has had several new relationships. I discovered the many scandalous information, and that he had lied saying that he had never assaulted other women in his clinic as he did to me. Did Drake get hard when he treated patients? Too late, I realised the dude was a disturbing predator, with flirting and sexual violations and manipulations to suit the monster's fantasies. I find out there are billions of them and they're dangerous to their surroundings.

Drake had lied that he had never acted so badly before towards a woman. But this was not the first time he had acted immorally towards others while treating them in his clinic. There was a pattern, with his many schemes. Secretaries and patients in his clinic were his primary targets. The primary targets were wealthy women he met as patients or having affairs with his secretaries, yea, like Cadance who is his secretary. He repeats the same behaviour in his relationships and his flirting, and the sexual violations were repeated against other victims, to suit his fantasies. Some women catch on early, but I found out too late. He is a master of taking advantage of others for his own benefit, and he continues perpetrating fishy scams.

My friend Selena, who is 43 years old got scared and told me, 'Doctor Schmidt is crazy. He flirted from the beginning and thought I was adorable. Doctor Luke Schmidt said, "You are very special. A beautiful woman like you, we must get such a lovely girl like you well." He commented aggressively on my body and sent inappropriate glances at me. He gazed at my big breast all the times. He kept saying, "Such a special beautiful woman deserves to be well—I must help you—you deserve me." And, "You must be every man's dream." Then the old nasty pink pig asked me, "Have you ever tried a real man?" Doctor Schmidt didn't respect my sexuality and instead offered me his sperm so I could get pregnant. I wanted to puke. This behaviour went on for weeks. I feared him. From the start, I was upset at his gross behaviour. I'm terribly traumatised by Doctor Luke Schmidt.

Fannie, 45 years old told me, 'Doctor Schmidt acts like he is Jesus. He fumbles blindly with his treatments. He creates false stories. He has a generally nasty way of being. He is out of reach and a man who thinks he is the navel of the world. He is loaded with lies and has no conscience. He has psychologically abused and manipulated me. And damaged my body and health a lot more.'

I wish I had known beforehand. I was traumatised to hear that Drake used the same loving words and way of playing with so many women. It's as a MeToo effect. Things became much clearer to me during my research and when I talked others. The pattern and methods he'd used in his hunt for women were all the same—we all had bad relationships, had or would get a lot of money, and were gorgeous blondes with big breasts. We were ill-fated women. Our ages were no obstacle to Doctor Bates/ Nilsson. If one of his marks didn't have money, he recklessly dumped her.

Women, you are not alone! Perhaps you once were a victim of a psychopath. I spoke with several other women who contacted me about

Drake. Talking to those who had been in the same mess as I was a liberation. *I was not alone!* Went through my mind. It's sad, though, that it happens to so many victims and then I spoke with Lynn.

'The worst I've ever tried was Doctor Luke Schmidt clinic. I trusted his promises of healing, trusted the man with such weight and charm to perform miracles. Instead, I got worse. I suffered excruciating pain after his many harsh treatments. I stopped. It cost a fortune. It's a money machine for his own gain. I'm clearer about my knowledge of Doctor Schmidt. He is lying. I highly doubt his abilities. His journals are incorrect! He's unethical, sloppy and slanders his patients. He spies on us on Facebook and has a group of women, including his secretary Cadance to run his dirty errands. He excludes you from the clinic if you write a critical review. He is a loose cannon. He has abused another patient, I know. More injured come out of the bush. It's grotesque! I read they have accused him of quackery in the past. That says it all. I'm speechless! What a dirty old pig.'

Caroline 47 years old.
'Doctor Luke Schmidt and his skills intrigued me in the beginning. Next, I had a relationship with him, which I should never have done. He scammed and took advantage of me. When I ditched him, he stole my entire portfolio with clients. Because he swindled me, I took a loss. What a beast! It's insane! I had it bad mentally for a long time afterwards. He finally lost his authority to treat patients. What a great relief.'

I realised Drake had sold Caroline the stolen machine, I have paid for, which Steven, Drake and I were fighting about in court.
I spoke with Dorothy, who said:

'At first, I thought Doctor Luke was impressive, and I was desperate for treatment. I was still in grief after I had lost my husband many years ago. I was captivated by him and his charm. I felt he was a fresh breath of air for me. He flirted wildly with me. Luke kissed me passionately many times during my treatment.

After I made a dispute about one payment, he dumped me. He told me never to show my face at his clinic anymore. He was ice cold to me. He treated me like the worst shit. You might as well not try to understand such a sickening guy. His is constantly bragging about everything. His supposed knowledge is suffocating. He is a scheming, lying moron. I have experienced nothing so awful of what he did to me. I'm 73 years old, so Doctor Luke Schmidt's behaviour is appalling!'

One day 41-year-old Madison called me and wanted to tell her brief experience of Drake.

'Luke Schmidt talks badly about all other doctors. He ruined me. I felt like my arm would fall off. This happened after he jerked my neck. I could knock him down. Idiot! Psychopath! From day one he started frantically flirting with me. He threatened to silence me, so I didn't dare report him. I don't know why this anxiety mentality in women makes it so difficult for behaviour like his to come to light.'

I had a brief chat with 33-year-old Maddy. We meet next day at a café, bought coffee and strolled to the nearby park. It's a vivid sunny afternoon while we sit on the grass listening to the birds chirping in the trees. She appears sadden and tells me her experience with Doctor Luke Samael Schmidt.

'I had a weird gut feeling when I met Doctor Schmidt and was unsure of him right away. He reminded me of something. Now I know why.'

'You must believe in your inner gut feelings.' I tried to calm her.

'I believed in all Luke's bullshit about help and support. He claimed he was the best. He is a monster, a narcissistic psychopath!' She is deeply upset, picking up grass and throw it away.

'Hidden narcissists typically behave gracious, and passionately to people around them in the public space.'

'Luke thought I was adorable. I didn't like him from the first time. He wasn't nice. I told my mother that others had experienced worsening conditions after his treatment. She had heard about an old quack case, but at that time it was under another name; she said to me.' Maddy was close to burst out in tears.

'It's true, Maddy, there once was. And he changed his name for a few years ago.' I confirm.

'Wow! When Luke Schmidt got too nasty, I stopped treatment. I've lived with a psychopath for some years. Nothing is harder! Getting away requires a strong psyche. The country has finally determined mental violence to be punishable. You can get a prison sentence.'

'Wauw, that's great, Maddy. Have you talked to a professional?'

'Nah, not yet. With my boyfriend Alex I discovered who he was. I've loved as I've never loved before—just the wrong one.' Then she is changing the topic.

'I learned to manage my inner pain. I recovered well with myself and the pain disappeared. I accepted Drake wasn't worth having.'

'Alex did something stupid to me. I was furious and upset and close to reporting him to the police for abuse. He raped me and did something ugly during sex. He held me tight. Staring at me with insane eyes, "Say you want to be with me, Maddy!" Alex kept yelling.'

'Whoa! How awful! If you're not mentally on top of yourself because of Alex, then it can drag on for a long time before you get better.'

'Jeez, I froze like ice. When Alex got sexually relieved, he stopped. I ran into another room and cried. He thought I was too sensitive and cried too much and turned the mistake on me.'

'There is a reason you cry.'

'Oh, my goodness, Mary! Then Alex wanted to discuss it again. "Why don't you hug me enough?" He brainwashed me and by the time we finished talking; I had forgotten what the subject was about.'

'Sweetie, Alex gets you to do something because he doesn't get the attention he wants. He suddenly must give you attention. He can't stand that or the defeat. It's all about him and *not you*.'

'The adoring attention I sometimes got for a few moments was enchanting. Alex manipulated me as he sat crying, "I'm a psychopath, sweet Maddy. What do I do?" I comforted him and felt sorry for him, then asked Alex, "Do you believe so?" "Yes," he answers. "It's not that

I want to kill anyone. I only think of myself. My needs. How I can get them fulfilled. I can't see my own mistakes, sweet Maddy." Next I said to Alex, "I knew your thoughts well." Then he promised to get help. I believed him. It wasn't true. He got mad when other men looked at me. He invented stories about other men and me to make me feel bad. I hate him. Then his tone changed slightly. "I love you, Maddy. I want our relationship to succeed." Alex moaned. Or he said, "I know we're not right for each other, Sweet Pea. However, I miss you dearly every day, Maddy. I miss hearing you laugh. Your smile. Your bewitching eyes. I think about you all the time." Then Alex smirked falsely.'

'Oh, my goodness.'

'When I had a new boyfriend, and Alex found out. He made me apologise a hundred times. I became deeply pitiful. A message from Alex popped up after our break. "You've probably moved on and are happier. I'm not, Maddy. Far from it. I miss you. You fill my head with thoughts all the time. No one can ever replace that love I've with you, my precious Maddy." He wrote. Shit! Will you believe it, Mary? I jumped into the trap and went back to him.'

'On, no! However, I know the feeling.'

'After a week, Alex behaved again as a psychopath. I feared of his gaze. I was anxious when I was out dining or in a cinema with him.'

'Drake was cute in many ways too. The rest has been awful in the bad column.'

'Mary, it was awful. I threw up when Alex touched me. I was shaking when he screwed me. He was good at giving me orgasms too, but lousy for sex. He screwed like a robot—emotionally cold. Ha-ha, I miss the orgasms, though.'

'Drake only gave me one pleasant thing in life. He was good at giving me a finger orgasm. That's what I missed—the orgasms. His hands. His hugs. Ha-ha, Maddy, buy a *magic wand*.'

'I had constant stomach pain. Anxiety attacks. I wanted to jump off a bridge.'

'It's awful, Maddy. I know the feeling.'

'Damn, I couldn't stop loving him. It mentally and physically screwed my love pattern. Everything screamed inside me.'

'You will go through many phases—coming back and leaving Alex again. We might imagine ourselves in love, Maddy. Typically, what you can't get is what you *want!*'

'When I talked to my girlfriends about it, they said, "Well, Maddy, that's not normal." I didn't listen to their advice, so they became tired of it.'

'Listen to those who are trying to warn you.'

'People can't stand being with someone caught up in that kind of drama. We are lovers. Then not. Then I forgive Alex.'

'It can be tough for people in your surroundings to understand.'

'Everyone considers me who as the crazy and evil one.'

'It's not *you*, Maddy.'

'Alex was my greatest love. But the person who hurt me the most.' She sniffles.

'He isn't doing you any good.'

'I've experienced nothing so hard before. It's beyond understanding.' She cries. 'They destroy all people around them. Alex don't care. He made me believe everything was my fault. Why would he want something bad for me? He is emotionally cold and fake!'

'They may be caring at first. The next moment, they give you an uppercut in the face.'

'I'll never forget the day Alex smiled crookedly when I got upset. He was so evil. I fainted. When he was with other women, he said, "You don't show me enough interest, Maddy." I didn't care for myself. I would do anything. Just so he would love and respect me. I humbled myself to get his love. It was degrading! Exhausting!'

'Maddy, I have an idea. Make two columns on a piece of paper—one *worthy* and the other *immoral*—and filled in the columns. Write what upsets you. I bet *it limits worthy*. Possibly it's only the orgasms he gave you. See it as a *task* you must solve. Get help!'

'I found some nasty pictures on Alex' phone—photos of him banging all kinds of women.

The same night he was screwing me, yuck, he wrote to another woman. Ewww, saying how in love he was with her.'

'Oh, my goodness! That's awful!'

'He went into town and banged her. While banging her, he wrote to me he wanted to have children with me.'

'He controls you until you're completely broken. Then you cannot fight anymore.'

'I dreamed Alex assaulted me. I was drowning. Water and fire! He is always present.'

'I had nightmares of Drake. Of being trapped in his cobwebs. Falling into deep gloomy holes. My heart was racing. The doctor suspected heart attack. They were trauma reactions—the outcomes of Drake's cruel conduct. Steadily, I stepped down. It's like being a junkie. Step out of it in small doses. Set small new goals, Sweetie. Go dancing. Enjoy friends.'

'I try! I'm still in the phase where I don't understand Alex and me not being together.'

'Stop talking about him. Show you're stronger than Alex. Forgive yourself. It takes time.'

'Mary, some days are worse than others. I get jealous when Alex finds a new one.'

'I know the feeling. I don't care. Let Cadance have the ignoramus.'

'I don't want Alex to be a dream man to another woman. It pains me.'

'Maddy, dear, he can't change. He can't be the dream man for someone else.'

'Alex only sees me as a loser. Geez, life is fragile, Mary.'

'I have completely detached myself from Drake. It required some work on my part. I once found a quote by Tahereh Mafi; All I ever wanted was to reach out and touch another human being, not just with my hands but with my heart.'

'Mary, I've experienced nothing so hard before.'

'Don't let that loser win over you. The psycho is not worth loving or crying over. Sweetie, you are not alone in the world! There is help there. You will be the *winner*.'

'Thanks Mary, it was nice talking to you. I must go. Take care and let's keep in contact.'

'Take care, Sweetie. You will manage it. Call me if you need it. I'm there for you.'

Too many women get anxious to make changes. I'm not afraid of Drake anymore. Look up with courage. You will walk the green path again—perhaps with a person who appreciates you for your luring way of being. With that person, you can look at the bright Moon and the glittering stars. You can have a romantic life. Don't give up hope. It's a challenge you must go through.

In about 2025, the world's population will be around eight billion. I repeat; A study shows that 4 percent of the population are psychopaths. Of those, 3 percent are men. That's far too many!

With eight billion people, that's a lot of *male* psychopaths.

CHAPTER 41

INFERNAL AFTERSHOCKS

> Grief is like an earthquake. The first one hits you, and the
> world falls apart. Even after you put the world together
> again there are aftershocks, and you never really know when
> those will come.
>
> —Unknown

Imagine an audible high energy sound- and shockwave going throughout your entire body. Imagine it as it's a similar phenomenon to the RAF Typhoon making a sonic boom during a flight, when it's breaking the sound wave. Even the 'pistol shrimp' causes a hushed shockwave effect when it shoots its claws into its prey. (You can google it and see the effect of it.) It's that massive. Strangely, it's also successfully used for treatment of various condition in the human body in the medical world, and very famous in Europe. Except for with such kind of treatment in the therapeutic industry it's not that loud and hard as the sonic boom. Though, I felt I was in the middle of the devastating shockwave boom the RAF Typhoon, meaning what Drake and Cadance caused on my persona.

As my heavy pen is sailing with gloomy black ink through the darkness of the clouds, my struggles with depression and anxiety begins as I scribble the scary path of my life onto the dark gloomy white paper. I still have some lessons to learn about managing these afflictions, but

I think doing so will be a true test of my own strength. The pen and paper are my only hope of surviving my shattered life, despite it's a rough time, and I hope I'll get through it. It's like climbing the highest mountain with the only rope I have left in life—helping me reaching my dream of once again living a good and serene living.

To me it was all about trying to follow the many rules, using common sense, and just keeping a positive frame of mind. I'm not a quitter and will never give up. But sometimes it's hard to keep from wanting to give up, so I'm trying to focus hour by hour and day by day. Following the pen as it sailed, scared and shattered, over the dark gloomy paper and through my past life and not dying for it was a challenge, because I felt I had only one more chance to survive. I didn't want to give up this challenge, even though my depression and anxiety had spiked. When the anxiety was kicking in, I tried to count down out loud from 100 and do breathing exercises. Sometimes it was damn hard, and I would lose to the anxiety and want to jump off from my balcony on the seventeenth floor, during my time I lived in Czechia, shortly before I moved to England. I was so scared that I had to lock all the doors that led out to the balcony, and next, I would be hiding in my bedroom. Most of my network had been destroyed as well, so I didn't have many people to reach out to. Sometimes—and this was mostly in the beginning, before I started feeling anxious—I would crank up some lively music. Typically, it would be Enrique Iglesias, and then I'd begin to dance. It looked silly, but I had a good time while I was at it. Often, though, I began to think desperately about Drake and about us dancing salsa together. My dancing to the tunes began to fade, because it triggered the depression instead of cheering me up. I couldn't manage anything that related to what we had done together.

There was also too much uncertainty to look at any type of future with Drake, so I tried to do one thing at a time and wanted to do it well. For me, it was a new target, a new mountain to climb with my one and only last rope in hand. I could use the robe to hang myself, or I could take the challenge to climb the tough and rough mountain and reach out again for the clear blue sky. I wanted to be able to smell the delicate aroma of the tropical flowers and breathe in the fresh air of the Croatian and Montenegrin black mountain. I wanted to touch the fluffy soft white clouds beyond the dark thick ones. I wanted to make my way safely through the heavy thunderstorms while my many endless tears flowed like heavy raining I've seen in Spain and The Philippines, flooding over from my once dry eyes. And as I got safely through that massive dangerous hurricane, I wished to grab as many glittering stars on the other side of the universe—holding them close to my heart for a new journey and gathering from them the new hope of having a happy decent life again. Therefore, I followed my weighty pen and let the smutty black ink float on the torn pieces of paper. I followed the dream of the ink to become shiny royal blue, so the paper would be whole again. I dreamed of seeing it transformed into a white sheet of paper, pure as the snow I once saw at the Benedictine Sisters Monastery, in Denmark when I walked to the graveyard and saw the new fallen snow lying on the stones, glittering as millions of diamonds when The Sun shined on them. I had no intention to jump into the Tatun volcano, I saw in Taiwan, which suddenly erupted with grey smoke. It was dangerous, so I rather wanted to reach the snow I could see on top of the peaks of the beautiful Mount Hermon I was about to climb in Israel.

Mark Twain said, 'I've had a lot of worries in my life, most of which never happened.' This was certainly not something I could boast about, and there are probably not many who could claim Mark Twain's words. More than ever, I was busy thinking about the many problems I've had—especially those I experienced with Drake over the last many years. Everything else that had happened in my life had eventually turned into microscopic and insignificant fragments.

What happened to Mary's psyche after she was dehumanized by Doctor Bates? Isn't it really a matter of how degrading Drake has been to Mary.

Even though he had given me all the discomfort he had given me, there was still something magical about him that kept attracting me. I couldn't let go of what I wanted with him. Being a caring, thoughtful, helpful, and sensitive woman made me not quite realize it was just illusory—simply non-existent hopes and dreams. At times, it was hard to set boundaries for myself and say no to his lying flattering. It was as if I had an inner jet fighter pilot, who constantly directed my attention to finding solutions to the forces of the universe and our problems as I floated in space.

Without the force of gravity, I couldn't stand on solid ground and stick to my decision that our relationship was over. There were far too many themes tumbling around in my confused mind about our bond and the work we wanted to do together but couldn't do because he wanted ultimate power over me and my money. The headline always ended up— 'Problems, Money, and Shortcomings of my person'. Maybe it was also that I thought it an advantage to be with him because of the prestige and status I believed he could add to my life—after all, he boasted so much about his knowledge as a doctor.

Perhaps my focus on troubleshooting only led me to grasp half of reality and not the real facts—in other words, that Drake was a true psychopath who was untrustworthy. In his world, the problem was always me—how I'd done things that were not right and how I wouldn't share my money and possessions with him. In his opinion, everything I did and said was wrong, or he'd say I was full of lies, so he played the victim and twisted the narration. His opinion and attitude that our relationship was unsatisfactory came to surface often. And on his side, that meant it was only me who had faults and was unable to think in full bloom. In short, from his perspective, I was just a mentally underdeveloped orphanage child who didn't understand the real world and that I wasn't very clever!

Maybe I wasn't so clever, but it's likely that few people question their daily experiences. Whenever there's a conflict or any disagreement, Drake tends to act in a repulsive yet unsurprising manner. To late I discover that he can't deal with reality, because it contradicts what he wants to be true, and he see the situation is real, even though it isn't. I accepted everything I personally felt and experienced within myself as being real and ethically correct. When I tried to talk to him about topics, I did it based on my best intentions and goodwill. Unfortunately, I hadn't always investigated things at that time and, therefore, had a hard time figuring out the illusion so that I could see how things were.

The more Drake told me a story of my faults, the more I believed it, even if initially I knew it's not true. Did our conversations solve anything for us at all? No, it didn't solve anything, because he was not interested in resolving anything or being introspective. So, didn't they just create more problems for me? Yes, but it was difficult to let go of him after so many years. After all, I'd once trusted Drake. In my quest to find the many projects he described and presented to me; I think he is not honest with me.

Behind many of my problems and my search for solutions, there was probably a frustrated death sentence of a dream I could not fulfil—a dream I blindly tried to fight, despite it being a lifelong suicide, instead of using my only rope to climb the rough mountain. Dreams of hope, happiness, a loving relationship and that things would turn out for the best stayed an unfeasible illusion. It was utopia that I tried to enchant my thoughts with. But my heart couldn't make sense of the difficulties. My brain kept sending rational signals to get me to stop this unattainable hopeless romanticizing of a phantom that did not exist. The difficult battle was between my heart and brain. When I wasn't with Drake, my energies were high. I thought then that I was happy again. I could easily do without him, and I did not need his presence. When he wasn't there, I was no longer afraid of him. Instead, I began to miss him.

It was interesting and very difficult for me to describe how a psychopath had gained power over another human being by yo-yoing between safe and unsafe in interactions. One cannot doubt the cunningness of his seduction and that enough truly was enough. It is something that goes beyond normal limits and a means of grotesque power he used on a fragile person. How many had he truly done this to?

Scribbling down the entire story of Drake and Mary was more than difficult, as was describing the infernal aftershocks with him. It was a tough topic I had subjected myself to. Where should I begin? Where should I end? It was a nightmare, and it—all his malicious behaviour— is still haunting me. I can't forget it. It's impossible to shake it off my body and out of mind. It's like a swiftly running crazy horror movie, playing repeatedly, and is a never-ending story with this guy. But for me, this would be the last part of the ten years where Drake Lucifer Bates had spooked my life.

I grasped that he was not the dream man I thought he was, because he can't change. I completely detached from him, I didn't talk or write to him anymore. It took me several years afterwards to get free of Drake, though, I'm a winner in the end. But truly, I was yet not free from him, because he kept on haunting me as the foul wolf in his dirty sheep's skin. I thought I would never again hear about or from him, but he still spooked me from behind his foul curtain. Mostly, I needed to get free of him, and I thought my story had an ending when I wrote, 'It required some work on my part. I would not let that loser win over me. The psychopath is not worth loving and Drake wasn't worth all my suffering.' When I stopped having contact with him, I got peace of mind. Or so I thought!

After our final breakup, many devious and hurtful aftershocks hit my life, even I thought I could be just friends with Drake, professionally and privately. Who was I trying to convince? Him or me? Because you can't be friends with Drake. It's *impossible*. Once he doesn't need you anymore, he burns his bridges behind him, and enters a total hate mode—despising the other person. That would eventually become my next nightmare with him. Despite the hatred he had for me, he still wanted something from me. I couldn't comprehend it; it was impossible for me to cope with his constant attempts to swindle me. He kept falsely courting me and constantly gave me renewed hope for a continuous relationship with him.

I was a little gullible when he kept on telling me he didn't want to spend time apart or be away from me. I was, of course, very flattered. So, I kept on thinking, *is there still hope for Drake and me?* Subconsciously, I knew very well, his words couldn't be sincere. Even a friendship between him and me would be doomed in the long run. What I didn't know was that he had several other relationships going on at the same time he was trying to hold on to me.

I can't deny that my female curiosity was huge when it came to find out what he did when we were no longer together daily. *Was he with other women?* I was stupidly jealous. *Can he manage without me and without my money?* I mused.

He still had no proper income, so he wanted to start a new clinic in United Kingdom. My curiosity needed to know about his doings and deeds. It was significant to me because I was thoroughly researching Drake Lucifer Bates, who had become to Luke Samael Schmidt, after our court case. I felt more like a James Bond spy than a woman still missing him inexplicably. I visited him few times at his new clinic, and he wanted me to work for him. Each time, I thought I got renewed happiness, as he would make me feel wonderful and appreciated. It was the best feeling in the world. But every time, I also received confirmation that my choice to hold on to him was wrong. These love meetings destroyed the inner strength I had, in the meantime, built up. Everything I felt, my thoughts, my gladness, my indifference, and my pain changed every single time.

My belief had, therefore, to be completely wrong. There was only one thing in my life I was missing, and it was love—the love and companionship I thought I could get from Drake. I realized the older you get, the fewer available healthy, successful, intelligent, and happy men there are. He had made me feel good even though he was a lot older than me. So, I kept on believing he was a great catch. But what I didn't know or wouldn't realise is that he was a wicked and predatory individual. He went from victim to victim and didn't form any real relationships with anybody. He used people! He had no real attachment or bonds to other people and took what he could and found a new victim. When I was with Drake, I began to feel anxiety. The more I clung to my willingness to continue having a loving relationship with him, the more I wanted to control the situation and send him to hell. This often resulted in greater anxiety, almost bordering on horror that I might never be with him again. My imagination would never end. I ended up being a totally hopeless brainwashed individual and thought that life couldn't exist without him. My mind would sometimes race wildly, and I began to show symptoms of neurotic anxiety. I thought often that I was going to die, especially of a broken heart.

Broken heart syndrome was thought to be a short-term condition; the latest evidence suggests otherwise. A stressful event, such as the death of a loved one, really can break your heart. In medicine, the condition is known as broken heart syndrome or Takotsubo syndrome. It is characterized by a temporary disruption of the heart's normal pumping function, which puts the sufferer at increased risk of death.

Broken heart syndrome has similar symptoms to those of a heart attack, including chest pain and difficulty breathing. During an attack, which can be triggered by bereavement, divorce, surgery, or other stressful events, the heart muscle weakens to the extent that it can no longer pump blood effectively. In about one in ten cases, people with broken heart syndrome develop a condition called cardiogenic shock, where the heart can't pump enough blood to meet the body's need. This can result in death.

It has long been thought that, unlike a heart attack, damage caused by broken heart syndrome was temporary, lasting days or weeks. But recent research suggests that this is not the case. A study by researchers at the University of Aberdeen provided the first evidence that broken heart syndrome results in permanent physiological changes to the heart. In terms of long-term risk, a new study on the condition published in *Circulation* now shows that the risk of death remains high for many years after the initial attack.[1]

When I moved to the United Kingdom, doctors believed I had suffered from broken heart syndrome. It gave me an explanation as to why I during the last year had suffered from sudden heart problems that would strike me like lightning from a clear sky several times over the following four years. The fear of dying became a lasting anxiety for me, as my heart unnecessarily went into overdrive and still does occasionally. Crazy nightmares about losing Drake forever came more often, and I typically woke up with a galloping heart, bathed in sweat, even though I felt like I was freezing. *What if he dies before I can say*

---

[1]   'Broken Heart Syndrome Was Thought to Be a Short-Term Condition: The Latest Evidence Shows Otherwise', *The Conversation*, 5 November 2018, theconversation.com.

goodbye? Fuzzy thoughts and questions bombarded my head. *Do I want to attend his funeral? Should he die alone in his sin without my forgiveness?*

Despairing, I often tried to find explanations for what had happened to my confused mind. What should I do to stop the problems of this dreadful palpitation? After all, I was usually a very sporty healthy person and not an overweight woman. Junk food was not on my menu card. I did not drink alcohol. But unfortunately, I smoked. The pros and cons of my acquaintance with Drake had to be found. Decisions had to be made about what was going to happen to my life. But who should do it? Who was in charge? Him, me, or both of us?

I knew that my relationship with Drake ended in Sweden that day when he said goodbye to me. I was convinced that we could easily have a friendly and professional relationship with each other. I did everything to be positive, show consideration, and forgive him for what he had done to me. But I learned that you can't maintain a friendship with him.

So, the battle to forget him was a massive ordeal. The constant pressure of deprivation made me more and more exhausted. I felt bad inside myself. The good mood disappeared, and I lost momentum and initiative. Lack of concentration and overview turned into a daily unbearable struggle. Overwhelming frustrations hit my mind. I was confused, and my own needs were ignored. The effects of isolation began to emerge, and I became paranoid of other people. The anger; the powerlessness; the guilt; and, not least, the shame overtook me for years. Slowly, I lost myself more and more. Outwardly, I smiled at others, but inside I was a as an active volcano, erupting of grief, self-pity, anger and loneliness, ready to set fire to the entire universe.

Within time, Drake had truly terrorized me. All the time I had been vulnerable, and he seemed to have liked the complete package of my vulnerability and the goodness I could give him. In many ways, I felt I had caused it all myself. This was the last thing I'd ever wanted to happen when, on our first meeting, he had asked me so many questions about my life. Foolishly, I had been to open from the beginning. And the future storytelling would be a chronicling of the many bad consequences that resulted from my having allowed him to do all those awful things to me.

It also took me many years to see through Drake's many conversation and manipulation about the mean things he said about Paul. And it haunted me. I didn't see it, but now it makes me outrageous, when I'm analysing this comparison, when he once said; 'Yikes, the sneaky old dude, Carl, thought he could put his ticket in by inviting you on a secret naughty date. Recall of the scene in *Pretty Woman*. Where the lawyer expect he could screw Julia.'

What I grasp is that Drake compares me with a whore, and he is the one inviting himself on the secret dates. He is a *gigolo*, financially supported by me, to be my lover. I believe he is the man-whore. A promiscuous man who has sex with his clients for money and has no regard for his sexual partners or the emotional value of his relationships. I was paying the salty dog whatever he wanted. In return for that, he gave me the false love I sought. That's how I perceive it today. This is precisely the 'ticket' Drake got.

'People like Paul stand as believers. You know? With the truth and lie ratio from before.' Drake once said and what will I get out of it later in life, when I'll grasp that it was Drake who was the less skilled and the master of manipulating?

Those accusations are more a description of Drake himself—especially the 10 percent lies counting more than the truth. It's not, as he claims, what Paul is doing to me—especially the above manipulation technique, involving the ration between truth and lies. Is that what others will remember? The truth is told and is so dull that it's forgotten? I'm not even sure if I will find truth in Drake's stories, because I believe the playboy's lie percentage is higher than 10 percent. Unfortunately, he gets away with it—every time.

I wanted to stay strong in my marriage and to my children and not be a weak person. In hindsight, I'll see that Drake was talking of himself and man sluts own sickening behaviour when he talked badly about Paul, the kids and my friends. Drake used the fear I had. I still can't find the many accusations regarding Paul and the plots the hustler came up with. It tells me more of how blind love can make you. In the aftermath, I will understand it's not Paul, who is a sicko, because he was enormously supportive, and still are, but I didn't see it.

It is mental abuse! Drake was not talking of Paul, but of himself. He told everything cryptic and scientifically, because it was difficult to understand a squid of his shit. I have spent years trying to understand the millions of conversations and letters from this devious horn dog. Though, I will get it—understand the behaviour of psychopaths. I'll comprehend he was a shifty, disturbing madness—a sneaky murky shadow around my fragile personality. Traumatised and angry with myself, I will realise I had allowed such darkness in my life, and in retrospect, I understand it was the grease monkey who wanted to save money by letting me pay for it all. I was living with a narcissistic sociopath, a Casanova, a man-whore.

When I thought I was healing with this philanderer and had an enjoyable life with him, I first realise it can't happen after I had done my research on whoremonger, where I find the scary truth and learn that what we spoke of was what he has done his entire life. He accused me of being a stupid, uneducated, and misbehaved orphanage child and of not understanding shit. It will frustrate me; I couldn't comprehend it back then. Such things happen in my strong affection and blindness to the whoremaster. Today I don't care. Let the man-whore think what he wants.

CHAPTER 42

Cyberbullying

> When a fool utters all kinds of insults against you in a social media group without even knowing you or without any worthwhile reason or provocation usually, they are merely sad and pathetic attention seeking trolls who we should all feel sorry for. They don't deserve our anger. They deserve our pity.
>
> —R. M. Engelhardt, *Coffee Ass Blues & Other Poems*

B eing loved by Drake one day and having him utterly hate me the next moment was impossible for me to understand. The salty dog broke me in half. I knew I was a good person. That was when I asked myself, is it true that there is only one step between love and hate? Is he going to turn on you and destroy your life?

Suddenly the playboy told the entire world that he only felt pity for me! What was that about? Swiftly, and in his wicked mentality, I was a scorned woman who had come into his life only to destroy the sneaky himbo. I don't enter people's lives to destroy them, but I do tell the truth if necessary. Drake destroyed himself. It's beyond my mental capacity to tell lies about others or think of myself as better than other people. I want to care for others and love them, that's how I am. Hearing about the cruelty of the words Drake said to others about me traumatised me and was one of the many massive aftershocks my damaged soul suffered.

I believed I truly had gotten peace from this he-bitch after his last shitstorm.

'You must stop this craziness of all these falsehoods you're writing about me,' I told Drake when I finally contacted him. Instead, he made me feel stupid and not good enough.

'Don't you understand that everybody knows you are full of lies?' he said proudly, adding. 'I've plenty of friends and patients who protect me from all your lies. It does not matter how many times I get knocked down I will always get back up! You're such a psychopath, Mary.' Ice-cold spikes ran down my spine.

It ended up in a massive fight with him. 'What the hell is wrong with you?'

'Stop lying, Drake.'

'I want you to stop all your lying shit about me.'

'Stop lying to patients, Drake.'

'You have no right to discuss anything of what I do or what I can do with others. What the hell do you know about it anyway? Nothing! I built all the businesses by myself. Me alone. Nobody else! Your knowledge is coloured by your selfish self, so shut the hell up. Stop writing to me. You have no good in you.'

'Thanks for your lovely comments, but I'm not stupid,' was my simple reply.

'Why can't you do as I say?' the hustler shot back. 'This is what comes of your disrespect. Maybe now you'll start using your damn silly head. Bitch!'

'I don't understand what you are talking about.' Gosh, I was so confused by him.

'You mark my words. I told you, if you cross me, there will be consequences.'

'The opposite of a bitch is a HE-BITCH'

'You are the lowest person one can imagine. Keep your dirty fingers off the keyboard. You are so full of it, Mary. Are you so stupid that you don't understand a shit?'

'I understand a lot more than you think. You are a damn scammer, Drake. Monkey shit!' I became angry. How else could I answer such a mean little man-child of a maggot?

'You never believed in me. You were never grateful for anything I did for you. Shame on you and leave me alone. You are sick in your head, Mary. I am gathering evidence against you and your lowly comments.'

'Drake, please stop being so mean.'

'There is nothing legally wrong in what I am doing. But shitheads like you must absolutely clap your dirty hands for no reason and hope I have a problem. How dare you, Mary?' He behaved like a scorned little man child in preschool class, pointing the finger at his enemy.

'You are so full of lies and deception, Drake. I almost must take off my hat for you. You are so good at telling false stories to everyone around you. Stop lying and misleading people.' I said even though I knew it was waste of my good energy to try to get him to stop lying.

'See yourself in the mirror, Mary. You will see the greatest liar and psychopath I have ever known. Liars like you believe every man is lying.' And so, he went on and on with his many mean messages.

'I have never been given such a diagnosis. Remember the psychiatrist in Iran told me I was completely normal. Only you always think everyone else is a psychopath.'

'You're always whining and complaining about how I want to make my money and business. You're just dragging me down in the mud, while I try to do everything. I told you so many times to keep your damn mouth shut. You are a no-good stupid bitch. This is all your fault.'

'Your sense of reality is immensely weakened. Bipolar, psychopathic, and manic fit your diagnoses much better. Seek medical advice, but maybe you can't be saved.' Enough was enough, and these were my last words. I never spoke to or wrote him again.

The hound doggie lied about everything constantly. Why did he do so? I had not expected to receive such a mean and twisted impact, and it was difficult for me to put into words what had happened. How could I then expect others to understand? After all, they had not even been in the same situation, nor had they felt the doubt or fear I'd faced. None of them had felt the insecurity that crept under my skin, eventually taking over my free will and my common sense during my time with Drake. They did not know how awful it was when he had affected my emotions so violently that I completely disappeared from the normality of my life. I sank deeper and deeper into the damn sucking quicksand. At first, I was incredibly angry over the persistent attacks from Drake, Cadance and his few followers. It mentally broke me down, as I never knew when the next attack would come. Drake, Cadance and the followers projected everything onto me, as if I alone had been the cause of all the problems.

In the beginning, I defended myself on all social platforms, where he and Cadance distorted and deformed the truth, writing horrible things about me. He had managed perfectly to manipulate—pulling the proverbial strings to control—a small group of women who believed in his many lies. Next, strange hateful stories popped up on several Facebook groups.

Can you imagine how many excuses and explanations I had to use to justify myself? The judgements swirled around like a sick virus of hatred that spread out in the cyberspace of his few female followers. I didn't understand any of it myself, and I didn't have any words for such hatred from others, who didn't know me. It was a constant pressure, and I felt bad inside, got very stressed and exhausted, and lost my good spirit, vigour, and initiative. My judgment was put to the test, and I often lost sight of the situation, and was frustrated and wildly confused. I realized how cruel people can be on social media. And they continue for years. Facebook has an unbelievably ugly bully culture, even though people didn't know me. It was pure terror! I felt as I was losing more and more of myself. My defence became more furious in the feedback I wrote to people I did not know. Basically, I should not be held accountable to anyone who didn't know the background of this whole emotional turbulence of anger Drake and his litlle group exposed me to. I owed the followers nothing. I owed Cadance nothing. I owed Drake nothing.

Then I realized that he and his group also cyberbullied those people who believed in me. Drake's and Cadance's and their followers, oh, yea, it was twelve specific people, who I ended up calling 'the Jesus group of followers'. Drake has a severe Jesus and God complex. None of his followers, nor Cadance even knew who I was or who those many other patients were, all of whom Drake and his group terrorized. Drake and Cadance and the group were crossing the line when they told private details about patients and about my life in a public forum. I felt so alone, knowing that this small group of people believed in all his fictional lying descriptions about me. He was restless in the way psychopaths are and he needed to blame everything on me and others. A dark shadowy hurricane was looming on Facebook, and a true witch-hunt was running more rapidly than a fire could burn me to hell. He is a dangerous man! He has too much power over others! He is as Hitler. As the Sinaloa Cartel Overlord El Mayo or the feared Pablo Escobar, hunting his victim to the death.

Cyberbullying is usually understood as a kind of bullying that includes peer aggression that's both intentional and continuous and involves an aspect of imbalance of power between a victim and a perpetrator or perpetrators. Despite the tool used (new media), cyberbullying often takes place within a traditional group (for example, a school class). However, cyberspace gives internet users the opportunity to attack other individuals—people known only through the internet. Targets include celebrities, teachers, totally unknown individuals, or whole groups of people. Involvement in such actions brings suffering to those victimized as well as potential negative consequences for the perpetrators.[2]

Drake deeply broke my heart, telling so many twisted lies to others in public forums, as well on all his social media outlets. I was outraged when I heard others talk about my childhood, my matrimonial secrets, and how I had never been his patient. He had broken all the rules of

---

[2] Pyżalski J Jacek, 'From Cyberbullying to Electronic Aggression: Typology of the Phenomenon', *Emotional and Behavioural Difficulties* Vol. 17 no. 3–4 (2012), 305–317.

doctor-patient confidentiality and denied my entire existence. He was just too harsh; it wasn't exactly what I expected from him after the intense love I thought we'd shared. Eventually, I had to look it all in the eye. That was how I got through the inferno of the burning desire I'd once had for him. However, I don't want to hide the facts that, at times, I cannot understand myself. Why do I sometimes still miss him? I would ask myself. That missing went on for too many years. Is it because I didn't achieve the ultimate with him? Or is it because he failed me so deeply that I am left confused—not understanding how humans can be so evil?

I had to realize the truth and try to understand where the problems, in fact, were buried. Was it him or me? I often wondered if, unfortunately, I was the person I knew least about. If so, I must admit that it was tragic and a loss for me not to know myself. Had I not learned to understand my own needs and desires? Had I not understood what I valued most and what was important to me in life? Until now, I had only been wrapped up in the intoxication of my crush on Drake and had invested most in him and not in myself. I had to understand the seriousness and importance of getting to know myself much better. I was born, I lived, and I knew I would die one day too. I am the only one of my kind, just as all other people are the one of their kind.

Why had I wasted part of my precious life on something so very rotten? I should not have done so and should, therefore, do better in the future. So far, I'd spent my entire life doing everything others wanted me to do and had learned nothing else. When it came to what others were asking me to do, I'd never asked myself, Is this right or wrong? Before I had never questioned what Drake wanted me to do for him. I'd ended up living a life with him that was more hell, then genuine and truthful love. It was a series of wrong decisions and a long-drawn-out suicide! I was punished for having put my life at risk.

Suicide had often been on my mind when I felt so alone in the world, but I couldn't overlook the consequences. Suicide was not an option, and I wanted to live my life and find it again. How could life be lived? It was important for me to understand how I could get my life back. I only wanted to have a happy living, but I couldn't get that with

Drake. I began to reach the mesmerising glittering snow I could see on top of the peaks of the beautiful Mount Hermon I was climbing in Israel. I began to understand myself and found my faults.

Creating my new own happiness was where my personal struggle really began. I asked myself the important question: How could I find happiness again after having been subjected to such deception? The burning desire had to be terminated. I no longer had confidence in any people, and I was scared, nervous, and lonely. I felt unhealthy and was malnourished and weak. In my critical state and low self-esteem, I isolated myself and tried to hide from the outside world. This was another personally destructive mistake I made, when it was happiness I had to find! I wanted to not live in the madness of deep depression and knew I should have paid attention to Sigmund Freud's suggestion. 'Before you diagnose yourself with depression or low self-esteem,' he wrote, 'first make sure that you are not, in fact, just surrounded by assholes.'

But I hadn't listened to that wise quote, and Drake kept haunting my imagination. He would not let go of me. Or was it that I would not let go of him?

I lacked a precise awareness of my own current situation and an in-depth understanding of where I would like to go with my future life. I wondered where I had gone wrong. Either someone else or I myself had to diagnose the problems that afflicted my life. I had to learn to control my own life again and find out what I wanted—what personal goals I wanted to set. What was my future working life going to be? How would I deal with having lost the family I'd lost? My friends? How should my relationships with other people be? And what about my spiritual life?

I hoped to truly embrace a quote by Richard Branson, where his words gave me a great deal of hope: 'Do not be embarrassed by your failures. Learn from them and start again.'

Yet, I was too embarrassed and shameful over my many failures. I have written about the many experiences I had while travelling around the world with Drake and how I felt while being a country-to-country refugee together with him. What did this mysterious man see in me?

In his eyes, I was only a bad orphanage girl, and he had impressed me with his many lies. He had the patience of a saint when it came to be controlling me, but he was hiding the truth about himself in his passive-aggressive shelter. That was exactly why I didn't figure it all out until it was past the point of no return. I was five years in before I started *looking* for answers or even knew there might be answers to look for. So, he had all the time in the world to use the manipulative tactics of a narcissistic abuser and make me suffer. I felt so cheap.

How much do I have to do for Drake to truly love me? This was a question that often ran through my mind. For him, it was all a lie. Nothing was real, and it was all an act. I had grasped that, somehow, he always seemed to get into a lot of trouble. And every time, he had the ability to find a way of slithering out of trouble successfully. He preyed on me because he knew I had suffered a lot of damage to my self-esteem and insecurity in my life and that I had a lot of money. He knew that all he had to do was give me his pretended love.

The next few years went on with the signs of the struggle I was facing. Health issues and depression were the maladies he inflicted and that fell over my body and soul.

In November 2018 I was thinking to myself, 'what do I do with the rest of my life.' I feared I would never fulfil my dream of meeting a new decent man or going on a cruise. I wanted to change my life and no longer live in fear. I haven't always been a cruiser. In fact, for much of my life, I was a total scaredy-cat of the idea of going on a cruise. I've been travelling so much since my younger days, but just cruising scared me. I was dead-set against the idea. Why? I was used to boating with Paul on our 450 Sundancer, around in the Danish oceans, in the largest archipelago in Sweden and cruising along the Norwegian Fjord. But on a massive cruise ship, I feared being pushed overboard. What if a crew member or even a passenger would drug me and assault me? The list of reasons why I would not cruise went on and on.

I had during the summer given myself courage and strength, to take up dancing lessons and to venture out into the wide world again. Well, I finally bought myself a business ticket for a two-month cruise around Hawaii and the Caribbean. Going on my first cruise ever I within the first days stumbled upon Daniel Detwiler. I found him to be a fascinating person, who also was single like me. A stunning filthy rich handsome tall man from London. His eyes shine as the blue Caribbean ocean and his movements as he walks his graceful stroll and when he swings me around on the dancefloor in a hot embrace, fascinates me.

He pulled me into his arms overlooking the blue Caribbean Sea and kissed me with a passion I had never experienced before. I could see myself spending months with him on the cruise ship. It was perfect with plenty of restaurants, pools and a lively life and dancing on the polished wooden floors. It was the biggest cruise ship I ever have seen, and we headed for Hawaii on our first part of the journey. It was a perfect life as I lay on the sun deck with Daniel, as we glided quietly through the transparent blue waters. Best of all, it was the best love of my life.

He is a true catch of a unique British gentleman. Not once had I to pay one dinner, a drink or anything when we were together for those two months on the cruise. We had been dating for one month and on our 28-Day Voyage in the Caribbean, Daniel had made a reservation at Giovanni's serving an elegant cuisine made from fresh and flavourful ingredients from Italy.

'I want to spend more time with you, Mary, when we come back to London.' He smiled.

Daniel and I spend a romantic spring vacation, three weeks in Scotland.

'Mary, I don't want to wait forever.' He sweetly smiles and pops the champagne.

'What do you mean, my love?' And I melt in his wonderful blue eyes.

'I want to live with you forever,' he said softly, handing over a glass of bubbles, 'I mean, as your husband.'

I was surprised and thinking quickly as he held his breath, waiting for an answer.

'Wow! Oh, my goodness. Get married when?'

'July or best in August' he said firmly.

'I love you, Daniel,' hugged him and whispered into his ear, 'yes, I will marry you, my darling.'

'I love you too,' he said and gave me a vast rock on my finger and kissed me, asking, 'where do you want to get married?'

'My favourite is St. Martin in the Fields Church on Trafalgar Square, in London.'

'There it will be.' And during the next three month we do all preparations for a weeding, that was meant to be. A marriage of two people who truly loved each other, a perfect union between a lovable man and his happy bride.

The minister was watching us and next turned to everyone, then looked at them solemnly.

'Dearly beloved, we are gathered here together today to join this man and this women,' he glanced at us and smiled. All I could see was Daniel and all he could see was me, until we both said, 'I do,' kissed and walked back down the aisle.

CHAPTER 43

GLOBAL MADNESS AND DARKNESS

> The funny thing is, when you don't let people disrespect you,
> they start calling you difficult.
>
> —Tom Hardy

The world has gone mad and has been plunged into a global darkness. Maybe the time has come for a new beginning on our planet when it comes to the way we behave. I would like to put my focus on the modern society when a catastrophic, feared pandemic began in Hubei province's Wuhan city in China in December 2019, before spreading around the world. Everyone's own behaviour has consequences for the world's situation, and the situation shows us that everything has a price.

Experts have looked back and found that the original cases of this new virus started in November 2019 and at a completely different region than where the first case was found in Wuhan. This is only the beginning of an immense global crisis. No one knows yet the severity of what is happening to the world's population and what the consequences on the global economy and health will be. The world's population was tranquil. I celebrated Christmas with Daniel, and all around the world, everyone celebrated a fantastic New Year 2020 and I with Daniel in London. In the first two months of the New Year, many people travelled on skiing holidays, especially to Northern Italy, France, and Austria.

Unbeknownst to any of us, it was the perfect way to spread the infection to the rest of the world, and nobody has yet realized the severity of the virus.

On 30 December, the Chinese authorities announced information about the new virus. Maybe even before Christmas, they should have hit hard with the closure of China's border to the rest of the world. It didn't happen because it was feared that doing so would cause unnecessary panic worldwide. No one knew yet that COVID-19 was a new deadly corona virus, which is a group of related viruses that cause diseases in birds and mammals. In humans, it causes respiratory tract infections that can be mild but that also can be lethal, like MERS or SARS. In twenty-one days, in 2002 and 2003, twenty-one countries were infected with SARS, with a mortality rate of about 11 per cent. With COVID-19, the Chinese doctor, Dr Li Wenliang discovered the first outbreaks, which he first thought was another SARS outbreak. He began discussing it with former fellow students in a chat group.

'Beware,' he wrote to the group. 'Our WeChat group has been closed. Latest news is that the coronavirus infection has been confirmed and the virus classification is ongoing. Do not share the information and ask your family and loved ones to take their precautions.'

Dr Li was picked up by the police and disciplined by his own hospital. He was told not to gossip falsely and was not given the opportunity to tell the truth, so his knowledge was kept secret. A group of whistle-blowers sounded the alarm. Dr Li Wenliang and two critical citizens—Chen Qiushi, a lawyer and citizen journalist and a Chinese businessman named Fang Bin—uploaded disturbing videos on social media of infected patients and doctors who were close to the edge of collapse.

'There are dead people in waiting rooms, on the floors and in hallways. Doctors and nurses are under pressure,' they told the world.

The two citizen journalists warned of the crisis. And suddenly, on 6 February and for mysterious reasons, Chen Qiushi disappeared without a trace. The day after, the first doctor died. It was Dr Li, who had tried to warn against the virus. On 9 February, the businessman Fang Bin and several other citizen journalists also mysteriously disappeared.

The crisis was fast approaching, and people were rapidly dying in China. No one cared for the dead who lay together with the living and sick. There were no vaccines or antiviral drugs to prevent or treat the infections. The hospital capacity was not enough to take care of all the sick. There was total chaos. At the end of January, the city was completely shut down, and the news was now being watched by the world. Aircraft was grounded, and businesses were closed. There was no access to the city, and the opportunity to get out no longer existed. The authorities had made drastic decisions and had chosen to close the doors. A massive iron ring had been laid across several cities, and Wuhan was trying to get control of the situation.

The city was on total lockdown. But it was too late. The infection had reached thirteen countries in a short time and 80 people had already died in China. Ten days later, the death toll was almost 600 people. And 16,800 persons in a single district were hospitalized. People collapsed on the streets and the queues were long in front of the hospitals. The streets were disinfected, and the authorities used violent methods to force people into isolation just because they had a fever. In some parts, residents recorded videos, showing how the front doors of homes were welded shut so people couldn't get out. The virus spread at crazy speed, and 1,300 people were dead within a very short time in Wuhan. It was a nightmare! By the end of March, China had almost 82,000 cases and little over 3,300 deaths.

It was a long and daunting experience when family members were hit. Mothers and fathers were lost. Young children lost grandparents or even their own mother or father if the parents were already afflicted with other life-threatening illnesses. The world was in chaos. The virus was a dangerous uninvited intruder.

In February 2020, fear spread as the epidemic spread in several countries, and several countries evacuated their citizens from Wuhan. By the end of February, the epidemic had spread to more than fifty-four countries. Nearly 3,000 people had died so far, and 85,400 had been infected.

It was peak time for skiing, and Italy was full of tourists. Italy, along with South Korea and Iran were currently among the hardest hit countries outside China.

At the same time, the world economy was on unstable ground. In mid-March 2020, China began to get the situation under control and to successfully mitigate the infection. The country's authorities reported that there were now only about 100 cases of infected patients. In contrast, the United States was facing tough times, and the rest of the world was beginning to bleed.

A few months after the outbreak in China, Italy became Europe's epicentre, with 2,500 dead and 31,500 infected, while several countries followed and were severely affected by the infection. Under normal circumstances, hospital care in Italy functions quite well. The nation is home to well-educated, highly skilled doctors and specialists. They fought well and did a fantastic job, but there was a lack of space in the intensive care units. The Italians were, to put it mildly, on the edge of the bed. Lots of tourists, including infected people from China, had been holidaying in the country at some of the most famous ski resorts during February. It was a violent crisis that had not been seen for many years and had turned into a health war against a virus that had turned the world upside down.

It was battle of life and death, and during March, the WHO termed the outbreak a pandemic. Freedom of movement was restricted, and all events were cancelled. Milan in Italy was on lockdown, and a state of emergency was declared. Everyone had to stay at home, and each family now had to manage on their own. Only one person could go out at a time to shop for groceries or pick up medication. Officers walked the streets checking the entrances to subways and checking people's documents for exit permits. The city ended up as a ghost town.

On 18 March, Italy's coronavirus deaths rose by a record 475 in a day. Nearly 3,000 had died so far, and 35,713 cases had been confirmed since the outbreak in the beginning of March. So far, more than 4,000 of those infected had successfully recovered. On the same day, China reported no domestic cases of coronavirus for the first time since the outbreak began. On 5 April, Italy has almost 125,000 cases, only 21,000 recovered, and over 15,000 deaths. In July 2020 they had 243,967 cases and 35,028 deaths.[4]

Spain, Austria, and France followed rapidly in the footsteps of Italy, with massive

outbreaks of sickness and death. 'We are at War. The enemy is invisible, and it requires our general mobilization,' said French President Emmanuel Macron, declaring France at war with the virus, as was the European Union. He proposed a thirty-day travel Ban for nonessential travel. Macron also commanded the French to stay at home for at least fifteen days and declared that the movement of French citizens would be tightly restricted. Anyone violating the order would face punishment. Only food shopping and essential activities were allowed. On 5 April, France has almost 90,000 cases, almost 15,500 recovered, and over 7,500 deaths. In July 2020 France had 174,674 cases and 30,152 deaths. Spain rapidly followed severe many cases and in July they had 307,335 cases and 28,420 deaths.[4]

In Europe and Scandinavia, most countries closed schools. Many were in lockdown, following the lead of the new temporary rules from France and Italy, as the infection spread with lightning speed within a few weeks after tourists had returned to their respective countries from their skiing vacations in Northern Italy and Austria. Then Denmark locked down and the week after followed United Kingdom. UK ended up in July with 293,239 cases and 45,233 deaths.[4]

The infection was by now also spreading to Canada and the United States. The entire world was in lockdown and in full readiness.

'I always treated the Chinese virus very seriously,' Donald Trump tweeted. 'And have done a very good job from the beginning, including my very early decision to close the 'borders' from China—against the wishes of almost all. Many lives were saved. The Fake News new narrative is disgraceful and false!'

In another tweet, Trump said, 'The coronavirus is very much under control in the USA. We are in contact with everyone and all relevant countries. CDC and World Health have been working hard and very smart. Stock market starting to look very good to me!' But the stock market was severely bleeding worldwide, and everyone was losing on that account. In July USA had 3,730,135 cases and 141,562 deaths.[4]

'Mr Trump has a habit of taking credit for supposedly healthy markets and doesn't always ground his claims in reality. Not a good day to invoke them as an indication the crisis was 'under control'—as we now know it wasn't,' reported an article in *The Independent* on 24 February 2020.

By early April, 206 countries and territories around the world had reported a total of

1,202,473 confirmed cases of the coronavirus COVID-19 that originated from Wuhan, China, and a death toll of 64,691.[3] In July 2020 was reported a total of 14,071,993 cases and nearly 600,000 deaths.[4]

World Animal Protection wrote:

> If we are going to stop future diseases that spread from animals to humans, and along the way mutate and turn into dangerous viruses - we must have put an effective end to our dealings with wild animals. Only a global ban can stop future epidemics. Unfortunately, Asia is at the bottom of the animal welfare area. Though China has now banned the consumption and trade of wildlife. Such legislation should be Worldwide. Too many wild and endangered animals are used for the entertainment industry, such as pets, food and traditional medicine. COVID-19 is a real threat and it will continue if not all countries tighten up on wildlife trade legislation.

China's supreme legislative assembly has now announced that it is forbidden to trade and eat wild animals. Shenzhen is, so far, the only city that has extended the ban to dogs and cats as well. This also applies to a permanent ban on breeding wild animals, dogs, and cats for food use. This is a great step on the road to better animal welfare.

---

[3]   Worldometer, 5 April 2020.
[4]   Worldometer, 17 July 2020.

But why am I telling all this? What does it have to do with Drake and Mary? You may well be wondering. I'm embarrassed by some people's unethical way of behaving during this tragic global situation we find ourselves in. The only thing Drake thinks of is himself, himself, himself. A serious threat from him suddenly feel on my head. He made grossly false accusations, just as a global threat fell upon all of us in our modern society when the virus COVID-19 is spreading rapidly. It's not surprising to me that I have once again discovered that this self-centred psychopath has come up with a new and appalling method of haunting others, only to save his own ass. I realized that, somehow, Drake always seems to get into a lot of trouble, but he also has the ability to find a way to slither out of problems successfully every time.

This time, though, he was in a dingy situation. He tried to put the blame on several patients, me and others for his massive downfall when he ended up in the black dirty pot. There he was dipped in ink by the British Department of Health and Social Care, smeared in tar, and then rolled in feathers over his unethical behaviour at his clinic. He had, for one, been reported to the police for sexual harassment and malpractice. Finally, the Department of Health and Social Care took away his license and closed his clinic, as he was a danger to the patients. Adding to this he broke the GDPR (General Data Protection Regulation). Patients complained to the Information Commissioner's Office about Luke Schmidt as he in public told spoke of patients which included their name and what they had complained about to the Department of Health and Social Care. Adding to that, the Department of Health and Social Care upheld their claims of malpractice and sexual harassment against Doctor Schmidt's patients and he was sentenced up to five years in prison for his many fences. I am delighted about these decisions, although it was, not without any cost for the patients. Aggressively, the scumbag and Cadance began attacking patients and me with various threats on social media.

This time I had Daniel on my side to support me. I refused to be seduced by Drake's and Cadance's pervasive hatred, their selfishness, and their unethical behaviour. Publicly and on social media, he also announced his intentions to sue a group of other people who had criticized him. More severely injured patients were now becoming his victims, including the Department of Health and Social Care and me, all of whom he allegedly reported to the police, according to his announcement. In his alleged reporting to the police, he reasoned that all of us had *falsely* notified to the Department of Health and Social Care. For some patients, Drake claimed they had *falsely* reported sexual abuse, making inaccurate claims against him and his business. In his opinion, everything was a conspiracy created together with the Department of Health, Social Care, patients, others and me.

Welcome to the real world, Doctor Bates or is it Doctor Schmidt. There must be a reason the Department of Health and Social Care did what they did. Hopefully, his shady infectious virus dies with his sins or with COVID-19. I choose to do as the Buddhists do during such times of crises and follow their sensible example—listen to Buddha's advice and take it easy.

By scribbling this narration, and during my obsession with research into men's psychopathic behaviour towards women, I figured Drake out in the end. It took too many years, but lastly I saw the real Drake Lucifer Bates, vs. the false prophet who's name now is Doctor Schmidt. He and Cadance are cowards and mean bullies that can't stop their cruel behaviour. It's his lifestyle, and Cadance follow in his footstep, I can see it clearly now. Drake or should I call him Luke, had planned it all from the beginning, when it started a sunny summer day in Spain and the storyline ended in 2020. I truly don't know who he is, but I know he is a massive liar with no honour, and he destroyed a lot in me. Fortunately, though, he failed to bring me completely down. Although he took away my dignity and my life will never be the same, nevertheless I learned from his evilness—from having lived with a dangerous psychopath. Thus, I finally discovered the strength to find out the truth about myself. I reached the mesmerising glittering snow on top of the peaks of the beautiful Mount Hermon in Israel. But, I wish I'd never walked into Drake Lucifer Bates clinic and never met the false prophet who calls himself for Luke Samael Schmidt. For a long time, I have only wanted my life back, and finally, I got it—by letting go of my previous narcissistic mean boyfriend and getting married to a true and honest British gentleman man as Daniel Detwiler.

The world is brutal and full of psychopathic, sadistic, two-faced people. Drake looked so normal on the outside, but I realised that, on the inside, he was a nasty maggot. Many times, I truly wanted to give up, but I am a *fighter* and giving up was never an option. It was difficult for me to understand and admit what was going on during those many years, because I couldn't understand that I had been so naive, senseless, and blind. It hurt me to know how much I had degraded and humiliated myself just to be together with Drake. I once lost myself, but today I'm a survivor of psychological abuse and Daniel helped me through the many nightmares.

Nightmares are not just scary dangerous dreams. They can be good for your self-awareness and health, even if nightmares are created to scare you. Dreams have been a great source of inspiration for many creative people through the ages. Sleeping people experience nightmares as exciting, and that's what my story is built on. The dreams took me into a fictional world where I discovered that one of the lessons in my unfolding is that nightmare monsters always look like monsters.

I had the craziest dream, that came on the very same night/morning that was the day I'd first met Paul, thirty years ago. I was supposed to move to Spain, but before then, I visited him in what was once our large mansion apartment in the centre of Copenhagen. Even though we were divorced, he wanted me to stay overnight. Suddenly, a lot of women came and had to try on these new clothes creations that he had designed. He ended up becoming a well-known fashion designer while still working at his large company. All the women kissed him passionately, and I didn't know if I should be jealous. In his bedroom, I found women's panties, jewellery, and several passports, for Pablo Escobar who was charged with sexual abuse. Then Paul took me to the company, and there we met Drake, who had become the drug Lord Pablo Escobar, picking up his new passport. Drake got angry when he saw that I was with Paul, so he ordered his goons to liquidate us.

Paul and I went into our toilet to bang, and afterwards we went home to Paul's. Out on the balcony, we walked up a high hill, where

Paul embraced me, and asked me when I would come back to him. I congratulated him on his new success and said that we could use my apartment in Spain as a summer residence. Then I woke up and looked at the phone on which I found a greeting from Paul remembering on our first day 30 years ago.

These were crazy dreams, and dreams probably have some strange monsters (Drake as Pablo Escobar) built in.

Maybe the reader remembers the importance of the Venus constellation in September 2010, when the entire narration began. It was magic, when the luminous full moon cast a bright clear light over the city in Jerusalem, while Venus and the stars glowed as the clearest and most beautifully polished diamonds. That specific year in September was special, when Venus stood at its peak and shone powerfully over the clear sky of Jerusalem's night.

As the Moon and the Stars, she was important in my life. And in April 2020, Venus was playing with my mind again. I'm fascinated with Venus, but I don't know why. This year, she will reach its greatest brightness in its evening apparition. On this breathtaking night, I stare intently at the clear night sky and at Venus, the divine Moon, and the Stars, thinking happily, *this is also the time I have finished my last chapter about Mary and Drake.*

From the south coast of the United Kingdom where Daniel and I use the apartment as a holiday home, we enjoy this apparition, which is exceptionally well placed and prominent, as we clinch our hands standing on the balcony and philosophize. *Is this a coincidence? Or are there more between heaven and Earth?* I'm thinking about, the first day Drake came into my life, when I fell in love with a mysteriously rasping sexy voice without seeing the man. As a chopped-of-headless chick, I must admit, I was not true to myself, and only thinking with my heart, instead of thinking with my otherwise normal functioning intellect. I am not perfect, but I'm real, humble and kind, so I paid the price because; Love was blind! Daniel and my love are not blind, it's real and honest.

Awakening from my strange dream on a beautiful shiny morning, clinching hand with Daniel next to me, I knew that this was my last nightmare with the previous lounge room lizard. I understood that Drake was the most dangerous, devious, and charming monster that I had ever met in my dreams and that the entire story was simply a horrifying nightmare, which Venus had saved me from. I wonder, if it was Drake or me who should never have been *born*?

My writing is not an excuse for the many inappropriate decisions I've made throughout my life. What I have scribbled down has allowed me to gain self-understanding about my actions. It helped me pull myself out of the nightmare of that life I created for myself during the period with Drake.

Through the clever pen, my thoughts and memories moulded on a piece of white paper. The pain, disbelief, and the darkness of everything were a gloomy nightmare, although you have only read a micro part of the massive abusive hell. A lot was too painful to re-live and write about, even I wanted you to know everything.

Going forward, I will have a new and better life with Daniel, and I'll continue in positive spirit netting good karma. I still don't understand why I jumped in the trap with Drake. When I go through all the context and knowledge I have gained, I get disappointed in myself for letting it happen and get angry of Drake's deception. I did *so much* damage to myself, and I'm angry at myself for the wrong choices I made.

Drake is a master manipulator, a true profile of a psychopath. I fell in love with a dream, but the man in front of me didn't exist, because I was only a source of supply for him. Too late, I found out what his smirking smile and eyes revealed—that he enjoyed when I gave him what he wanted. It energised *him!* It drained *me!* He became my puppeteer and did not understand the puppets feelings, because he was as smooth as an evil electric eel, living on the muddy bottom in his murky swamp.

Drake questions nothing about himself and believes he does no wrong. *He brainwashed me through psychological violence*, then constantly quibbled and twisted everything. When I tried to hold on to a confrontation with him, he would shift the focus to something else, so I would become extremely confused. He spoke in circles, blocking any clear dialogue, and spoke about things with no action or constructive solution to accompany the words.

Drake's many personalities express themselves in his tone and imitation when he wants to start a quarrel. I can't tell if he'll be Dr Jekyll or Mr Hyde. He can be kind and accommodating for one moment, and that part I loved about him. But then he'll suddenly be vicious and patronising the next. He limited my control and isolated me, so often I doubted myself, my intuition, and my senses. Often, he behaved identical to a spoiled tiny child, then he feels superior to me and others. A selfish seductive and controlling person, absorbed by wealth, power, and grandiosity, who likes to receive special treatment from everyone. Only Drake knows everything best and only his rules apply!

Moody, Drake has high energy and creates drama to get attention. He's jealous and never gets enough from one woman, because his emotional life is superficial, and he has difficulty with closeness and intimacy. He's dishonest and denies any knowledge of wrongdoings.

With a smirk on his face, he would accuse me and others of always misunderstanding everything, would mock me, telling me I was wrong anytime I confronted him. One minute, I was pretty and clever, and the next moment, I was immensely stupid, ugly, fat, and wobbly, and needed a body tone or a facelift.

Drake made it look as I was always in the wrong, because he was *never* the problem. In his world, he made me feel I wasn't good enough, claiming I had several evil demons and was not worth loving. He was a perfect master of writing love letters, though, and I took them all in with pleasure, which caught me in his spin. I'm sure that most of it is recycled from previous or other exciting women he was writing with. Everything was about him—his wishes, his life, *his needs*! Worst of all, it was always his money—not mine—even though he didn't have a single dollar. It took me years of frustration and confusion before I grasped his devious intentions. It convinced me I was wrong about all I had done in my life with him and seemed that things were opposite of how they really were.

After our final break-up, it took many years to get back to myself. As a woman in a hot bond with Drake, it was difficult to get out of such a toxic relationship, because I believed him. I allowed it all—everything he did to me, because I had a massive burning desire for him. If he could take advantage of me, he stayed and would not let go of me, even when he was together with Cadance, where he passionately kissed me in his clinic, and before I left the place. It has been difficult to comprehend the games he played with me and with other people. I finally lost interest in his drama and stopped talking to him and accepted he would never change. No one could help him escape from his own sickening game. When he no longer could benefit from me, he went on to another woman, because he will always need a fresh victim, and cannot live alone.

*   *   *

It's my goal to let the pen scribble the last word in this story about Mary and Drake—ending this poignant chapter of the past nearly ten years of a haunted life with a narcissistic psychopath. I will forget everything and let the end of the beginning to be where the beginning now ends. The past is a simple illusion and the present is to live in happiness—to love the future of my life, together with Daniel Detwiler. When trust is broken, *sorry* means nothing.

One day I found a great text written by an Unknown person; It took me a long time to understand what it means to forgive someone. I always wondered how I could forgive someone who chose to hurt me. But after a lot of soul searching, I realised that forgiveness isn't about accepting or excusing their behaviour... it's about letting it go and preventing their behaviour from destroying my heart.

Drake or rather Luke, means nothing to me. He was mainly a ghost in a dreadful nightmare. I had put my hands and my life into his otherwise lovely tender hands when he moulded the clay, when I was as a soft lump of clay in his tender hands. In his lovely warm hands, he broke the fragile moulded pottery into millions of fragments. He can no longer hurt me, and I humbly must conclude I'm not a psychopath. I forgive him for all his sins he did to me. Of all his lies I've heard, 'I love you' was my favourite. Now I've peace from Drake.

Sadly, it took me too many years to figure out Drake's many scams—his mistreatment of using of fragile women for his sickening play. I'm a survivor of his meanness and it *freed* me from *the hidden shadows of Doctor Drake Lucifer Bates.* Maybe I was too strong for him—even though I was also weak in the moment of desperate love, in a complex life, where I was manipulated by the man I had a Burning Desire for.

Life is as a Japanese cherry blossom tree in full bloom. The flower falls off the tree to the ground with the slightest breeze. Then life is over for this delicate blossom. When you have withered and fallen off the tree's crown and are resting dead on the ground as a lifeless flower, it's too late. Cherish every moment in life! You'll only experience it once! Take care of your life.

> The most important relationship we can all
> have is the one we have with ourselves.
> The most important journey you can take is one of self-discovery.
> To know yourself, you must spend time with yourself, you must not be
> afraid to be alone. Knowing yourself is the beginning of all wisdom.
>
> —Aristotle

Lightning Source UK Ltd.
Milton Keynes UK
UKHW011948080321
380016UK00012B/1526/J